AT LAST THEY WERE TOGETHER . . . TO
LOVE . . . AND TO FACE THE TRUTH HE
HAD HIDDEN FROM HER . . .

Throwing her arms around Eben, Lucy clung to
his shoulders. "You're angry because of what I said to
Thomas. My temper upset you. That's true, isn't it?"

Her face, just inches from his, was flushed. Her
eyes were puffed and red. Eben felt her hot breath
against his cheek. At that moment, he did not want
her in the least. She seemed almost a stranger to him,
though in some recess of his mind he knew he loved
her and would feel that love again when the shock of
the evening had passed.

"There are things you don't know, Lucy."

"I'll learn, Eben. I swear. You'll be proud of me."

"Oh, Lucy!" Her eagerness touched him profoundly.

"What is it? Tell me." She stopped suddenly and
stepped back from him. Appalled, she covered her
mouth with her hand. "You're in love with someone
else."

"No."

"You're lying to me, Eben. I can see it in your
face."

"I have a son." He spoke without thinking. "About
Delphia's age."

"But you can't. You told me . . . Amanda . . ." Her
shoulders sagged. "Then there is someone else. Another woman you prefer before me."

With a sigh of resignation, Eben took her in his
arms and began his story. . . .

Tomorrow's Journey

Drusilla Campbell

A Dell/Banbury Book

Published by
Banbury Books, Inc.
37 West Avenue
Wayne, Pennsylvania 19087

Dell ® TM 681510, Dell Publishing Co., Inc.

ISBN: 0-440-08618-3

Printed in the United States of America

First printing—October 1982

For my father
Willard Newlon Green

PART I

Chapter 1

The moon was low when Amanda dried her tears for the last time. Rising from her bed in the stillness of the hot room, she put on a robe that trailed the floor behind her as her gown had on the misbegotten day when she had married Eben Hopewell. She caught a glimpse of herself in the long glass mirror. Tiny and frail, her blonde hair white in the gloom, her peignoir the color of old lace, Amanda thought she might already be a specter.

She slipped silently between the sleeping forms of her slave companions, Biddy and Dora, and stepped out into the hallway. The candles in the wall sconces had guttered, leaving the long expanse as black as a hole in space. Amanda did not hesitate at its edge, not even as she heard the scratchy sound of mice skittering off to their own dark hideaways.

The ancient hinges of the front door groaned faintly. She stopped, held her breath, waited to be discovered. There was not a sound. She sighed, her breath escaping in a tremble. Her feet barely touched the warm, damp stones of the flagged terrace as she ran. The expanse of tended grass stretching out from in front of the house and down the hill to the water was freshly cut and fragrant. That wonderful scent of mown grass stopped Amanda short. She turned to look back at Wild Rose.

The rambling and dilapidated frame mansion was only a dark shadow against the purple sky, but Amanda saw it as she remembered it best. She had only happy memories of the days before her arranged marriage. When she was seven or eight, her Grandfather White still lived at Wild Rose and was its master. She remembered a Christmas she and her parents and her brother Hiram had spent in the then magnificent old house. Her grandfather, sensing that it would be his last Christmas, had determined to make it the grandest holiday ever. The eaves of the house had sparkled with tiny candle lamps, and in the front hall an orchestra played for dancing on each of the festival's twelve nights. The cooks worked around the clock in shifts, producing the delicious aromas of vanilla and sugar and browned butter. Platters of delectables were borne to the guests by liveried footmen in white, their skins as black as bitter chocolate. It was a gala Amanda would never forget. All the rooms of Wild Rose were opened wide that season, refurbished and made comfortable for the guests who came from Savannah on a chartered boat to spend the holiday on the island. Amanda White had been the little princess of a fairyland populated by handsome people who loved and petted her. Now, years later, barefoot in the new-mown grass, she held her breath, remembering what it had been to dance from group to group in a dress the color of heaven, her blonde curls bouncing adorably. Her smile had been exquisite, her laugh a bell sound. The world had loved Amanda in those days.

She whirled away from her memories and ran

down to the bay without looking back at Wild Rose
again. At the shoreline, she followed a narrow path
beside the water. It curved around the little bay and
went into the woods. After crossing a narrow point of
land, the path opened out on a place where the channel separating the sea islands from the Georgia mainland was wide. Amanda stopped and looked at the
glassy water. Its surface gave no hint of the strong
currents dragging from below. But Amanda knew.
Once, on a trip to the mainland, Hiram had dropped
her doll overboard, and the tide had pulled it away
from her reaching hands. Dolly could not swim and
neither could Amanda.

She walked in at the water's edge. Behind her, on
the other side of the woods, a cock crowed and Wild
Rose began its slow awakening. Her robe swirled
around her ankles.

I love you, Hiram, she thought. Remember the
time you took me snake hunting and Elizabeth, their
mother's slave companion, found out? Remember the
Christmas when Granddaddy dressed me like an an-
gel?

"I'm coming, Granddaddy."

Now the water lapped against her thighs, its
touch intimate and exciting. Inside she was already
liquefying. Near the shore the channel bottom was
muddy, but farther out it became gritty and sometimes sharp stones stabbed Amanda's feet. Even this
she experienced as a pleasantly erotic sensation. Her
tiny breasts lifted and the nipples tightened as the
water caressed her. She recalled Eben and instantly
longed for something she could not name. The yearning overcame her like a swoon and she cried aloud, a
terrible sound such as a spirit might make, trapped
between this world and the next. The water nudged
her feet and lifted them. Her eyes were open, and she

saw the purple night, the horizon colored mauve and grey and silvered gold as the water lifted her and carried her along on its crest. With her gown billowing around her and her hair spread out about her head, already she seemed to belong more to water than land.

They found Amanda's body that afternoon, caught in the weeds and roots that grew at the water's edge. In a rage of grief, Hiram locked himself in his room and refused all offers of comfort. Red-eyed and weeping, Elizabeth, Biddy and Dora prepared her body. She was buried beside her grandfather the next morning, before the heat began. By midafternoon of the same day, Suzannah Hopewell Paine and her son, Patrick, were heading back toward Savannah on the channel boat.

There were frequent stops, and their somber voyage lasted for almost two days. Mother and son hardly spoke. For a six-year-old, Patrick's reticence was astonishing. Instead of carrying on a normal nonstop dialogue about this and that, he spent his time staring from the bow into the distance and whittling a scrap of wood with a small knife Hiram had given him when they first got to the island.

Suzannah wondered what his thoughts were. Her own memories of the last week were vivid, sometimes to the point of pain. Yet she returned to them again and again, unable to stay away. She saw Amanda with the baby, screaming her harridan's rage at the tiny, dead creature. The noise had been enough to awaken Patrick. Until she had sent him back to bed, he had stood behind her skirts, watching the terrible scene: the dead baby, Amanda screaming incomprehensibly, Hiram and the slaves immobilized by shock. Suzannah feared for Patrick after such a night. He had seen and heard things that could misshape an impressionable mind. Apart from his silent, contemplative mood, however, he seemed unaffected by what had occurred that night. Still, she feared for her son. In his short life he had watched or been part of domestic scenes terrible enough to break or ruin most children. She knew it was impossible that he had come through them all unmarked.

Patrick was a more complicated child than Suzannah had imagined before their stay at Wild Rose. His extraordinary independence in that hostile environment had impressed her. Now that Wild Rose was behind them and Suzannah had time to think, she could see that Patrick had been made stronger by his experiences. But there was a streak of rebel in his makeup, too. She knew he had not inherited this trait from his father, James Shawn. She watched him from her seat aft in the channel boat and could see with special clarity his resemblance to both Shawns and Hopewells. It was unsettling to see James Shawn's square Yankee jaw and strong mouth coupled with her own sea-green eyes and the unmistakable, brooding Hopewell brows. Surely the day was coming when someone else would look at Patrick and see that he could not possibly be Travis Paine's son.

Dear God, she thought, when the time comes, when he asks me, help me to find the words to tell the truth. But how could she explain to an innocent boy that the man whose name he bore was not his true father? His blood parent was James Shawn from Cooper's Mountain.

Would she ever see James again? Would the boy ever know his father?

Suzannah's brother, Valentine, had made it clear that if she and Patrick returned to Amoset he would make trouble for them. And Suzannah knew better

than to test him at his word. Like the rest of the
family, Valentine was half mad. Suzannah supposed it
was as much a family trait as moody brows and green
eyes. Valentine might do anything now that he was
set on proving himself in the arena of Hopewell Mills.
Until he was brought down by his profligate ways,
Suzannah and Patrick could not risk a return to
Amoset. And since she had no reason to visit Boston,
it seemed likely that years might pass before she met
with James Shawn again. It was even possible that
they would never. . . .

She did not want to think about any of this, and
she was irritated with herself for being morbid. She
must force herself to look on the bright side of things.
But it had never been more apparent to her that the
Hopewells, from her parents Sarah and Martin to
each of the children, were a family born in the
dimness of a sorrowing moon. It was as if the gloom
of some crime had cast a shadow over all their lives
and would continue to do so until it was confessed,
the sin atoned for.

Suzannah and Patrick arrived in Savannah unan-
nounced, so she hired a carriage to take them to
Eben's home on Ross Point, overlooking the river.
Though the sun had set an hour before, the air was
still hot and muggy, like a great unmoving pool
through which the carriage rushed them home to Jasmine Gate.

How can I tell Eben about Amanda? What can I
say? She wondered whether she should lie about the
baby. It would be a gentle lie, a loving falsehood to
make her brother's pain easier. But he trusts me, she
thought. I must tell him everything.

"When we get to the house, Patrick, I want you
to go upstairs with Belle right away," she said as the

carriage turned into the entrance. "I'll be up when I can."

"I don't like her, Mama. She has mean hands."

"Mean?"

"When she picks me up, she pinches sometimes. And her nails are hard." Patrick rubbed his arm in recollection.

Suzannah felt a new emotion. Anger. It came as a relief after two days of brooding grief. "Are you sure she hurts you on purpose?"

"You mean for sure? Well, it seems like . . ."

"Just stay away from her hands and do as she tells you. But if she hurts you, even if it seems like an accident, tell me." Suzannah was distracted for a moment. Then she added, "I don't know how long Belle will stay on at Jasmine Gate. Now that Amanda's . . . gone, she might as well go back to the Whites." Her voice trailed off as she began to consider some of the ramifications of her sister-in-law's death.

Patrick interrupted her. "What will you tell him, Mama?"

"Tell whom?"

"Will you tell Uncle Eben about the trick they tried to play with the baby?"

She stared at him.

"Remember, Mama? I heard Elizabeth and Uncle Hiram talking in the hall." Patrick wrinkled his brows. "Did you forget I came and told you that?"

"Of course not, darling." She took his hands and held them tightly in hers. "And I'm glad you told me. But now that it's over, I want you to forget you heard Elizabeth and Uncle Hiram. I want you to forget all the words you heard them say."

"It didn't make sense, Mama. First Uncle Hiram said. . . ."

She grabbed him close. "It didn't make any sense

so it will be easy to forget. You must never speak of anything you heard or saw at Wild Rose. And you must promise not to break your word on this." She held him away from her and looked directly into his eyes. "Do you promise, Patrick? On your honor as a young gentleman?"

"Yes, Mama." After a moment, he ventured another question. "But what will you tell Uncle Eben? You have to tell me, Mama. That's fair."

He was such an earnest little negotiator that she could not disguise a smile. It was her first in many days. "I shall tell Uncle Eben the truth, Patrick. That's all there is to tell."

But it was more difficult than she had imagined. No sooner had she stepped into the pool of colored light that filled the foyer of Jasmine Gate than Eben was beside her, hugging her, begging to know about his child. "Is it a boy or girl, Suzannah? And how is Amanda? Tickled, I'll bet. When may I visit?"

On the pretext of busying herself with Patrick, Suzannah avoided having to tell him the truth so suddenly.

"Leave the boy to Belle, Suzannah, and come into the study. I was about to have a brandy. May I pour one for you?" He headed off toward the study, but all at once he stopped and turned back to his sister. "You're here early, aren't you? The baby must have come ahead of schedule. There's nothing wrong is there?"

She ignored his question. "I will have that brandy, Eben. The trip was exhausting in the heat. And the insects were a fright! I swear I may never adjust to Georgia. There is something unwholesome about the climate." She hurried past him into the study, untying the ribbons of her high-peaked bonnet as she went. The slat-shuttered French doors to the terrace were open. She walked to them and stood staring out across the gardens to the river, inhaling the sweet, heavy fragrance of jasmine. The silence between them became ponderous. When Eben brought her a glass of wine, she took it without saying more than a quiet thank you.

"Tell me."

She did not look at him as she spoke. She knew that if she had to see his face as he heard her words, she could never tell the truth. He would blame himself for Amanda's death. She knew that as surely as she knew it was not his fault, but the fault of two old men intent on arranging a marriage for profit and without regard for the childlike girl or the driving, stormy man involved.

"The baby came from somewhere on the plantation, Eben. Amanda was never really with child, though of course she found it easy enough to pretend. She had only to dress voluminously and keep you from her bed until the time when the real baby was expected. Since you were here in Savannah, I suppose she thought it would be easy enough to fool you into thinking the baby was yours. Her mother made all the plans, not anticipating that I would be on the island when it happened. Then when Mrs. White became ill and knew she would die, she shared the plan with Hiram. It became his responsibility to see that everything went as arranged." Suzannah had memorized these lines on the trip north. They were intended to convey the truth as quickly and unemotionally as possible. Yet now that she had actually spoken them, she realized that there were unexplained gulfs between each concisely put fact. She looked at her brother, an expression of helplessness on her face. She expected to see surprise or anger in his eyes. Instead, he slowly nodded his head.

"I think I always knew she wasn't. . . ."

"The baby died, Eben. It choked to death."

"Poor bastard," he muttered softly. "How is Amanda taking this?"

Suzannah's voice dropped to a whisper. "She was hysterical. From my room I could hear her screaming, screaming. . . ." Suzannah's voice trailed off as she remembered the words ringing through the rickety old house: Mama, Mama, come and get me!

"What was she screaming?"

"I . . . didn't hear. It was just noise. Hiram was with her until she fell asleep. Then," Suzannah sipped her wine, stalling, "in morning Dora and Biddy couldn't find her. We looked everywhere for her."

Eben groaned and turned away, covering his face with his hands.

"One of the yard boys found her in the afternoon, floating in the swampy water near the mouth of the inlet. She had drowned, Eben. I am so sorry."

Chapter 2

Long after Suzannah had kissed him goodnight and retired to her room, Eben Hopewell sat staring at the empty fireplace, idly swirling the brandy in his glass.

Amanda was dead. He had never loved her and had even wished himself free of her. Yet now that she was gone, he felt a deep regret for the failure of their marriage. In the early years before her mother's death and while she was still considered too young to marry, Amanda had been an endearing poppet of a girl. If she had failed at the day-to-day requirements of wifehood, if she had shown no skill for hostessing or housekeeping, if her conversation had been limited to girlish gossip, it was also true that Eben had never wholeheartedly given himself to the task of helping her mature. He knew in his heart he had never given Amanda the tender support she craved from him and to which she would have responded eagerly. In the beginning, her nature had been hopeful and sunlit. Like a garden. But he never could love her and she knew it. The more she knew it, the harder she tried to please him and the more pitiful she grew in his eyes. Eben had been eager to rush to Marianna's side or up to Boston and Lucy's arms. There had always been other women whose needs, as well as his own, he put before Amanda's. As their years together grew in number and her personality became more snappish and petulant, it was easier, always easier, to walk out the door and leave her alone.

On the mantel, a china clock struck the hour of nine. Eben glanced up at the instrument's blue face. Amanda had brought it with her from her parents' home because she said it matched her eyes. That was true enough, Eben always had agreed. What he could not say was that Lucy Shawn Kilmaine's eyes were almost the same brilliant azure, and whenever he looked at the clock he thought of her. Its chimes wounded him with every hour they struck. His body and head ached with guilt.

He'd killed Amanda with his disinterest. If he had been faithful and generous and, above all, loving with his young wife, she would still be alive, still garden-bright for him. If he had been patient instead of flying off the handle at the least provocation—a foolish word, a girlish spite—Amanda could have grown and learned from him. Instead. . . .

Eben put his head in his hands, but though his body hurt with the need to cry, his eyes were dry. Their burning shamed him, for it seemed to mean that, despite his grief, he did not truly care that Amanda was gone.

What had Lucy said to him?

Suddenly, he recalled a conversation they had had years and years earlier. He might still have been a student at Yale when he happened to meet her while riding his horse on Cooper's mountain. She had been put out because he had dismounted and walked beside her up the road past the old church. What had she told him? "You Hopewells are all the same. You use people, Eben, just like your father. You use them and when you're finished with them, you drop them and walk away. You care nothing for what they suffer."

But the last time they were together, she had told him that this wasn't true, that she had been wrong. Lucy, he thought, despising himself even as the words formed in his mind, I am free to love Lucy now.

But, of course, this was not true, as he quickly reminded himself with a fresh wash of guilt. Amanda was dead, but Marianna, his tragic mistress, remained in her little villa on the South Coast Road. And there would always be Christian, his son by her. His son. This reminded him of Amanda and the poor baby that was not and never had been his. At last he wept. Not for Amanda, but for the child he had never quite believed in. Flesh of his flesh. Bone and blood of his own. The longing to hold and own a child before the world without shame or explanation, to say this child is mine and I am his, was an emotion so strong in Eben that for the moment it was sufficient to drive away guilt and grief. He thought of Christian, and suddenly nothing would console him except a few moments with the boy.

He hurried from the house to the stable and saddled his mount. From her room upstairs, Suzannah, lying sleepless, heard the hoof beats on the cobbled drive and guessed where her brother was going.

On the South Coast Road a mile or two from town, he slowed his horse to a walk. Then he stopped on a bluff overlooking the dunes and the ocean. A sliver of moon hung overhead like an ornament in the spangled sky. He stared at its reflection on the calm waters, wishing he were still at home, grieving for his young wife as he knew was right. She had killed herself because his love was insufficient. To Eben, who

had never raised his hand to her or threatened her
with violence, this was the same as murder. Now he
regretted his hasty departure for Marianna's. He
wished he had stayed at Jasmine Gate, forcing the
tears until the china clock struck dawn. He wished for
so many things, for second chances in the way of
love. Yet, despite all this, he continued his midnight
ride to Villa Caribe. The sense of his worthlessness
and the futility of life and love engulfed him. He
hated himself bitterly.

Villa Caribe was a small stone house set
discreetly behind ten-foot-high stone walls in the
midst of a bountiful garden. It was situated a quarter
of a mile from the coast on a rise of land at the end
of a narrow track. It had been Marianna's home for
most of the years she had known Eben. It was he
who had arranged to have it built and furnished.
Within the walled enclosure, behind iron gates, there
was a stable. He roused a boy who was sleeping in
the hay to tend his horse. As he entered the house
through the front door, Bess, Marianna's only house
servant, was in the foyer to meet him. Dressed in a
nightgown and wrapper, the old black woman's fat
face was wrinkled from sleep and cross as an ornery
cat.

"Mr. Eben," she cried, snapping her toothless
gums in reproach, "this whole house be sleeping. Why
you coming here at this hour of the night?"

He walked past her and into the sitting room.
The terrace doors overlooking the sea beyond were
shuttered. At the sideboard on which Marianna kept a
decanter of his favorite brandy, he poured himself a
drink.

"Don't scold me, Bess," he said after several swallows. "Where is Mrs. St. Clair?"

"In her bed, of course! Where do you suppose she is? Off dancing the cotillion?" Bess tugged her wrapper more securely about her waist and pointed at the clock. "Look there. It's after midnight. You don't expect me to wake her up, I hope. That poor little thing needs all her sleep. What she suffers. . . ."

Eben did not want to hear about Marianna's pain. Grabbing the decanter from the sideboard, he went out of the room and started up the stairs. He met Marianna just coming down.

She held a taper in her hand. In the candlelight it seemed as if the signs of her illness had dropped away and she was the girl he had met long ago in a brothel and sworn to love forever. But she descended the stairs slowly and when she was close to him, Eben could see how lined her face had become and how frail her appearance.

"Eben, my dear, I am glad to see you." She stood a step above him but was so petite that she still had to stand on tiptoe to kiss his cheek.

"I told him I don't think he's got no business coming round here at this time of night when folks are all in bed and getting the sleep they needs and deserves. I told him. . . ."

"Thank you, Bess," said Marianna quietly, smiling. "I will be fine and you must by all means go back to bed."

"But Miz Marianna, you need your rest more'n any of us. You don't want all this excitement in the middle of the night!"

Marianna's tone was firm. "Bess, Mr. Hopewell is the master of this house. Have you forgotten? He may come to call when he wishes, and he knows that I am always happy to see him."

Bess looked resentful and shot Eben a snarl of pure displeasure, but she waddled to the back of the house where her room was located. Her mutterings were silenced by the slamming of the hall door.

Eben sprawled in a large and comfortable chair in the sitting room. He had finished his first drink and was halfway through another.

"She's right. I should not have come." His brows knitted as he stared into his glass. "Go back to bed, Marianna. I'll talk to you in the morning."

"As you wish, Eben. But I would prefer to stay with you. I meant it when I said that I am always happy to see you."

"But you are not well."

She stood behind him and rubbed his neck soothingly in a way she knew he liked. "I am quite well at the moment, Eben. Besides, I cannot imagine feeling so ill that I would send you away."

He leaned against her hands, feeling the tension seep from his body. It was wrong to come to her, but it was right, too. The contradictions spun in Eben's head and mingled with the dizzying effect of the brandy. In broken sentences, he blurted out the truth about Amanda, sparing himself none of the responsibility. When he was finished, Marianna came around in front of him and knelt at his feet. She was so close that he could see the tears in her amber eyes.

"Why should you weep? Amanda was nothing to you."

"She was your wife."

"I didn't love her."

Marianna shook her head a little. "Perhaps not passionately, but I believe you cared for her and I know you were good to her."

With a bitter laugh, he pushed her aside and went to the sideboard. He poured another drink. "How can you say I cared for her? Before I even married her, I put you in this house and vowed to care for you." His voice was hard and brittle.

"It is possible to love more than one person, Eben. I believe you loved us both." Marianna rose painfully from her knees and went to her favorite chair near the window. With his back to her, Eben could not see how slowly she moved, but he heard her labored breathing.

He put down his drink without finishing it. "I'll carry you upstairs."

"It doesn't matter, Eben. You are all I care about. You and Christian are all of life to me." At the sound of his son's name, Eben's eyes filled with tears. Marianna saw them. "About the baby, Eben, I'm sorry for that, too. But . . . I confess I never wanted you to have someone else's son. I was afraid that if Amanda's child was at all winning, it would lure you away from Christian."

"I think Amanda knew about Christian and thought of the . . . ruse as a way to win back my love from him."

"It would have happened, Eben. You would have loved that white baby more than Christian."

He was furious at the suggestion. Pointing upwards, toward the room where the boy slept, he declared, "Christian is my first-born. And the child of our love. How can you suggest . . . ?"

"Sit here beside me, Eben. Don't let us be angry with one another at this sad time."

He began to pace. "I won't be cajoled or coddled by you, Marianna. You think my love for Christian is inferior. That's what you're saying. You believe I can't love the boy because he's black."

She sighed. "I never said any of that, Eben."

"You think I'm ashamed of him."

"Not ashamed, never that. But, after all, you cannot claim him publicly. I know you wish you could."

In a burst of passion, Eben threw his glass against the sideboard. It shattered. "What the hell do you know about my wishes?"

"Eben, *chéri*, I only meant . . ." She tried to rise from her chair, but an unexpected spasm of pain struck her. Uttering a small, inadvertent cry, she fell back against the cushions. Eben stared at her.

"Why do you look at me that way?" she gasped.

"Where is he?"

"He's sleeping, Eben. Don't disturb him, *chéri*. He's just a little boy."

"I am going to prove you're wrong. I may be a bastard as well as a murderer, but I love my son and I am willing to prove it."

"Think, Eben. Think. Don't do anything you'll be sorry for in the morning."

Eben strode to the foot of the stairs, then turned back to her, saying, "In the morning all Savannah will know that Christian St. Clair is the full son of Eben Hopewell."

"No, my darling! You can't do that," she cried. But he ignored her and rushed out. His heavy boots made an angry noise on the stairs and then on the floor overhead. She heard Christian's door bang against the wall as Eben opened it. "No, Eben," she whispered, tears slipping down her cheeks. She tried to rise, but a terrible lassitude came over her and she sank back in the chair, listening to the beat of her heart.

Eben brought the boy, still dressed in his white nightshirt, downstairs. Marianna had never seen her lover in such a state of fury. She was frightened of him, and frightened for him as well. Lying in Eben's arms, bewildered and still half asleep, Christian looked from one of them to the other.

"I know you love him, Eben," she said, rising from the chair at last and trying to take Christian from him. "You needn't prove your love this way."

"Why not? Why not prove it to the world?"

"You'll be ruined. And think of the pain you will bring to Hiram and his poor father. Give me the boy, Eben. Please, Eben, put him down. Wait. Wait."

Too late. Eben was already out the front door and striding through the garden toward the stable. He set Christian down in the hay while he saddled his horse. Then, lifting the drowsy youngster in his arms, he mounted and rode out the gate without looking back. When he reached the South Coast Road, he kicked the horse into a gallop, wheeling him off to the right and down a sand dune to the water's edge. In front of him on the saddle, clutched in the crook of his arm, Christian squirmed and turned to look up at his father with large amber eyes the color of his mother's. The sight stung Eben, and he kicked the animal again so that its hooves flew across the hard, wet sand. The gritty sea air bit into his skin.

"Father, where are we going?" Christian's voice trembled with excitement. He was close to tears. "I'm afraid, Father."

Eben was as oblivious to Christian's words as he was to the night and the sea. One obsession controlled his mind completely. He would be finished with the lies, the hiding, the duplicity that had driven his wife to a desperate hoax that finally had made her life such a misery that only death seemed comforting. And if Marianna thought he was ashamed of Christian, he would prove otherwise to her. Once and for all, he would stop hiding. He would present the boy to the world and call him son and to the devil with those who pointed to his tawny skin and curling hair. Whatever was required and for however long it took, Eben swore he would be done with lies.

"Father!"

The word penetrated Eben's consciousness, the first and last thing he heard before the horse, catching its hoof in a hole in the sand, lost its balance. Its right front leg doubled under and it pitched forward, flinging both Eben and Christian over its head.

Chapter 3

Eben and Christian landed in the sand. Apart from minor bruises, aches and strains, they were unhurt. The horse, however, had broken its leg. As Eben, carrying his son, returned on foot to the Villa Caribe, he could hear the screams of the suffering animal as the wind carried them down the long, empty beach after him. At the house, he deposited Christian with a tight-lipped and silently condemning Bess. Taking a pistol from its rack in the hall, he walked back and put the beast out of its pain. It was midmorning by the time Eben finally returned to the villa.

Marianna was resting upstairs, and he did not disturb her. He felt ashamed and as stupid as an adolescent for the way he had carried on. Rousing Christian from his slumber, driving the horse dangerously and, finally, killing the animal through carelessness. This was not the behavior of a man Eben could admire. Coupled with the circumstances of Amanda's suicide, the events of the previous night filled Eben with self-loathing.

Once before he had experienced these depths. Long ago on a visit to Savannah with Martin Hopewell, he had discovered the truth about the man he had admired and sought to emulate. His father had been responsible for his grandfather's death. Now, lying on the daybed in his room at the Villa Caribe, Eben recalled all the details of that visit and of the weeks that had followed it when he had sunk into madness. He had learned that his father was a monster and had fled from that knowledge to the edge of suicide, certain that the same was true of him. Wondering how he could ever escape his father's evil, he had stood on the high rocks overlooking the Amoset River, his gaze fixed on the boiling rapids below. He had wanted to leap and be lost forever, but finally he had turned away, knowing that death was too easy. After that, Eben had converted his hatred into pure energy and stormed into the world. He had made a fortune in the name of Hopewell and spread the fame of his family throughout the Southern states.

Now he asked himself what was the use of it all when the truth about himself was as he had feared all along. He was as much a monster as Martin Hopewell. His actions were proof of this. His heartlessness had driven Amanda to take her own life, he had terrified Christian and he had destroyed an animal so faithful and good that it would have run for him until its heart exploded.

Eben stayed at the Villa Caribe for two days. During that time he saw almost nothing of Marianna, who spent hours alone in her room looking out at the sea. Sometimes he and Christian took a meal together, but the boy was obviously nervous in his father's company. The ride on the beach had shown him that Eben could be a dangerous man. This new reticence in Christian was agony for Eben. He longed for words to explain what had happened that night, but Christian was not yet five years old and there was no way he could be made to understand. It seemed to

Eben in his depression that this was his doom, his fate, the way it would always be for him. It seemed that there would never be anyone to whom he could explain the twisted braiding of his emotions.

Lucy. As he wandered aimlessly about the villa gardens or sprawled in a chaise on the terrace below Marianna's window, his guilty thoughts turned irresistibly to Lucy Kilmaine in Boston. Would she understand him, or was he deluding himself about her as he had about himself? He saw Lucy vividly in his mind, and sometimes the longing for her reached a painful intensity. But fast in the wake of this hunger came shame and guilt. He would hear Marianna stirring in the room above and hate himself the more.

Although his and Marianna's relationship had been extremely ardent in the beginning, after a few years Marianna's illness had made sexual intimacy difficult. Even when she seemed well, Eben could not forget how she sometimes suffered. This awareness had made him acutely sensitive to the fragility of her delicate, almost childlike, body. When they embraced, he was afraid of hurting her. Foolish as it was, he believed she might break in his arms like driftwood kindling and so his embraces had become more gentle than passionate over the years.

But he loved Marianna more than any person he had ever known, for she had never failed him. Ever since he had rescued her from her half-sister's brothel, she had devoted her life to loving him and providing him with all he desired. She had made the Villa Caribe a haven for him. There, his daily tension and inherent anger and melancholy dissipated and became inconsequential. Marianna asked nothing of him, and so he gave her all he had and was refreshed. When Christian was born, a child with golden skin and amber eyes who was as beautiful as his mother,

Eben believed that he could accept whatever life might bring to him from then on. A son, an innocent new soul made from his own corrupt body, was the greatest gift he had ever received.

Yet he had risked the boy's life on a crazed midnight ride. He had terrified the child he loved more than himself. And for what reason? Despite his inebriated declarations to Marianna, he would never have claimed Christian publicly. If he had been cruel to Amanda while she lived, he could not humiliate her memory. Nor could he shame Gregory White, his father-in-law, the man who came closest to fulfilling his need for a father. Therefore, if he could not openly acknowledge Christian as his son, of what use was all his talk of fatherly love? Was he so self-indulgent that there was no love on which he would not turn his back if it seemed expedient to do so?

Such were the twists and turns in the maze of Eben's thoughts, a maze in which he was both the monster and the questing hero.

On the morning of the third day, Suzannah sent him a message saying that Gregory White wished to see him. Reluctantly, Eben left the Villa Caribe and rode to town.

He found his father-in-law in his office at the bank. Although it was not yet noon, Gregory White was fully absorbed in the work of the day and did not immediately look up as Eben entered the comfortable pine-paneled office which had been the setting for many happy times between the two men.

Finally, Gregory raised his head. During the past year, he had lost both his beloved wife and his daughter. Grief had lined and aged his ruddy face. Without smiling or speaking, he motioned to the chair facing his desk. Eben sat down obediently. White was a large, handsome man in his late forties, a distinguished-looking man with bright, intelligent eyes and dark, silver-streaked hair. In happier times, he smiled frequently and was known by everyone as a man of hearty and jovial temperament. But on this morning his expression was somber. He put down his stylus and meticulously took the time to straighten the edges of the papers piled in front of him. When this was done, he stared at Eben for a long moment.

Under such close scrutiny, Eben wanted to turn away, but he forced himself to return his father-in-law's gaze. At the center of his passionate temperament, there was a core of pure, hard Yankee in Eben Hopewell. Now the Yankee would not let him continue to avoid the results of his actions. To have done so would have meant tightening the twisted knot of guilt around his heart that was already threatening to destroy him.

Gregory was the first to speak. He prefaced his words with a long, deep sigh. Turning his chair, he faced away from Eben as he spoke, his eyes fixed on the window behind his desk that opened onto a small green and floral garden. A pair of slaves in blue working clothes were on their knees beside the flower beds. As he watched them weeding and snipping the withered blossoms from the plants, he said, "You are, of course, my daughter's heir. I have just been looking over the applicable documents and thought now was the proper time to discuss them with you. I trust I have not interrupted whatever important business kept you out of town."

"I have been too ashamed to come here."

Another sigh. "I'm not surprised. Or perhaps I am. It is hard to know precisely one's feelings at a time like this." Eben started to speak, but Gregory would not allow him to interrupt. It was as if he had planned his comments, practiced them, and was determined to have them said before any word from Eben could change his mind. "I told you once that I believed Amanda would mature and make you a good wife. I wasn't lying to you in order to assure your marriage. Nor was your grandfather. Theron and I both believed it at the time. But later, particularly in the last three or four years, I began to see that I had made a great mistake."

"Sir, the guilt is mine. I bear it all."

Gregory turned to face him. One eyebrow raised, he said, "You do?" He laughed shortly. "I was not affixing blame, Eben. Merely responsibility. I think there's a difference. I should never have permitted Amanda to marry. Now that she is . . . gone, I can say that there was something wrong with her. I've known it for some time. For that reason, I was able to excuse, even understand, the business of your mistress, the seamstress Marianna St. Clair."

"You knew about her."

"Why, certainly I did, Eben. What do you take me for? It was Amanda who was slow-witted and not I. Of course I knew about the St. Clair woman, and so did half the city. But I tolerated it because I felt that I had persuaded you to marry Amanda under false pretenses. I should have known years ago that she was like her grandmother."

"Sir?"

"My mother was a childlike woman, very like Amanda. Even their pretty appearance was much the same. But her life was different from Amanda's. She was married to a man of great wealth but country manners. He had no need of a wife with any wit. She bore him children and cared for them with the help of slaves. That was sufficient activity to make my mother's life a happy one. Her day to day existence on the island involved nothing more challenging to her intelligence than a barbecue or fete."

"Nothing can excuse what I did, Gregory. If you are being kind to me out of sensitivity to my feelings, then I tell you that you need not be. I have spent the last three days in the kind of painful self-examination that . . ."

"I am not interested in your guilt, Eben. My own is sufficient." For a few moments, White busied himself with glancing through the papers on his desk. When he spoke again, a light shone in his moist eyes. "As you know, at the time of your marriage to Amanda, I provided her with a generous dowry that included several thousand acres in the center of the state, the property we call Seven Springs. There was also some tobacco land to the south and several thousand dollars in shares."

Eben stood up. "I don't want any of it."

"There is also the jewelry she inherited from her grandmothers as well as that which came to her recently from my wife. A few emeralds, some rubies, a rather fine diamond tiara."

"I said I don't want it."

"You don't really have much to say about it, Eben. Your wife died and as her heir it is all yours." Gregory pushed the papers toward Eben. "Read them. You were rich to begin with. You are doubly so now."

Eben felt himself growing hot. "I will not profit by her death. If you think I would, you do not know me, Gregory."

"Oh, I know you, Eben. Better than you know yourself at this point. You are crazed with grief and shame and guilt now, but . . ."

"I said I don't want it."

Gregory shrugged and rubbed his eyes. "Even if

you don't sign, it is still yours. Shall I call in our lawyer to convince you?"

They stared at one another again. This time Gregory White's unflinching gaze was more than Eben could bear. He collapsed into the chair and covered his face with his hands. When he could trust himself to speak, he said, "I care for only one thing and that is your good opinion of me. I know it is lost forever. I have been a fool, Gregory. A fool and a blind man, but I cannot undo anything I have done. I can only ask that you find it in your heart somehow, someday, to forgive me for what I did to Amanda." He looked up. "Is that possible, Gregory? Or do you hate me so much . . .?"

"I do not hate you, Eben. I pity you."

"I don't want pity."

"Why not? It is an honest feeling on my part. I pity you because you are an enemy to yourself. You have been a second son to me, but . . ." Something occurred to Gregory and he stopped short. After thinking for a moment, he said, "Of all of us, I think Hiram's grief is the most acute. It is he who suffers the greatest pain now. Be careful of him, Eben. I don't know what he might do."

Eben nodded and stood up.

"Eben, about Amanda's dowry . . ."

"It is yours. Have our attorneys draw up the documents. I will sign it all back to you." He closed the door on White's protest.

Once outside the bank, standing on the sunny Savannah street, Eben was at a loss. He didn't know where to go, what to do. His talk with White had been different from what he had expected, but just as bad. Though there might be no outward break between them, Eben knew their intimacy was permanently destroyed. They would be polite. They would be friendly. Nevertheless, the loving comradeship was gone forever.

Though it was nearly noon and perishingly hot in Savannah, the main street of the little city was crowded and noisy with the clatter of wheels and hooves on cobbles. The footpath was crowded with merchants and tradespeople and slaves hurrying about on their errands, calling out and talking among themselves. Standing on the steps of the bank, Eben was oblivious to this industrious confusion. When acquaintances raised their hats to him and offered their condolences, he paid no attention to them. Instead, his mind was fixed on Hiram White and what suddenly had become his first concern. He had spoken honestly with Gregory, and now he must do so with Amanda's brother. He must seek out Hiram and attempt to mend the breach between them.

He found Hiram at the threshing mill. The mill had been a thriving business for some years, largely due to Hiram's determined pursuit of the rice trade from the island plantations. It had been his idea to institute a regular traffic of flatboats down the Savannah River. The boats traveled in and out among the most northern of the sea islands where many of the rice planters, having no mills of their own, were quick to take advantage of the service. Hiram paid cash for their crop, then threshed it himself and sold it to the highest bidder.

As Eben emerged from the hot and dusty pine woods that separated the mill from the river road, Eben saw Hiram at the boat landing supervising the unloading of a flatboat that had recently arrived from the islands. Before approaching him, Eben held back, taking the measure of his brother-in-law as if he were a stranger. Hiram White was several years younger than thirty-three-year-old Eben, but his boyish appearance made the age difference seem even greater than it was. He was of medium height and had broad shoulders and a barrel chest. Seen from behind, dressed in his large straw hat, jodphurs and high boots, he had the immovable appearance of a tree trunk set firmly in the ground. Watching as Hiram struck the handle of his whip impatiently against his thigh and yelled out orders to the bare-chested slaves, Eben knew his brother-in-law was a man who must be handled carefully. Despite his jovial smile and open farmer's face, he was hot-tempered, satisfied only when things were going his way.

"Hiram," Eben called as he swung out of the saddle and handed the reins to a slave. "Hiram," he called again.

His brother-in-law turned slowly as if he doubted his senses. As Eben walked toward him, Hiram did not speak. His expression was flat, impassive. When they were a few feet apart he said, "What do you want?"

"We must talk, brother. Alone."

"I don't believe we have anything to say to each other." Hiram looked at the flatboat and, seeing something amiss, gave several curt orders, his voice loud and crackling with hostility. Then he turned back to Eben. "And I am not your brother. I am no one's brother anymore."

"We have to talk, Hiram."

"Why?"

"Not here. Alone." Eben looked around. He and Hiram were the only white men at the mill. The slaves were hard at work, but he knew they were listening to their masters. When the day was over, they undoubtedly would return to their shanties with several versions of what they had heard. In a few days time, all of Savannah would know the details of the meeting between Eben Hopewell and Hiram White.

Hiram, who did not regard slaves as human beings, was unconcerned with what they heard. "Anything you have to say, you can say it here."

Eben's hands doubled into fists and he pressed them hard against his thighs, forcing down the anger he felt rising in him at Hiram's insulting tone.

"I haven't got all day, Hopewell."

"You're making this very difficult for me."

"I'm gratified to know that. Now, what do you have to say?"

"It's about Amanda, of course. You must know that I never wanted such an awful thing to happen. If I had known about your scheme with the baby . . ."

"What would you have done? Would you have given up your nigger mistress and that yellow bastard?"

The question stopped Eben. He could not answer.

Hiram's face reddened with anger. "Obviously, we have nothing to say to each other. Get off this property."

"I'm part owner, Hiram. You can't drive me off my own land when I have a right to be here."

"Very well. I will leave." Hiram strode away toward the mill, but Eben followed him. Near the double doors of the entrance, he grabbed Hiram's arm.

"Listen, Hiram, I don't pretend that what I did was admirable. I'm not here to offer up excuses for the unforgivable. There was never such a mismatched couple as Amanda and me. We never should have been married."

"I knew that from the beginning, but I had to

pretend you didn't treat her like shit from the barn-
yard."

"That's a lie. You know I was good to her."

"You shamed her and set her up for ridicule. You
made her the laughingstock of Savannah."

"Try to understand me for a moment, Hiram. Just
try to imagine what it was like being married to a
girl, a child who never grew up. . . ."

"You turned your back on her and went to that
pig."

Eben took a step forward. "Don't call her that."

"Why not? Does it give you pain to hear the
truth? She's a whore, a nigger whore, Eben Hopewell.
My brother!" Hiram spat out the words and strode
into the mill. Eben followed, yelling over the grating
sound of the turning mortar.

"I didn't come here to have you insult Marianna.
But if it makes you feel better, if you have to do it,
then insult me."

"Nothing will make me feel better except to see
you as dead as Amanda," Hiram sneered. "You really
did manage to avoid it all, didn't you? You were up
here in Savannah and never had to see her, that
pretty girl with her face and skin all bloated like a
fish belly from being in the water. And you didn't
have to stand there while they put her in the ground
without even the honor of a decent burial because already the heat of the island was making her stink." In
the darkness inside the mill, Eben could not see his
brother-in-law's face, but he knew how he was suffering. Hiram's voice trembled with pain and rage combined. "She never was good enough for you, was she?
She did her best to please you, but nothing was ever
enough. You wanted some mannish, school-talking
Yankee bitch. Or that other one." Eben tried to interrupt, but Hiram drowned out his words. Now that he

had begun to speak his mind, the words poured from his mouth like a poisoned stream held back too long. "I knew Marianna St. Clair back in the days when her sister kept that fancy house on the river road. I paid for her once myself. Did you know that? Did she ever tell you how she turned that little brown butt around to me?"

Eben slammed his fist into Hiram's face before he knew what was happening. Blood gushed from the younger man's nose. Hiram's mouth dropped open in surprise and then he began to laugh, a vicious, satisfied sound. Like a dog with his teeth sunk deep in the neck of a rabbit, Hiram knew that it was he and not Eben who had drawn first blood.

He backed away, but continued to speak. "Has she told you? Did she tell you she liked it?" One hand reached for where his whip was jammed through a loop on his trousers. "Did she tell you how good I tasted?" Hiram laughed, loud and hard.

Eben made a lunge for him, but Hiram blocked him with a blow from the butt end of the whip. Eben's temples rang with pain, but in his rage he could ignore almost any hurt. He hurled himself against the stocky younger man, throwing them both onto the floor, which was dusty with rice husks. Hiram beat against his shoulders and back with the end of the whip as Eben groped for his throat and set his thumbs against his windpipe. He pressed hard and his victim's laughter gurgled and stopped. Hiram's eyes widened and were suddenly full of tears. Eben relaxed his death hold.

Hiram sobbed. Despite the fury of the last few moments, despite Hiram's venomous verbal attack, Eben's rage evaporated at the sight and sound of his weeping. His own eyes watered uncontrollably, and he reached to embrace the man he had wanted to kill just an instant before. They were closer than ever in their lives as they clung together and wept for the child-woman each had cared for in his own way.

It was Hiram who spoke. "Why wasn't it enough? Why?" In the shaft of sunlight that shot through a break high up in the mill roof, his face was shiny with tears. "She never knew. She never believed me. I loved her just the way she was."

Chapter 4

On the first day of November, Suzannah received a letter from James Shawn in Amoset. Early that day, Belle had brought her the mail as she sat in her bedroom at Jasmine Gate. When she saw the familiar handwriting, the bold up and down strokes without flourishes or decoration, her hands began to shake. She was glad to be alone where no one could see the flush of excitement that reddened her cheeks as she slit the envelope with a silver letter opener. It began:

> My dear Suzannah,
> I am writing you on the advice of your sister-in-law, Margaret Duffy. She and I agreed that you and Eben must be told the desperate state to which Hopewell Mills has sunk under the administration of your brother Valentine.

It was a long letter. She read it twice, at first paying little regard to the message. She had hoped for some word that James loved her and wanted her back in the North for his own happiness. The slightest allusion to their relationship would have thrilled her, but the letter was the sort of businesslike message that a casual acquaintance would have written out of concern for the family. Not until the second reading did she begin to absorb James' depressing news.

"We both must return to Amoset," she told Eben that afternoon when they were alone. They were walking in the garden behind the house after the midday meal. The setting was idyllic. Flower beds of vivid pink and white and yellow bloomed everywhere and the air was fragrant with the honeysuckle and jasmine that twined profusely among the branches of the trees. From where Suzannah and her brother stood, the view of the Savannah River was wide and tranquil. All of this could not calm Suzannah's agitated nerves, however. "From what James said, we have no time to lose."

Since their intimate and revealing conversation one afternoon several months earlier, Suzannah and Eben had not spoken of the secret relationships that figured crucially in their lives. Still, when Suzannah spoke the name of her former lover, the father of her son, she knew her voice was trembling and that Eben understood the cause.

"I trust James completely," she went on after a moment, walking a little ahead of Eben so he could not see her face. "He would not have written were the situation not urgent."

"Tell me what he said."

"Some of it will hurt you, Eben." Not only had Valentine squandered the family wealth, but the mill's good name had been damaged, perhaps beyond repair. And there was more. Suzannah faltered, wondering how to begin.

Eben, sensing her discomfort, said, "I assure you, Suzannah, though Valentine's mismanagement worries me and makes me angry, I am not hurt by it. To tell you the truth, I expected something like this from him. Our brother never surprises me much anymore." Eben knocked his pipe against a tree trunk and a shower of sparks dropped to the moist earth like tiny fireworks.

"It was a long letter. And not just about business. It seems . . . Eben, do you recall that for many years there have been violent attacks on young women in Amoset? And do you recall that all of the women, in addition to being mill operatives, had something else in common?"

He wrinkled his brow. "They were blonde, weren't they? Pretty young women with blonde hair."

"That's right."

Eben laughed suddenly. "Surely you are not going to tell me that our Valentine was the culprit. He may be a worthless . . ."

"It was Foster McMahon, our former overseer at the mill. He was the one who committed the murders."

"That brute! I never did like the man, but how was he found out? How can anyone be sure?"

"It seems that all along the focus of his . . . madness . . . was Lucy, Eben. Lucy Shawn Kilmaine."

For as long as she lived, Suzannah would remember the progression of emotions that traveled across her brother's face. At first he was incredulous, then enraged and, finally, anguished. "She is lost!" he cried, turning away.

Instantly, Suzannah embraced him. "He didn't harm Lucy, Eben," she assured him. "But James wrote that she is badly shaken by the incident."

"What happened? You must tell me everything."

"McMahon kidnapped her off the Boston streets when she and little Delphia were shopping. He took her to Amoset and tried to use her to extort ten thousand dollars from Valentine. He claimed the mill owed it to him."

"She is worth all that and more." He stared grimly at the placid river. "I would have paid as much as I could lay my hands on."

Suzannah leaned against the low stone wall separating the garden from the slope of lawn that stretched to the riverside. "Valentine refused to pay anything. James had to go after McMahon himself. He and a young Irishman from the Gully, a magician named Mickey Quick, discovered that McMahon was hiding in that wretched old tavern outside town. Lucy was with him, and so were his wife and his son, Simon. There was a fight and James killed McMahon."

"By God, I'll do some killing myself! What in the name of God is the matter with Valentine? How could he risk . . .?" Eben began to pace furiously, his boot heels making a sharp, ringing noise on the flagged path. His teeth were clamped down so hard on the stem of his pipe that a line of white marked the contour on his strong, square jaw. Beneath glowering brows, his sea-green eyes darkened stormily. "She could have been murdered. Or worse! And God knows what it did to her spirit, locking her up, making her a prisoner." He wheeled toward the house, calling back to Suzannah over his shoulder. "We'll go north immediately. I'll send Prospero to check on ships. If we have to, we can go by carriage. I must see Lucy!"

"Stop, Eben," Suzannah cried, hurrying to him. "Wait." He glared at her. "There is more, Eben. Walk with me. And listen. You have to know it all." She reached for his hand and held it tightly. "James was not as hard on our brother as you might expect. He said that Valentine probably did not have the money to pay McMahon."

"That is preposterous."

"Think for a moment. We both know Val. He's a foolish gambler. He takes too many risks. And he has never truly cared for the mill and its affairs. According to James, he has so mismanaged everything that the business has sunk into an abyss of debt."

"All the more reason to leave for the North immediately. Affairs here are such that I . . ." Eben's voice faded and he stared moodily at the river, unable to finish his thought. It seemed impossible, but for a moment he had entirely forgotten Amanda, Gregory and Hiram. Even Marianna had slipped from his consciousness as soon as he had heard of Lucy's plight.

"What about Marianna?" Suzannah asked gently.

"I will have to return to Savannah because of her and because of our son, of course. But since Amanda's death and my falling out with Gregory and Hiram, Marianna and Christian are all that hold me here."

"Shall I tell Patrick we're going?"

Eben nodded. "I'll make the arrangements."

But that evening as he rode along the coast toward the Villa Caribe, it occurred to Eben that it might be awkward if he flew to Lucy's side. Her husband, Thomas, might become suspicious. And he knew that to leave now, while Marianna was suffering, was the kind of self-centered behavior that had brought grief to his friends and family before. Still, his concern for Lucy overcame these thoughts. He told himself that Marianna had been ill for so many years that his departure now could make little difference to her condition. Anyway, no matter how bad she felt, he knew she would never ask him to stay in Savannah. He had only to mention family and business and finance and Marianna would wish him Godspeed. Furthermore, when he told her, as he suddenly decided he would, that he would use the visit as an opportunity to find a school in Boston for Christian, Marianna would never complain. Years before, they had settled the matter of the boy's education. Much as she did not want to lose her son's companionship, Marianna had agreed that if Christian were ever to have an opportunity for a happy and productive life, he must be educated in the North.

But when he spoke to her of these matters later that evening after a light meal on the candlelit terrace, Marianna's reaction surprised him. Her pretty face hardened, and she asked him to stay in the South.

He tried not to be angry. Marianna asked so little of him and gave so generously of herself. He must be calm and patient with her. He could persuade her to his point of view. She was ill, but that was no bar to understanding.

"Mrs. Paine can go. You've told me many times that your sister is the equal of any man where matters of business are concerned." Marianna ran her fingernail along the fold of her napkin again and again.

"This is different, Marianna. Valentine can be a violent man. He threatened Patrick."

"I am asking you not to go, Eben. Not yet." Her large amber eyes met his. "Please."

Despite his resolve, Eben grew impatient. But even as he felt his pulse quicken with the beginnings of anger, he was shamed. Marianna was gentle. If it came to a fight, he knew how quickly she would capitulate to his wishes. It was not in her, he thought, to demand her own way for very long. "If you knew how important the mill is to our family, Marianna, you would not trouble me with whimsical demands."

She flinched, and he could see clearly the hurt in her eyes. He thought she would accede to his wishes then, but she continued to surprise him by saying, "This is no whim, Eben."

"Look, Marianna, I swear I won't be gone long and I will be attending to more than just Hopewell family matters. I plan to make the arrangements we spoke of concerning Christian's education. Soon the lad will be ready for schooling." He patted her arm. "Six weeks or two months. I won't be gone longer."

"I don't want Christian sent north."

"My God, Marianna, what in the name of heaven has gotten into you? We talked this through years ago, and we agreed that for the boy's sake it is best." He stopped suddenly and gripped her forearm tightly. "What is it? There must be something more to this, something you haven't told me. What has happened to make you behave. . . ."

She tugged her arm away and stood up. As she walked to the corner of the terrace and looked across the dunes to the sea, she said quietly, "I want to go home, Eben."

"This is your home."

"No. It is where I live. There is a difference."

"You can't mean you intend to go back to Martinique? I will not permit it, Marianna. I want you here."

She turned and looked at him, smiling a little. "Do you really, Eben? We have been so much to one another and for so long a time, let us not begin now to tell lies."

Eben felt a twinge of panic as he sensed the conversation slipping from his control.

"I love you. I want you near me. What in the name of God . . .?"

"I want to go home to die." Her voice did not

quaver, nor did her eyes leave his face. Her serene stoicism confounded him, and he could think of nothing to say for a long time.

"I don't believe you," he said at last. "No one can tell when they are going to die. That's all mumbo jumbo and superstition."

"You know nothing of such things, *chéri*. I do not manage your mills and banks and railways for you. Pray do not claim to live within my skin and know all that I am privy to." Her expression was maddeningly peaceful.

"There is nothing the matter with you. You are tired and you have some kind of arthritis. You've seen several doctors and they all say the same thing. Beyond that . . ."

". . . there is so much more."

He refused to heed her. "Anyway, you can't go back to Martinique. What about Yves, your half brother? He hates you. It isn't safe."

"If Yves St. Clair were still alive, I would not go."

"He's dead? How can you possibly know that?"

"I have had a letter from Aimee."

"That old whore!" Angrily, Eben poured himself another glass of wine, slopping it on the white tablecloth. He drank it down in a single swallow.

"I remind you, Eben, that when we met, I too was a . . ."

"You were different." Confused, slightly drunk, he ran his hands through his thick, dark hair.

"Aimee is in Havana now. In the same business, I presume. She simply said that Yves had died in a shooting accident last year."

"More than likely someone did the world a favor and put a bullet through his head."

She smiled. "Perhaps, *chéri*. At any rate, he is gone and now I may return."

"Have you only stayed here' with me because he was still alive?"

"*Mon amour,* how can you ask? You know I am here because of you. I love you, Eben, but our time together is like the sand in a glass. It has all run through."

Though he knew she loved him still and that what she wanted might even be the best for both of them, Eben was too stunned to react in any way that was not defensive. He got up from the table and strode to her side. Grabbing her, he said, "You won't take my son."

"You are hurting me, Eben."

"I don't care. Did you hear what I just said?"

"He is my son as well as yours, Eben."

"But I won't permit you to take him down to that island and lose him to a bunch of superstitious old Africans."

She laughed at him with what sounded like real amusement. "Those Africans, as you call them, are his cousins and aunts and uncles. His heritage is on Martinique."

"And here, too, Marianna. And in Massachusetts. You cannot deny that. You only want him near you for selfish reasons. You want to cling to him for as long as you can. And that is all very well while you are alive. But if it is true that you are . . . dying, what will become of the boy when you are gone? His black blood shows, Marianna. If he stays in the South or in the Caribbean, they will make him a slave and you know it. Is that what you want? To see him in bondage like the rest of his race?"

"He has his papers, Eben. They prove . . ."

"You know perfectly well that documents can be lost or destroyed. In a place where there is no law, they can simply be ignored."

Her eyes filled with tears. "I love him so, Eben."

"Then stay here." He sat down, convinced of his victory over her.

For some moments they said nothing. From her corner of the terrace, Marianna's sighs were like the movement of the wind through the sharp-tongued grass. The moon had not yet risen, but near the horizon the sky was softly, luminously grey. In this light, the sea across the dunes was the color of tarnished silver. High in the eaves of the little villa, a mockingbird began a song.

"Do you swear to love him always, Eben?"

"Don't do this. Please, Marianna."

In the faint light he could see that she was smiling at him, and he recalled a feeling he had felt for her in the early days of their love. Then, as now, she seemed to possess within her tiny frame the knowledge and wisdom of the ancients. Beside her he was and must always be an innocent.

When she began to talk, her voice was in haunting counterpoint to the mockingbird's joyous caroling. "In another time, a different place, we could have loved magnificently, Eben. But here and now, as if the ways of the world were not enough to separate us, I also bear this curse in my blood. I inherited this disease. Sometimes I think I have been ill since the moment I was born. But in another world," her voice broke, "I would have borne you many children and stood beside you through all the storms of life. As it is, however, I can scarcely move without pain, and all I have done by loving you is break Amanda's heart and bring shame to your family and grief to hers. I never wanted any of that, *mon amour.*"

"Stay, Marianna." His voice was a whisper.

"I will go, Eben, and you will be free at last. And when you think of me, you will remember the early times when I was not weak and pitiful and old before my time."

"How will you do it? Who will care for you?"

"Bess will come with me. You can make the arrangements, can't you? We will go to New Orleans and take a ship from there."

"I cannot permit this."

She shivered and sighed. "Don't let us argue any longer, Eben. I have given you the boy. Now let me go."

"Not alone."

"If I am careful, I can pass for white. Bess will come as my servant. We will be safe enough."

"It is too dangerous for you."

"But you must go to Amoset. You said a moment ago. . . ."

"I was a fool a moment ago. I have been a fool most of my life. But of all the things I have ever done, loving you was the wisest."

"My darling." He went to where she stood and they embraced. Her body was like a delicate piece of china, a thing so fragile it might break in his arms.

"I will take you back to Martinique. Christian and I both will go."

"It will take months, Eben. And it is not necessary. I do not ask this sacrifice of you."

He almost laughed at her choice of words. "Sacrifice? This is nothing. Less by far than all I wish I could do for you."

"Eben . . ."

"I want to do this, Marianna. More than anything in the world. Suzannah must tend to Valentine herself."

Chapter 5

Arrangements for the trip had gone smoothly. Two
days after Suzannah had received the letter from
James Shawn, she and Patrick had boarded a ship
which took them from Savannah to Boston. Now, as
they traveled by carriage along the heavily trafficked
road from Boston to Amoset, it seemed as if November had been holding its breath, waiting to delight
them with its lingering splashes of autumn color. Although she had been away from New England for
only a few months, Suzannah had forgotten the un-
rivaled beauty of that region and was able to view it
through the eyes of a newcomer. She too held her
breath, exhilarated by the scenes that welcomed her.
She saw a white stone church in a stand of flame-
colored maples, a farmhouse beside a still pond, a
hillside shimmering with treasure: ruby, bronze and
gold.

The joy that possessed her was so intense that
she wondered how the others in the carriage could
fail to be affected by it. The businessman, the traveling salesman and the elderly matron in widow's
weeds passed the trip in a long doze, however, and

did not appear to notice anything. Only she and Patrick felt the electric thrill of energy running like sap in the brisk air. She was continually laughing aloud at Patrick's antics, then shushing him quiet when his six-year-old comments on the world became, as they inevitably did, too loud and rambunctious.

Then, as they approached Amoset, everything changed. Quite suddenly, Suzannah's mood shifted and shadows of dread moved in at the edge of her excitement. The leaves on the trees were no longer vibrant, but tired, and dulling to brown. For the first time, Suzannah became aware that winter was settling in. The chill in the air that had been so invigorating now seemed merely cold. She wrapped an extra lap shawl around Patrick and pulled her own wool cloak more tightly about her. Soon she must face Valentine, her mother and perhaps even Martin, her father.

Glancing sideways at her son, she saw the little line of worry that had formed on his brow and guessed that he too was wondering what to expect. "Don't worry," she whispered in his ear. "You'll be glad to be home. Remember, you never did anything wrong, Pat. Nothing. You have as much right to be in your home as anyone. And just think, soon you'll be near your special mountain."

He smiled faintly, and she knew he did not entirely believe her. It was Patrick who, however inadvertently, had caused his uncle to fall the length of the great stairway in the Hopewell mansion. And it was Patrick whom Valentine had threatened. It was difficult now to recall Valentine's precise words, but the message remained clear in Suzannah's memory. Valentine hated his nephew and had sworn to see him punished.

But the fall and the threat had occurred months

earlier when Valentine had demanded control of the mill, believing he could manage it better than Suzannah. Now he had been proved incompetent. Suzannah wondered if Valentine's latest humiliation had made him impossible to deal with, more of a danger to the family finances than ever. Or would she find him chastened and willing to listen to reason? Gloomily, she considered the days ahead of her.

The Hopewells were, she thought, turbulent and complicated people. Even she could not be called normal, with her love of business and her independent attitude toward society. What chance had Patrick to escape a family heritage wrought of instability and wildness? Was there hope that his Shawn strain of clear-thinking Yankee yeomanry might be sufficient to rescue him from the passionate misadventures of men like his uncles? She prayed it would. Though generally skeptical when it came to religion, Suzannah resorted to prayer where her son's welfare was concerned. She clasped her hands together, closed her eyes and, giving the appearance of a woman drifting off to sleep, prayed for her little boy as she would never have thought to pray for herself.

Sarah Hopewell met them at the door.

"My dear child!" she cried, embracing her daughter. "Thank God you have come."

Although the familiar reek of brandy emanated from Sarah Hopewell, Suzannah was astonished to see how well she looked. For the first time in years Sarah was dressed in something other than a peignoir. Her pale hair was properly, even elaborately, dressed, and instead of her customary mule slippers she was wearing shoes and hose.

"Your brother has lost his mind, Suzannah. He's in there right now." She pointed to the door of Martin

Hopewell's study. "I don't know what he's saying to his father, but it must be dreadful. All the news is terrible. Have you seen the mill? Do you know?"

Suzannah nodded. Yes, she knew the worst.

At the coach depot, Suzannah and Patrick had hired a carriage to take them across town and up to the knoll on which the Hopewell mansion had been built with a commanding view of the river valley. When they came to the mill, she made the driver stop. Was it possible? She stepped down from the carriage and hurried to the entrance. The huge iron gate was closed and on it hung a sign: *These premises for lease or sale.*

"What does it mean, Mama?" Patrick had begged to know, tugging on her sleeve for attention. "What word is p-r-e . . ."

She couldn't answer. She had been struck silent by the sight of the abandoned mill, its yard full of leaves and debris blown in by the sharp autumn wind. The door of what once had been Ingrid Shawn's little schoolhouse hung by a single rusty hinge and creaked as it swung back and forth. The impression Suzannah got was of flimsiness, as if the mill were a model made of paper and paste and might topple over in the first storm. As she was standing there, the midday factory bells rang out, heralding the dinner break. In years past, the mill's double doors would have opened wide and dozens and dozens of laughing, talking operatives would have rushed across the mill yard, through the gate and down Front Street for their boarding house meal. But this day nothing happened at all. The mill was dead and Suzannah was its only mourner.

"You have to do something," Sarah Hopewell was saying now. "I believe your brother is intent on ruining us."

Ignoring her mother, Suzannah turned to the Irish servant who was holding her hat and coat. "Take Patrick into the kitchen, Mercy, and give him something to eat. Then he is to go upstairs. It's been a difficult journey."

"A nap, Mama?" Patrick groaned.

"A little one. I'll be along to see you when I can."

"Where will you be, Mama?"

"I must speak with Grandfather and Uncle Valentine."

Patrick shook his head. "I don't want you to."

Sarah tried to take his hand. "Darling, Grandmama will look after you. There's no need to hand him over to servants, Suzannah."

Patrick shrank away from her and grabbed a fistful of Suzannah's skirts.

"Well, what's got into him?" huffed Sarah, all outrage and dignity.

"He's afraid of you, Mama. Is that so surprising?" Suzannah looked down at her wide-eyed boy.

"That is absurd! I am his grandmother."

Suzannah smiled, suddenly realizing how familiar it all seemed. She was home again, where nothing and no one was ever normal, no reaction ever as expected. Months ago she had left her mother stewing in drink, a self-willed exile in her closed, malodorous bedroom, adoring Valentine and hating everyone else. Now the same woman wondered why her grandson, for whom she had never spared a moment in the past, disliked and feared her.

Sarah was pouting. "Don't laugh at me, Suzannah. Don't smile that knowing smile. I know I have not always done right by you in the past, but that time is over now. Since you left, I have been reconciled with your father."

"I do not believe it."

"Doubt all you wish, but I am with him every day now. I read to him and talk of this and that to keep his spirits up and occupy the hours. Really, Suzannah, you should be grateful. He is your father. And what kind of a life has it been for him all these years since he was taken prisoner by that madwoman from the mountain? He's lived in that study of his without anyone but the India Man to care for him. Crippled. Silent." Sarah raised her eyebrows haughtily. "I am his wife and I take my duties seriously." She reached for Patrick again. "I am also this boy's grandmother. I have only one grandchild and I intend to do right by him henceforth. How could you let me stay in my room all that time when I should have been down here?"

"You blame me?"

"As a daughter you have been less than perfection. You were always too willful and importunate for your own good."

Suzannah fell into a chair, laughing. How many times had she heard the same words from her mother? How many times had she been blamed for being herself when what she said or did met with Sarah's disapproval? But now, instead of being frightened or intimidated, the repetitious scenario amused her. It was like a comic scene from a ridiculous melodrama so badly acted and conceived that it could only entertain. Now she knew that no matter what her mother said to her, Sarah no longer had power over her. Suzannah felt strong and brave. She laughed wildly, genuinely, until tears came to her eyes. Had she not glimpsed the look of fear on Patrick's face, she probably would have continued. Grabbing him up in her arms, she hugged him tightly.

"Don't be afraid, Patrick. Go with Mercy and stuff yourself on Cookie's wonderful chocolate cake and tell her I said to make ice cream for tomorrow. Stay in the kitchen as long as you like. You need not go with Grandmama. And please, my darling, don't be afraid." Her smile had an almost girlish gaiety. "Beginning today, you are going to have a wonderful time in this house. I promise. I promise."

Leaving Sarah speechless, Suzannah strode confidently to her father's study and, without knocking, opened the door. The first thing she noticed was that the room was no longer kept as cold as it had been in the past. A pleasant fire burned in one of the fireplaces. Valentine was standing in front of it.

"You've come back," he said.

"Indeed I have." By the light of the fire and the mantel lamps, Suzannah could see that her brother was exhausted. He spoke with the familiar arrogance, but she was not misled. She saw it as a sham intended to protect what little might remain of his self-esteem.

"You are just in time to hear what I have to say to our father. Say hello to Papa, Suzannah." Valentine took her hand and led her to the big overstuffed chair in which Martin Hopewell was seated. Of all the moments since her arrival, this was the one most difficult for Suzannah. A flood of vivid and terrible memories washed over her. She recalled beatings and scathing rebukes, kisses and adoration and, like a worm born in the heart of a fruit, an ugly and inexpressible truth.

Martin Hopewell, an obscenely bloated man who had lived out of the sunlight for so long that his skin had turned a deathly shade of white, stared at his daughter with no sign of recognition.

"Father, it is our darling Suzannah. The managerial wizard."

"Val . . ."

"Why deny it, Sister?" Valentine shrugged and smiled thinly. "I would be the first now to admit that as a businessman, I am totally miscast." He tugged on her hand, pulling her closer to Martin. "But enough of me. Give our father his kiss, like a dutiful daughter."

She bent forward, her lips just grazing the old man's cold brow.

"He doesn't know who I am."

"Don't be too sure. I think it suits his purposes to play the idiot. And it should not surprise you, Suzannah. This family lives by pretense and masquerade. We are none of us what we seem."

Despite this warning, she chose to ignore Martin. "Come across the hall. I have been to the mill and now we must talk."

"But that is just what I am doing. I am about to inform our father of what I have done. After all, he is still the titular head of the Hopewell dynasty."

"He doesn't need to be told. It won't make any difference to him."

Valentine made a face. "For shame, Suzannah. Where is your loyalty? Would you conceal the truth from the man who gave you life?"

"Really, Valentine, your archness is not . . ."

"To begin with, I have sold the mill machinery, the looms and such, to Hathaway. His people carted it all away last week. A pity you missed the event. Quite touching, it was."

She sat down.

Valentine smiled as he spoke, but Suzannah could not tell whether it meant that he relished the bad news or whether it was intended to conceal another less happy emotion. Shame. Or desperation. Or even fear.

"Last June, after you and Patrick went away, I wasted no time instituting my own regime. As you knew I would, I fired the Yankee men and women who were unwilling to work for lower wages. In their stead, I hired Irish from the Gully."

"Unskilled workers."

"The few Yankees who were left became teachers for the new hands. Unfortunately, I suppose I underestimated the challenge of the work and the language problems. All this should please you, Suzannah. Your point of view is vindicated."

She listened without comment as he told her how first one and then another contract could not be met by a mill staffed by untrained workers. Those wholesalers who did receive Hopewell Mills' staple product, the coarse cotton called immigrant cloth, complained about the quality and some refused to pay full price for the goods. Bales of raw cotton began to pile up in the warehouse and then in the mill yard, unprotected from the weather. The heat and moisture of the Amoset summer ruined the stock before it could be sold to other mills. Covered with mildew, it had to be thrown into the river. Valentine, unable to meet his payroll, began to lay off employees. He had hoped to keep the mill in operation with a skeleton staff of operatives, but soon even these were forced to look elsewhere for paying work.

"And then the wolves moved in. Sensing my weakness, they closed in on me. Suddenly, I was surrounded by creditors from as far away as New York and Philadelphia who thought it best to collect while they still could."

"How much, Valentine?" While her brother had been speaking, Suzannah had begun to make rapid mental calculations. It was unthinkable that the mill would be lost and the family reputation sacrificed with it. As Valentine supplied the details, she added columns of figures in her mind, calculated percentages, and weighed the odds in favor of Hopewell

Mills. "I presume you have personal debts as well. What do they amount to?"

"A great deal. Some of them have been paid." He shrugged again. The annoying gesture had become habitual in recent years. "There were gambling debts and. . . ."

"You were always fond of gaming with your Irish friends."

"But not just the Gully. It's true that I lost a sum of several thousand to Jamie Teig and his cronies, but I also made some investments."

"How could you do this to us, Valentine? Did you think we were made of money?"

By now both of them had forgotten Martin Hopewell, who was sitting motionless in his easy chair, the pupils of his thick-lidded, somnolent eyes staring impassively at the geometric design of the oriental carpet. Across from him and to the right, Suzannah slumped in her chair, her expression haggard and drained of prettiness. She appeared gaunt and older than her years.

"Why didn't you send for me before matters came to this? How could you be so . . . foolish?" Brother and sister stared at each other. Valentine shrugged again. "Damn, Valentine! What's the matter with you? Don't you care about what's happened? Is it possible you wanted this from the very beginning? To ruin us?"

"Do you care what I wanted?"

"I am your sister, Valentine. For years you have assumed that I am your enemy and intent on robbing you of your birthright. But it's all been in your imagination. How can you ask if I care? Of course I do."

"I don't believe you." He gestured toward Martin who still gave no sign that he was present. "I think you and he and Eben wanted me out of the business from the start. I was never quite smart enough, never ambitious enough to satisfy you. Because I wanted my fun, some recreation and entertainment, you looked down on me, made me out the inferior. It's your fault if I failed in running the mill, Suzannah. Yours and the old man's. Neither of you ever gave me the chance to learn what I could do."

"Listen to yourself, Val. I hear the same lies and excuses you've used all along. Why can't you understand that no one has ever wanted to hurt you? You have brought all this on yourself."

He threw back his head and laughed. "You sound like him. Like our inestimable father. Well, let me tell you something. I am glad for everything that has happened. All my life I have hated that beastly mill as much as I hated him. As far as I am concerned, they are one and the same. Martin Hopewell and Hopewell Mills. And I'll tell you something else. I wish the mill could be destroyed, that flood or fire would take it and demolish it completely. I wish it could be wiped off the face of the earth."

"You don't know what you're saying."

"Don't I? Look at him." Valentine walked to within inches of Martin and pointed. "What do you see? I'll tell you what. A monster. He's a bloated mass of corruption with no right to life or breath. Crazy Edythe tried to do him in, but even she couldn't succeed, though God knows her plan was clever enough. Imagine a little old lady wily enough to outfox the great Martin Hopewell. She hated him as I do, and she did her best to punish him for what he is. Now I am going to finish her work. If I cannot kill him, I can destroy the only thing he ever cared for." He stared at his father. "Do you think he loved you, Suzannah? You're wrong if you do. He thought you were pretty, like a valuable possession that he could say was his. But he never loved you and he never loved our poor mother. He couldn't. He hasn't got a heart. Inside there," he jabbed a forefinger into Martin's chest, "there is nothing. Nothing."

Slowly, Martin Hopewell raised his eyes and looked about him.

"Come away, Val," urged Suzannah. "We'll talk somewhere else." Her eyes fixed on her father, she reached for Valentine's hand. "Leave him. Leave . . ."

But Valentine did not notice or care that Martin was now conscious of all that was happening in the room. "He cannot be destroyed because he has no heart. But the mill, the mill lives and breathes with his soul. That's why I hate it, why I wish to God I had burned it to the ground."

Like an awakening giant, Martin lunged forward and rose.

"Sweet Jesus," muttered Valentine, stepping back.

For the first time in many years, Martin Hopewell stood on his feet without support from anyone. He looked at Valentine with an expression that struck Suzannah like the cold hand of terror. Suddenly the room seemed as icy as that cave on Cooper's Mountain, and she wanted to run before it was too late, before the hand could grip her tight and hold her frozen in fear. But she could not move. She saw her father's hand upraised, his fist like a stone.

"Get out," Martin whispered, striking Valentine across the ear once, then again and again. "Leave me," he said in a voice as rough as stones dragged across gravel. "Leave me before I kill you."

Chapter 6

Valentine tore out of his father's study and ran across the foyer and up the staircase, Suzannah close on his heels. When he reached the door of his own room, he turned to confront her, his face livid.

"You have your own way now, Suzannah. The mill is yours. Such as it is." Pushing through the door, he hurried into his dressing room where Robert, his personal servant, was brushing down his clothes. "Stop what you're doing and get me a traveling case, Robert. Make that two cases. Then go down to the stable and tell them to prepare the new wagon. I'm going on a trip."

"In a wagon, sir?" Robert was incredulous. Though he was accustomed to Valentine's peculiarities, there was something fresh and urgent in the air today, and his curiosity overcame his servant's good sense. "Where are you going in a wagon?"

Valentine ignored the questions and began throwing handfuls of clothing from his bureau onto the bed.

"But, sir, let me. . . ."

"Do as you're told!"

Robert hurried out of the room, nearly colliding with Suzannah, who was still standing in the doorway. When they were alone, she asked Valentine the same question. "Where are you going?"

He was sorting through piles of shirts and sweaters and underclothes and spoke with the rapid, clipped enunciation of a man determined to have his own way. "I am getting out of your life. That's all that matters, I think."

"Oh, Val, it's not. You know it's not! I've said before and I will repeat it until I am hoarse: I care for you. You are my brother and I am bound to you. At least tell me where you're going. You don't intend to live in the Gully do you? There's nothing for you there. You know you'll only gamble and . . ."

"Shut up, Suzannah."

She was about to reply when, with no warning even to herself, she burst into tears.

"Oh, my God," he groaned. "Leave me in peace, Suzannah."

Of all the things he might have asked, this was the one thing she could not do. The weeks on the island, the emotional parting from Eben, the long trip from Savannah, the horrendous scene with her father, and the heart-stopping shock of the mill's decline were an accumulation that all at once exhausted and defeated her. She sank down on Valentine's bed, weeping.

"Damn you to hell, Suzannah!" Valentine flung a handful of shirts across the room and sat beside her. For a long time the only sound in the room was her sobbing. "Please don't do that," he said finally, giving her shoulder an awkward pat. It trembled beneath his hand and, for the first time in years, Suzannah seemed vulnerable to him. He was torn by conflicting emotions. On the one hand, there was the jealous hatred he felt for her and for what he believed she represented. On the other hand, he could not forget that she was and always would be his little sister. Surprised by a sweet memory, he put his arms around her and held her while she cried.

In the early days before Martin and Sarah had begun to use them as pawns in their adult battles, before they had been taught mutual distrust and envy, the three Hopewell children had loved one another intensely. On an afternoon like this, but long ago, when Suzannah was no more than three or four years old, she had come to Valentine, broken-hearted. A beautiful child with brown hair as thick and plush as mink fur and teaspoon-shaped green eyes that made him think of damp spring mornings and new leaves on the sugar maple, she had thrown herself into his arms and sobbed out her terrible story. It was strange, but now, so many troubled years later, Valentine could still recall the source of her grief. Martin Hopewell had found her favorite doll out of what he considered its proper place. To teach his daughter a lesson in orderly living, he had stood behind her with a switch in his hand and forced her to throw the doll into the incinerator behind the house. Then, as now, Valentine had held her until her tears were spent.

Though he was still angry and bitterly jealous of her, it didn't seem to matter so much anymore. "I'm going west, Suzannah," he said quietly. "I have a little money left, and with the wagon and supplies, I'll do well enough. I know that whatever happens to me, it can't be worse than staying here."

She was wiping her eyes with the hem of her skirt and sniffling like a little girl.

"Here," he said, handing her a handkerchief.

"Thank you." She blew her nose.

"I've been thinking of this for some time," he went on.

"It's a wilderness, Valentine. And with such dangers! Indians, animals, outlaws. It isn't safe."

This amused him. "Neither is Amoset. At least not for me."

"Where in the West?"

"I don't know. As you say, it's a wilderness. Just the sort of place for a man like Valentine Hopewell to lose himself."

"Will you write me? Just a note to say that you're well? And promise I'll hear if you need anything."

It was in his mind to say that after this there would be no communication between them. But when he looked at Suzannah he did not see the same woman who had stood before him countless times, humiliating him with her superior manner and unshakable confidence. Instead, he saw the little girl of his memory, a child with springtime eyes. He realized that if circumstances had hardened Suzannah, she could not be blamed. He saw with a new clarity that his sister was a remarkable woman whose competence, vigor and courage had maintained the family in times of crisis. Undoubtedly, they would do so again. He nearly laughed aloud imagining how, the instant he was gone, she would rush to her little office and probably not emerge until she had struck upon some plan for saving the mill. An hour before, he would have hated her for this quality of single-minded diligence. But the scene in Martin Hopewell's study had restored and rejuvenated Valentine's spirits. For once he had been honest. If he had not succeeded in destroying the mill, at least he had spoken the truth to his father and renounced once and forever the hypocrisy of their relationship. He was free of the old man at last.

"Will you write?" she asked again, still snuffling a little.

"Enough to reassure you."

"Oh, Valentine, be careful!"

"It is you who must take care, Sister. I am leaving you here with them." He raised his eyebrows and gave a mock shudder, then rose from the bed and began once again to sort his belongings.

"Will you see Mama before you go?"

"I suppose I must." Up to this point, Valentine had not considered Sarah. Even now, his mind veered from the thought of her. He could bear any danger, any tribulation in what was called the Wild West, but anticipating a final encounter with his mother filled him with dread.

"Shall I send her to you?" asked Suzannah as she stood up and walked to the bedroom door.

Though his heart screamed no, he nodded. "I might as well get it over with." Alone after Suzannah's farewell, Valentine stopped packing and went to stand at his bedroom window. It was late afternoon and the westering light was brassy. From where he stood he could see that the grass in the front ellipse had turned brown and the maples at its border were nearly bare.

I'll go south and then west, he thought. Away from the cold.

This scheme pleased him and suddenly he felt hopeful. He was even excited about the prospect of a future far from Amoset and the Hopewells.

From another part of the house he heard a noise. It sounded like a shriek. Mother, he thought. When it came to Martin, Valentine's feelings were clear-cut. He despised his father completely. But where Sarah was concerned, his emotions were complex and contradictory. He hated her. He loved her. He pitied her weakness, yet at the same time it disgusted him, as did his own. Although she had ruined him with her clinging, he blessed her for caring.

When Sarah rushed into his room a few moments later, she was all in a dither and smelled of spirits. Seeing his traveling case and the clothes piled on the bed, she wasted no time with questions, the answers to which she could guess well enough.

"You can't go away and leave me, Vally. I'm your mother, and haven't we always been close? I love you, son. I've always loved you the best. You and I, we're alike. We understand each other. Not like the rest of this family." She sniveled and plucked at his arm, begging him to turn around and face her. "I don't know what happened between you and your father and sister, but whatever it was, you must not let it trouble you. Don't leave me because of them. I can handle your father and Suzannah. You belong here. The mill is half yours."

"One third," he corrected her.

"Don't be ridiculous. Suzannah is a girl. She has no right to any of this."

"I disagree, Mama. She's wonderfully competent."

"Too much like a man, if you ask me."

"Which I did not."

"Valentine!"

He turned on her, clenching his hands behind his back. Hate, love, anguish, resentment all churned in him. He wanted to scream at her, to beat her down, to fall into her arms and cry and be a child once more. Instead, he told her, "I am going west. We won't see each other again."

"You don't mean it," she whined, reaching for him. "My baby, did they hurt you so much?"

He could only smile. It was a horrible farewell, but like the scene earlier with his father, he knew it

was liberating him. As a man who sheds his chains
link by link savors each small victory, he pushed beyond the moment, foreseeing a time when he would
be totally free.

"You can't go. I won't permit it!" He pulled away
from Sarah, leaving her to stare at her empty hands.
"You are my baby," she wailed.

"Suzannah is the youngest, Mother."

"It doesn't matter. You are the one I love. I never
cared for anyone else. You were such a pretty little
boy. You held my hand and clutched my skirts so
sweetly. You adored me, Valentine. What has
changed between us?"

He sighed. He wanted to speak cruelly to his
mother and thus repay in part the multiple grievances
he had against her. But now that he had the opportunity, he had lost his taste for vengeance. Looking at
her, he no longer saw the mother who had coddled
him and clung to him and denied him his independence. She was just a pitiful old woman, and a drunk-
ard at that. The churning had ceased and he was
calm at last.

"I am going west to find what I can never find
here. I'm going looking for my self-respect, Mother.
My manhood."

A little while later, at the foot of the stairs, Valentine encountered his nephew. Seeing his uncle, Patrick turned to flee, but the man's strong arm stopped
him.

"I didn't mean for you to fall, Uncle Val," Patrick
blurted as he tried to free himself. "Mama was
frightened. And I knew you were going to hurt her."
Strong for his age, he almost broke Valentine's embrace with his furious squirming. "Let me go!" he
panted.

"You must promise not to run from me. There is no need to be afraid. Not now. Have I your word?"

Patrick studied his uncle with solemn eyes and after a moment, he relaxed.

Valentine let go of him and they both stepped aside as Robert came down the stairs, loaded with traveling boxes. "Tell William to bring the wagon around to the front," said Valentine. "And have the cook pack some things. Beans. Flour. Non-perishables." He turned back to Patrick, who had been listening to these orders intently.

"Are you going on a trip, Uncle Val?"

"Out west, Patrick."

The boy's eyes grew round. "Into Indian country?"

"Perhaps."

"You better take a gun, Uncle."

Valentine laughed. Had he ever before felt this good? He was a young man again with the promise of the future set banquet-style before him. He wanted to do everything, feel each sensation, reject nothing that life might offer from this point on. "Before I go, I want to tell you something, Patrick. It's about what happened the night you and your mother left here."

"I didn't mean for you to fall," the boy said again.

Valentine shook his head. "I ask you to forgive me, Patrick, for what I did to your mother and for the terrible things I said to you. I cannot leave unless I know you pardon me. I could never hurt you. You must believe me."

Patrick considered a moment, then beamed. "I'm glad you didn't hurt yourself, Uncle Val." He thought a moment. "Do you really want to go away? Don't you like it here anymore?"

"No. It's not the place for me."

Patrick rolled his eyes as if he understood. "But it's better than Savannah. And St. Simon's Island. Did Mama tell you what happened down there?"

Valentine was listening to the sound of wagon wheels on the gravel drive.

"Did she tell you Uncle Eben is coming back here, too? Even he hates it down there. Uncle Val, do you like slaves? I've got another uncle. His name is Hiram. He says . . ."

Valentine began to laugh. Grabbing up Patrick, he spun him around until the boy squealed and giggled with the thrill of it. Out of breath, they hugged each other tightly. "I'll miss you, Patrick. You're the only one I regret leaving."

A moment later he sent the little boy off to help William and Robert load the wagon. After ducking into the kitchen to see that the supplies he had requested were packed and ready to go, Valentine stood once again in the wide, cold foyer, marking every detail for the last time. He could hear his mother sobbing upstairs, but felt no temptation to comfort her. When Suzannah came to stand at the balustrade near the top of the stairs, they did not speak. But the look that passed between brother and sister was as eloquent as any words either of them could have put together at that moment. Coming from behind Martin Hopewell's study door, he could hear the voice of the one they called the India Man, Mr. Harahsi, who cared for his father.

Glancing back up at Suzannah, he saw that she was even more beautiful as a woman than she had been as a child. He was struck by the miracle of such beauty in the offspring of a monster like Martin Hopewell. Encased in white fat, riddled through and through with hate, his lizard eyes blind to everything lovely and good, Martin had nevertheless helped to create some beauty that would live beyond him. The thought encouraged Valentine. Vowing to forget his father, he raised his hand to his sister in farewell, then went outside to where the loaded wagon awaited him.

Chapter 7

Valentine drove his wagon to Muldoon's pub in the Gully. The Irish had been his only real friends, and he wanted to say good-bye. The Lavender and Lily had been severely damaged by Selectman Stoat and his cronies when they thought Muldoon was harboring the murderer of the young women in Amoset. But after it had been proved that Foster McMahon had committed the murders, and not Mickey Quick, Stoat had seen to it that the pub was refurbished.

Once a shanty, the Lavender and Lily now had an air of respectability that surprised and vaguely displeased Valentine. In fact, the entire area called the Gully had become considerably more affluent. In a few years' time, no doubt, the streets of the Gully would be cobbled and the crowded hovels and lean-tos razed to clear the way for substantial mercantile operations, offices and businesses. The blacksmith's hut, O'Leary's, would be rebuilt in stone and mortar. The cooper and the cobbler would have proper storefronts with professionally-lettered signs. Eventually, the central thoroughfare of the Gully would have a name like Center or Division or Main Street. There would be a milliner, a theater, and a fancy goods store to help the increasingly prosperous new Americans spend their money. Though he wished the Irish well, imagining these changes depressed Valentine's spirits. Many of his happiest times had been spent in the ramshackle Gully, and he knew there would be no place for him when progress came to the area.

Indeed, it was best that he was moving west.

Immediately upon entering the Lavender and Lily, he was greeted by a chorus of salutations from the dozen or so Irishmen at the bar and tables. Coo Magee, the barmaid, brought him a free grog, courtesy of Muldoon.

"Cor, ain't it good to see you, Mr. Hopewell," she said as she set the mug in front of him on the bar. "You've been a stranger to these parts. Don't hardly seem the same without you!" She was a big, buxom girl, untidy in a stained and spotted apron, her brown hair unruly about her broad face. When she smiled, she showed the spaces where several front teeth were missing. This disfigurement did not inhibit her smiles, however, which were given freely and spontaneously and had a way of making her appear almost pretty. "That your wagon out in front?"

"Where you going, Master Hopewell?" asked Jamie Teig, the gambler whom Valentine had made rich a few months before by losses amounting to more than a thousand dollars. He was sporting a garish brocade waistcoat across which was festooned a heavy gold-link chain. Despite his new finery, Valentine noted that Jamie still smelled like a gin house and worse.

"Looks like a long trip to me," commented Muldoon as he wiped the polished bar with a swirling motion. "Leaving town are you?"

"I'm heading west. I just came in to fortify myself and say good-bye. I don't expect to return to Amoset."

There were noisy, incredulous exclamations at this news. Only Muldoon seemed to understand. A while later, as he filled Valentine's glass a second time, he said in a low voice, "I hope you know we bear you no ill will in the Gully, Master Val. It isn't for all of us to be industrial wizards."

Valentine was grateful for the kind words. It seemed that in all his life, it was only the folks of the Gully who had not disappointed him. Upon taking over management of the mill, he had hired as many of them as he could. Though the wages he had offered were no more than the pittance paid the Irish by other mill owners, like Hathaway and Shackley, workers had flocked to his door because he was well-known to be a friend of the Irish. But in a few months he had fired them all, and many without wages. Several hundred Irish were returned to their chronic state of unemployment because Valentine Hopewell had ruined the mill. Surprisingly, the people in the Gully bore him no grudge. There was an almost general sympathy for the black sheep of the Hopewell clan, the perennial failure.

"Does Victorine know you're off?" asked Muldoon.

Valentine shook his head. For the last hour, his mind had been skirting around the issue of Victorine and Hart, his mistress and her son. Their son.

"You might at least say good-bye to the darling girl, Val. You can say what you like about Victorine, but she's a faithful woman. These many years she's held you true, though you can believe there have been offers a faithless girl would not have resisted." He raised an eyebrow in the direction of Jamie Teig. "That one, for example."

"That hideous old man?" Valentine flushed, imagining Victorine in the arms of the gambler.

"Since you paid him off and made him rich—by Gully standards, anyway—there's plenty of colleens would share his bed."

The thought disgusted Valentine. He was too distracted to reply. While the owner tended to his other customers, Valentine stared at the whorls in the oaken bar, his thoughts wandering back through the years he had known Victorine. Their affair had begun as no more than a careless pairing such as often took place between masters and servants. He repaid her with a few baubles and a gold piece or two and promptly forgot all about her as he went off to try a year at divinity school. But he was a failure at Harvard, as he was at everything else he tried. It amused him now to think that Victorine's fidelity was, in a way, his only success story. In 1835, unbeknownst to him, she had borne him a son. And in 1842, when Valentine was again living at home and entertaining himself in the Gully, she and the boy had returned to the Amoset River valley.

Initially, Valentine had wanted nothing to do with either of them. In time, however, Victorine had worked her female sorcery on him. Apart from her irresistibly kissable mouth with its glossy, pouting lower lip, she was not a pretty girl and, until he had educated her in matters of hygiene, she had smelled no better than Jamie Teig. Despite these flaws, he had returned to her arms again and again, finding her more and more necessary to his contentment with each embrace.

Eventually even the boy had won him, and this still amazed Valentine. Though horribly deformed by an accident of birth, Hart's beautiful face marked him so clearly as a Hopewell that it would have been pointless for Valentine to deny the blood between them. The whole Gully knew that Hart was his son.

Valentine had come to think of Hart as a kind of symbol, for the contrasts which were so apparent in the boy represented the divisions Valentine was aware of in his own being. Though his family might call him a failure, a definite disfigurement of character for a Hopewell, he knew that if he could just find the right time and place he would do well for himself. There was a wisdom in Valentine, a kindness and a generous nature. In the company of simple, undemanding folk like Victorine or Coo Magee or Muldoon, these qualities showed themselves and received the honor they deserved. Gradually, Valentine's affection for Hart had become part of what bound him to Victorine. Though he had broken his ties with his legitimate family, there was still the matter of Hart and Victorine to deal with before he could leave Massachusetts.

He dropped a coin on the bar.

"Are you off, lad?" asked Muldoon. He extended his hand. "The best of luck to you then." They shook hands solemnly.

Out in the street, the sound of farewells still ringing in his ears, Valentine climbed onto the wagon and turned the team down one of the Gully's narrow, rutted lanes that ran between clusters of decrepit shanties. When he came to Victorine's, he stopped, climbed down and tied the horses to a sapling growing near the door. He entered the hovel without knocking.

Victorine was crouched on the ground before the fire, prodding the embers. Hart was beside her.

"It's you," she said.

"Aye."

"I didn't expect you, Valentine. There's not much to eat, I fear. Shall I send Hart . . .?" She stood up, brushing her heavy skirt of dark immigrant cloth. She was surprised by the look on his face. "Well, what ails you, I'd like to know! Have I sprouted two heads?"

She was a big woman, a strong woman. He wondered why he had not noticed her sturdiness before. He saw that she would not cringe from shooting a rifle or skinning a bear if called upon to do so. He suddenly saw her in a dozen demanding situations and realized that Victorine could handle almost any challenge set in her path. Why had he never noticed this before?

He glanced at Hart who was staring at him, confused by his father's sudden appearance and strange quiet. True, the boy was deformed, but he had learned to compensate for his twisted shoulder and hip. Though he looked clumsy in the saddle, he had learned to ride quickly and well when Valentine taught him. And however little he spoke, there was no doubt that he was smart. Val laughed aloud, realizing that within his beautiful head, Hart was as clever as any Hopewell.

"Holy Mary, what's got into you, Valentine Hopewell? Don't stand there laughing like a loony. Are you drunk?"

"Ah, Vicki," he said, still laughing.

"Vicki is it?" She came near and sniffed. "You been beerin' it with Teig and the rest of them, haven't you? Well?"

He grinned at her. "But I am not drunk, m'lady."

"Then why are you spouting this blarney. Vicki and m'lady indeed!"

Hart tugged on her skirt and urged her toward the door of the shack. When she saw the wagon, Victorine's voice became harsh. "It's good-bye then? It's parting that amuses you?"

"Do you care if I go?" he teased. He liked Victorine's high spirits and quick temper. It amused him to be coy with her if only for the pleasure he got from kindling the flash in her eyes and the flame in her round cheeks. More and more it seemed she was a woman that a man of the West would be a fool to leave behind. "Would you miss me, Victorine?"

"Not hardly!" she declared, tossing her head. "You know what I'll do if you leave me, Valentine Hopewell? I'll marry Jamie Teig."

"You would not!"

Now Victorine laughed. "Ah, but I would, my darling boy. And though I might think of you when I spread my legs, I'd spread 'em wide no less!"

"Don't talk like that around the boy."

"Why not? Does he think his mother's a lady?"

"You have a strumpet's mouth, Victorine."

"Ah, so now it's Victorine. Gone away is Vicki!" She turned her back on him and poked a long-handled knife into a chunk of bread. Ignoring the grownups' talk, Hart took it from her and began to toast it over the fire.

"You're a wretched woman, you know that?"

She smiled. "I've been told the same by one or two. But I've learned to live with it."

"I'm going west."

"Oh? And what is that to me? I crossed the Atlantic in the hold of a death ship when I was only twelve years old. Do you expect me to be impressed by a man who rides off into the setting sun in a fancy wagon loaded with provisions? Fare thee well, Valentine Hopewell."

He grabbed her arm above the elbow, pulling her close to him. "I will not go alone."

"And who is it will be going with you?"

"I want you by my side, Victorine. And Hart, too."

The boy dropped the knife. The bread fell into the fire.

"Clumsy clod!" his mother cried, but she did not trouble to rescue the bread from where it lay, blackening among the coals.

She shook her head slowly from side to side as his words took on substance. Looking about the single room of the shanty, she spoke softly, almost to herself. "To tell the truth, I'd given up even dreamin' for this. I thought that when your family got together they'd . . ."

He silenced her with a gentle touch and drew her near. Hart, hovering close by, was brought into his parents' embrace. "You are my family, Vicki. You and Hart are my family. We'll go south during the winter months and then head west. We'll just keep going until we find a place to stop. Then we'll be home."

Chapter 8

As Valentine had guessed, Suzannah wasted no time trying to sort out the mill's myriad financial problems. Late on the day of her brother's departure, she and a pair of strong servants went down to the mill to collect all the documents and ledgers from the office and counting room. Transporting the reams of paper and dozens of account books took several trips, but eventually the transfer was completed and her home office prepared. When the last load had been carried up the hill, she remained behind in the mill for some time, walking from floor to empty floor.

She recalled how she had felt after her father's disappearance, when it became clear that she must either learn about Hopewell Mills' affairs and become its manager or let the family business fall into ruin. Her first reaction had been pure and undiluted terror, for she felt the task was too great. Suzannah had only the scantest of educations. Like most men of his time, Martin Hopewell thought it a waste of money and contrary to nature to school young women. In Amoset's Mrs. Mortimer's Academy for Young Ladies she had learned to sew well and to play the piano and sing. She could speak a little French and German and do a few basic mathematical calculations, but

certainly accounting would be beyond her! And she
was sure she would never feel confident when speaking of contracts and bills of lading and all the other
technicalities of manufacturing. Nevertheless, neces-
sity had forced her to overcome her self-doubt and set
to work. As the months passed, she had become not
only competent, but proficient.

Those had been exhilarating, empowering
months. Now, standing in the vast, empty room that
had once contained dozens of huge timber looms
painted green, she felt again the pulse of the huge
mill. It moved through her bones and muscles,
causing her spine to straighten and her jaw to firm.
Though logic told her the task was impossible, she
knew she would find within herself whatever was
needed to save Hopewell Mills from ruin. To do otherwise would be the same as letting a part of herself
die. Valentine might not see the difference between
the mill and Martin Hopewell, finding them equally
corrupt, but Suzannah could make that distinction.
Hopewell Mills was also an extension of herself and
Eben. Each of them had worked to keep it going, had
sacrificed a part of life to assure its success.

In her office at home, she closed herself in and
became immersed in a sea of numbers. For three
weeks she worked every day until late at night, her
spectacles making a reddened dent across the bridge
of her pretty nose. Sometimes she did not even emerge
from the depths of her obsession to take meals. They
were brought in on a tray and forgotten, so great was
her concentration. The work was arduous, but Suzannah was happy. After those idle, discontented months
in Savannah and on St. Simon's Island, it was wonderful to be challenged once more. She was no longer
merely one of life's ornaments, but had become vital
to her family's survival. The responsibility made her

stronger daily. Engrossed as she was, there was no time for Suzannah to think of James Shawn. And when her sister-in-law, Margaret Duffy, came to welcome her back and spend an afternoon, she was too distracted by lists of credits and debits to enjoy their visit fully.

Only Patrick was welcome in his mother's austere little study with its simple Shaker furnishings. Although there had been little rain and no snow, a cold wind had torn the few remaining brown leaves from the trees and the boy sometimes stayed indoors. He would bring his picture books and drawing materials into the study and quietly occupy himself in front of the fire. From time to time, mother and son would look up from their work and smile at one another, but conversation seemed unnecessary. On their trip south, Patrick and Suzannah had developed a mutual respect that made their relationship more than usually close. Now when he roamed Cooper's Mountain on milder days, she no longer worried for his safety. On St. Simon's Island, Patrick had shown himself to be more competent and trustworthy than many adults. For his part, Patrick, having heard his mother's defense of the slaves before the implacable Hiram and now realizing that it was she and not his uncle or grandfather who controlled the mill, recognized in Suzannah a model he sought to emulate.

Observing all this, Sarah Hopewell grew more and more cross. After Suzannah had been home a week or so, she ceased to pretend any affection for her daughter. She did not mind saying to whomever would listen that she was ashamed to have such a mannish girl and was humiliated by her unseemly behavior. It would almost be better to lose the mill, Sarah thought, than to have a daughter so shameless and brazen. The family had plenty of other sources of income, didn't it? She had heard that Eben was a brilliant businessman. Why wasn't he tending to the mill?

"I have told you before, Mother," Suzannah said with a sigh one morning as she and Sarah breakfasted together, "Eben had urgent business in New Orleans. There was no way he could come here. And anyway, I am more familiar with the mill than he."

"Well, you shouldn't be. Can you imagine how ashamed I was last Sunday night at church when Beatrice Strickland asked me where you were and I had to say you were working. Working! On Sunday, of all days. Why, Reverend Strickland must think you are a godless pagan."

"I am sorry if I have embarrassed you, Mother."

"You don't mean that. You know you don't."

"Very well. I am not sorry."

"Don't take that tone with me, girl. I am your mother and don't you forget it. I know shameful things about you. . . ."

Suzannah, who was trying to read a letter from Eben that had arrived early that morning by special courier, was more than usually aggravated by Sarah. Her voice was sharp when she interrupted. "I am not ashamed of anything I have ever done, Mother. As a matter of fact, I am actually proud of having managed, very often in spite of you, to have a happy and satisfying life." She glanced down at the letter again. It was six pages long and closely written.

Sarah huffed in outrage but decided to ignore her daughter's tone and words. Changing the subject, she said, "What is so urgent that your brother must send a letter by special messenger. Is he made of money?"

"It has to do with restoring the mill."

"Oh really? Then you deign to take instruction from someone?"

Suzannah smiled narrowly, an expression more telling than a frown. "Eben and I are co-workers, Mother."

"You foolish girl. Listen to yourself! Co-workers indeed." For a moment she watched Suzannah read. Then curiosity overcame her petulance. "Well? What does he say? If you may be a co-worker, then certainly I have the right to know. . . ."

"We have decided not to retool for making immigrant cloth. Eben does not like our dependence on such vast amounts of Southern cotton." Though she would not let her mother know, Suzannah was rather confused by Eben's long letter. He gave no hint of what he had in mind to replace the manufacture of the highly profitable immigrant cloth. She had complete faith in her brother's business acumen, however. Once she was assured that Hopewell Mills' financial obligations were met, she would follow his recommendations exactly. Suzannah read on. Eben did not expect to return from the South until the following spring; until then the mill would have to stand idle.

Sarah was outraged when she heard this news. Her unhealthy mind, permanently affected by years of addiction, first to her nerve tonic and then to alcohol, saw trickery where none was practiced and insult where none was intended. After breakfast, she went upstairs to her room and, taking a cut-glass decanter from the little washstand near the window, drank directly from it. After several large, burning swallows of brandy, her body was suffused with calm and a mellow sense of confidence. She drank again, then put the decanter away and began to pace the length of her bedroom.

She hated her daughter and admitted it to herself without guilt or shame or even much emotion. She had given Suzannah all the love a girl had any right to require from a mother, but time and again the child had betrayed her. She was willful and heedless of conventions created for the protection of women. Her masculine love of business and power was despicable. In Sarah's mind, it seemed clear that Suzannah intended to take permanent control of the family business. Gradually, as she paced and returned to the washstand for more brandy, Sarah realized that Martin must be informed of all this. No matter what it took, he must be made to rise from his chair and leave the darkness of his study. He must throw off his dependence on Mr. Harahsi, the India Man. Once again Martin Hopewell must become the man she remembered with sudden fondness.

Even on the day of their wedding Sarah had not loved her husband, and she certainly did not love him now. But she convinced herself, with the aid of the brandy and a will that was in some ways as strong as Suzannah's, that a deep and everlasting bond held husband and wife together. They must cling to one another before their plotting and ungrateful children brought them to ruination.

Immediately after Suzannah's hasty departure from Amoset a few months before, Sarah had opened her bedroom door and given up her life of inebriated seclusion. For the first time in years, she had begun to take an active interest in household affairs. Since she was frequently in an alcoholic stupor by midafternoon, it was not uncommon for her to give an order in the morning and deny it a few hours later. Lifting their brows in long-suffering resignation, the Irish servants made adjustments and muddled along in much the same way they always had. Once Valentine had taken over the management of Hopewell Mills, Sarah had begun attending church and prayer meetings. She even had taken part in several benevolent causes when she had been sober enough to remember. Surprised and intensely curious, parishioners of Reverend Strickland, particularly the wives of the other mill owners, whispered about her behind their hands. How sloppy she often looked, they commented with raised eyebrows, and didn't she reek to the heavens of spirits! But Sarah was oblivious. So proud was she of being Valentine Hopewell's mother that she strutted like a peahen, even when her plumage was soiled or mismatched.

She had not immediately returned to her husband's company. But one day in the middle of the summer, Sarah ventured into his study with a copy of *Ivanhoe*, which she proceeded to read aloud whether he wanted to hear it or not. Surprisingly, her visits, which had become more and more regular and sometimes lasted for several hours, had revived Martin Hopewell somewhat. It was possible to believe from the glint in his eye and the way he had of glancing at the clock when the time for her visits approached that he actually looked forward to her company. When she was not reading to him from a novel or a book of poetry, she had a newspaper in her hands. Because Martin never spoke, and therefore never criticized her, she had become increasingly at ease with him. Her manner became outspoken. Though no one had guessed it before, Sarah had an opinion about almost everything from women's rights, which she deplored, to labor regulations, which she also opposed. If Martin Hopewell ever became exhausted by Sarah's virtually nonstop conversation, he gave no sign of it. His expression was always the same: still, morose, his eyes half shut.

Now she stopped pacing, took one last swallow of brandy and went downstairs, determined to rouse her husband from his stupor. All that summer and autumn she had observed him growing stronger. He had gotten up out of his chair and confronted Valentine. Horrible as that moment had been, some good had come of it. Sarah now knew that her husband could hear and comprehend what was said to him. And if he could stand, he might be able to walk. When that happened, the mill would be his once more.

PART II

Chapter 9

The north wind blew ceaselessly as November gave way to December. Day after day the skies were grey and low, but there was little precipitation. For the first time since Suzannah could remember, there was talk of drought in Massachusetts. The Amoset River and its hundreds of tributary streams and rills were at the lowest level in anyone's memory. Ponds had become little more than pea wallows, and there were stories of brackish wells. Although its manufacturing function had ceased, Hopewell Mills continued to generate power which it then sold to other mill owners in town. But as the dry, cold weather continued, it was feared that power would have to be cut back. The cataracts of the Amoset, normally a churning white water, were strangely, ominously calm in comparison to other years.

During the second week in December, Margaret Duffy came to visit for a few days, bringing her two children and Simon McMahon. Margaret, a woman who grew plumper and prettier with each year that Suzannah knew her, found in the weather a lively topic of conversation. "I could hardly believe my ears last Sunday, Suzannah. Bigelow Duffy, my eminently sane husband, was actually offering up prayers for

rain like some Indian shaman. And what is more, his
congregation joined right in. You should have heard
the amens! It reminded me of the prayer meetings
Travis and I were dragged to when we were children.
I told Bigelow afterward that I hoped the rain would
come soon so that we could go back to sounding like
Episcopalians." She pulled a face. "It doesn't hurt the
church to be dignified. That's my opinion!"

Margaret had hundreds of opinions which she
delighted in expressing whenever the opportunity
arose. Though Suzannah thought she must be rather
trying as a marriage partner, as a friend she was un-
surpassed. She was kind, generous and tolerant. And,
for one who had lived all her life in rural towns and
villages, she was surprisingly worldly. But sometimes
her generous heart gave Suzannah misgivings. Margaret believed in the innate goodness of people to
such an extent that she frequently took risks. Hobos
knocking on her kitchen door were treated benevo-
lently and sent on their way with knapsacks full of
fresh bread she had made herself and slabs of bacon
intended for her family's supper. Twice in recent
years she had made a home for wayward girls whose
families had ostracized them. And now the widowed
May McMahon and her son, Simon, were living at the
vicarage.

"You worry too much," Margaret told Suzannah
when her sister-in-law expressed her fears about Foster McMahon's son. "He's just a boy, after all. The
same as my Alexander." The three young people
could be seen through the front drawing room windows rolling hoops across the dry grass of the ellipse
in some sort of competition. From time to time, the
sound of their laughter reached the two women as
they sat by the fire in the comfortable room, sewing.
"And they seem to get along very well."

Suzannah was unconvinced. "There is something about the boy's appearance. A sneaky quality, I think."

Margaret made a face. "For shame, Suzannah. You're blaming the boy for the sins of his father, I think. You know better than most that we cannot choose our parents."

"That's true, of course. And yet, even I who," she thought for a moment, searching for the right word, "dislike my father, must admit that I have some of his qualities, Margaret. I cannot deny it."

"That is no reason to condemn Simon. We must be fair. Every one of us deserves a proper chance in life. Two if need be."

The women were quiet for a time, their heads bent over their handwork. The only sound in the room was the ticking of the porcelain clock on the mantel above them.

"May is responding wonderfully," Margaret said as she bit off a piece of thread and held out her embroidery hoop to examine the work. "Did you know she's an excellent needlewoman? Why, her work makes this look like a schoolgirl's sampler!" She put down the hoop and took off her thimble with a sigh. "Try as I might I will never be a domestic paragon. Bigelow did not do well in that department when he married me!"

Suzannah laughed. "But in every other regard, he is very lucky."

"I wish you were married, Suzannah. It is the only true happiness for a woman."

"I doubt that, Margaret. I always have. And anyway, must I remind you, of all people, that I *am* married. Your brother is my husband."

Margaret snorted. "Not hardly, I would say."

A squeal from the ellipse distracted the women

for a moment. The game of hoops had become a chase. Simon was running after Louisa, beating back Alexander as he staged a mock rescue.

Suzannah commented without thinking. "I don't like that."

"What's the harm? Didn't your brothers chase you and pull your pigtails?"

"Hmmm. But Simon is not her brother and my hair was never like Louisa's. So golden. She seems to light up the landscape this dreary time of year."

Margaret shook her finger at her sister-in-law. "Do you mean to say because that monster Foster McMahon had an . . . obsession with blonde women, his son must not be permitted to play with Louisa? Really, Suzannah, where is your charity?"

"Am I really so awful?"

"Well, not awful. But rather unkind. Believe me, Suzannah, I have watched the lad carefully these last months and so has Bigelow. If we had the slightest reason to distrust him, we would find him another home. After all, I am not about to endanger my own darling children. But if there is a chance we can help him. . . ."

Suzannah nodded, suddenly tired of the subject and wishing she were not always so quick to see or imagine faults in people. She was struck for a moment by how much the years had changed her. Only a few years before she would have been willing to trust Simon. She would have defended him to his critics, reminding them that he was only a fourteen-year-old boy longing for a chance at life like everyone else. But now just the sight of his long-legged, scrawny body and the small eyes and mouth made her restless and uncomfortable. Although in the face of Margaret's charity it shamed her, she had a sudden urge to check the silver drawers. Simon had the look of someone who was waiting for an opportunity. To do what? Suzannah could not guess, but no amount of assurances from Margaret could shake her discomfort.

For a time they watched the children on the lawn. Nine-year-old Louisa was chubby like her mother, but her rose complexion and glistening corn-silk hair, so thick it fought against the bindings of its plaits, were evidence that she would one day be a beautiful woman. Alexander, two years her senior and very much impressed with himself as a boarding school scholar and class proctor, had his sister's fair coloring, but where hers was as delicate as a flower, his was ruddy. Watching him tackle Simon and roll on the grass in a laughing scuffle, it was obvious that Alexander was a boy good at games and destined for leadership.

"How proud you have a right to be, Margaret. Your children are so fine." Suzannah had no desire for more children, so she was surprised to hear a touch of envy in her voice.

Margaret heard it, too. She touched her sister-in-law gently on the knee. "And I can say the same for Patrick. You know, Suzannah, he is extraordinarily competent and adult for a little tyke. Don't you notice that?"

Suzannah agreed, and for a little while they talked of Patrick's independence on St. Simon's Island. "I would have thought the atmosphere which, though beautiful, was rather sinister in some ways would have frightened him. Instead, he immediately made himself at home. It even made me a little sad because I realized how quickly I will lose him to the wide world."

"Some folks say fatherless boys suffer from restriction. Their mothers are generally overprotective, it's said. I see it all the time among the widows and sons in Bigelow's congregation. I've always thought such clinging ways were unhealthy. But you go to the opposite extreme, I'm afraid." Margaret shook her head emphatically. "I would never let my children have the sort of freedom to wander that you give Patrick. I thought you told me you were going to forbid him to go alone up the mountain?"

Suzannah was about to make an excuse, but she stopped herself and spoke honestly. Margaret was the one person in the world with whom she could do this. "I have to let him go, Margaret. I don't know how to say it, but it's almost as if that mountain is in his nature."

Margaret's smooth brow wrinkled and she clicked her teeth a time or two as she stared at her neatly booted foot, which was resting against an andiron. She could feel the heat from the fire as it slowly penetrated the thick leather sole.

"Suzannah," she said after taking a deep breath, "I think we should be more honest with one another."

"But I am."

"Well, I know I am not being completely frank with you. Not as I should be." Margaret looked at Suzannah. "You should know that I have known about you and James Shawn for years." She put out her hand. "Don't interrupt me, please. I want to say this. I'll feel so much relieved if I do. Ever since I stayed with you for Patrick's long delivery, I have known. You were in a delirium for a while and called for James Shawn. I had to hold you in my arms to muffle your voice against my shoulder for fear the midwife would hear. They're all such gossips, those women. So you see, I have known for years that Travis is not Patrick's true father. But I kept silent because . . . because I couldn't blame you."

"I never wanted you to know, Margaret." Suzannah's hands twisted in her lap. "You know, until this moment I never felt guilty or ashamed or. . . ."

"And you mustn't now. If I shock you or if I seem to favor infidelity, please forgive me and accept my assurances that in . . . the normal run of life, in simple cases where uncomplicated people are involved . . ." Her voice drifted off and she looked unhappily into the fire. "I never understood why you married my brother in the first place, Suzannah. It seemed the most unlikely pairing in the world."

"There was a time when I loved him, when I loved him passionately, Margaret. You must believe that."

"I do. You loved Travis and somehow he made you feel ashamed for it."

"Why do you say that? How could you know . . . ?"

"Because I watched our father do the same thing to him when I was a girl. Father thought it was his duty to kill what was purest in Travis. He destroyed his loving nature as surely and as keenly as a swordsman cuts out the gizzard of his enemy. Poor man, he knew no other way."

"Margaret!" In a rush, Suzannah embraced her friend, knowing they had never been more important to each other. Lucy Shawn Kilmaine had been Suzannah's girlhood friend, but those easy adventurous times had not been enough to hold their friendship together when they grew into women and their differences became apparent. With Margaret, the differences between them were part of the attraction that bound them together. Lucy had never trusted Suzannah or believed in her, but Margaret Duffy did. Her loyalty was so great that she could see into and beyond people's actions to the core of human feeling in each one. She could even find pity for her father, who had scarcely acknowledged her existence or their relationship.

"You are my dearest friend," Suzannah whispered. "And I bless you for your goodness."

The ticking clock gradually invaded Suzannah's senses. "It's almost four," she said.

On the ellipse, the children were nowhere to be seen and the oval of grass was deep in the shadow of Cooper's Mountain. The sky had grown overcast.

"We might have rain," Suzannah observed.

Margaret resumed her needlework. "Well, I hope so. As I say, Suzannah, the sight of all those proper Episcopalians sounding like camp meeting folk distressed me sorely." She grinned. "Still, if their prayers work. . . ."

Just then Louisa and Alexander burst into the room. Simon was with them but somewhat in the rear. He looked envious. It was the only word Suzannah could think of to describe his expression. She couldn't blame him. Poor lad. A charity case, his father a monster. Seeing him in this light, she regretted her earlier suspicions of Simon McMahon and resolved to be more hospitable.

"Come in, Simon," she invited. "Don't be shy." Then she turned to Louisa. "What were you saying about Patrick?"

"Is he back yet?"

"Back from where, dear?" asked Margaret.

"He was just going somewhere. Doesn't matter." Alexander tugged on Louisa's sash. "Come on you! Cookie's made your favorite chocolate cake."

"Wait one moment, if you don't mind!" In a flash, Margaret had become imperious, the unbending autocrat. The metamorphosis amused Suzannah, but she hid her smiles. "Do I detect an eagerness to fly,

Alexander? What are you afraid your little sister will say?"

Alexander kicked Louisa. "Now you've done it. He'll put crackers in your bed like he did that other time."

Suzannah interrupted. "Who did that?"

Louisa was petulant, and instantly, to win an ally, she leaked a little of the truth. "Last time I told you Patrick went up the mountain, he got even by putting crackers in my sheets."

Suzannah and Margaret looked at each other and laughed.

"You mean he's gone up the mountain today?"

"Yeah, he went before lunch."

"Don't say 'yeah,' Alexander."

"And he hasn't returned?"

All three children shook their heads.

"I'll go look for him." Suzannah folded her handwork and put it neatly in her sewing box. "This may take a while. Will you mind dining alone?"

"Of course not, my dear."

At the door, Suzannah turned and said softly, "Thank you, Margaret. Thank you for being my friend. My honest friend."

She had a good idea what path her son had taken up Cooper's Mountain. Most likely it was the same one she herself had used in the days of her childhood when she had spent a lot of time commuting between Lucy's home and her own. It had been years since she had taken that particular path. Some distance up, it skirted a cleared space where a portion of Crazy Edythe's cabin still stood. From just within the fringe of the woods, she stared into the clearing, remembering the time she had tripped and fallen right in the middle of it. The old woman, who had been standing

guard over her hovel, had ranted and giggled in-
sanely. Now Suzannah shuddered and hastened away
from the memory. Her russet cape and hood were
drafty and she could feel the cold moving in toward
her bones. The hillside path was steep as it came out
of the woods and climbed around the uppermost end
of a deep, wide hollow. In the spring, it was a
meadow filled with sweet greenery. Cold as she was,
she stopped at an exposed point and looked down on
the expanse of dry grass that stood up like whiskers.
She remembered how the meadow had smelled that
day when she and James Shawn had lain together as
lovers for the final time. The air had been decorated
with birdsong and the serenade of insects.

She had gone a quarter of a mile or so beyond
the meadow when she began to call Patrick's name.
After the third or fourth call, she heard a reply. Sec-
onds later, Patrick emerged, skipping down along the
path. A short distance behind him was James Shawn.

Chapter 10

The first thing James Shawn noticed was the expression on her face. She looked wounded, accusing, ready to panic.

"He shouldn't be out so near dark," she said crossly.

"I know that, Suzannah. But Patrick and I saw a deer." James was dressed in homespun country clothes, muckskin pants and a linen shirt with wide sleeves. A soft-brimmed leather hat covered his fair hair.

"Mama, they looked real sick and kinda weaker than usual. You know? It's the drought. Everything is dry and dying." He looked at James. "Isn't that right, Senator?"

Suzannah would not allow herself to smile at her son. "I care more about you than I do about the deer, Patrick. I have told you many times . . ."

"It's my fault, Suzannah. Don't chastise the lad on my account." James grinned at her boyishly. Then he tapped Patrick's shoulder. "Better get on ahead, boy, while I try to make your mother smile."

"I've spoken to Margaret," she blurted when Patrick was out of earshot. "She knows. She knows everything."

James nodded. "She told me she did on the day I wrote you that letter about Valentine and the mill. Since then I've been unable to get you out of my mind."

They were looking down the path, their attention seemingly fixed on Patrick, who was already some distance away.

Ignoring James' declaration, Suzannah said, "He loves this mountain. Like you do. When I see him from a distance, my mind plays tricks and I seem to see you as well. The way he carries his head is you and the lazy sort of swinging gait is you, too. It is a miracle that only Margaret knows he is . . . yours. I see you in his face sometimes and. . . ." She didn't finish.

"What, Suzannah?"

"Never mind. It's late."

"Tell me."

"He almost breaks my heart sometimes."

She turned and opened her arms to him. They held each other for a moment that both of them would remember for the rest of their lives. It was an expression of regard so deep and necessary to each of them that it meant far more than simply love. For James, it was as if a part of himself long empty were now filled. It seemed to him that to do nothing more than hold her was the truest happiness.

She pulled away and hurried down the trail, fiddling as she went with the strands of hair that had been loosened from their pins. But when she heard his voice behind her, she was compelled to stop and listen.

"I'm forty-three years old, Suzannah. And you, though you may not care to hear the truth, will be thirty next year. Our lives are passing us by. I am aware of it every day now, as if death were stalking me."

"Don't say such a thing, James!"

"I don't want to waste the feeling I have for you, Suzannah. It may be wrong by some men's standards, but by mine, here and now with you, the only wrong for us lies in denial."

As he reached for her, he saw her shrink back just an instant, waver, then relent. Her mouth beneath his was full and softer than he had recalled. But the lemon scent in her hair was the same, the feeling of her body in his arms unchanged. His need for her was aroused quickly, as it always had been. Slipping his hands within the folds of her russet cape, he stroked his palm up her rib cage to the base of her breasts. For an instant he stopped there, savoring the anticipation of her response when he would touch her breasts. He and Suzannah had been intimate on only a few occasions, but it seemed that their love affair had always been a permanent part of their reality. He remembered vividly her touch and the taste of her skin. It had always been easy to arouse her by touching her there ... and there ... and there.

She jerked away quickly. The wounded, accusing look was back. "Go home, James. Your family will wonder what has kept you."

He ignored her command. "When, Suzannah? You want me. You know you do."

"Never. I don't know."

"When?"

"I don't deny I love you, James. But I have lived without you for seven years, and I have survived." He thought he heard a faint touch of irony in her voice. "I have been happy with only my work and Patrick to enrich my life. If I were a different sort of woman, I might have pined to death from loneliness. As it was,

I missed you to the point of pain for a long time. I thought I'd never stop hurting. Only my work and Patrick kept me alive. And now you ask me to risk my hard-won contentment."

"Life is full of risk."

She laughed shortly, bitterly. "You are too glib, James."

"I need you, Suzannah."

She shook her head. "I can only mean trouble for you, James Shawn. You're an important man now. Soon your fame will spread farther than Massachusetts. When you are governor . . ."

"I haven't even been nominated yet, Suzannah."

"And you never will be if there is even a hint of scandal. I am a liability to you."

"You give me energy. I see you and it's as if. . . ." James thought for a moment and then smiled. "As if I were shot by lightning."

She made a face. "It sounds quite dangerous.'

"You are."

"No, James." Her eyes filled with tears. "Don't call me dangerous or bad because your touch sets me afire. I can't help it."

"But you are dangerous because the dream of you is no longer enough. You are necessary to me, now. Like food and water."

"The shame and the hurt . . . I could not live with the threat to our reputations, with the scandal." High in the trees the wind whined. She shivered and wrapped her cape more closely about her.

"Trust me, Suzannah."

She laughed and shook her head. "Don't grin at me, James Shawn. Don't try to beguile me. You know I would trust you with my life. But with this I'm not so sure."

He was still smiling. "Go home, Suzannah. In a

few days I'll get word to you." He touched her fore-head lightly, pushing back the thick curls that had fallen loose. "I will see to everything, my darling. And no one will know. Trust me."

Suzannah and Patrick reached their home just af-ter dark. Margaret met them at the front door looking quite cross, her arms akimbo like a fishwife. "Patrick Paine, this is the second time you have nearly frightened me to death with your excursions up the mountain! You've missed supper, and caused your mother to miss it, too."

"He's all right, Margaret. And so am I." She nudged Patrick ahead of her into the foyer and toward the stairs. "Tell Mercy I said you should have a bath and supper in bed," she called after him.

"Is that all you're going to say to him? Have a bath?"

"Rest easy, Margaret. He was perfectly safe. We met on the path. He was on his way home." She looked about her in some distraction.

"What's the matter, Suzannah?"

"Nothing, Margaret. Nothing. It's only . . . busi-ness. I have business on my mind."

"You need to relax and forget the mill for a while. You can't continue to overwork like this or . . ."

"I'll be all right, Margaret. Leave me alone." She spoke sharply, scarcely noticing when her sister-in-law recoiled slightly. "Leave me alone," she muttered again and hurried up the stairs after Patrick.

She sent her maid away. She had no appetite and she wanted to be alone as she prepared for bed. Free of its pins, her dark, wavy hair fell to the middle of her back. As she had on thousands of nights, Suzan-nah brushed it out with long, slow pulls of the pearl-handled brush that had been a gift on her sixteenth birthday. But tonight, the comforting ritual stirred rather than sedated her. She sat for a long time, lost in her thoughts and memories. At last, unable to relax, she put on a warm woolen robe and hurried a few steps down the hall to Patrick's room.

"Are you awake, son?" she asked, opening the door a crack.

"Uh-huh."

She went in, closing the door softly behind her, and sat on the edge of Patrick's bed. With the covers pulled up about his chin and only his head sticking out, he resembled an infant tortoise.

"Were you up at the Shawn homestead today, Patrick? Is that how you came to meet the senator?"

Patrick nodded.

"I told you to stay away from there. Don't you think that poor Helen Shawn has enough. . . ."

"She likes me, Mama. We're friends now."

"Oh, Patrick, that doesn't matter. You disobeyed me. You know what I told you."

"But she *likes* me." He sat up, eager to talk. "And I like her family too, Mama. Senator Shawn is always real nice to me, and I like to talk to him because he knows the mountain even better than I do."

"What about the rest of them? Have you met the whole family?"

"Only Miss Ingrid. She used to be the school-teacher at our mill."

"You haven't seen Lucy Kilmaine?"

"No, ma'am. She's in Boston. That's where she lives."

Suzannah sighed. "You must promise me something, Patrick. And I mean for you to stick to this promise. Do you understand?"

"Please don't tell me I can't go up the mountain, Mama. I really like it up there."

"I know you do, and I suppose you may continue to visit. But always tell me where you're going, Patrick. And promise, swear to me that if anyone else is up there besides Ingrid or her parents, you will not go in or even say hello. Promise that if Lucy Kilmaine is at the homestead you will hurry home."

"But why, Mama? She has a little girl named Delphia, and Mrs. Shawn says that when she comes to visit we can ..."

"Promise, Patrick."

"Oh, Mama, why? It's not fair!"

"Life is not always fair, my love. You must promise not to make friends with Lucy or her daughter. And don't question me about it."

But even as he sulkily swore to obey, Suzannah knew the day would come when he would be unable to resist the temptation to know all the Shawns. When that happened, she was certain Lucy would recognize him as James' son.

In bed that night, she tossed restlessly until long after midnight. Such sleep as she enjoyed was full of confrontation scenes and dreams where she was running, running, always running, but toward a goal she never knew.

Next morning, she slept later than usual. Even the pealing of the mill town's bells did not awaken her. When she joined Margaret in the dining room, she was so groggy that her breakfast fell like a lump of coal to the bottom of her stomach and sickened her. Though Margaret watched her carefully, her casual remarks about the dry weather and the excellent breakfast gave no hint of her concern. But when they were finishing their coffee, she finally asked, "Would you like me to go home, Suzannah? Is there just too much confusion with the children and all being here? I know how hard you have to work and . . ."

"Please stay, Margaret. I was rude last night, I know. I was very tired."

"But I heard you walking through the house at all hours."

"I couldn't sleep." Raising her eyebrows, Suzannah made a helpless gesture with her hands. "I had bad dreams."

In her office, the desk was covered with paper towers, each pile demanding her urgent and immediate attention. But instead of working, she lay down on her narrow, upholstered chaise longue and stared out the window behind her work area. Her office was on the first floor and faced across the side yard garden where the bushes looked scarcely alive. It was still overcast, but there was no wind that day. The winter sky was washwater grey.

She must have dozed off, but all at once, something startled her. She sat up abruptly. Eyes wide, she stared at the window. A face looked back at her.

"Simon!" She jumped up and ran to the window. It had been nailed shut for the winter and would not open. She craned her neck to the left to catch a glimpse of the boy, but he was gone around the corner of the house. After a moment or two, she began to wonder if she had only imagined he was spying on her. Perhaps he had been part of a dream.

She tugged irritably on the bellpull and ordered coffee even though she did not want it. The most important thing, she told herself, was to keep active and not permit her imagination to run away with her. Nevertheless, Simon's face had been so clear, the expression of greed in his squinting eyes so unmistakable, that the more she assured herself it was unreal, the less convinced she became. She began to imagine that the boy was following her, spying on her wherever she went. How could she hide away for an hour or two with James Shawn when her every move was being pursued by that boy, the son of Foster McMahon?

When it came, she drank her coffee in several scalding swallows. The bitterness made her eyes water, and the knot of food in the pit of her stomach steamed and swelled and rolled in acid. Could Simon have followed her up the mountain the day before and seen her in James' arms? No, that was a preposterous thought. He had been in the house with Margaret. Suzannah herself had welcomed him into the drawing room. She held her head in her hands, squeezing her eyes tightly shut. What was wrong with her? Why did she continually see Simon's leering grin before her mind's eye? Had she dreamed his face at the window? Was there really something sinister about the boy? Had his face at the window been real or simply part of a bad dream? Unable to tolerate the crowding uncertainty any longer, she put on her cloak and went outside to look for him.

The grounds of the Hopewell mansion were easily large enough for a child to hide himself, but there were several specific places she guessed would hold more interest than others. She went first to the stable and asked one of the boys who worked there if he had seen Simon McMahon. He hadn't, but he suggested that she look around the other side of the pond. There was a dilapidated lean-to where winter feed was kept, and the stableboy recalled having seen Simon there the day before.

Thanking him, she hurried across the property toward the low side where the largest pond was located. In summers gone by, it had been a swimming hole for Eben and Valentine until the snapping turtles had driven them out. Now, seen under a dirty sky, it had a grey metallic cast and looked as lifeless as the plants and bare trees around it. It was not a pretty place.

Some instinct made Suzannah step more softly as she approached the shed. It was not that she intended to spy on Simon, but there was a warning in the dry, cold air, and she dared not ignore it. When she was a yard or so from the open door, she heard a sound from inside the shed. She stopped in her tracks, expecting an animal to run out at her. All had grown still. Only her breath was noisy.

Another two steps forward and she could see Simon in the shadow cast by the shed's overhang, lying against the bales of sour hay and stale feed. He wore a blue coat. Though his head was thrown back, his eyes, as small and mean as his father's, were fixed directly on her. His trousers were unlaced and hitched down below his pale buttocks. He held his penis in his hand and was stroking it in a quick up and down movement as he stared at her.

Chapter 11

"But it's perfectly normal, Suzannah," declared Margaret. "Disgusting as it seems to you and me, Bigelow tells me that there are some young men of Simon's age who do it frequently." She covered her mouth to hide her embarrassment. "As much as once a day."

"But it was . . . different from that, Margaret." Suzannah paced up and down in front of the drawing room fire. "I know more about men than you might suppose. Long ago, my Aunt Bronwyn taught me about life and men. She used to give me little lectures in the afternoon over cream and crackers. I believe I know as well as you what is normal and what is not. All I am trying to make you understand is that what I saw in that wretchedly gloomy, damp and moldy shed definitely was not normal." She shuddered, remembering the boy's hot, red eyes and the little grimacing mouth.

"What did you do?"

"Turned and ran back here, of course."

"You look a fright, I'll guarantee that."

Suzannah frowned. "How nice of you, Sister."

"You must rest. Then we can discuss this sanely and with some objectivity."

Margaret rang for a servant and ordered a basin

of warm water so that Suzannah could refresh herself, and some hot irons to warm her bed. They went upstairs.

"I don't want to sleep, Margaret. I have work to do." Nevertheless, she stood still as her sister-in-law unbuttoned her dress and helped her slip it off. "If I don't sort through those dreadful letters Valentine sent our creditors. . . ."

"What you need right now is sleep. You were up half the night. I heard you, remember? Now I don't care how important that mill is, your good health is more important still. You have to rest, Suzannah, or you'll make yourself sick. Then the mill *will* be in trouble!"

Suzannah washed her face and hands and put on a long flannel nightdress while her maid prepared her bed. When the maid left, she sank gratefully into the cloudy softness. Enveloped in warmth, all the fight went out of her.

"There is something I want you to do for me, Suzannah," Margaret said as she finished tucking the blankets around her.

"Mmm?"

"You must hire a detective to look for Travis."

Suzannah tried to sit up, but Margaret wouldn't have it. "You can't go on like this," she continued, sitting down on the edge of the bed. "You are beginning to sound like an elderly spinster living half in a dream world. Now I grant you that Simon may not be a very attractive child and he certainly has a dreadful history. I don't deny that. Nevertheless, in all the time he and his mother have been at the vicarage, I have never known him to behave in the slightest untoward way. There hasn't been one single solitary incident. . . ."

"Yes, Margaret, yes. Your point is made." Suzannah sighed, but sleep was out of the question now. She looked at her sister-in-law. "What has all this got to do with my sending a detective after Travis?"

"If he is alive, you should know it. If he is dead and you are a free woman, you should know that, too. Suzannah, my dear, I am telling you this all for your own good. If ever there was a woman who needed a man, it is you."

Suzannah turned on her side and tried to get comfortable. "You are talking nonsense. I don't need a man when I have the mill and Patrick."

"That is not what I mean, Suzannah."

"Lord, Margaret!" Suzannah couldn't help grinning when she saw Margaret's blushes. "You are so genteel. I gather you believe I need bedding!"

"Don't make fun of me, Suzannah. I know you're more worldly than I and that I must seem frightfully prim. But I remind you that just because I do not speak of these things easily, it doesn't mean I don't know what I'm talking about. A minister's wife sees and hears a great deal."

"All right, all right," Suzannah chuckled. "You've made your point, Margaret."

"If you don't hire a detective, I will!"

"That is extortion, Margaret. I suppose I have to do it now since I know perfectly well your budget cannot stand the strain. I would have the ruin of your family on my conscience."

Margaret hugged her. "My dear Suzannah! I know you won't regret it. It is always better to know than to wonder, wonder, wonder."

Margaret rose from the bedside and, after drawing the curtains on the dormer windows, she lowered the lamps that burned on the three tables in the room. It was the same bedroom Suzannah had lived in all her life. She had restored the furniture and brightened the chintz a few years earlier, but essentially it was unchanged. During her girlhood years, she had lain in this very bed at night, dreaming of a future rich in love and adventure.

"I saw James Shawn," Suzannah whispered in the darkened room. "He says he does not want to waste the years and our love. He says they are too valuable."

Margaret took her plain woolen shawl from its hook by the door. "And what do you say?"

"I'm afraid, Margaret."

"Ask yourself what you want, Suzannah. What do you truly want?"

"Him," she replied swiftly and so softly that Margaret almost didn't catch the word.

"Then have him, Suzannah. Have him."

Several days passed. Margaret, her children and Simon returned to the vicarage in Marivale. Gradually, Suzannah's mood settled down. She saw little of her mother, who spent hours with Martin every day, and Patrick was content to play with the servants' children or roam the hills when the wind wasn't too bitter. She lost herself in her work again. From time to time, however, she could not keep from putting down her stylus and turning to stare out the window across the dry, brown expanse of yard. Her mind wandered far beyond, up the mountain, and sought the heart of James Shawn. Was he at the homestead or had he returned to the General Court in Boston? Had he reconsidered his hasty proposition and seen that it was unwise? A part of her hoped he had so that she could be free of him again. If she could focus on nothing but Patrick and her work, life would seem simple again. Since their meeting that afternoon on the mountain, she had scarcely known a calm, clear day. Emotions and longings she had learned to repress rose up and demanded her attention. She could not ignore her yearning for James' strong touch, for the tremors of sensation that came back to her with painfully tantalizing clarity.

Only her work was adequate distraction. The easiest task so far had been unscrambling the financial records. Her calculations showed that Valentine, who never had been very good at numbers, had overlooked a clerical error. The mill had a little more money than she had originally thought, and this was a great relief. What troubled Suzannah more than finances now was the damage Valentine had done to the mill's reputation for reliability and honesty. He had been so underhanded and cheap that there wasn't a buyer in Massachusetts who trusted the Hopewells anymore. Somehow, if the mill was to recover its prestige, creditors and wholesalers and other businessmen must be cajoled into trusting them just one more time.

She was considering how this might be done when the outside door slammed shut. Suzannah heard the unmistakable sound of Patrick's running feet and then, just outside her door, a little sliding noise on the polished wood floor.

A knock.

"Come in, Patrick."

He opened the door and peeked in. "How did you know it was me?"

His face was flushed and glowing from the cold. Just the sight of him pleased her. "I have magic eyes. I see through doors."

"Do you know what I have in my hand?" he teased.

"A frog."

"Guess again."

"A stone."

"Do you give up trying, Mama?" He beamed at her.

"A letter for me from Senator Shawn."

Patrick's mouth dropped open. "How did you guess?"

Taking the envelope from her son, she said, "I told you, I have magic eyes."

The deep forest that covered most of Cooper's Mountain crept close to the Hopewell mansion in some places. In others it was remote, separated from civilization by meadows or open woods. The big stone house sat on its knoll facing southeast. To the right, beyond the cobbled yard behind the house and in the middle of a sloping meadow, was the stableyard where the horses, their gear and pullings were kept. Behind the stable, the grassland continued for a hundred yards and trees began to appear. At just the point where the true forest began, there was a huge old oak in which Eben Hopewell had once built a splendid tree fort and declared, if only to himself, that it was invulnerable to either savages or desperados. The tree house had been his kingdom and he had maintained its floor and roof and ladder until Yale called him away to more adult matters. Eventually he forgot the tree house and it fell into disrepair. But as Suzannah approached it now from deeper in the forest, having taken a circuitous route, she was amused to see how well, and with what an eye for camouflage, James Shawn had repaired it. There was even a ladder made of rope and wood that swung down to welcome her the moment she stood beneath the oak and called out softly, "James. It is I."

He had made the aerie secure and comfortable. As she crouched and looked about her at the quilt spread out neatly, the crock of wine, the apples and cheese wrapped in cloth, he pulled up the rope ladder, securing their privacy.

"Sit down," he said, "or you might bump your head."

Obediently, she went to the corner farthest from him and, using the wall of the tree house as a backrest, sat with her legs pulled up and her full worsted skirt wrapped tightly about her knees.

"Well?" he asked. "What do you think? Would Eben mind?"

Instead of answering, she asked her own question. "Do you remember the other time we met here?"

"I can't forget it."

"I almost expect to hear Travis prowling around below." She gave a shudder that was half amusement and half horror, recalling her behavior of years gone by. Hugging her knees, she stared at the plank floor.

"Do you want to leave?"

"Do you want me to go?"

"I want you to do what is in your heart to do. I want nothing of you that cannot be freely given. You know what's right, Suzannah." He reached out to stroke her smooth, dark hair, but she pulled back.

"James, how can you?" She frowned at the floor rather than look at him. "You know that what I want has nothing to do with what is right."

"Just stay here and talk to me. There can be nothing wrong in that."

She looked up at him quickly to see if he was teasing her, but his expression was serious.

"I received a letter from your brother Valentine."

"You? After what happened?" He pulled an envelope from his jacket pocket and handed it to her. As he did, his fingers touched her wrist. She drew back, startled, and the letter dropped. Confronted with such an obvious sign of the electric tension between them, they laughed nervously.

To fill the silence, James spoke about the letter. "Valentine said he wanted me to understand why he had refused to pay off McMahon when he was holding Lucy for ransom. What's more, he wanted me to know that he bore me no malice for having beaten him up."

"You did that?"

"In your foyer. Your mother was there and was ready to kill me for it."

Suzannah could not help smiling as she imagined the scene. With Lucy safely home in Boston, McMahon dead, and Valentine far away, the nightmare of the past few months took on a fictional quality. Now she could be amused at the thought of Sarah's impotent consternation while Valentine lay sprawled on the marble tiles with a bloodied nose. Almost instantly, however, she regretted her lightheartedness.

"I'm sorry, James. I didn't mean to seem callous. It was an awful time for all of you and I regret my brother's behavior more than I can say. You had every right to fight with him. Murders have been committed for less."

"If it had turned out differently, I might have killed him. I don't know." James folded the envelope in half and then folded it again. He glanced at the postmark. "This was mailed from down in southern Pennsylvania. He didn't say where he's headed or what his plans are. Only that he's sorry. He said he had no alternative but to deny me the money."

"That's true enough. As far as Val knew, the mill was bankrupt."

"And it's not? That's good news, Suzannah! Not just for you, but for all of Amoset. Does that mean you're going to reopen?"

They talked of the mill and city affairs as if they were two old, but essentially casual, friends. After the first few moments, Suzannah lost her shyness with him and dropped into the relaxed familiarity that had made them friends as well as lovers even in the Marivale days when their passion was at its peak.

She told him, "Even if Valentine's original figures had been correct, the mill still would have been saved. My diamond is in a Boston bank, and if Eben thinks I should use it for the retooling, I'll be happy to. My Aunt Bronwyn gave it to me to insure my independence. It's done that, so if it becomes necessary for me to borrow against it for the mill, then, of course, I will do so. The mill comes first."

James did not answer. He was looking at her so strangely that she blushed.

"What's the matter? Why do you stare so?"

"I was thinking of you when you were a little girl, trying to make this astute businesswoman match up with that shy, wild child!"

Suzannah laughed. "I am glad you can remember that far back."

"I loved you from the start, I think."

She was shocked. "James! I was a child."

"I know. But I loved you anyway. I was shamed by my feelings, but at the same time I think I knew there was nothing I could do about them. I loved you. That was that."

Suzannah wouldn't hear of it. "I was a friend of Lucy's. If you loved me, it was as you loved your own daughter. I would have known if there were anything else."

"You were too busy stalking Indians and finding hideouts. You and Lucy thought you owned Cooper's Mountain. But my wife knew, I think." James made a wry face and shook his head. "I'm not a Calvinist, but sometimes I almost believe that our destinies are mapped out for us from the start. Loving you was something I had no control over."

"Don't say that." She sounded almost angry. "I don't believe in preordination. What we do, we do of our own will. If you love me, it is because . . . you choose to. As I choose to love you."

They sat for a little while in silence. Outside the treehouse, the wind was rising. The great oak swayed gently.

"It's as if we were in a little boat," Suzannah said as the tree house rocked.

James rose to his knees and opened a trap in the roof. Overhead through the bared oak boughs, the sky was darkening.

"Leave it open, will you?" she asked.

"I think it's going to rain."

"At last. I feel myself withering from the drought."

"You'll get wet." As if the weather had taken its cue from James' words, there was a flash of lightning and to the west, from behind Cooper's Mountain, came the roll of thunder. James laughed. "Van Winkle's dwarves are playing bowls."

"At last," she said again, looking at him. Valentine, the rain and the mill were far from her mind.

They stared at one another, smiling faintly. In the moment before they kissed, it occurred to Suzannah that if she had not liked James Shawn so much, if the casual give and take and humor of his company had not been so pleasant to her, she would have forgotten him long ago. But because their pairing was comprised of more than yearning and sympathetic sensation, it was almost as if what James had said were true. The threads of their lives were destined not just to meet but to interlace like the woof and warp of an elaborate pattern. To ensure this, fate had given them more than passion. They were friends as well.

Chapter 12

In May of 1844, Eben Hopewell arrived in Amoset with his son Christian by his side. Knowing the value of first impressions better than most men, Eben had hired the most splendid custom-made carriage in Boston for the trip. To insure the maximum effect, the vehicle was pulled by a matched quartet of bays. When they drove into the mill town on a busy Saturday afternoon, Eben made sure there were many pauses and full stops along the way to insure that the townspeople would know whose carriage it was. When he stopped at a confectioner's shop on Front Street, a crowd gathered to admire the coach and horses and to stare at the tawny-skinned child sitting inside.

"That you, Mr. Hopewell?" Eben recognized a man who had once worked on accounts at the mill.

"How are you, Botts?" he inquired, shaking hands. "It's a long time since we met. Your family is well, I hope?"

Botts shook his head. "I had to take them all down to my kin in Maryland, sir. When I get work, I'll send for them."

Eben went into the store, followed by Botts. He handed a coin to the confectioner and tucked a paper packet of sweets in his pocket. Making certain his voice was loud enough to carry to the other customers in the shop, he said, "Come see me in a couple of months if you're still needful of employment, Botts."

"You opening up the mill again, sir?"

"Well, of course. What else did you think?" Eben paused at the edge of the walk. A footman opened the carriage door. "What is the gossip these days regarding Hopewell Mills, Botts?"

"We thought you'd sell it, sir."

"Botts, you can tell your friends that Mrs. Paine and I intend for the mill to be operating at full capacity again by the fall." He shook the accountant's hand firmly. "That's a promise, Botts."

Continuing toward home, Eben remarked to himself that running into Botts had been a piece of good luck. Within a day or two, there would be a dozen different stories circulating with regard to Hopewell Mills. Everyone would be confused, including the other mill owners, and that was just what he wanted.

As they approached the mansion, Eben pointed out town landmarks to Christian, hoping to relax the boy by involving his mind in something other than nervous anticipation of the meeting ahead. As he pointed out the stacks of Hopewell Mills, it occurred to Eben that perhaps only he was uncomfortable with the prospect of introducing Christian to his family. The boy had been quiet and calm throughout their long trip, giving no clue as to what might be going through his mind. If he was nervous about his new life, Eben had no way of knowing. Eben was not worried about Suzannah's welcome and he knew Patrick would be excited to have a cousin playmate. But he wondered what Sarah would do when she saw Christian's golden skin, his wide, expressive mouth and flaring nostrils, the startling amber eyes. And Martin? Eben resolved that until he began school in September, Christian would be kept away from his racist grandfather.

Originally, he had planned to enroll the boy in a Boston school immediately. But he had changed his mind, knowing in his heart that the child had to be suffering from his separation from Marianna. Eben could not look at him without feeling the pain of that loss himself. It would be too harsh to send Christian out among strangers just when he needed family affection and reassurance the most.

Having decided to bring him home to Amoset for a few months, however, Eben was confronted with the problem of how to keep the boy in the same house as his grandparents without exposing him to humiliation and suffering. The more he thought about this, the more clearly he recognized the dangers ahead. Somehow, Christian must be prepared. But it was hard to find the words. Everytime he tried to bring up the subject of Sarah and Martin, he found himself unable to do so. Now they were in Amoset and their splendid carriage was wheeling up the long, curved driveway to the mansion. He must explain to Christian about his grandparents before it was too late.

Eben cleared his throat. "Chris, do you remember yesterday when I told you your Grandmother Sarah was a strange woman?"

Christian nodded in response.

"You mustn't mind what she says to you, son. I'm just warning you." Eben cleared his throat again. How could he say it? How could he tell a five-year-old that he would be hated for simply being himself? "She might say mean things or ask questions you don't like answering." Eben stared out the window, catching a first glimpse of the massive house on the knoll. The grey stone was now framed by bright green maples, oaks and elms, and decorated with the pink blossoms of the cherry trees around the ellipse. There were flowers crowded gaily in every bed. The whole scene, laid against an azure sky, was too pastel pretty to suit Eben. To be fairer to Christian, to prepare him for Sarah and Martin, it would have been better if it had been winter. In that season, the mansion was more itself, cold and forbidding, like a chiseled lump of granite come to rest on a barren hillside.

"*C'est jolie*, Papa," said the boy, his voice excited. "*Très jolie!*"

"Don't be fooled," Eben blurted, grabbing Christian's hands. "Aunt Suzannah and Patrick will be your friends, but beware of the others. Stay away from them, son."

Christian's face, heart-shaped like his mother's, wrinkled in perplexity. He had lived all his life in the security of the Villa Caribe. The danger to which Eben alluded was impossible for him to understand.

"Trust me, Christian," said Eben, pulling the boy onto his lap and holding him close. "You'll understand when you're older. But for now you must believe what your father tells you."

Suzannah and Patrick were standing in front of the porticoed entrance. Patrick waved his cap and jumped up and down with excitement.

Suzannah admired the carriage with a raised eyebrow. "I am sure you impressed the locals," she said, as Eben stepped down and hugged her. "But there are those who would tell you, the bigger the carriage the larger the debt."

"You old Yankee woman you!"

She pushed her brother away. "Yankee woman, yes! But old, never!" She looked in the carriage and put out her hand. "Welcome, Christian. I am your

Aunt Suzannah." With her other hand, she brought Patrick forward. "And here is cousin Patrick. You are five and he is seven."

"Come along, Christian," said Eben a little impatiently. "Hurry, son."

"Hush, Eben. Why don't you try to be easygoing for a change? Try to understand what it must be like to be five years old. It is very young, Eben." She smiled at Christian and drew him close. "While I get to know Christian, why don't you go up to see our mother?" She gave Eben a knowing look.

"I thought you wrote that she comes downstairs these days."

"Yes, she does. But I encouraged her to stay in bed today because I thought it would make things a little easier." She glanced down at Christian. He was staring at Patrick, who returned his curious gaze without flinching.

"Where have you got us sleeping?" Eben asked as they entered the house.

"The servants opened up and refreshed your old suite. With the little sitting room attached, there is plenty of room for both of you." She kissed Eben's cheek. "You look drawn and exhausted, my brother."

"I'm worried." He glanced at Christian.

"I don't believe there is any need. The servants have been told not to mention him, but to treat him like family. Just to help us out a bit, Margaret Duffy will be here in a few days with her children. Little Christian will be surrounded by loving family."

Eben was watching his son, who was still staring at Patrick. "God, I hope I haven't done the wrong thing, Suzannah. He seems so little here. So vulnerable." Like his mother, he thought.

"Don't worry, Eben. It's a trick children have

that catches adults off guard. I swear, sometimes I think nature intends for us to underestimate them."

Eben's eyes were turned toward Christian, but he was remembering Marianna as he had last seen her, standing on the dock, watching as their ship weighed anchor and moved away from Fort au France. She had been wearing a bright yellow and green cotton dress that fit snugly about her hips and reached almost to her feet. Like all the other native women gathered at the dock, her head was wrapped in a scarf of matching fabric. He had bought the clothes for her on the day before the ship's departure. Though they were simple garments of coarse weave, the purchase had pleased her as much as the jewels and silks he once had lavished on her. He recalled how she had waved her straw parasol that was decorated with paper flowers. She had been smiling, but he would forever remember her as sad, tiny and vulnerable as a violet.

Suzannah nudged him gently toward the stairway. "Get along, Eben. I swear, never was there anyone like you for blue moods! Patrick and I are going to take Christian for a walk and then we'll show him his room and the playroom on the third floor."

"Playroom? In this house?" Eben laughed in disbelief.

Suzannah looked pleased with herself. "When I brought Patrick back here last autumn, I swore in my heart that this would be a happy home. And somehow, despite all that *they* might like to do, it has been a happy place. You'll see. You won't regret bringing Christian here."

It was not until many hours later that Suzannah and Eben had a chance to talk. While Eben had gone upstairs to speak to his mother, Suzannah and the little boys had taken a long walk about the grounds and house. The newcomer was shown the stables and ponds, the duckhouse and chicken runs, the vegetable gardens, the orchard, the beehives, and even the old lookout above the mill. Near the end of the afternoon, they came inside and toured the bedrooms and playroom, the kitchen and pantry.

"These are *our* stairs," declared Patrick, grabbing his cousin's hand. He opened the door to the narrow servants' staircase that connected the four floors of the mansion. "If you go around the other way, you have to see Grandmama!" Patrick made a face. Catching a glimpse, Suzannah almost laughed aloud.

Christian would be all right. Patrick and the back staircase would see to that.

Meanwhile, upstairs, Eben made polite conversation with his mother throughout an interminable afternoon tea. He accepted her condolences and answered her questions about Amanda and the White family. Then he listened as she nattered at him about Valentine. "I declare I miss that boy so much it hurts. You should have children, Eben. Then you'd understand my meaning." About Martin. "Your father is ever so much better and I half expect to see him up and about and managing things again." About Suzannah. "There is something unnatural about that girl. And the way she takes to men's affairs!"

To all her comments, Eben responded in noncommittal terms, holding back his true thoughts and emotions as if they were stallions he must control at peril of his life. What he saw of his mother that afternoon did nothing to assuage the loathing he felt for her. Although she was properly dressed and her room well-aired, her mean, resentful nature poisoned the atmosphere with an acrid odor only he could smell. She insisted they dine alone together in her room. Fearing that if he refused she might come downstairs,

Eben agreed. But the food almost choked him, and by the time he could decently excuse himself, he was suffering from painful indigestion.

He found Suzannah in her office.

"Do you work every night, Sister?"

She shrugged and looked slightly guilty. "It's become a habit, I'm afraid. Something to do."

"Well, I offer you an alternative tonight. I'm serving wine in the front drawing room in ten minutes. If you can tear youself away." He started to close the door, then added, "The spectacles are quite beguiling, Mrs. Paine."

When she appeared in the drawing room fifteen minutes later, she was carrying several mill ledgers and a sheet of paper covered with long columns of figures.

"I don't want to work!" cried Eben, taking everything out of her arms and handing it to a servant. "These belong in Mrs. Paine's office."

"But, Eben, it will take only a moment, and I need. . . ."

He shook his head as he poured a large tulip glass of champagne for her. "I'll see all of that tomorrow. Tomorrow I'll *want* to see it. Now I want something else." He pushed a chair nearer the fire for her. "Sit down, Sister. Let me tell you what I have in mind for Hopewell Mills."

Their conversation lasted well into the morning hours and between them they drank two bottles of the best champagne the wine butler could find in Martin Hopewell's cellar. As Eben told her his story, Suzannah's mind wandered sometimes. She thought how much she loved her brother. She recalled their first really intimate conversation, the one they had shared while riding in the carriage between Savannah and Augusta. She had begun to realize then what a joy a brother could be. He honored her with his trust and she reciprocated with hers. It was a kind of sacrament between them. No matter what their differences, they were brother and sister. And being that to the fullest extent gave each of them strength to draw on.

"I didn't tell Christian that his mother was going to die, but he sensed it from us, I think. That's when he started acting shy and timid. Inside the walls of the Villa Caribe, he was as bold as a warrior, but the world alarms him. I saw that right away.

"Marianna, Christian and I went by private carriage to New Orleans. Bess, the old black woman who used to belong to Grandpa Theron, came with us." Eben took a sip of wine and stared at the carpet. "We were lucky in New Orleans. The wait for a ship was less than a month. We spent the time in a little pension in a quiet part of town. The place was discreet and remote enough from the more traveled paths that I could relax and not worry about meeting someone I knew. I have done a great deal of business in New Orleans over the past ten years, Suzannah, and I am well-known in several prominent homes. But after a time, I became less concerned that someone would recognize me with Marianna or Christian. I remembered that I was a widower and free to do as I wished. After the first two weeks or so, we spent our mornings driving around the city as all the so-called aristocrats do."

Suzannah looked up. "And did you meet any of your associates?"

He nodded. "I didn't care. Being with Marianna and Christian day after day as I was, I realized that they were my family. After that, something in me refused to hide them or be ashamed. I loved her, Suzannah. I still do, and I no longer wish to conceal that truth. I had to be honest in New Orleans, and I am determined to continue to do so. That is why, if our mother or father find out about Christian, I won't deny him. If we can avoid a confrontation, so much the better, but if not . . . well, Christian is my son. I love him."

Eben talked about Martinique, recalling for her how the Caribbean island had struck him with the rawness of its color. Too much red and black and green and blue. The blinding sunwashed blue of sea and sky was still painful to remember. Even under the bowering trees, he had not been able to escape the glaring color. Flowers like bloodstained trumpets hung in streams from the branches, and in the shady places, a sinuous blue-flowered vine tangled with everything it touched.

"Marianna insisted on going back to visit the sugar plantation where she was born. It's become so overgrown that we had to get someone to take us out there and make a way through. It was the eeriest moment or two I've ever lived. We were coming through what was almost a wall of those tangled blue flowers and it was hard for the horses. They were restless and making everyone nervous. The trees and lianas grew low and overhung the path, so our guide and I were cutting them back with machetes. And the air! God it was still. It stank so of decay that I didn't want to breathe. Then suddenly we were through it and there was the house. The walls and chimneys and porches were crumbling away, getting softer with every rainy season. And those vines, those inescapable vines, were growing all inside and out of the place. It was clammy and damp in there, as if death were breathing on us."

"Eben!" Suzannah laughed and shifted her position. "You make me nervous with all that talk. You aren't superstitious are you?"

"I don't know. Maybe I am. During those weeks with Marianna at Fort au France I learned one thing: those Creole people have a touch of wizardry in them. As soon as we got to that island, Marianna began to change. She dressed like a native woman and while I stayed at the hotel with Christian, she found a place to live in a part of town where there were several families who remembered her mother. It was a shantytown, Suzannah. Worse than the Gully. I tried to make her stay somewhere more . . . substantial, but she insisted that she wanted to be with her friends. I would have bought her a house, but she didn't want it. She wanted to be with others like herself. She called them her friends, but I know she hadn't seen any of them since the day she left the island as a little girl. Still, there was a feeling of kinship about the place, I must admit. And Marianna was happy there. After a while I began to sense that I was somehow in the way. Then I knew it was time for me to go."

Marianna had said to him, "Go now, *chéri*. Before we are sad together."

"But what will happen? Who will care for you?" He had been blinded by tears.

"My friends will care for me when it comes to that. But for now I can be useful. At our home I was too idle."

"But you had your needlework, Marianna. You did that."

"Not in the last year, my darling."

It had been a dappled day of sun and cloud, and they were standing side by side at the end of a little spit of land that extended like a solitary finger pointing north into the sea. Below them was a curve of beach and a few rocks against which a light surf broke.

"Go home to Amoset, Eben. And take Christian. Take him with my blessing. I see how all of this unnerves him, and I know you are right. He belongs in the North with his father. Martinique is the end for me. With you, he can have a beginning."

Eben looked at Suzannah frankly. "I must tell you, Sister, that for all I loved Marianna, at the end I was eager to leave her. It took every bit of her strength to fight the pain. I knew she was suffering and I wanted to leave her. Does that sound monstrous to you?"

"Only honest. I think I would feel the same."

Eben laughed. His eyes were shining. "Oh, Suzannah, let me be completely honest with you then! Let me confess that I feel tonight like a man reborn." He eased the cork on the second bottle of champagne; it hissed and then exploded. "I am, as of this very moment," he laughed again as he filled her glass and his own, "free of the South for the first time in my life. And so are you and so are all of us. I have sold out all my southern holdings, even the railroad I loved. My father-in-law, Gregory White, was just as happy to see me go. He gave me an excellent price on everything."

Suzannah was stunned. "Not Jasmine Gate!"

"No. I stopped short of selling the house, but I gave Gregory a lease. If there comes a time when we want the house, it can be arranged. I couldn't part with Jasmine Gate. It reminds me of Grandfather Theron."

"Everything is gone?" Suzannah whispered.

Eben finished off his glass and set it down firmly. "The long and short of it is that the Hopewells are now a fully solvent Northern family."

"You have some plan? You must have a scheme of some sort, Eben, because if you do not, it seems to me . . ."

He grinned. "Drink your wine and stop worrying, Sister."

She pointed back toward her office. "You didn't want to see the numbers, Eben, but when you look . . ."

"Drink!" he ordered.

She complied and then began again. "See here, Eben, I have been managing this mill for . . ."

"And you still do, Suzannah. Only when we re-open, it will not be the same kind of mill it was. I hope to convince you that Hopewell Mills is going out of the business of making immigrant cloth and into the business of fine cotton piece goods."

Considering this, she absent-mindedly finished her wine and held out her glass for more.

"First," said Eben, "I believe that if we want to survive in the business of milling cotton, we must look ahead to a time when it won't be easy to get Southern cotton. Cotton will go way up then, and even immigrant cloth will be expensive to make. Looking ahead, imagining how this country is going to go in the next twenty or thirty years, I can see only one set of buyers that will remain relatively stable. The rich ones. My dear Suzannah, the wealthy will continue no matter what cataclysms befall the government. The faces may change, but the class itself is eternal. We can't go wrong if we aim our product to the rich. With them, it doesn't matter how much the price goes up if the goods are quality."

He leaned forward eagerly. "I got the idea when I was in New Orleans. I had a little free time one day and wandered into a shop devoted entirely to the sale of piece goods. I was astonished by what I saw,

Suzannah. There are hundreds of different shades and varieties of fine cloth available in the world. Silks embroidered with real gold, velvets with pile an inch deep. Suddenly I realized that what our mill should produce is the finest cotton cloth in America. And it should be available in prints and with embroidery."

Midway through his story, Suzannah had begun to nod her head. By the time he was finished, she was enthusiastic. She had seen some beautiful cloth during her stay in Palermo with her Aunt Bronwyn. All at once she remembered one of her aunt's nightdresses in particular, which had been made of a sheer but sturdy cotton from North Africa. Though surely there would be problems involved in implementing her brother's plan, Suzannah knew from instinct that it would work. As he told her more, her mind darted ahead and around, fully energetic for the first time in months. Or was it years?

She sipped her champagne and leaned against the deep cushions. The mantel clock struck two, but she didn't hear it. She was filled with a sense of well-being unparalleled in her experience. For all that he had been through, Eben was stronger now than ever before. Not for an instant did she doubt that he had within him what it took to make a success of his dream. And she knew she would work comfortably and well with him in this new version of Hopewell Mills. She closed her eyes and thought of the years ahead with something like pure pleasure. With work to challenge her and James to love her, she would find her greatest happiness.

Chapter 13

"This is the nicest time of year in Boston," Eben remarked to himself as he walked from his rooms at the Yale Club in the direction of the Kilmaine residence on Moon Street. It was early summer, when the afternoons were not yet too hot and the mornings still bore a sweet nip of chill. As he waited for the traffic in Dowell Street to clear a little, he noted that the shops all around were spruced up for the new season. Boston had the feel of a city wanting to forget economic hard times as quickly as possible. The atmosphere was one-hundred percent Yankee-American, with people on the move, destinies being grabbed for. The crowds of men, women, children, animals, carts and wagons, the pleased-with-itself racket the city made, exhilarated Eben. He found himself standing there on the corner, grinning like a looney.

Ever since that morning, when the matter of his son's schooling had been settled, Eben had been in the grip of an uncommon ebullience. In a few months Christian would begin his education. Certain now that the boy would be happy in the Quaker Academy's environment of calm discipline and generous instincts, Eben felt as if a weight had been lifted from his mind. But this was not the only reason for his good spirits.

At the foot of Moon Street, he stopped to buy a huge bouquet of summer jonquils and daisies from a flower girl. He glanced at this watch. He was early by almost half an hour.

The moment he had arrived in Boston, Eben had sent a brief note around to his friend Thomas at the Boston Globe offices. A hastily scrawled invitation to lunch the next day at the Kilmaine home came by return messenger. Now here he was down at the bottom of Moon Street with thirty minutes to idle when what he really wanted to do was rush up the street, throw open the door and squeeze Lucy until she squealed. Short of that forbidden joy, he could not bear to arrive unexpectedly. At no time before the magic hour of one could he put on the mask he knew he must wear throughout that afternoon. By one, he would have to be ready to hide completely his passion and adoration for Lucy, to remember that he was Thomas Kilmaine's friend. Challenging as all this pretense might be, he knew he would be able to manage. But not before one. It was the hour he had been thinking of, preparing for, focusing on since the day before. Eben sat down on an iron bench in a little square a block from their home, waiting, watching the passers-by.

Lucy dropped her earring into the folds of her rose-patterned skirt and, fumbling for it, she muttered an exasperated, "Damn!"

"Perhaps you need eyeglasses, Lucy," commented her husband from the other side of their bedroom. He was studying his reflection in the tall glass on his dressing room door. He frowned briefly as he tugged down on his waistcoat in an effort to cover his thickening waist.

"Shall I tell Mrs. Tippits to stop making desserts for a while?" asked Lucy as she tried the earring again. The single pearl drop reminded her of a tear.

"No need to say anything to Cook. I'll go riding twice a week. And now that Eben is here, I shall invite him to ride with me." He glanced at Lucy and saw that she wasn't listening to him. She didn't really care what he said. Her mind had gone off to that woman's place where it often went, and his presence in the room was merely a distraction.

There was a time when this awareness had possessed the power to wound him terribly, and he had wept a time or two in the privacy of his study. Now, however, he did not care much one way or another. The Lucy he had loved and married was gone forever, and the woman with whom he lived and who went by her name was someone for whom he felt no significant regard. But the memory plays tricks, and just as Thomas was noting to himself how little he cared, his heart was stung by the memory of Lucy on the night they met. Blazing bonfires had ringed the skating pond near Hopewell Mills, and the ice had been crowded with pretty girls in heavy whirling skirts and bright, knitted scarves. He had come upon her as she stood in the midst of her operative friends from the boarding houses, talking about workers' rights. That vision of her was so brilliant that it had burned forever into Thomas' memory. If ever he could get beyond that raw place and put behind him the poignant sense of loss it evoked in him, he believed he could be free of Lucy Shawn. Until then he would see her as he remembered her, curls of fairytale silver and gold haloing her head like a medieval painting, the features pretty, the expression skeptical. In that moment, she had seemed to embody the hope of womanhood, the destiny of her sex.

Now she thought of nothing but the child, Delphia, who was six and beginning to chafe under her mother's smothering attentions. Although he spent little time with his daughter, Thomas thought he understood her rather well. He was fairly certain of the kind of rebellious and difficult young woman the gently restless little Delphia would become.

I won't even be here, Lucy, he thought before he could stop himself. Perversely, thrilling in the forbidden, he tasted the thought again: I won't be here, Lucy.

Once Thomas had become disillusioned with his marriage, he had begun to create a fantasy of freedom in the West. With the passage of time, it had become clearer, keener, more enticing. Often, now, he dreamed of the West even as he slept, seeing himself as a solitary man on horseback, roaming and writing about what he saw. In the beginning, he had thought he would like to own a little rural newspaper, but soon that thought had become too confining. Now he realized he wanted a life where nothing and no one would have a hold on him so that he could be the truly impartial observer he aimed to be.

"Is something the matter, Thomas?" Lucy was dabbing herself lightly with a bit of cotton she had dipped in violet water. "You've been staring at me for almost five minutes."

He was not exactly lying when he said, "I was thinking about the *Globe*. I've almost had it with Henderson and his damned editorial policies. The man won't let me write the truth about slavery. Or about the economics of this city, as if Boston were the Holy of Holies, Mecca of the god Mammon. . . ." He turned back and disappeared into his dressing room for several moments.

Although he continued to talk to her, Lucy could not make out his words and soon ceased to listen. But her thoughts stayed with her husband. Lately Thomas had been having excitable outbursts of anger, and she was concerned about his health. His mental health, she corrected herself, recalling a conversation with Miss Dorothea Dix, the champion of the mentally ill. The conversation had taken place during a dinner party at the Moon Street house a little over a year before. Eben had been there. A day later they were lovers.

"As we were meant to be," she whispered at her image.

But it was months since they had last been together, and in the meantime there had been McMahon.

"Damn!" she muttered, squeezing her eyes shut. So far she had been having one of her good days and not once, until that moment, had Foster McMahon's name come into her mind. But now, without warning, her whole body began to tremble as she relived the days she had spent as his captive. She felt as if she were made up of billions of minute particles, all of which had begun to vibrate and move about erratically.

The violet-scented cotton dropped from her hand and she clutched herself around the waist, bending forward as if to close herself away. She hugged herself tightly, for it seemed that at any moment the trembling might go mad and she would begin to fly apart in all directions. Foster McMahon was dead, but he had left her a legacy of fear that she knew she would carry to her grave.

The spasm passed after a few moments and she

was able to finish dressing without further incident. But for Lucy, the luncheon ahead, the meal she had planned to perfection in every detail, was spoiled. The edge was taken off it, as her father used to say. Suddenly, she could think of nothing positive about seeing Eben Hopewell. They would spend the afternoon trying not to look at one another. They would yearn from a distance and conspire for a single moment when their fingertips might touch. Despite Amanda's death, nothing had really changed for them. What difference could her death make to them while she and Thomas remained firmly married? Lucy saw that she would probably spend the rest of her life in helpless, hopeless longing for Eben Hopewell. The thought almost undid her.

"Damn!" she muttered, giving the leg of the dressing table a fierce little kick as she stood up. Downstairs the grandfather clock struck one and the doorbell chimed. As she opened the bedroom door, Lucy heard the housemaid, Maureen, saying, "Good afternoon, Mr. Hopewell. Welcome back to Boston."

Chapter 14

Late the next morning, after she had seen to the management of her home, Lucy Shawn Kilmaine donned a light knitted cape and matching grey gloves and hurried down to the shopping area on the square at the foot of Moon Street. The Kilmaines' neighborhood was now almost entirely Irish. Thousands of immigrants were making their way across the Atlantic from Ireland to homes on Moon Street, and behind them were thousands who might follow. Only a few of these families, such as Lucy's next-door neighbors the Flynns, owned their homes. The others rented apartments in the two-story brick houses. In scarcely more than a year, the shopping area around the square had taken on a distinctly foreign atmosphere. There were strange dialects and accents in every shop where Lucy stopped to make a purchase or admire from afar.

For the most part, the proprietors were not Irish, but came of Yankee stock. The greengrocer, the chemist, the cobbler's young assistant, all of them treated Mrs. Kilmaine carefully and inquired respectfully after her health. Each face looked uniformly downcast and pitying. It was an uncomfortable situation. They all knew that Lucy Kilmaine had been kidnapped from under their noses one beautiful day the year before and taken away and held hostage for money. And Lucy knew that they knew. Nevertheless, decorum demanded that all of them pretend the nightmare had never occurred.

"And how are you feeling today, Mrs. Kilmaine?" asked the thin little woman who tended the ladies' counter in her husband's dry goods store.

"I'm very well, Mrs. Schriber. Lovely weather." Lucy watched Mrs. Schriber nod her head, then shake it, then nod it again, her gaze fastened to the countertop as if she had heard the worst from Lucy's very own lips. "Mrs. Schriber, I wonder . . . have you any spectacles for ladies? With magnifying lenses in them?"

Mrs. Schriber became Mrs. Business. From a shelf in the dark recesses of the store, she brought forth a large cardboard box filled with wire-rimmed spectacles in several degrees of magnification. Using the glass of the countertop as a mirror, Lucy tried them on. Mrs. Schriber looked on for a moment, but when the door jangled open and another customer walked in, Lucy was left alone.

She wanted to cry. The spectacles made her look like an old woman. Now, for the first time, she could see clearly the lines in her face. How could Eben possibly care for her when she looked at least forty years old? She was only twenty-eight. How dare life mark her so early? What chance did she have if even her own face betrayed her?

She put the glasses down and stared into the case beyond her aging reflection to the beautifully beaded shawl that was displayed inside. Its colors of blue and green were like a peacock's tail. With a rush of hunger, she wanted it more than anything else in the world. It was as if the artist who created the shawl had said, "Look, here's just the thing for Lucy Kilmaine. This shawl will cheer her up and make her young again!" It was so beautiful and so definitely made with her in mind that she could not help feeling happy just looking at it. What would it be like to wear such a magnificent garment?

"Mrs. Schriber," she said, "may I try on the shawl?"

Mrs. Business became even more serious. "If it was anybody else who asked me, Mrs. Kilmaine, I would have to say no. But seeing as it's you, I can say that this is a very special drape and quite expensive." After removing it from the case, she leaned closer, watching as Lucy opened the ornately decorated square of blue wool and put it across her shoulders. "Costs fifty dollars, that does," she said softly.

Lucy didn't hear her. The wool was so soft she thought it must be cashmere, and the vivid green satin lining caressed the nape of her neck as would a lover's fingers. She could only sigh.

"How much is it, Mrs. Schriber?"

Mrs. Business looked annoyed. "I told you, madam. Fifty dollars."

Lucy was aghast. She had not imagined it could be so much. Quickly, she slipped it off her shoulders and gave it back to Mrs. Schriber. "I'm not interested, of course. I'm sorry to disturb you."

"What about the spectacles? Not interested in those either?"

Lucy shook her head and hurried out of the store as quickly as she could before the temptation to have that shawl overcame her. She went into a little confectionary shop on the corner to have a glass of chocolate and a sweet cake. One window faced the street, and in front of it was a small table where a customer could sit. From there, she could watch the pedestrians and traffic and get her mind off everything that was upsetting her. More than Eben, more than memories of McMahon or unhappiness with Thomas, more than her stinging eyes and the blurring headaches, not being able to afford the blue-beaded shawl seemed the greatest wrong of all. As she sipped her chocolate, it seemed to her that she deserved that shawl after what she had suffered in the past year. The blue shawl would lift her spirits every time she wore it, and for that reason alone it was worth the fifty dollars. Such logic would not impress and certainly never convince Thomas Kilmaine, who prided himself on thinking clearly at all times. He did not much believe in feelings that sprang from intuition and could not be registered on some scale or graph.

She doubted that he even knew how miserable she was. Most of the time, Thomas lived in his own world. When he entered hers he was clumsy and gave every impression of being eager to escape. She could not begin to tell him how her heart ached. It seemed impossible to explain the fear she had lived with every day since McMahon had kidnapped her. If she were to say that she saw McMahon's face in the crowd again and again and that half the time she could feel him following her, she knew Thomas would scoff at her and make light of her illusions. "Women," he would mutter, shaking his head. If she were to ask him for the shawl, he would refuse and belittle her in his apparently gentle way for wanting it in the first place. She knew this very well, but the desire for the shawl would not abate. She must have it.

Just as I must have Eben. The thought jolted her mind back to the previous afternoon and the luncheon which had been both terrible and wonderful and nothing in between. She stirred the milk in her glass and clouds of dark chocolate swirled up from the bottom. A serving girl brought her a plate on which were several elaborately frosted bite-sized cakes, filled with creams and fresh fruit. She selected one and nibbled on it absent-mindedly. As she looked out the window, her vision blurred, this time by design, and instead of the busy street, she saw the enclosed porch at the rear of her Moon Street house.

The white wrought-iron table was set with fresh flowers and blue and white china. There were open windows on three sides, which gave a pleasing view of the walled yard. The little gazebo and the shrubbery and trees and vegetable garden Lucy had cultivated were limited to a relatively small area, but the outlook was as soothing as a country vista. At least Lucy hoped so. She had planned this meal a dozen times a dozen in her mind, yet she was certain that something would go wrong. And it almost did. So jangled was she by Lucy's feverish directions and implorings for perfection that Mrs. Tippits made a cream sauce instead of a fish sauce. Maureen had to rush down to the bottom of Moon Street for more butter at the last minute. Hearing this, Lucy flew into a rage for which she knew she would spend the next month apologizing.

When Thomas came home from the *Globe* about noon, she curbed her impatience, but she never stopped being excited. The moment she saw Eben standing in her foyer looking dark and strong, her excitement rose to such a breathless height that she actually was afraid for herself. She could hardly taste the white fish in its delicate lemon butter sauce.

Thomas and Eben took turns dominating the luncheon table conversation, which was literate and interesting. Though it always would seem strange to Lucy, her husband and her lover truly enjoyed each other's company. While the men talked, she watched her lover form his words and imagined his lips touching her bare flesh. Whenever he looked at her, she would tingle with warmth and melt inside.

"I wanted to free my slaves, those I inherited from Grandfather Theron, but the law in Georgia wouldn't let me," Eben told Thomas. "I was required to sell them or give them away. I arranged for Gregory White to have them under the condition that Hiram White would never become their master."

"I thought you liked the man," said Thomas, pouring his guest another glass of wine. "What changed your mind?"

As briefly as he could, Eben told Lucy and Thomas some of what Suzannah had reported of the conditions at Wild Rose on St. Simon's Island. "I knew that I could no longer live in Georgia or any other place in the South until this matter of black and white is settled and justice is done."

"You have become an abolitionist, my friend?"

"Not that exactly. As you know, I'm not particularly fond of political or social movements. I leave such matters to you and Lucy."

"Lucy!" Thomas laughed disparagingly, but not unkindly. "This young lady hasn't been involved at all since we came to Boston. I thought you would quickly espouse some cause or other, Lucy. Everywhere I go, I meet feminists and abolitionists who tell me there is much work to be done. But Lucy doesn't care. . . ."

"It isn't that, Thomas. I told you that until Delphia is older . . ."

He shook his finger at her. "And I've told you: Women make altogether more fuss than is necessary over this mothering business. Think of poor Eben's

Amanda." He touched his friend's arm. "I am truly sorry."

Eben acknowledged the condolences, but clearly he did not wish to dwell on grief. He seemed eager to talk about his plans for the mill. She tried to listen to what he had to say. She had spent many years as an operative at Hopewell Mills, so the affairs of the mill town were always interesting to her. Causes with high-sounding names like Abolition and Feminism carried little meaning for her, but the day-to-day affairs of women working in the mills, wage-slaves her father used to call them, were of great interest. But not today. Today there was only Eben.

"Sarah Bagley will force hearings in the legislature this year," said Thomas. "She leads an association of women from the mills called the Female Labor Reform Association. If your new mill has a workday that lasts one moment over ten hours, you'll be in trouble from Miss Bagley. She may not manage to win over all the wise old men of the General Court, but I went to hear her speak once and I assure you, she is a woman to be reckoned with."

"Thomas, in the new mill no woman will labor more than ten hours. Although I do hope to work the place twenty-four hours a day for the first several months, ten hours is the limit of the workday."

Thomas laughed. "Your outfoxed competitors will accuse you of denying the right of overtime employment to your workers."

"Let them try. I'm telling you, my friend, this is a mill of a new sort for Amoset. Suzannah and I intend to prove that manufacturing can be a humane institution. And still make a profit." Eben took a sip of coffee.

Lucy stared at him.

Who cares! she wanted to yell.

She craved him so much she thought her body could not stand it. From neck to knee, all those parts now covered in dark pongee silk and grape-colored lace, Lucy was quivering. Her hands and arms and her head on its pretty neck moved gracefully enough, but a pulse vibrated through her stomach and thighs. The flesh between her legs seemed very hot and when she pressed her thighs together, the feeling became even more intense. The fact that she noticed such symptoms of desire was surprising to begin with; a year earlier she would have ignored rather than faced them. But now she was excited beyond her wildest imaginings. She glanced back and forth between Eben and Thomas, who were still in earnest conversation. Without thinking, she grinned to herself. What would they think if they knew the lascivious thoughts she was entertaining at that moment?

Now, in the confectionary shop, Lucy finished her glass of chocolate and dabbed her lips daintily with a napkin. She looked normal, but inside she was still whirling, giddy with the memory of that long afternoon's hot wanting.

After a while she had become certain that Eben was aware of what she was feeling and was also excited. Heedless of the risks, she had begun trying to catch his gaze and hold it until just the instant before Thomas noticed. As the meal drew to a close and Thomas seemed unaware of his wife's flirtation, she became bolder. The element of danger, the sustained sexual tension unalleviated by the briefest touch made Lucy distraught and reckless.

Like a shopkeeper, Eben inquired after her well-being.

"I am well enough, Eben. Thank you. No physical harm was done to me."

"Even so, it was a terrible ordeal for our Lucy,

Eben. McMahon was a monster. But as you can see, she has come through it with her usual marvelous courage. If she were an ordinary woman, I'd hate to think of the hysterics. But Lucy has shown her pluck."

"But you don't look well, Lucy." Eben studied her more closely. "I think you have a fever."

As a matter of fact, her head was throbbing and suddenly she thought she might be ill.

She stood up. Now there were stars, dots of light, burning her vision. When she drew her hand across her brow, the dots of light became a comet's tail that ended in a terrible, thick ache. She looked at Eben. Her blue gaze clasped his brown and held him captive for a smoldering instant before she fainted into his arms.

Chapter 15

"You embarrassed me, Lucy. Not to mention our guest. And if you were so ill yesterday, why were you out gadding in the shops today when I came home early to see you. I expected to find you indisposed, not disappeared."

"I had not disappeared, Thomas. I merely went to the shops for one or two necessities." She fiddled with the vegetables on her plate.

"You bought spectacles for yourself, I hope!"

"No, Thomas."

"Why not, I would like to know? I suppose you would prefer to visit a doctor and pay him his rent money so he can tell you what we both already know. You need eyeglasses, Lucy."

She pouted and pushed her dinner plate away. At her end of the table, Delphia ate in silence as she watched her parents.

"I did see something beautiful, Thomas," Lucy ventured to say a moment later. "At Schriber's Store, in the glass case at the back, there is a most beautiful beaded shawl made of cashmere. It's blue, Thomas, like the sky at home. And the lining is green silk, a pine foresty sort of shade. It is the loveliest thing I have ever seen, Thomas."

Kilmaine narrowed his eyes. "Yes, Lucy?"

"I want to buy it."

"What do you mean you want to buy it?"

"I want to use my own money."

"What money is that, Lucy?"

"The money my father has been giving me, the little presents."

Thomas looked cross. "I thought we agreed that I would only consent to your receiving money from your father under the condition that you would save it toward some item of special importance. You know I dislike the implication behind your father's gifts. I am more than able to support you and support you well, Lucy. You are not a poor girl who needs money from her family."

"But Papa believes a woman should have a little money that is all her own."

"And you want to spend this money, your private cache, on a frivolous shawl?" With his disappointed eyes and glum lower lip, Thomas resembled a hound. "What can you be thinking of, Lucy?"

She looked over at Delphia. "Are you finished, dear?" She rang a little glass bell beside her place and Maureen came into the dining room. "Take Delphia up to Brownie, will you please? I'll come up for a few moments when she is ready for bed."

When they were alone in the dining room, Lucy folded her hands before her, breathed deeply a time or two, and then tried to explain to Thomas how she felt.

"Ever since those days with McMahon, I've felt so awfully down. It's been as if my life is over before I am even thirty. And it does no good to tell myself this isn't realistic thinking. I know it is not and yet I feel this way. Like an old woman, a dirty spoiled thing."

Thomas leaned toward the candle flickering between them. "You know you are nothing of the sort, Lucy. Whatever that man was, you are . . ."

She touched his hand lightly. "Thank you for being kind, Thomas. I know I shouldn't feel soiled by McMahon, and yet I do. I always will. I am so downcast, Thomas. I think that if my life should end tomorrow . . ."

". . . a blue-beaded shawl would not make the slightest difference."

"But it would! Not for you or a person like you. But for me it would make a difference. Thomas, somehow I feel it was made with me in mind."

He shook his head and rang the servants' bell. "I forbid it, Lucy," he said as Maureen cleared the plates from the table. "I forbid you to waste money on frivolous clothing. If you are so mad for spending, use your account to pay an occulist. After that display yesterday afternoon, I cannot have you falling into the arms of every man in the neighborhood."

Lucy did not bother to argue. She knew it was hopeless.

The next morning, after Thomas had left for work and Brownie had gone off with Delphia to the park, Lucy went upstairs to dress. Although she took particular pains to make herself attractive that morning, the activity, which should have taken an hour at least, was accomplished in less than thirty minutes.

For the rest of the morning and all afternoon until her nap at three, she kept busy with her needlework. From the sewing room window, she could see all the way down Moon Street. The wide view of street and houses and square made the sewing room seem more secure on days when McMahon dominated her thoughts and she was imagining him in every face she glimpsed. But today her thoughts were all for Eben and the blue shawl. Would he come today?

She was so distracted that she jabbed her finger several times with her sharp embroidery needle. Finally, she noticed that she had gotten a dot of blood on the white linen.

"Damn!" she cried, throwing down the handkerchief. Loops and rolls of pastel embroidery cotton spilled onto the floor. An instant later, a tin of needles clattered after them. Angrily, Lucy stooped to pick them up, but halfway through the task her eyes were burning, and not even the thought of Delphia with a needle in her little foot could keep her at the task. Uttering a sigh so deeply resonant that it seemed to express the accumulated sorrows of humankind, she turned her back on industry and went to stand idly at the window, her hands clenched behind her back.

"If you do not come to me today, I shall die of grief," she whispered.

But though she waited and watched throughout the afternoon, Eben Hopewell did not come up Moon Street.

At dinner, Thomas looked up from his soup and said, "You are unusually quiet this evening, my dear. Is something the matter?" His voice was perfectly pleasant and conversational, but Lucy heard innuendo and resentment and ridicule in it.

"Do you take pleasure in making me unhappy, Thomas?" She sighed and pushed her plate away.

"Good Lord, woman! Are you still fretting about that shawl? Why, I nearly had forgotten it."

Maureen cleared the soup plates and replaced them with a sorbet for the palate, but Lucy was uninterested in food. The wretchedness that had been stewing in her for the past two or three days had deadened her taste and given her a queasy stomach.

That, combined with another headache, made eating impossible.

Thomas could see that she was ill. "Let me have the cook fix you a tray, Lucy."

She eyed him belligerently.

"Well, if you prefer to suffer . . ."

She pushed her chair away and stood up.

"That's better, Lucy. Much more sensible. I'll be up in a little while, my dear. To check on you."

Thomas watched Lucy as she left the room on Maureen's arm. He ate his meal alone, but Lucy occupied his thoughts completely. Thomas was a man who did not believe in doctors, but for the first time in his life, he was considering getting help. He had been watching Lucy and lately her appearance and odd behavior had begun to worry him. While he told himself that she might need a tonic or a rest somewhere to cure what must be a physical ailment, he could not avoid thinking of her mental condition as well. Lucy's mother, Helen, was notoriously peculiar, and then there was that lunatic woman who had locked up Martin Hopewell. Was Crazy Edythe related to the Shawn family? Suddenly, it occurred to him that Lucy's mind might have been affected by her recent experience with McMahon.

If Lucy had become unbalanced as a result of the kidnapping, then Thomas knew it was in some measure his own fault. He had not given her much consolation because he thought that by trivializing the incident, she would forget more quickly. The more he thought of it, the more culpable Thomas became in his own mind. And not merely for Lucy's ill health.

He thought about their marriage and gradually he assumed the full burden of guilt. He staggered beneath it, but he would not set even the smallest portion of it down. From the beginning, their troubles had been of Thomas' own making. He never should have married a young firebrand like Lucy Shawn and brought her away from her home and into the city. What's more, he had done all he could to reject who she was and shape and mold her into his own pretty image of a wife: intelligent but docile, witty but demure. And in bed. . . .

Their marriage had died there first, and Thomas knew it. No matter how unrealistic his other assumptions of sole guilt might be, he knew that as a lover he had failed his young wife. He remembered how on their first night together she had screamed aloud and struggled as he clasped her tightly against his heavy chest. He had thought it best not to coddle his young wife, not even in the bedroom. Her little girl's voice had pleaded with him to stop, pleaded with him not to hurt her. The memory of that first night had stood between them through all the years of their marriage. Even now, when they no longer shared the same bed and the conception of Delphia seemed more and more a miracle from an almost mythical past, the memory of that night filled Thomas with sorrow and shame. He had been a brute with the woman he had loved and sworn to cherish. Was it any wonder she had changed toward him? Was it a surprise that marriage had become a misery for both of them?

He stayed up late that night, sipping a port he had intended to save for a special occasion.

The next morning, he went to work early. He left orders that a doctor should be called in and that until he arrived, Mrs. Kilmaine was to rest. But the doctor's wife sent word by messenger that her husband had gone down to the shipyards about a man with a broken head and was not expected home until that evening.

"I told her to please have him come around as soon as he got home," Maureen told Lucy. "Was that all right, madam?"

"Yes, I suppose so. But there is nothing wrong with me, Maureen. I assure you of that." Nevertheless, as Lucy thought it might be nice to spend the day napping and playing invalid, she let Maureen assist her as she climbed back into bed. At least until Eben came, it would suit her well enough to laze. Fluffing pillows, bringing books, opening and closing the window shades, Maureen assumed her nursing role. "Everything is fine, Maureen. I am quite comfortable, I assure you." She had to say it several times before the girl finally hovered away and out of the room, leaving Lucy to her longed-for sleep.

But it would not come. Passing her hand across her brow, she realized that her skin was hot. Along with her heartache, she must have contracted a fever of some kind. No delirium accompanied her illness. Like the eminently Yankee woman that she was, Lucy was organizing her thoughts. One by one, she lined up her sorrows, trying to dissolve them by logical analysis. For once in her life, however, this would not work. Her distraught melancholy was ungovernable.

As the morning inched toward noon, she could think of nothing she had not considered a dozen times before. She loved Eben and longed for him with a physical need that was ruining her health and threatening her self-respect, but she couldn't help herself. Again and again, she thought, I am tired of always being so strong. Just this once, I want to be weak.

She was eating a light lunch when Eben was announced. She pushed the tray away when he came in and, forgetting gossip, ordered Maureen out of the room. As soon as the door had shut, Lucy was on her knees on the bed, her arms opened to him.

"At last," she whispered as he held her against him, his arms encircling her waist.

"Let me look at you, Lucy. Maureen says you've been ill. Is it true?" He cupped her face in his hands. "You're burning up!"

"It's nothing, Eben. Fevers are common in the summertime." She took his hand and put it against her breast. "But my heart . . . feel my heart, Eben?" She fell back into the pillows and stared up at him. "I love you, Eben. Knowing that you are my beloved, it's been more and more difficult to live with Thomas these last few months." She reached for him. "Come down here and lie beside me. Please."

Instead, he laughed softly and drew a chair to her bedside. "You may not care for your reputation, Mrs. Kilmaine, but I do."

"Spit on my reputation!"

Eben burst out laughing. He couldn't help giving her the embrace she wanted. She was the dearest girl in the world with her courage and her defiant vulgarisms. But when he held her as if she were made of glass, she twisted in his arms until their mouths were only inches apart. He was suddenly unable to resist what, just a moment before, honor had told him to forebear. He pressed his open mouth against hers and kissed her deeply. His palms tingled as he fought to keep them safely on her back when all he could think of was the pounding in his groin and the feel of her skin beneath his fingers.

"Please, Eben," she whispered against his ear, her lips caressing the sensitive shell. "Let us live dangerously for once."

He held her away with a groan. "Not yet, Lucy. There will be a better time and place for us. And I have to talk to you. Before we go any further, there are some things you must know about me."

"All I must know is one thing, Eben. Only this: I love you. These months apart have been a test, and I have learned from it. I have learned that I love you more than anything. More than Delphia, Eben. More than my own good name. I would sacrifice anything for you. I would suffer for you if necessary. Love me, Eben. I adore you. Without you, with only Thomas for the rest of my life, I shall die, Eben. Please, Eben." With one hand she opened the laced front placket of her nightdress, revealing her small breasts and firm, dark nipples. With a sigh, Eben dropped onto the bed beside her. His mouth and tongue and fingertips pulled and gently tormented her breasts until they ached. She reached to unlace his trousers for him.

The night before, Thomas Kilmaine had decided to buy the shawl. Despite a head that throbbed from too much heavy, old port, he had gotten up early the next morning so that he could make the purchase before work. He had taken the box with the shawl in it to the office, intending to bring it home at the end of the day. But around midmorning, he had begun to dwell on how happy this purchase was going to make his wife and how good her happiness was going to make him feel. Finally, he decided to forgo his usual lunch with the other journalists for a quick meal at home. As he entered the house and hung up his coat, he was mildly sorry to see Eben's coat on the peg. But then again, it would be pleasant to give such a generous gift to his wife in the presence of another man. Though eventually the money would come from Lucy's personal account, there was no reason for Eben to know that.

He had to admit that it was a beautiful shawl. A lovely piece of workmanship, without question. And the colors, blue and green, suited Lucy's coloring to such perfection that the shawl did, indeed, appear to have been made with her in mind. On the landing outside Lucy's bedroom, he paused to take the wrap from its box and drape it across his arm.

Perhaps the shawl could become the symbol of rejuvenation in their union. From this day, there would be a new beginning, he thought as he opened the bedroom door.

Chapter 16

The only sound was the whisper of the blue-green shawl as it slipped from Thomas' arm onto the floor.

"My God," muttered Kilmaine. "My God."

There passed what seemed to Eben a freeze in time, a protracted moment when neither Thomas, Lucy, nor he moved. Then Thomas turned and left the room. The door closed behind him with a soft, precise click.

Eben leaped from the bed, fastening his trousers.

"Let him go, Eben," cried Lucy. "It's better this way. I can't go on being divided. I can't live as two people." She reached out her arms to him, but he did not see her. All he saw was the look of outrage and betrayal on his friend's face. "Stay here, Eben," wailed Lucy as he opened the door. "You think he cares, but he doesn't."

Eben whirled on her. For a moment, he forgot that this was Lucy, his beloved, the shining golden girl who owned his heart. He saw only a selfish woman intent on having what she wanted most. "I am his friend. Whether he loves you or not doesn't matter. I know he cared for me."

He found Thomas in his study at the end of the hall. He was standing in front of one of the bookcases, running his finger along the titles. He appeared as calm as any librarian.

"You've come to explain," he said quietly, without looking at Eben.

"Thomas, I won't lie. I've loved Lucy for years. Since we were children back in Amoset." Eben stepped closer to his friend. "I know that nothing can excuse . . ."

"Do you know what I've been doing?" Thomas interrupted, resuming his perusal of the bookshelf. "I've been wondering which, if any of these volumes, I could not live without. I have Emerson, Shakespeare, Pope, the writings of a dozen noble philosophers. Look here." He pointed out a set of books bound in dark leather. "These are the Greek plays of Aeschylus, Euripides and the rest. They are great works, I'm told. Tales of love and hate and betrayal. . . ."

"Don't ignore me, Thomas. Turn around. Let us have our confrontation scene like they always do in those plays. Let it be out in the open between us."

But Thomas continued to ignore him. The bookcase ran the length of one whole wall of the study. As he walked beside it, he pointed out the books that held special meaning for him. "Look here. This is my family Bible. It was brought to America by my great-grandparents, back before the Revolution. They came from Ireland. Galway. The same country as my neighbor Mr. Flynn. America is becoming a nation of Irishmen."

Kilmaine's irrelevancies infuriated Eben. He had charged into the study prepared for angry words, a fight, or even the challenge of a duel. But this mind-wandering, careless, literary talk was something he could not deal with. His hands sweated and he rubbed them hard against his trousers.

"A family Bible has some value, I suppose. On the inside cover are all the births going back several generations. Even Delphia's name is here. I suppose I should value this Bible, but I don't." He looked at Eben for the first time. Surprisingly, there was no accusation in his glance, only a mild perplexity. "Strange, isn't it? I am a man who has loved books and collected them all my life long and yet now I find there is not one, not even this Bible, that I care to take with me."

"Take?"

"Yes. Take." He stared at Eben as if what he saw was a puzzle and not a man. "Were you ever my friend? Or was it always Lucy who brought you into this house?"

Eben sank into a chair and covered his face with his hands. "I don't know anymore. I wish I did. All I know is that you have been my good friend. I never calculated. . . ."

Kilmaine wasn't listening. "I suppose I should have guessed. The way she became all flustered at the mention of your name should have been a clue for me. But I assumed," he laughed without smiling, "that you made her nervous because she had once been an employee in your mill. How naive I am." Thomas tugged on the bellpull behind his desk. "Well, what do you think? Should I take the family Bible with me or leave it for my daughter?" He thought of something and peered closely at Eben. "She is mine, isn't she? You say you've loved Lucy a long time. . . ."

"Of course, she's yours! God, Tom, I feel like a bastard. What can I say to you?" Eben thought of the pain he had brought on all sides: Amanda, Marianna, Lucy and Thomas. As he sat, head in hands, staring down at the polished toes of his boots, it occurred to Eben that the more he despised his father, the more

surely he was like him. The kind of good man Eben
yearned to be would have resisted Lucy's arms and
told her the truth about Marianna and Christian as he
had intended to do. But he was not a good man and
never could be.

Maureen knocked and entered the study. "You
rang, Mr. Kilmaine?"

"Yes, Maureen. Will you get me the carpetbag
from the attic? The old one with the brass fittings."

The servant's eyebrows shot up, but she swallowed her curiosity and hurried out of the room.

"Where are you going, Thomas?" asked Eben,
watching Thomas take papers and documents from
his desk drawers.

"I don't know precisely."

"Don't leave Lucy. No matter what you think
now, she's a good woman and she cares for you."

Again Kilmaine laughed humorlessly. "She cannot care much or she would not have made a cuckold
of me."

"It isn't her fault. It was I. I pressed my advantage unfairly. I . . ."

"Don't bother trying to explain. Whatever you
say is irrelevant now."

"But I have to make you understand! You can't
go off and abandon her. And what about Delphia?
She *is* your daughter."

At last Thomas showed signs of anger. Always a
cool and rational man, a man of orderly habits and
precise ways, a man strong and inflexible in his opinions, passion seemed all at once to get the upper hand
in him. When he spoke, there was a current of quiet
rage beneath his words.

"Delphia is my daughter. Lucy is my wife. But I
don't care. She has done the unthinkable, humiliated
me, violated my trust in a way I can never forgive. In

an hour's time I will be gone and I will never return or even look back with regret. There is nothing here I value."

"Delphia. . . ."

"She doesn't care much for me. If she were a boy, it might be different. I might even take her with me then. But as it is, a girl is better off with her mother. Even a tramp like Lucy."

Eben jumped up from his chair. "She is not that! I told you, Thomas, I took advantage. . . ."

Lucy suddenly appeared in the doorway. She was still in her trailing nightdress, and her silver-gold hair clouded about her head and shoulders like a halo. She was crying.

"I heard what you said. You have no right to call me such names, Thomas. I am not a bad woman."

She stood before them, weeping unrestrainedly. Neither man spoke until Eben gathered his wits and said, "Go back to bed, Lucy. You are ill."

"Don't tell me what to do! Don't you know how sick to death I am of being lectured to and ranted at about every subject under the sun? I may be a woman, but don't you know that I am also a human being? I am willing to take responsibility for my own actions. You've treated me like a child from the beginning, Thomas. And now you are doing the same thing, Eben. It is too much! Too much!"

Maureen returned with the carpetbag. Her mouth was a little round "oh" of surprise, her eyes wide with unconcealed curiosity. She dropped the bag at Thomas' feet, watching Lucy all the while.

"What's the matter with you?" Lucy snarled.

"Mrs. Kilmaine . . ."

"Get out! Damn you, get out of my sight!"

"Lucy, I've told you not to swear in front of the

servants." Thomas stepped forward as Maureen scurried into the hall.

"There you go again with your lectures on the right and wrong way of living. I don't care what you tell me. If I choose to, I will swear like a navvy. I will stand on the rooftop and curse the God in heaven if it suits my mood!"

"There is nothing to be gained by any of this, Lucy." Eben touched her shoulder, but she whipped away from him.

Thomas was smiling as he said, "I will think of you both from time to time. But not with envy. Oh, no, Eben, I do not envy you this woman. I have loved her, and I know she can only bring heartbreak."

"Shut up!" All at once, she was on Thomas, pounding against his chest with her fists and screaming. The words spewed forth volcanically. "You priggish man! You fish! I wanted to be a good wife. In the beginning, I cared for you deeply. But you killed my feelings with your cold certainty, your unfailing righteousness, your insensitivity. You say you loved me, but that's a lie. A lie, Thomas. You only loved what you imagined I could be when I was modeled after your perfect image of a wife. I had to do as you told me, think as you thought. I could not even call a doctor without begging your permission. Do you remember when Delphia was so ill with a fever? You scolded me for bringing in the doctor. You would have rather seen that child suffer than unbend a single inch." Lucy tried to laugh, but the sound was mixed with weeping. "Now you're going away. Well, I don't care! Do you hear me?"

Thomas turned away from her and spoke to Eben. "I will not leave Lucy destitute. The house is in her name and I will arrange through our banker for a sum of money to support Delphia." He glanced at his wife as if what he saw disgusted him. "Everything is yours, Lucy. The house, the furnishings, everything." He gestured behind him. "Even the books are yours. And when I am gone, you must consider me gone for good. You will at last have the freedom to think and act independently. You may curse the servants with impunity." He picked up the carpetbag and went to the study door. "Now, you will excuse me. I am going to pack."

Eben made a move to follow him. "Don't bother, Hopewell. I have nothing I want to say to you."

Thomas Kilmaine stepped into the hall. Then an afterthought occurred to him and he turned back to speak to Lucy. "About the shawl. I got to thinking last night, and you might see some humor in this, that I have often been hard on you. Last night after you left the dinner table to come upstairs, I saw that you were truly ill and realized that I had not seen you smile in some time. That's why I bought you the shawl. I thought it would be a tonic for you. I even thought, and this certainly will make you laugh, that it might bring us closer together."

"I don't want it."

"But it is yours now, and you must wear it. It's a beautiful piece and suits you very well."

"I'll throw it away."

He shook his head, smiling thinly. "No you won't, Lucy. You're vain enough to keep it and wear it, despite the fact that every time you do, you will be reminded of me and of this day."

When he was gone, Lucy and Eben stood where he left them. They said nothing for a long time. Down the hall they could hear the sound of drawers opening and closing, doors slamming, the groan of the water pump. From outside on Moon Street rose the raucous laughter of drunkards staggering home and the rattle of carriage wheels on the cobbles.

At last Eben asked, "Are you all right, Lucy?"

She nodded.

"You'll catch cold."

She shrugged.

"Let me ring for Maureen and have her help you back to bed."

She looked at him in sudden panic. "What about you? Where are you going?"

He sighed. It was his turn to lift and drop his shoulders in a hapless gesture of troubled confusion. "To my club, I suppose."

"After all of this, you'd leave me?"

"Lucy, I can't stay here. You can't expect me to after what's happened. I'll see you tomorrow or the next day. I think it's best that we each be alone for a while."

She threw her arms around him and clung to his shoulders. "You're angry because of what I said to him. My temper upset you. That's true, isn't it?" Her face, just inches from his, was flushed. Her eyes were puffed and red. Against his cheek he felt her hot breath. At that moment, he did not want her in the least. She seemed almost a stranger to him, though in some recess of his mind he knew he loved her and would feel that love again when the shock of the evening had passed. Now, however, he could not wait to escape her. His feelings must have shown, for her temper flared defensively and she railed at him. "You've ruined me and now you can't abide me. I've lost my husband and now I am losing you!"

Her arms were about him, her hands locked behind his head. He tried to disengage himself. "I love you, Lucy, but this is not the time for us."

She pressed her head against his chest and wept

again. "Yes, yes, say you love me. Say we can be together always. Just you and me and Delphia. Say that we can, Eben. Say that I am yours forever. Swear it to me, Eben. Unless you do, I won't be able to sleep or eat or live another moment. I adore you, I . . ."

He thought of Marianna. He remembered Christian. "It's not as easy as that, Lucy. It is all so complicated."

"But it isn't! In a few years time we can be married. No one will doubt that Thomas is dead if we wait a decent interval of years. Such second marriages occur all the time. I can be patient, Eben. I know I can."

"There are things you don't know, Lucy."

"I'll learn, Eben. I swear. You'll be proud of me."

"Oh, Lucy!" Her eagerness touched him profoundly.

"What is it? Tell me." She stopped suddenly and stepped back from him. Appalled, she covered her mouth with her hand. "You're in love with someone else."

"No."

"You're lying to me, Eben. I can see it in your face."

"I have a son." He spoke without thinking. "About Delphia's age."

"But you can't. You told me . . . Amanda . . ." Her shoulders sagged. "Then there is someone else. Another woman you prefer before me."

With a sigh of resignation, Eben took her in his arms and began his story. Never in a thousand years would he have chosen such a time to speak of Marianna, but at the moment there seemed to be no alternative. He experienced an enormous sense of destiny having taken over his life. He had become no more than a moving piece on a board controlled by capricious forces beyond himself. He told his story quickly and awkwardly. But as he spoke, an image of Marianna came into his mind, and he knew it was important to describe her well. Perhaps Lucy could be made to understand that Marianna was no ordinary woman but a delicate, dark flower, a rare prize he had discovered and treasured and honored from his soul. To do less than try would be to dishonor Marianna, and Eben was through with dishonor.

When the long telling was over, Lucy said, "You are in love with a colored woman. All the time you were caring for me, you were loving her, too. And a child? You have a child by her?"

"He is in Amoset with Suzannah."

"A half-breed child?" She began to walk about the room, shaking her head from side to side. Occasionally, she would look back at him as if she did not believe the words she had heard with her own ears or expected him to recant them.

"I love him, Lucy, and I mean to raise him and give him a good life." Though he wanted to touch her, he was strangely afraid. All at once, she seemed to have a wall around her.

"When you lay with me, did you think of her?"

"How could I? I was consumed by you. When I am with you . . ."

"I don't believe you. When you made love to me, I couldn't help but think of Thomas. A little bit, at least. I thought how different you were from him, how much more gentle and passionate. How can you say she was never in your mind?"

"Lucy, she wasn't. But even if she had been, it doesn't matter now."

"Oh, but it does!" she cried shrilly. "You were married to Amanda while you loved this . . . whatever she was. And you were tied to both of them when you and I were lovers. If you can divide your affections three times, why not four or five or even six? Is there any limit to your perfidy?" She uttered an angry little cry full of heartbreak and confusion. "No wonder Amanda destroyed herself. You must have made her life a hell."

"You don't know what you're saying, Lucy. You are feverish. Let me call Maureen."

"You are a villain. A philanderer."

"I am neither of those things. And in your heart you know it. Let me come back tomorrow. You'll be better then and we can talk more rationally." He tried to steer her toward the door, but she shook him away in fury.

"Don't touch me! Don't ever touch me again! I thought you were different from your father, but I was mistaken. In your own way, you enjoy the manipulation of people, the control, the cheating as much as he. Don't bother to deny it. I won't listen."

In the darkening study, Lucy looked ugly to Eben. Her flushed face was drawn down by deep, angry lines and her mouth twisted into a gloating distortion of a smile. He stared at her. There was nothing to say. He saw that no matter how he tried, her heart was set against him in the way it had been years earlier. The tide of fate had dragged them back to where they had stood ten years before on Bonfire Night. A boy. A girl. A wall of misunderstanding and distrust between them.

He wanted to say that he loved her, yet he was no longer sure that it mattered. It even flashed in his mind that he might be better off without Lucy Shawn Kilmaine in the long run of things. He turned away on this thought. As if some giant hand had reached within his belly and scooped out half of him, he felt suddenly sick and empty, robbed to the vitals of what had given his life a meaning beyond mills and railroads and profits.

Muttering good-bye, he escaped from the room at last.

PART III

Chapter 17

Summer, 1851

He seemed taller now because there was no fat on his
bones. His was a lean, sinewy body with ribs that
showed, but he had strong legs and broad though
somewhat bony shoulders. His clothes, the rough
homespun breeches and shirt, the forlorn remains of
a soldier's coat with jaded braid, hung on his body
like rags on a strawman. With his broad-brimmed
leather hat pulled low to shade his face from the
southwestern sun, Travis Paine—Yale alumnus of outstanding promise, architect, husband—was indistin-
guishable from any of the silent, bearded men who
traveled the southwest deserts and mountains alone,
pulling behind a laden burro. His face was browned
to the color of clay, and his dark eyes had squinted
into harsh sunlight for so many years that they were
now permanently small and narrow. His nose, once
straight and elegantly supercilious, had been broken
some time back in a Mexican bar. Travis could not
remember what the fight was about, but since then
his aristocratic nose was flattened and shoved a little
to one side of his face, giving his expression a peculiar

cast that put off the men who met him briefly along
the ways that lonely men walk.

He carried with him an old Bible that had been
his father's. It contained the Apocrypha, and Travis
often read the story of Suzannah and the Elders as
if the descriptions had been written of Suzannah
Hopewell. They reminded him of how she always had
tempted him with her body, from the very first day
they met in the hay barn during a sudden storm. She
had been wanton in her sensuality. Like a spider's
sticky web, the promise of love had captured him before he could summon the will to run. He had been
caught by her. And now his life was ruined.

For years he had been walking the trails. He had
traveled along the eastern seaboard and then across
the prairies and down into the Southwest. He worked
when it was necessary to sustain himself, but he preferred to keep out of the way of towns and settle-
ments and live off fish and game and wild plants. In
the late 1840s, Travis did a stint with the army, serving under the command of Stephen Watts Kearny and
his U.S. Army of the West. He fought the *Californios*
at the battle of San Pasqual and had the scar of a
sword through his side to prove it. When his enlist-
ment was up, he started north, following the rumors
of gold near Sacramento. The central valley through
which he now walked was harsh and hot. A white sun
scorched the flat, alkaline land, which was populated
by coyote, snakes and scorpions. From sunrise until
evening, the path ahead rippled with heat as if the
sky and land were melting into one another.

One evening just after sunset, he fell asleep on
the trail. His feet kept moving, but he was nonetheless asleep. He didn't hear the warning of the night-
hunting rattler in his path, but he was startled to his
senses by a flash of pain as its poisonous fangs stabbed

his ankle. Travis screamed and fell as the reptile slithered off into the sagebrush.

Travis had been on the trail for many years, so this was not his first snakebite. He dealt with the wound carefully and skillfully. Using his old red bandanna as a tourniquet, he cut off the flow of poison up his leg and sucked the wound. But he knew from past experience that even though the wound was clean, he would suffer from it. Ahead of him lay hours of sweats and hallucinations. Hoping to ease the discomfort as much as was possible in such a hostile environment, he threw together a hasty lean-to that would shield him from the next day's sun and lay his bedroll on the dusty ground.

As the moon rose higher that night, it seemed to Travis in his delirium that the desert was a beautiful place, like the landscape of the moon might be. Only half-conscious, his vision blurred and painful, he saw that the mountains to the east had a grandeur in their barrenness, a majesty in their harshness. When he awoke in a sweat, his leg swollen and pulsing, the sky was full of a bloody sun. Throughout that day and the following night, he drifted in and out of dreams in which the landscape was sometimes mountainous and green and beckoning, at other times as hot and dry as hell's own garden. The rattler had been a big one and full of death. Travis imagined he could feel the venom poisoning his body vein by vein.

He fought to live. He struggled out of nightmares full of distorted memories and visions. He heard himself moan and did not recognize the sound of his own voice. By dawn of the second day, however, the worst was over. He lay still, watching the morning light stain the horizon pink and gold. Now that the pain in his ankle was bearable, he became aware of a raging hunger that filled his belly. He knew he could not lie in the dirt much longer, but he found that the snakebite and its attendant suffering had stolen his will. The mere idea of continuing his journey up the parched, empty valley exhausted him. Not even the promise of gold could make him endure the harsh light of another month of suns. In his lean-to, he sat up and scratched himself. During his illness, he had been bitten all over by tiny insects. Now his body was covered with itching, red welts that broke and bled when his nails touched them. Sunlight, arid miles, snakes, insects. No amount of gold could be worth all this.

He stood up, resting his weight gingerly on the injured leg. As he did, he glanced up and to the east. The yellow mountains lined the horizon to the north and south as far as he could see. Somewhere, he thought, there must be water and grass. And trees. At a higher elevation, it would be cooler, and there would be shade to lie in. He was sure that a garden of ease and greenery lay just beyond his vision. He imagined he could smell the pines and hear the rush of fast water. He must go now. He must hurry.

But one step on his swollen ankle convinced him that he could not climb the mountain paths. His burro had wandered off and was nowhere to be seen. He needed new supplies and rest. In pain, but with an excitement that was novel enough to make him ignore it, Travis returned to the mission settlement at Santa Theresa and negotiated the purchase of a burro and several weeks worth of supplies. When the proprietor of the trading post inquired after his destination, Travis had no answer for him. He wasn't sure himself. All he knew was that he must escape the sun and heat and find a place where trees grow.

Travis left Santa Theresa and traveled across dry, rocky stream beds, dusty valleys and through foothills covered with scrub, hacking his own trail up hillsides covered with oat grass and manzanita. With every step he took farther into the Sierra Nevada Mountains, he could feel the temperature dropping off by fractions. A week out of the village and the air felt different in the mornings. There was a zest to it. And his ankle ceased to throb. He slept well at night and awoke refreshed.

But his daily thoughts were not unlike those he had gnawed on for most of his sojourn in the West. The years had altered his appearance drastically and had carried his feet to alien regions, making him familiar with danger and hardship. Nevertheless, Travis was not much changed within. He still dreamed of monumental prizes and all the glory that might have been his. And he still brooded over the wrongs done to him by Suzannah Hopewell.

By early June, the heat in the foothills of the Sierra Nevada was already intense. In the meadowlands and on the open hillsides, the outgrass was browning and everything was covered with a blue-green haze of dust. The buckeye growing in open places blossomed with cones of delicate white flowers, and here and there were low, thorny bushes bearing clouds of dark blue blossoms.

Two days into the foothills, Travis found a river flowing down from the eastern mountains. When he bent to drink from it, the water was so cold that it hurt his throat and stomach. No doubt about it, somewhere to the east rose mountains so high that they lay beneath snow for half the year. He decided to follow the river toward its source.

As he continued east, the path grew steeper and sometimes veered so far from the river that the sound of the water was only a grumble. He was sure he was

on an Indian trail, for every day or so he came across
signs of encampment. Travis was not in the least disturbed by this. He had encountered Indians before
and had not suffered badly at their hands. More important, he had been told that the Indians he might
meet going this way were peaceful, gentle people.

Twisting and turning, the path he followed always led back to the thunderous river, falling steeply
amidst boulders as big as houses. One day from a
rocky lookout, he caught sight of a peak covered with
a thick cone of white. It rose to the south, and mo-
mentarily Travis doubted the wisdom of following the
river. The flanks of the mountain to the south were
covered with a forest of conifers through which no
sun or touch of heat could penetrate. The sight almost
led him to abandon the Indian trail and set out overland. But reason prevailed, and he continued upriver,
turning his back on the mightiest mountain he had
ever seen.

Travis rounded the curve of a hill and was
startled to find himself entering a forest of yellow
pine and incense cedar. Although the dust of the
foothills was still underfoot and this unexpected forest
was inadequate to fulfill his dreams, Travis was comforted by the hardy trees through which he walked.
His mood so improved that once, as he washed his
feet in the cold river, he surprised himself by hum-
ming an old hymn he recalled from his childhood.

Finally, he came upon a valley of white fir and
sugar pine that made him sigh with contentment.
Beautifully shaded forests fringed the meadows, and
there was an abundance of game and water everywhere. Here he built a little shack from fallen wood
and wide sheets of bark, and for the first time since
leaving Amoset, he did not think much of Suzannah
or the wrongs done to him in the name of love. The

time or two she did cross his mind, he could dismiss her easily. Lying back on the soft earth, hands clasped behind his head, he contemplated instead the vision of mountains etched in obsidian against a sapphire sky.

He had not forgotten the goldfields. But having tasted the summer climate of the foothills, he didn't care to pan for gold in air that was like a blast from a primed boiler. He could wait for a few months and strike it rich in a cooler season.

The days of summer passed in easy succession. Once or twice a week there were rainstorms that kept the meadow grass a brilliant shade of green, and wildflowers bloomed until August beside every stream. It was for Travis a contented time of life. He had no wish to see it end. Nevertheless, it was astonishing and unsettling when the thought of staying permanently in the mountains occurred to him not only once, but with increasing frequency. Although he had never spent a winter in the mountains, he did not imagine it would prove much more difficult to bear than any other experience of hardship. And through the worst weather, there would always be spring to anticipate. But then he thought of gold lying in nuggets on the ground and stream beds glittering with yellow sand, and he knew the time must come for moving on.

One day, not far from where he had made his camp, he came upon the trunk of a fallen tree, an immense giant whose core had been hollowed out by fire. Now only a long, round tunnel of wood remained. Lying on its side, it was tall enough that Travis could stand comfortably within its circumference. Whenever he passed the tree, he could not control his architect's imagination which for so long had been deprived of an object. One afternoon, he sat on a stump for hours, looking at that tree trunk and imagining the kind of house he might build for himself. Although he rationalized his fantasy by calling it no more than a mental exercise for a brain too long permitted to lie fallow, he was forced to admit it was more than this when it stayed with him for days on end, invading even his dreams.

As a young man just beginning his architectural studies, Travis often had dreamed about the work he was doing. His nights were filled with monuments of his own design, with libraries, cathedrals, amphitheaters and great railway stations. He imagined his buildings would mark the hub of the modern world and house the rich and mighty. Never once in those halcyon days did it occur to Travis Paine that he would spend his talent on tree trunks. Thinking this as he sat on the stump, he suddenly was awash with bitterness. Like a thunderhead, the emotion blocked his sunny thoughts and, once again, all he could think of was Suzannah and how she had ruined his life and stolen his promise.

After that, he stayed away from the fallen tree for a number of days. But he couldn't do so for long. Early one morning, after a night spent dreaming of houses, he went to the tree and paced out measurements for a cabin that would lie adjacent to it. He cut several pines and, using his burro, dragged them back to the site of the hollow giant. He worked hard, spurred on by cooling days and brisk mornings. Although he assured himself he had no intention of living in the cabin—like making the plans, the building of it was only an exercise—something drove him to finish it before the cold weather began.

While he worked, he thought of what life would be like in such a place. If he chose to graze horses or cattle or sheep in the lush meadows during the warm

seasons, the huge, hollow trunk would be an adequate
barn in the winter. He made the cabin large enough
for comfortable living and even included a stone fireplace taller than he was. Then, unable to stop, he
built a plank table and benches and a raised sleeping
platform. When he was finished, the steep-roofed
little dwelling was comfortably habitable.

His work done, Travis chafed from idleness. Ac-
tivities that had pleased him earlier in the season left
him feeling restless and out of sorts. He spent several
nights in the cabin, but he realized he could not live
there alone, not for a week and never for a winter
season. One morning, after a particularly chill night,
some Indians passed through the clearing. They
stared at his strange house with curiosity, and one old
man tried to explain by signing that in the winter the
snows fell to a depth ten times the height of a man.
But Travis was only partially attentive. Instead, he
eyed the Indian girls wistfully. If he were not a married man. . . .

That night he could not sleep. The wind was
loud in the trees, and its mournful lament seemed to
dig into his soul and twist it like a vise. Perhaps it
was sleeping in a roofed house again, perhaps it was
the sloe-eyed Indian girls, but whatever the cause, he
lay on his mat thinking of Suzannah. The more he
tried to drive her memory out of his mind, the more
firmly it took root. The joy of loving came back to
him, and also the desperation of knowing his love was
doomed. He had loved her, and she had betrayed him
in the arms of James Shawn. Even now, so many
years later, it hurt him to recall his last meeting with
Suzannah. He was bitterly ashamed of what he had
done. Still, he thought, trying to excuse himself, she
had made a cuckold of him. What alternative had

there been for him but to punish her wrongdoing in a way that she would never forget?

He remembered the blood and her body squirming beneath his. As each moment of their final hour together returned to him, he relived it in vivid detail. Finally, he could bear it no longer. Throwing off his blanket, he leapt to his feet. His memories had poisoned the atmosphere of the little cabin, and now he could not wait to be gone from it. He must fly from the mountains as he had fled from the alkaline desert, as he had fled from Amoset.

The goldfields had been his original destination, and before dawn that day, he resumed his trek toward them. He regretted having to leave the cabin, but Suzannah and his own guilt had changed his feelings about the place. It no longer offered him peace and solitude, only the same bitter memories he had been trying to escape for years.

To avoid the foothills and desert valley as long as possible, Travis took a northern route up over the tableland where already there was ice in the morning and a bitter wind that smelled of glacial snow. When he had been on the trail for almost a week, he left the tableland and descended into the river gorge. Now, at the end of summer, it was only a quiet stream, but it flowed through the most spectacular scenery Travis had ever seen. Sheer granite walls rose on either side of its banks, dwarfing the man and his burro.

As Travis emerged from the verdant mountain forests in late September, the desiccated woodlands and fields where no rain had fallen since April were like a glimpse of hell. At that moment, despite the threat of winter and bitter memories, he almost turned back to his mountain cabin. The heat of the hills was intense, fiery. Even the worst winter could not make him suffer any more than did the blazing sun. But he trudged forward, his jaw set, his eyes and face burning and red.

He was only three days north of Sonoran Camp when he knew he could not continue. He had been forced to shelter in a cave all one long day when a fierce rainstorm, the winter's first, came to the Sierran foothills. Walking was impossible in the deluge. Tucked away in the snug cave, he could think only of his cabin in the mountain valley. Gradually it came to him that, with or without his bitter memories of Suzannah, he belonged in that place as he had belonged in no other. The little house was his. He had made it from his own strength of arm and imagination. To let old thoughts, ancient guilts and grievances drive him from it was to deny the dreams of greatness that had energized his youth.

He wintered in the foothills, and when spring arrived, he returned to the mountains.

They were even more magnificent than he had remembered. In those few months away, he had forgotten the immensity of the granite crags and the frigid barrens of the high slopes where nothing grew but short, hardy grasses and lichens in every color of the spectrum. He had forgotten the thundersome noise of the snow-fed river as it rushed over immense boulders. He had forgotten the walls of water, like beaded veils, falling hundreds of feet from the tableland to the floor of canyons carved from ice. The higher he climbed, the more these sights and sounds inspired Travis. He urged his burro to move faster, always faster. It was now in his head to reach his log house before the Indians began their summer in the mountains.

One day, as he stared into a pool where he had dropped his fishing line, Travis realized that he had

not thought of Suzannah in weeks. He closed his eyes
and tried to see her face. He knew her eyes were the
color of this deep, still pool, but he could think of
nothing else about her looks. At last her face was
gone.

And what of the great deeds, the masterpieces of
architecture that would never be realized because
Travis Paine had chosen mountains and not the fortune wheel of the mother lode, that vast casino of
dust and dirt? Were they gone forever, too, as was
the image of his wife's face? Though he could not
quiet a tiny, persistent voice that said he still was
meant for greatness, Travis determined not to listen to
the refrain. He set his mind on the mountains, the
cabin and the long, comforting summer ahead.

One night he walked longer than usual and did
not make his camp until hours after dark, and only
then because a dense fog had dropped over the forest.
Even Travis, whose eyes saw in the dark like an Indian's, could not be sure of where to place his foot
from step to step. He didn't bother with a fire that
night. His walking day had lasted more than sixteen
hours and he was exhausted, content simply to roll in
his bedding and close his eyes. Yet once he lay down,
he could not relax. He began to wish he had continued walking, for something about the woods in which
he lay disturbed him. They were preternaturally
silent under the gown of fog. He listened for owls or
night predators, but heard nothing except the steady
drip of moisture.

He drifted into a deep slumber at last, and when
he awoke he thought he was dreaming.

During his sleep, the mist had lifted and
cloudless skies sailed over the forest. The sunlight, re-
fracted a million times off every drop of moisture, was
like the light of stars. At first, the brightness hurt his

eyes and made him turn away. But he looked again, hardly daring to trust his vision.

He had wandered into a forest meant for giant folk to walk in. The trees in the grove where Travis lay were huge, bigger than any living thing he had ever seen. From where he sat, they rose about him on trunks so big around that fifty men, their arms linked, could not have spanned them. They towered hundreds of feet above him, the first branches occurring fifty or sixty feet from the ground. The sight awed Travis, elevated him to a state of reverence unlike any he had experienced, even in his sanctimonious youth. The feeling consumed him, erasing the Travis Paine who had entered the grove in darkness. The transformation begun by the deserts of the West and continued by the mountains found completion in the morning forest.

He slipped from his bedroll and, without stopping to drag on his boots, walked to the nearest tree. Beneath his feet the ground was cool and moist and spongy, with an aroma of fertile changes. He reached out to touch a tree trunk, but tentatively, as if the forest were a great cathedral and the trees forbidden icons.

Beneath his palm, the bark was as soft as hair and the color of a red setter dog. Bits of it crumbled in his fingers. Looking up, he saw the giant stretch out its arms and clasp hands with its brethren. The only thing higher was the bright blue sky itself. Like the architecture of an ancient cathedral, the trees drew his gaze toward heaven.

Without warning, his eyes began to water, and soon he was sobbing like a child, his face in his hands. Tears of relief. In those few moments of gazing upward, he had lost the last of the burdens he had carried with him from his old life. Never again would he wonder if greatness would be his, for here, when he least expected it and in the most remote of places, it had come.

For several days, Travis remained in the grove of giant trees. He hadn't intended to stay for more than a day, but the time had passed quickly and peacefully; there had been no desire to go. He did not cry again, nor did he think of the past. Instead, he lived each day from moment to moment. He lived according to his needs and with a calm that would have astonished men who had known Travis Paine in cantinas and wretched boarding houses. The comrades from his soldiering days would have marveled at the change in him. The meanness left his face, and his narrow, suspicious eyes widened as he saw the world without anger or guilt. When the time came for him to move on toward his cabin, he walked with a lighter step. The animals of the forest stopped their grazing and turned to watch him. Their ears flicked up at the sound of his step, but they showed no fear. Even his singing did not alarm them. They seemed to know that Travis Paine belonged to the mountains as much as they, and if his cry was a strange one, it was nevertheless full of joy.

Chapter 18

In the years since Thomas Kilmaine had left his wife
and child and disappeared into the West, Moon Street
had been greatly changed by the tides of immigration
that rolled across America. Moon and the other streets
in the neighborhood had become solidly Irish in character. The men and women whom Lucy Shawn Kilmaine met in the shops on the square at the bottom
of Moon Street spoke their English in lilting accents
entirely unlike the flat cadences peculiar to the part
of Massachusetts where she had been born and
reared. She liked the sound, unfamiliar though it was
at first. And she liked the Irish with whom she had
frequent dealings. Brownie, who had cared for Delphia throughout her infancy and childhood, had gone
on to other charges in other nurseries. Maureen was
still with them, however, her Irish grin no less wide
than it had ever been.

As Lucy cast a critical gaze about the front
drawing room and saw that all was in readiness for
that evening's guests, she realized that Maureen finally had learned to dust the picture frames without
being reminded. It only went to prove that anything

was possible! When the mantel clock chimed at five-thirty, she was startled. With all the fuss she had been making over the house and furnishings that day, she had entirely forgotten her own appearance. If she hurried, there would just be time for her to change out of her coarse cotton duster and spend a few minutes tidying her hair.

At thirty-eight, Lucy was still an attractive woman, and her shining silver-gold hair remained her dominant feature. As she looked at herself in the mirror on her dressing table, however, she was only too aware of the changes time had wrought while leaving her hair unaffected. There were lines about her eyes, and her mouth, bracketed by creases, was now more stern than pretty. She felt an instant pang as she recalled her youth and the beauty she had taken for granted. But she forced the thought to the back of her mind, reminding herself that it was no wonder she had aged. Life since Thomas' departure had not been easy. She worked hard.

He had left the house in her name, an extraordinary occurrence in times when, under most circumstances, only men were permitted to own property. Despite all his other failings, however, Thomas had never held with the popular view of female inferiority. Therefore, his departure from tradition was not surprising. He also had made generous provisions for Delphia's rearing and education. Nevertheless, Lucy had been alone for only a short time before she realized that if she intended to survive in Boston independent of her family, she must discover a means of earning money.

Six months after Thomas' departure, when she was just twenty-eight years old, a sign went up in front of Lucy's little house on Moon Street announcing that there were rooms available. She might not have had the courage to take in boarders had her father not announced his intention to move from his club to the more comfortably family surroundings of her home. With James residing there much of the time, Lucy was able to overcome her natural fears and insecurities about running a boarding house. She quickly found that she had the organizational ability required of a woman whose breakfast table, stretched to its full length with all its leaves in permanent place, seated half a dozen paying adults, as well as James, Delphia and herself.

Maureen complained that with the attic rooms converted into sleeping chambers and strangers in and about the house all day, there was too much work for one servant. Rather than jeopardize economy with another full-time servant, Lucy had taken on more and more of the domestic chores herself. In 1851, when Mrs. Tippits fell sick with influenza and almost died, in addition to her other duties, Lucy had cooked all the meals herself and had been praised for her efforts. While Maureen's labor had not greatly increased and Tippits had been appeased with a slightly higher salary, her own work took up more and more time. If she was no longer glowing with the bright vigor of youth, it was no wonder. Most days she was up before dawn and the last one to bed, her eyes drooping before she could pull back the covers.

Despite the drain on her energies, Lucy did not regret that she was a woman living without a husband. Not once in all the years did she wish that Thomas had stayed in Boston. Not once did she long for the days when they had been together as husband and wife. The marriage, she knew, was best over by whatever means. In an enlightened world, her feminist friends were quick to tell her, a world where women and men were equal, it would have been possible for Thomas and her to part amicably.

To those friends, she had never spoken the name of Eben Hopewell. Lucy was certain they would not have been so quick to praise her independent and courageous spirit if she had. Even among the suffragettes she admired and supported, there was a strong code of right behavior, a propriety never ignored or challenged. The truth of her affair would have shocked them and made her an outcast. So she never mentioned Eben. Indeed, after the first months following their wretched parting, she had succeeded in putting him out of her mind. But it had been difficult. No matter how she blamed him, calling him faithless and despicable, she could not make her accusations stick. She knew she had driven him away as much from pride as from outrage. And what was pride, she asked herself in those early months, compared to years alone and loveless?

Delphia had made the difference. The boarding house kept her body too exhausted for desire, but it did nothing for her heart. It was Delphia to whom Lucy had turned when all her unexpressed love cried for an outlet. Although the girl had made it clear that she did not care for sheltering and coddling and that, in fact, she resented her mother's overheated affection, Lucy had loved her to distraction anyway.

Thinking of Delphia, Lucy threw down her hairbrush and sank back in her chair, sighing. Why was nothing simple? Why was life continually throwing hurdles in the way of her peace of mind?

Ever since the day before, Patrick Paine, having completed his first year of study at Harvard College, had been a guest in the boarding house. In a few days' time, he would accompany the Kilmaines to Amoset, where they were going to celebrate Helen

Shawn's birthday. It would be Lucy's only visit in many months and, until Patrick had appeared, she had been looking forward to it. She had been thinking what a lot of good it would do Delphia to live on the mountain for a time and learn the country ways. But seeing Patrick for the first time in over a year, watching him at mealtime and in conversation with James or Delphia, she had grown increasingly depressed. Now she could think of nothing pleasant when the boy's name came to mind.

He seemed to be in love with Delphia.

But that alone was insufficient cause for the morbid dread Lucy felt on seeing him with her daughter. If he had been any other young collegiate, or even an Irish boy from up Moon Street, she would have smiled tolerantly and dismissed their flirtation as childish. Patrick and Delphia had known one another for many years, ever since not long after that first day when he had appeared in the clearing before the homestead and made friends with Helen Shawn. Affection between the two of them was quite natural. Or would have been, except. . . .

The doorbell rang, distracting her. Lucy's guests were arriving. Tomorrow would be soon enough to consider the matter of Patrick Paine.

In the foyer, she discovered a young woman weeping while half a dozen other women gathered about her offering sympathy. Only one seemed less than kindly. The critical woman was a thin-lipped individual with rather fierce blue eyes and a prominent, imposing forehead.

"I don't believe we gain a thing by wearing those outrageous bloomer costumes," she was saying crossly. "Unless humiliation and hounding on the public streets counts for something. Look at you. Not only have you wasted a considerable sum of money on that costume, but your own dignity and that of our cause has suffered as well."

"What is it, Sadie?" asked Lucy.

"Oh, ma'am," wailed the girl in the bloomer costume, not waiting for Sadie to explain for her. "I was coming up the street and a crowd of little boys . . ."

"Irish devils if you ask me!"

"They followed me, calling me names. I ignored them. I've heard it all before. Then they began pelting me. . . ."

"With rotten fruit!" cried Sadie. "Look at her pantaloons. The girl's a frightful sight!"

This was indeed true. The bloomer costume, knee-length tunic belted at the waist and worn over wide, tight-cuffed Turkish-style pantaloons, aroused controversy and insult wherever it was worn. In this case, the pelting of soft, rotten fruit had left sticky smears all across the back. The unpleasant odor of decaying vegetation permeated the air in the foyer.

Lucy called Maureen. "Take this young woman up to Delphia's room and find something for her to change into." She touched the girl's shoulder. "What is your name, dear?"

"Eliza Pomeroy."

"May I send someone to your home for fresh clothing, Miss Pomeroy?"

At the mention of home, the young woman became highly agitated. "Please, ma'am," she begged, "they mustn't know where I am."

"Who must not?" asked another woman, who had just come into the house. She was a tall, plain-faced woman with dark hair and sharp, intelligent eyes. Her name was Susan B. Anthony, and it was she who would chair the meeting that night. "Are you afraid, child?"

"If they were to know, my brothers would kill

me. They told me not to come here tonight. They made me swear I wouldn't leave our home."

"You broke your word to be here?" Miss Anthony asked.

"Did I do wrong, ma'am? I know it's wrong to lie, but sometimes, well, what else can we do?"

Lucy and Susan Anthony glanced at each other, their eyebrows slightly raised. Eliza Pomeroy was typical of the hundreds of otherwise honest women who were resorting to lies and deception in order to become part of the movement of women for rights under the law.

"How did you hear of us?" asked Lucy, escorting Eliza to the foot of the stairs.

"Oh, ma'am, your fliers are all over our neighborhood. Half the women I know can speak of nothing else." She smiled and her tear-stained face brightened. "I made this bloomer costume as a kind of protest, ma'am. And because it's so hard, you see, to do the kind of work I do with the babies . . ."

"You're a mother?"

Eliza laughed and blushed. "Oh, dear me, no. The twins are sisters of mine. Ma died last year when they were born and since that time, I've seen to their tending and made a home for my father and brothers. But the work is hard, you see. It seems my arms are forever loaded up with babies and laundry and lamps and . . . well, last month I tripped on my skirt on the stairs and fell down half a flight. 'Tis lucky the baby in my arms wasn't killed or the house set on fire."

"You intended to wear the bloomer costume at home?"

Eliza nodded. "But when my brothers found out, they were furious. They told me to burn it. They

think it's shocking for a woman's legs to be shown so
clearly."

"More shocking than falling down a flight of
stairs, killing the babies and setting the house on fire,"
commented Susan Anthony dryly.

Eliza was instantly defensive. "They can't help it,
Miss Anthony. Pa and the boys go to the United Shoe
Factory every day. They don't know anything about
women's work. They don't know how dangerous it
can be." Her eyes filled with tears. It was obvious she
loved her brothers and father. Disobeying them was
nothing she did either gladly or with ease.

"Never mind for now," soothed Lucy. "You're a
brave girl and you've done nothing wrong. Go upstairs with Maureen. She'll make you comfortable in
other clothes. When you're ready, come down and
join the meeting. There isn't much time. I suspect
you're not the only woman here tonight who has to
be home promptly to avoid arousing suspicion."

The feminists were gathered in the front parlor
that overlooked Moon Street. By the time Elizabeth
Cady Stanton called the meeting to order, the room
was crowded to capacity. Even with the double doors
open and chairs filling the foyer, there was insufficient
space for the numbers of women. Some sat on the
stairs while others made themselves comfortable on
the floor. Delphia, who arrived at the last moment,
squirmed her way onto the settee beside her mother.

Mrs. Stanton rapped several times with her gavel
and at last the enthusiastic crowd was silent.

"I am filled with joy when I see you all here this
evening. Although I will not have an opportunity to
speak to each of you and learn your names, I want
you to know that I am fully conscious of what you
risk in being here. But I ask you to consider the alter-
natives. Are we to remain chattel all our lives? Are we

to accept the fact that we have no rights over our property or our children, and that even our own bodies belong to our husbands and fathers and brothers? Are we to accept a code of dress that is in no way practical or comfortable? Corsets that suffocate us, miles of petticoats and skirts to trip upon? In short, my dear friends, our lives and liberty are more than worth any risk we have taken to be here tonight." The crowd of women cheered at this point and began to clap their hands in unison, creating such a din and racket that the house throbbed with it.

As Lucy looked at the glowing, excited faces crowded into her home, a shiver of pride passed through her. She found herself recalling the years when she had been a mill operative and met in secret with other working women to organize a group called the Spindle Sisters. It seemed a very long time ago.

"Before I introduce Miss Susan B. Anthony," Elizabeth Cady Stanton said, "let me say that during the four years of this decade, our cause has grown tremendously in strength. But our road to liberty is not an easy one. To give you some idea of what I mean, I call upon Sadie Doolittle to share with us her experiences in Akron, Ohio. Sadie?"

As Sadie Doolittle told her story, no one spoke and all eyes were turned on her attentively. No woman in the room, regardless of age or social station, failed to appreciate the sacrifices of her sisters as they traveled the country, organizing and unifying women behind the cause of personal liberty. The names of their heroines were well-known, and around some of the more familiar had grown stories and histories that were half myth, half truth. One such was the black woman Sojourner Truth, of whom Sadie was now speaking.

"She was born a slave in a little village on the

Hudson in the days before New York freed all its slaves by law. All her life she has worked tirelessly, not only for the freedom of her race, but of her sex as well." Sadie went on to say that Sojourner Truth had been on the podium in Akron when the heckling began. The men in the hall had become so raucous that none of the women could silence them. "And then that brave woman stood up and turned the force of her eloquence on the crowd." Although Sadie Doolittle was hardly a great orator, she had witnessed the power of Sojourner Truth. As she set the scene and spoke the words she had heard from the black woman herself, her voice became more resonant, her expression more intense. The crowd in Lucy's drawing room and foyer was enraptured, taken for a moment back to that noisy, crowded meeting hall in Ohio.

The hecklers tried to boo down Sojourner Truth, but she was unintimidated. She raised her bare, black arm. "Look at my arm!" she cried. "I have ploughed and planted and gathered into barns and no man could lead me—and ain't I a woman? I could work as much and eat as much as a man—when I could get it—and bear the lash as well! And ain't I a woman? I have borne thirteen children, and seen most of 'em sold into slavery, and when I cried out with my mother's grief, none but Jesus heard me—and ain't I a woman?"

In the foyer, the listeners broke into Sadie's delivery with rousing applause and huzzahs. Although in general the crowd was orderly and ladylike, there were some who could not contain their enthusiasm. They stamped their feet hard in rhythm until Elizabeth Cady Stanton almost broke her gavel pounding them to silence.

"Let me remind you, ladies," she cried out over the noise, "we must never forget who we are and the gentle sex we represent. There is nothing we can gain by emulating our rowdy brethren."

Properly chastised, the crowd became quiet. After a few concluding remarks from Sadie Doolittle, Susan Anthony was introduced.

"As you know," she began, "the Massachusetts legislature, spurred to action by Senator James Shawn, whose daughter has made her home available to us this evening, passed a women's property act this year. And though this is a cause for celebration, it is only a beginning. There is much work to do throughout the nation if women are to have the right to own and keep property in their names." Anthony reminded the meeting of the many ways in which they were still considered inferior to men under the law. Gradually as she spoke, a spirit of restless, angry dissatisfaction crept in. It spread from woman to woman as a spark might jump from tree to tree, ultimately igniting a whole forest into blazing light. By the time she got to her plan for organizing a petition campaign in New York state, the women in the room were fully with her, willing and even eager to throw down everything and tramp from county to county.

"But this plan will not succeed without funds. It is my intent that sixty women will be chosen, one from every county in New York. They will act as captains and see that in each hamlet and town there are petitions advocating reform of laws pertaining to women. Women must have the right to control their own earnings, to keep their children with them in case of divorce. And they must have the vote. But Albany will not heed us unless they are confronted with the signatures of thousands of women and men from every corner of the state. To accomplish this, there must be sufficient funds to provide transportation and lodging and printing and food. If our captains starve

or fall dead in the snow from exhaustion, our cause
will not be won. If we cannot rise together as a sex
now when the call is out, we will never succeed in as-
suming our rightful . . ."

The front door flew open.

Three strapping young men in their twenties bellowed, almost in unison, "Where the hell is our
Eliza?"

Chapter 19

"This is my home!" cried Lucy. "You are welcome here only so long as . . ." She made her way through the crowded chairs and benches to the door.

One of the Pomeroy brothers hooted and another, the largest and probably the eldest from the looks of him, said, "We want no part of this immorality. Just give us back our sister."

"This is a peaceful assembly, and she came here of her own accord. She is a free American and has that right!"

"Where is she?" The eldest glared into the crowd until he saw Eliza on the stairs, trembling and trying to go unnoticed. "Get down here, girl, and come on home with us. You've been told . . ."

"I want to stay."

"What's that?"

"I want to stay. Please . . ."

"You need not apologize for wanting the freedom to think and act for yourself," Sadie Doolittle chimed in from the far side of the foyer.

"You're among friends here, Eliza," cried another.

"If you do not leave my house immediately, Mr. Pomeroy, I will be forced to call a constable."

Eliza began to cry as her three brothers, ignoring

the protests of Lucy and the other women, shoved their way through the crowd toward her. One brother grabbed her by the arm and wrenched her to her feet, causing her to fall forward. The crowd gasped as the man continued to drag her in the direction of the door.

When Eliza's sobs became cries of pain, Sadie Doolittle hurled her body against the eldest brother, breaking his grip on the girl's arm. Instantaneously, over the cries of Susan Anthony, Elizabeth Stanton and Lucy Shawn, half a dozen women attacked the Pomeroy brothers, lashing out with their fists and swinging their handbags. As the meeting was degenerating into a riot, the front door opened again and this time James Shawn appeared on the threshold.

"What in the name of . . . ?"

"Father!" cried Lucy, rushing to his side. "These men will not permit us to assemble peaceably. They broke in here and . . ."

"If you're the father of this hen, you'd best learn to control her," snarled Eliza's eldest brother. "And if she and the others don't stop contaminating . . ."

"Contaminating! How dare you speak so? You're stupid ignorant brutes, no better than Simon Legree."

"Hush, Sadie. It does no good to speak in anger." Elizabeth Stanton came through the crowd to stand beside Lucy. "Miss Pomeroy wishes to learn more about her rights, Senator Shawn, and these brothers of hers, whom she tends and cares for like a servant, are loath to have her educated." She turned to Eliza who stood cowering, dressed in an ill-fitting gown of Delphia Kilmaine's, beside her brother. "Have you had any schooling, my dear? Can you read?"

Eliza lowered her eyes. "A little," she replied.

"It's against the laws of God to educate a female." Pomeroy indicated the crowd. "Just look at this gaggle of geese. Why aren't they home caring for their husbands, brothers and sons as the Bible teaches?" He sneered, an expression of deepest loathing. "This spectacle disgusts me as it would all decent, God-fearing men. I will not have my sister spoiled by unnatural ideas. When I get her out of here, I'll beat this nonsense out of her, and not a court or a judge will find fault with me."

Eliza began to sob again, for she knew, as did each woman in the room, that what her brother had said was true.

"She can stay here, Father," said Lucy.

"Would you like that, girl?" asked Shawn. "Stop crying now and answer me."

"It doesn't matter what she wants," shot back one brother.

"Well, Eliza?"

The girl looked from Lucy to her brothers and back to Lucy. She gazed around the room at the dozens of female faces with their various expressions of anger, consternation and curiosity. "The twins," she murmured softly.

"Aye," said Pomeroy, "you might well think of those whose lives depend on you. Our mother died quietly only because she knew her babies would be safe in your care. She is in heaven, but even in that place there is grief. The grief of a mother for her neglected babies, for her unnatural daughter who would rather play at mannish games than stay where she belongs."

Eliza went limp.

"You can bring them here," assured Lucy, knowing the awful battle raging within the young woman. "You need not abandon them. Bring them here with you."

"No, Lucy," cautioned James, his hand on her arm.

"But, Father . . ."

"You cannot destroy this man's family no matter how you may feel, Lucy. What you recommend is kidnapping."

Elizabeth Stanton agreed. "It's true, Lucy. If Eliza wishes to come to our cause of her own free will, that is one matter. But this other means the destruction of a family."

Susan Anthony, a woman noted for her pragmatism, added, "The resulting publicity would damage our cause. And no matter what, we must always bear in mind our ultimate goal, Lucy."

Eliza had stopped crying. Beside her hulking brother she appeared so frail that for a moment, Lucy almost believed the popular notion of a woman's helplessness.

"I'll go home," Eliza said quietly. But instead of turning in silence to leave the house, she looked at her brothers one by one, her jaw firmly set. "But I only go because of those baby girls. And if you think I mean to keep silent after this, you are entirely wrong. I don't know how I'll do it, but I mean to fight so those poor babies will not grow up in a world where brothers are forever bosses and women nought but chattel."

Lucy, glancing at Susan Anthony, saw a little smile on the woman's face.

Eliza continued. "And if I may have my bloomer costume back . . ."

"Eliza!" the eldest Pomeroy roared. "I forbid that immoral . . ."

The plucky girl whirled on him. "What I wear in our home, for the safety of myself and the babies, is my business. Mine alone." Looking somewhat older and certainly more self-confident than she had earlier that evening, Eliza turned to Lucy. "Mrs. Kilmaine, forgive me for the disruption of your home and this meeting. And for all you offered, I cannot express my gratitude sufficiently. Do not think me weak because I choose to go with my brothers."

Impulsively, Lucy and Eliza embraced, and among the onlooking crowd, there were some whose eyes were filled with tears. Many had taken chances of one sort or another, risking the alienation of their husbands, brothers and fathers, to attend that evening's organizational meeting. Even the most insensitive among them could empathize with Eliza's situation. Delphia handed her a bundle containing the fruit-stained bloomer costume. After a long look at the crowded room, Eliza and her brothers were gone.

Later that evening, when the women had departed, each one promising to solicit funds for the New York petition campaign, Maureen served a late supper in the dining room. Over a pleasant meal of cold meat, fresh vegetables, biscuits and fruit, Susan Anthony, Elizabeth Stanton, Lucy, Delphia and James Shawn discussed the meeting and, in particular, Eliza Pomeroy.

"You see, Senator, what we are up against. Even many abolitionists disapprove of the women's cause. While they decry the enslavement of the black race, they are blind to the bondage of women." Susan Anthony took a banana from the fruit dish and examined it curiously. "What is this?" she asked, holding it out before her. "And how is it eaten?"

Lucy laughed. "It is called a banana. You peel the skin off. They come from the tropics. Occasionally you can find them in the marketplace. I confess they are a luxury, but I was so pleased when you accepted the offer of my home that I couldn't resist the extravagance."

Elizabeth Stanton said, "Although we had not met before tonight, Mrs. Kilmaine, your name was well-known to me. Your efforts with Sarah Bagley on behalf of the mill workers' ten-hour legislation have made you famous beyond your sphere."

"Even before that," said James proudly, "my Lucy was the leader of a successful turn-out of mill operatives in Amoset." He laughed. "I confess that when she was younger, I often feared for my outspoken offspring." He touched Lucy's hand affectionately. "Perhaps you guess how proud I am of her."

Lucy blushed a little and shrugged off the praise with a discontented sigh. "Better to be proud of all the women who have labored without success. Miss Anthony and Mrs. Stanton, I have often thought the cause hopeless."

Susan nodded her head. "But still, like the rest of us, you continue to fight."

"I half expect to meet my Maker with a placard in my hand," laughed Elizabeth Stanton, "and babies tugging at my skirts!"

It was good, Lucy thought, to laugh aloud and share the common tribulation. Though the work was exhausting and rarely showed substantive results, it was to this as well as Delphia and the boarding house that she had devoted herself since the departure of Thomas and Eben. For a time, when Thomas was still with her, she had thought her days of activism past, left forever behind amidst the spindles and looms of Hopewell Mills. But she had awakened one morning when Delphia was small, overcome with a restless longing to become part of the world again. Boston was a turbulent city, noisy with the voices of discontent and reform. Abolitionists, educationists, feminists and workers, both men and women and black and white, were speaking out. And on that long-ago morning, it had seemed to Lucy that they called to her in tones of challenge she could not ignore. That very day she'd sent a letter off to Sarah Bagley, asking to participate in her Female Labor Reform Association. As much as anything else, this activity had helped to drive Eben Hopewell from her mind and set her free of him. Catching a glimpse of herself in the long mirror on the wall opposite the dining table, Lucy saw a woman no longer young and girlishly beautiful, but one who had proved she could survive and even thrive by the use of her own wits and energy. There was satisfaction in that, she thought. Great satisfaction.

"And what of you, Miss Kilmaine?" Susan Anthony was asking Delphia. "Are you as committed to our cause as your mother?"

"Of course," replied Delphia quickly. "I know how hard my mother works. I know that immigrants like our neighbor Mr. Flynn can vote while you and she and I are denied that franchise because of the supposed weakness of our minds. I know that I have to study millinery when in my heart . . ."

"Yes?" Elizabeth asked. "What would you prefer to study? Medicine? The Law?"

Delphia shrugged. "I'm not sure. But I *am* convinced that there are more important matters in the world than feathers and veils on ladies' hats!"

Lucy said nothing. She was thinking that Delphia's chief complaint was in having to work at all. She would have preferred being the lady for whom the hats were made. Lucy felt a little guilty but, knowing her daughter as well as she did, it was unavoidable that the thought should pass through her mind.

"But at least you will have a means of earning your own livelihood, Miss Kilmaine," said Susan. "In that alone you are fortunate. I find in my travels that so many women are utterly helpless and untrained. Is it any wonder that men seek to close us behind locked doors, relegate us to the company of children and servants?"

"But what of the women who prefer the domestic life?" asked James, rolling his napkin neatly into its ring. "Must they become, per force, lawyers and doctors?"

"Of course not!" replied Elizabeth. "It is a matter of choice. We only ask the right to choose our lifestyles, just as men do."

The doorbell rang at that moment, and soon Maureen brought Patrick Paine into the dining room. Before he could be introduced, Elizabeth Stanton said, "Of course this must be your son, Senator. The likeness is quite striking."

Lucy's spoon dropped onto her plate with a clang.

James shot a glance at her, then responded, "My children are all daughters, madam. My only son, Talleyrand, was killed in the mills. Long ago."

"Forgive me. I assumed . . . How foolish of me."

"Allow me to introduce Patrick Paine." James smiled. It was a proud expression that made Lucy grit her teeth and turn away. "Patrick is an old family friend."

Chapter 20

At eighteen, Patrick Paine was a handsome young man marked with a Yankee brand. He was tall and slim-hipped, and his lean, chiseled face was accented by high cheekbones and the unmistakable browline of the Hopewell men. But unlike his Uncle Eben, whose appearance in youth so often had been glowering and tempestuous, Patrick's eyes that were sometimes blue and sometimes green sparkled with merriment as well as intelligence. He was a boy of easy moods and an unflaggingly cheerful disposition that was, it seemed to those who knew him, recharged by challenges. He had a wide, expressive mouth, white, even teeth and a smile that radiated confidence. His long hair, which was frequently untidy because he moved through life at breakneck speed and hardly stopped a moment to consider his appearance, was sandy colored. In the sunlight, it shone with lights of silver and gold.

It seemed to Delphia that she had known Patrick all her life. Sometimes even he forgot that their friendship had begun only after he had been made welcome at the Shawn homestead on Cooper's Mountain. In the months following his and Suzannah's return from Georgia in '43, his mother had devoted

most of her time and energies to the desperate plight
of the mill. Although he was never neglected and always knew that when he needed her his mother
would be there for him, Patrick took happy advantage of her preoccupation. Evading whenever possible the tutor hired to prepare him for school, he
gave himself over to the mountain he had always
loved.

As he grew older and more thoughtful, Patrick
often wondered what it was about Cooper's Mountain
that called him so irresistibly. Before he reached his
tenth birthday, he knew every path and trail and hidden glen as well as any man, and felt no fear of anything that dwelled there. He sensed that on the
mountain neither man nor beast would harm him.
Particularly, and most perplexingly, he was drawn to
the Shawn homestead and the strange woman who
lived there. Almost always alone, old Helen, the rec-
luse, possessed a quality of centeredness that fascinated Patrick. Although he told others he wanted to
be her friend because he pitied her aloneness and
knew the work of the homestead was hard on her,
what really drew him was the way, like him, she
seemed to belong on the mountain.

Their first encounters were violent on her part.
Helen Hildebrand Shawn wanted no part of Suzannah Paine's boy. She threw rocks to drive him away
from the clearing, and once she sent her big hound
dog after him. But Patrick continued to return, and
ultimately she gave way to him. After their first visit,
they were often together. Helen, whom Suzannah had
once described as a natural mother, a nurturer, could
no more resist the merry lad than he could ignore the
call of the mountain and homestead. At first, their
friendship flourished in secret. And then, to the surprise of her family, Helen introduced him as her

friend at a Shawn reunion. After that, he was often a part of their gatherings. He felt as much at home with the Kilmaines and Shawns as with his own mother and uncle and grandparents in the cold stone house on the knoll.

Although she watched somewhat nervously as his allegiance to the Shawns grew, after one or two attempts, Suzannah did nothing to stop her son. And when he came home with tales of the adventures he had shared with James Shawn when the senator was able to get away from Boston, she said nothing to discourage the affection developing between the boy and the man.

Patrick thought he must have been in love with Delphia forever. It seemed to him some miracle of fate that they could get along so well together and enjoy so many things in common. When they were very young, he had laughingly told her that she was like his sister. But now, at eighteen, his emotions were less purely friendly, more complex and troubling.

He loved her.

As he sat at the Kilmaines' dining room table and watched her, he was not listening to the talk of petitions and voting rights. He never wanted to look at anything else when she was in the room, and he didn't care what anyone was saying unless it pertained to her. She caught him staring at her and the corners of her pretty little mouth quivered slightly with the hint of a smile. She was sixteen and, to Patrick's eyes, perfect in every way. Her hair, once cornsilk yellow, had darkened to brown. Her blue eyes, however, had always been changeable. Although they were often merry, impudent and sparkling with intelligence, still they were capable of turning dark and hard when she was angry or upset. She was a stubborn girl, spoiled by her mother's attentions, but Patrick was willing to put up with her pouts and demands and the sullen, angry moments when she thought of no one but herself. He thought he understood her, for they were both children who had been abandoned by their fathers to the care of strong-willed mothers. But whereas Patrick had his Uncle Eben to turn to and, in recent years, James Shawn, Delphia looked to no man for advice or help.

During a lull in the conversation, Patrick spoke up.

"Mrs. Kilmaine, may I take Delphia out for a while this evening?"

"It's late, Patrick. Almost nine." She was about to say no when James interrupted.

"Let the children go, Daughter. Patrick here's just finished his first year at the college. He can be trusted with Delphia."

Lucy's mouth made a pinched, narrow line.

"Come, come, Lucy," said James, chiding his daughter gently, "these two have known each other since they were children. Let them have their fun."

"Where are you going?"

"Across the river. To Cambridge, ma'am." Patrick sensed Lucy's dislike of him and wondered at it. She had never been cold and unfriendly to him until the past year, when he had come to Harvard and begun to visit the Moon Street house frequently. At the heart of her dislike he recognized, without consciously acknowledging it, a mystery that with each year became more puzzling. "You've heard me speak, ma'am, of my cousin Alexander Duffy? He's my best friend, ma'am, and I would like Delphia to meet him."

"Alexander is the son of Bigelow Duffy, the rector at St. Thomas' in Marivale, Lucy," James explained. "A fine boy, from a fine family."

"Oh?" There was an awkward silence. Then Lucy said irritably, "Very well, then. Go. But see you watch after Delphia, Patrick. I am not as much impressed with the responsibility of college boys as my father is."

Delphia was giddy with relief. "I am so glad you rescued me, Patrick. I cannot tell you how tedious I find this endless talk of feminists. As if there were nothing in the world but voting!"

They hired a carriage at the foot of Moon Street and were making their way slowly through the crowded evening streets of Boston. Delphia leaned against the rolled back of the carriage seat and sighed. In her violet costume and with her curly hair tucked under a smart bonnet which she herself had made, she was as demure and pretty as a flower. Patrick suddenly was seized by a tremendous desire to kiss her. He leaned forward. Guessing his intent, she pushed him away gently with the palm of her hand.

"Remember what my mother said, Patrick. I should hate for her to be any more disapproving of you than she already is."

"Why won't you let me kiss you? And don't lecture me about your mother. If it suited you, you would do whatever you wished and the Devil take your mother!"

"Patrick! Save such talk for college boys."

"It's true. You know it is."

"I know nothing of the sort, and I think you are frightful for saying such a thing." She patted her skirt primly. "Besides, I've told you before, I don't care for kissing."

"You mean you don't care for kissing me." If there was anyone who could dampen Patrick's good nature it was Delphia, who could just as easily fill him with unrestrainable joy. He sulked a moment, staring out at the street, which was thronged with pedestrians and animals and vendors as well as vehicles of every size and shape. But he could not resist her for long, so he tried again. "If anyone should be permitted the favor of a kiss, it is I. Aren't I your best friend, Delphie? Haven't you said so a thousand times since you were still in baby clothes?"

She looked at him out of the corner of her eye. "I suppose if I should ever decide that I care for kissing, you would be the one most likely to know it first. But you may as well stop hounding me about it, Patrick, for at this very moment I haven't the slightest desire to kiss you or anyone."

"Oh, very well," he declared, throwing himself into one corner of the carriage. "I will not make a fool of myself for you or any woman."

As was often the case, Delphia's manner changed abruptly. Whenever she thought she'd gone too far, she would wheedle him back to cheerfulness. "Don't be cross with me, Patrick. You know you are my dearest friend. How can you be so nasty to me, all huddled in your corner like some mole?" Her little mouth was sullen. "You don't care a whit for me, no matter how you rave. When all you think about is kissing, you can't see how worried I am."

If she was concerned about something, Patrick had seen no hint of it before that moment. He half suspected her of pretense, but he loved her too much to pursue this line of thought. Instead, he begged to know what was troubling her.

"It's Mama. I am awfully worried about her."

It was in Patrick to say that if anyone did not need worrying over, it was the indomitable Lucy Shawn Kilmaine. For sheer strength of will and determination, Mrs. Kilmaine outshone even his redoubtable mother. But he kept his opinion to himself.

"There is something bothering her," Delphia continued. "I know there is. And I'm sure it's serious."

"Your mother works hard, Delphie. And she has many responsibilities."

"Oh, I know all that. It's something else. I think she might be ill." Delphia looked at Patrick, and for the first time he saw in her expression a hint of genuine fear. He grabbed her hands impulsively, wanting more than anything to ease her mind.

"Your mother is a strong Yankee woman, Delphie. She works too hard. She's tired. The senator says . . ."

"I know she has awful headaches. I've seen her when she didn't know I was looking, pressing her palms against her eyes."

"She might need spectacles. My mother wears them."

"She has spectacles, Patrick. But she says she can see as well without them, so they just lie there in her drawer."

"Well, no doubt she knows what is best for herself. I wouldn't worry if I were you." The carriage wheels clattered over the Charles River bridge. Patrick pointed out his window. "There's the college, Delphie. Alexander's rooms are just beyond."

On Brattle Street, the carriage stopped before a large old house. In one of the front windows, there was a sign that said, "Rooms for Students" and in smaller lettering beneath, "Only Upright Young Gentlemen Need Apply. References Required."

Delphia hesitated. "Should I go in?"

"It's all right. I know Mrs. Robertson. She keeps a nice drawing room. I'll take you in and introduce you to her, then I'll go up and get Alex. I can't wait for you to meet him, Delphie."

"Well, after all I've heard—Alexander this and that and everything—I hope I'm not disappointed."

After she had been introduced to the keen-eyed Mrs. Robertson and invited to make herself comfortable in the front drawing room, Delphia Kilmaine quickly lost her animated manner and permitted her true feelings to show on her pretty face. The feminist meeting had worn her out. Then, as if to test her patience to the maximum, Patrick had begun his pesky talk of kissing. She blamed Harvard for this. Before, when he was a country boy attending a small academy in Amoset, Patrick had been nothing but her best and dearest friend. There had been no pleas for kisses until he came to Harvard and mixed with older, more sophisticated fellows. Once, at the end of a particularly fine outing to the Botanical Gardens, she had permitted his lips to graze her cheek, but ever so lightly. Apart from that, Delphia had forbidden any physical intimacy between them. The excuses to explain her aloofness were easy to summon and quite believable. Patrick knew as well as she that the times they lived in were harsh for a woman who stepped so much as a hairline out of the mainstream of accepted behavior. Delphia's reputation was her most valuable possession, one she would require for the rest of her life if she hoped to make anything of herself. Patrick understood, and yet he persisted. Lately, it had gotten so they could not be alone for more than a few moments before his talk came around to the subject.

On those rare occasions when Delphia turned her thoughts to self-analysis, she felt horribly guilty for not returning Patrick's affection in the way he desired. She told herself he was so good, so handsome, so funny and interesting, so magnificently rich that she must be addled not to love him. These admonishments did no good, however. No matter how she

tried, she could not force herself to feel anything
more intense than a warm, sisterly affection for Patrick. Sometimes she thought that they were just *too*
close and knew each other so well that the surprises
necessary for love were impossible between them. But
what had given her the idea that surprise was an essential ingredient for love? She could not answer that
question either, but she knew, she *knew*, that without
surprise and adventure and a sense of the unknown,
she could never love anyone.

Except herself, of course. Although occasionally
she was assailed by doubt or niggling guilt, at the
base of Delphia Kilmaine's personality was an abiding
sense of her own importance in and to the world. She
believed she had a right to have whatever she
wanted. Neither the straitened circumstances of her
life on Moon Street nor the tedium of learning a milliner's trade could discourage her from this. On the
contrary, with each deprivation and every hour of unwilling labor, she became more convinced that what
she wanted was what she must have. The problem
was that she just didn't know what that was.

Irritably, she stood up and paced the drawing
room, wrinkling her pert nose with distaste for the
plain, shabby furniture and sentimental ornaments
she saw around her. Though certainly genteel and un-
questionably proper, the drawing room reminded
Delphia of all the things she hated in the world.
Struggle, economy, monotony.

In that case, she thought, why not let Patrick kiss
you? Why not let him fall in love with you? He was
halfway there already. As the heir to the Hopewell
fortune, he could guarantee her a life of luxury and
ease. If she wished, he would travel with her to the
farthest edge of the earth, carrying her away from
monotony and into the arms of one adventure after

another. But to do this would be a betrayal that even someone as self-obsessed as Delphia could not countenance. He cared for her. He was her friend. She could not cheat him, for she sensed that in so doing she would also cheat herself. Patrick Paine was a given in her life, an essential part of her existence. He was like a brother or a favorite cousin. If she married him on the pretense of love, he would soon know it. Proud as he was, that knowledge would drive them apart.

The mere thought of alienating Patrick filled her with an aching emptiness that verged on nausea. She recalled, dimly, the day her father had left. What lingered in her mind was not his farewell kiss or his request that she grow up beautiful and good. She remembered begging her father to stay, begging him to forgive her for whatever she must have done to anger him. She remembered the rising wave of sickness that had overcome her as she watched his carriage disappear. Her stomach had cramped painfully and she had doubled over, the sorrow spewing out of her, soiling her dress, pooling sickeningly about her little white-booted feet.

No, she could not cheat Patrick. She could not risk driving him away as she believed she had driven away her dear father.

Chapter 21

Upstairs in his room at Mrs. Robertson's, Alexander Duffy was packing books in a traveling box.

"You'll be doing me the greatest favor if you take these with you, old man." He spoke in the flat, drawling voice considered the height of vocal fashion by Harvard's older and more experienced students when speaking to "youngsters" like Patrick who, after completing only one year, were considered just slightly human. This condescending manner had offended Patrick at first, especially since Alexander had been his closest friend for years. Now, however, he accepted it as a natural part of collegiate life. In a year or two, he would adopt the same tone himself when speaking to a fresh, green crop of "youngsters."

"But Aunt Margaret is expecting you in Marivale, Alex. What shall I tell her?"

Alexander tied the traveling box with a length of heavy twine. "I'll be home no more than a week or two later than I originally had intended. If she doesn't understand, I'm sure my old gentleman will. He'll make her see I couldn't turn down an offer to study with Professor Pierce privately. You know as well as I do that Pierce is number one in the mathematics department. It'll be excellent preparation for Berlin."

Alexander had graduated from Harvard that June with the highest honors in mathematics, and he intended to go on to advanced studies in Germany the following year. "Ease Mater's mind, will you, old man. She does tend to cling a bit."

Patrick said that of course he would do that, but in his heart he confessed to feeling the same sense of sorrow when he anticipated his friend's departure. To change the subject, he said, "I have Miss Kilmaine downstairs. I want you to meet her, Alexander. Can't you stop packing for a few minutes and come down? Mrs. Robertson has agreed to serve a little supper for the three of us."

Alexander laughed. "Ah, the benefits of filthy lucre! You must have crossed her palm with plenty of silver to make her budge after eight o'clock in the evening."

Patrick blushed. It was true. He had stopped by the boarding house that afternoon and made all the arrangements, counting on Lucy's permission to take her daughter visiting in the evening. There would be wine and small sandwiches and fruit, and even a cake which he himself had bought.

"You think a lot of this young lady, don't you?"

Patrick nodded. "She's a jewel, Alex. The rarest and sweetest . . ."

"Whoa! She takes my breath away already. I don't know if I can stand to meet the living vision of all things good. The old pump," he patted his heart dramatically, "ain't up to it, old man."

"Oh, come on, Alex. Take a moment off, will you?" Patrick moved restlessly about the small, simply furnished room. A few days earlier, the place had been full of Alexander Duffy's presence. Ribbons on the wall had proclaimed his participation in crew regattas on the Charles in which Harvard had defeated

Yale not once or twice, but several glorious times over. Around the mirror near the door had been pinned sketches of his pals on the baseball team that played regularly on Cambridge Common. And over the narrow, monkish bed where he could see them night and morning, he had pinned a dozen sheets of paper on which were scribbled theorems so complex, so utterly incomprehensible that they gave Patrick a headache. But all of this had been removed, packed or thrown away, and the room gave scarcely any hint of having housed a man of Alexander Duffy's larger-than-life proportions.

Physically as well as intellectually, he was formidable. His shoulders and back were broad enough for any burden and his long, heavily muscled legs, as straight as birch trunks, helped to make him a splendid athlete. Even Patrick could recognize his classic good looks. Alexander was like one of those Greek statues he'd seen exhibited at Boston and New York galleries. His chocolate eyes, large and liquid beneath heavy lids and thick dark lashes, had a somnolent gaze that belied the active, wide-awake mind behind them.

"Listen, old man," Alexander continued, ignoring his young cousin's eagerness to rejoin Delphia in the drawing room, "I want you to do me a favor while I'm abroad."

"Of course. Anything."

"I wish you'd take our little Louisa under your wing a bit."

Patrick laughed. "Louisa is my senior by two years, Alex. I'm not sure she would appreciate my paternal concern."

"Oh, well, you know women. Whatever their age, they need taking in hand from time to time."

The son of Suzannah Paine doubted this generalization but chose not to disagree.

"Why are you suddenly so concerned about her?"

"It's Simon McMahon. I heard from my old gentleman that he's been hired on as a day laborer around Marivale, but he's still living at the vicarage with his mother."

"So?" Patrick and Alexander had known Simon McMahon since the terrible day years before when his father had kidnapped Lucy Kilmaine and held her for ransom.

"I never did think Mater had any business bringing those two into our lives, but you know her. She is convinced it is her duty to instill high ideals in everyone she meets."

Patrick made a face. "Be fair, Cousin. My aunt is a good and kind woman."

"Oh assuredly she is that! And she opened our home to that boy and his mother out of the pure Christian charity in her heart. But that does not mean I have to like Simon McMahon or trust him near my sister."

"What do you mean?"

Alexander put down the papers he had been sorting. "I'm not sure, Pat. But in her last letter Louisa said she was finding it increasingly hard to escape his attentions. I don't know precisely what that means. Women are such vague and airy creatures, aren't they?"

"Well, you needn't worry about her while I'm around."

Alexander clapped him on the back. "Thanks, old man. I knew I could count on you. It's about time the girl made a suitable match, and I don't want McMahon compromising her in any way."

"Surely my cousin is too clever to permit. . . ."

"Don't forget who Simon's father was, Pat. Despite all Mater's conviction that he's a reformed and thoroughly blameless youth, a veritable prince among paupers, I can never forget the adage, 'Like father, like son.'"

"I'll do all I can, of course. But now, can't you stop your packing and come downstairs? If I know Delphia, she's champing at the bit by now. She doesn't like to be kept waiting."

"Very well. I suppose Miss Delphia Kilmaine is one of those inestimable creatures for whom I can't really hope to prepare myself. I must just go down and face the brilliance of your own truest love. God knows I should be prepared. I've heard enough about her these past years." On his way out, he stopped in front of the oak-framed mirror to adjust his cravat and smooth back his thick, dark hair. Then he turned toward his cousin in the doorway with a grand gesture. "Lead on, MacDuff. Lead on!"

Downstairs, Delphia was indeed growing restless and irritable. She watched in silence as a servant laid a supper table near the window and stirred the coals in the grate, although it seemed to Delphia that the room was already overheated. In the warm air of the drawing room she could smell the clinging odors of cabbage and sausage mingled with the sugary aroma of baking. After the servant had gone, she went to the window overlooking Brattle Street and, drawing aside the lace curtains, tried to open the casement. It was stuck. She tried again, making a little exasperated sound in her throat.

"Let me do that for you." She whirled in surprise, not having heard the door open. "Mrs. Robertson does not believe in fresh air," commented Alexander Duffy. He came up beside her and gave the frame a sharp, upward blow. The window opened easily. He turned and smiled broadly as he made a half-mocking little bow. "Miss Kilmaine, I believe?"

It was a moment Delphia would never forget. Until the day she died, she would remember how he looked and spoke and even the smell of something faintly lavenderish. When she was an old woman, she would still be able to close her eyes and see his face looking down at her with a humorous, slightly condescending smile. And his eyes! Oh, those eyes that made her giddy in the stomach and weak in the knees! Suddenly her head was full of impossible things she knew she would never dare to say. At the same time, she knew she would die if she had to hold them back.

She whispered, "Yes," and put out her hand to steady herself. But her eyes never left his face. If the servant had not returned just then with laden trays, Delphia might have fainted or fled from the room. As it was, the interruption afforded her the moments she needed to regain her composure. By the time the three friends were seated and Patrick was pouring her a small glass of sweet wine, she felt her confidence returning.

"My cousin tells me you are a milliner," Alexander said.

She cleared her throat, took a sip of wine and replied, "I loathe the work."

Duffy laughed. "Well, Patrick, it is just as you said. She is a woman of firm opinions and outspoken ways." He turned to Delphia again. "Tell me why you hate it and then tell me why you stay at it."

"What good are all those veils and bows and artificial flowers?"

He admired her hat a moment. "I would guess you had a fondness for such fripperies, Miss Kilmaine."

She colored. "Well, of course I do. Every woman does. What I meant to say was, what use can there be in spending ten hours every day locked in a room and decorating hats for women who have no appreciation of the work involved?"

"They pay you, don't they?"

"In a way." She stared at her hands and chewed her pretty lower lip, wishing she were not such a tumble-tongued idiot. Tonight, at least, she seemed unable to make even the simplest idea clear. After a moment, she added, "Anyway, one must work, and this is as good as any other employment, I suppose."

Alexander Duffy raised his eyebrows in surprise. "Surely for a young woman of your charms—you don't mind my saying that, do you, old man—marriage would be the most hospitable career. Why must you bother with millinery at all?"

"Her mother is an ardent feminist, Alex. It would be hard for Delphia to avoid working." Patrick poured more wine for himself and his friend. "Mrs. Kilmaine's boarding house is a haven for free thinkers of all sorts, really. Isn't it, Delphie?"

Thinking of the undignified scene that had taken place in her foyer earlier that evening between Eliza and her brothers and the enraged crowd, Delphia frowned. She was grateful that Alexander had not been there to see it. She did not answer.

"Perhaps you do not care for such free thinking. Is that possible, Miss Kilmaine?"

"Call her Delphia, Alex. It's all right isn't it, Delphia? After all, he's my best friend. And since he comes from Marivale, he's almost like a neighbor of your family. He can use your Christian name, can't he, Delphie?"

She smiled, feeling suddenly shy and unprotected. "Of course," she replied, as she prayed in her mind for the calm to get her through the evening. Maybe when she was home and alone in her own room, her heart would cease its fearful pounding. The drumming was so loud she wondered why Alexander Duffy didn't comment on it.

After that, mercifully, the focus of the conversation shifted. The two men discussed a recent event at the college that had been bruited about the town that week by all the newspapers and gossip mongers. Professor of Chemistry John White Webster had been accused of the murder of Dr. Georgius Parkman, an important member of the Medical School faculty. The details were particularly gruesome, but when related in Alexander's sophisticated, bantering tone, the story seemed one step removed from reality. Until, that is, he told Delphia, apologizing for the truth, that Dr. Parkman had not been found. Not in the usual sense of the word.

"Would you prefer me not to continue in this vein, Miss Delphia? I know a woman's sensibilities are more tender than a man's."

"No, please finish your story. I must admit, I'm fascinated to know."

"Very well, then, but stop me please if I go too far. Just today I heard that after Professor Webster had kept his laboratory locked for several days running with the furnaces blasting at full power, a janitor became curious and entered the premises without Webster's knowledge. Then he called in the authorities. They found a bit of thigh bone and pelvis."

"Oh, Lord," gasped Delphia, sinking back in her chair.

"But that is hardly sufficient to convict Webster," said Patrick doubtfully.

"They also found Parkman's false teeth, Patrick."

Alexander looked at Delphia, who had gone pale at the gory details. "I've upset you, Miss Kilmaine. What a knave I am to have mentioned it at all. Can you forgive me?"

"It's nothing," she protested. "It is just a little warm in here, that's all."

"Ah, you are generous. No wonder my cousin thinks the sun and moon rise out of you. Now that we have met, I see that Patrick was not exaggerating when he described you. I must confess that originally I had dreaded this meeting between us. In fact, I have been avoiding it on the assumption that Delphia Kilmaine could not possibly be all that he said she was." He leaned a little toward her and, as if she were his equal in age and education and not a sixteen-year-old milliner's apprentice, added, "These first-year lads just in from country academies have never been known for clear thinking. Quite naturally, I thought . . ."

Patrick stood up abruptly, knocking over his chair, but he seemed not to notice his gaffe. "Perhaps we should be going, Delphia. Your mother might worry."

Instead of responding immediately, Delphia sat where she was and continued to stare at her plate with its cake and fruit left untouched.

"A little more wine before you leave," suggested Alexander. "It will promote a good night's sleep, or so the medical men tell me."

"It's late, Alex, and I think . . ."

"Just a suspicion, Mr. Duffy," whispered Delphia, pushing her glass toward him an inch. "Just a suspicion."

"Delphia is not accustomed to spirits, Alex," said Patrick, righting his chair and sitting down again.

She looked at him grumpily. "Just a little more cannot hurt me, Patrick. Why are you suddenly so full of do's and don'ts?"

"That's right, Cousin," added Alex teasingly. "I'll be gone to Berlin in a few months' time. Would you have me waste these few hours I have to get to know your young friend?"

"Berlin? You're going to Germany?"

"Indeed I am. I've been awarded a fellowship with Heckler at the university there. He's one of the foremost mathematicians of our time."

"You won't be coming back to your family in Marivale?"

He laughed. "It's Patrick here who loves the mountains and the Amoset River valley. I have no particular fondness for the rural scene, however. I happily anticipate a lifetime spent in cities."

"Cities," she repeated. "I like cities, too."

"Another outstanding attribute. Delphia Kilmaine, you are indeed a remarkable woman. Most of your sex prefer the quiet life of backwaters where no hint of adventure ever stirs. For myself, I itch to see the world and know its secrets."

Patrick sounded even more out of sorts when he said, "I think I shall find running Hopewell Mills quite an adventure. There are those who say that industry and the challenge of progress are the greatest adventures of all."

Alex laughed and leaned across the table to pat his cousin's hand. Patrick jerked away and stood up again. For the first time in his memory, he did not like Alexander Duffy. His collegiate haughtiness, that air he had of knowing what was best for everyone had hurt Patrick. He became aware of a pain, the heart of which he could not precisely locate. All he knew was that the meeting between Delphia and Alexander Duffy had not come off as he had hoped, and he wished he had never initiated it in the first place.

Chapter 22

It was five-thirty a.m., time to get up. Delphia rolled
onto her back, her eyes open. In the early sunlight,
the dogwood tree outside her window had cast a
ghostly shadow on the ceiling above her body. She
felt as if she had not slept all night. Her body felt
weak and foreign to her. A burning tear slid to the
corner of her eye and slipped down her cheek. Her
eyes felt as if someone had ground sand in them.

She groaned and turned, twisting her sheet
uncomfortably around her legs. She kicked to free
them and groaned again from the effort. Her light
cotton nightgown tangled as she tossed from side to
side and gathered itself in a knot at her hips so that
she had to turn again to loosen it. Doing so, she felt
the top sheet pull loose from the bed and her bare
toes touched the harsh wool blanket.

"Damn," she muttered. The cursing had begun,
as her mother's had in the first years of marriage, as a
clandestine rebellion against the strictures of her society, the millinery shop and the grinding tedium that
seemed to dominate her existence. She muttered the
curse again and punched her pillow. Burrowing her
damp face into its softness, she almost wished she

would suffocate and thus escape the forces that were
closing in on her.

As it had more or less constantly all night, Alexander Duffy's face appeared before her. Alexander
Duffy. She had been hearing his name for years and
yet now when she whispered it aloud in the chilly
morning, there was newness and promise in the sound.
Alexander Duffy. It was the name of a man who would
travel far, seeking adventure on every continent, a
man whose mathematical genius would serve as a key
to not only the world, but all the wonders of the uni-
verse as well. With a pang of remorse, she recalled
how young and callow Patrick had looked, standing
beside his older cousin. Compared to Alexander's, his
ambitions and aspirations seemed insufferably mun-
dane.

She rolled over again, kicking off the troublesome
sheet and blanket. But it was cold in the room, and
when she tried to cover herself again, the hopelessly
unmade bedclothes caught about her legs like some
restraining garment devised for the madwomen Miss
Dorothea Dix was always telling Lucy about. The
thought of the two women engrossed in conversation
particularly enraged Delphia. She was furious with
herself for thinking it, furious with her mother for
knowing Miss Dix, and furious with all the right-
eously enflamed women of Boston who came and
went, filling her dining room and front parlor with
their earnest advocacy for this or that cause.

"What about me?" Delphia muttered aloud as the
hall clock chimed six. She would hear a knock on the
door in just a moment and her mother's voice softly
calling her to work. "Damn!" In that moment, with
her body mummied in sheets and blankets and her
eyes burning with grit, Delphia knew she could never
become a milliner and commit her life to drudgery,

no matter what the consequences. In answer to the question, "What about me?" came the answer, "You deserve to get what you want just the same as anyone else."

Dorothea Dix wanted to save the mentally ill. Elizabeth Cady Stanton wanted women to have property rights. Susan B. Anthony wanted the franchise. Very well, Delphia Kilmaine could agree with all these causes in theory. But for herself, for what her heart and soul required for their flowering, she wanted something else.

She wanted Alexander Duffy.

"Are you awake, Delphie?" came her mother's soft voice as she opened the door an inch and peeked in. "Not up yet? Hurry, child. Madam will not tolerate lateness. You know that."

Delphia snuffled.

"Are you all right?"

Another snuffling sound.

Lucy came into the room and walked to her bedside. "What happened to the bed, Delphie? It looks as if you've been fighting with it."

"I can't go. I feel sick."

Lucy touched her forehead. "You don't seem feverish. What's the matter?"

Still not looking at her mother, Delphia answered, "My stomach. It's my time."

"Oh." Lucy hesitated a moment. "Madam does not tolerate absence any better than she does tardiness, Delphie. And with so many young women looking for work, she might not hesitate to terminate you."

"I feel sick, Mama." She looked at Lucy with red-rimmed eyes and a face that was, for a sixteen-year-old, haggard.

"You've been crying, Delphie. What is it?" Lucy

dropped to her knees at the bedside and grasped her daughter's warm hand. For the moment, she had forgotten the demanding Madam Aubry and the fifty dollars it had cost to get Delphia into her milliner's apprenticeship. As it had years before, the thought of Delphia in pain and suffering left Lucy defenseless, possessed by fear for her only child. "Tell me why you were weeping. What is it, Delphie?"

The girl's only reply, and it was not entirely a fabrication, was, "I hurt."

Imagining that she had spent the night weeping from that pain peculiar to women, Lucy said, "I'll send Maureen up with a hot water bottle to hold against your stomach. And a little later, I'll bring up some brandy. And don't weep anymore, darling. You know it never lasts more than a day or two. You'll soon feel bright again."

Lucy straightened the bedclothes, firmly tucking and mitering the corners of the sheet and pulling the blanket down tight under the mattress. As she smoothed the covers up about Delphia's shoulders, she saw that her daughter's eyes had again filled with tears, as if the slightest touch summoned up a fresh wave of pain.

"Sleep, darling. It's the best thing for it. I'll send word to Madam that you're ill. I think she'll understand this time."

But out in the hall, Lucy was less certain of the milliner's sympathy. This was not the first day her daughter had missed. Throughout the winter, Delphia had suffered from colds and inflammations and assorted other ailments, each of them requiring at least a day or two of bed rest. Madame Aubry never took these absences in her stride. She would argue in her stubborn Gaelic way that she was not in the business of running a benevolent school and if M'amselle Del-

phia could not work regularly, she must be replaced
by someone who would. Thus far these remonstrances
had been largely noise and temperament on the
French woman's part, but Lucy knew that eventually
she would put a finish to Delphia's training, and without a qualm. Madam was a businesswoman first and
foremost.

At the end of the upstairs hall was a long, narrow
room lined with cupboards and shelves in which were
kept the household linens. The woodwork was made
entirely of cedar, which lent its sweet, woodsy aroma
to all the sheets and pillow slips and blankets. Lucy
was gathering fresh linen for the room already va-
cated that morning by Elizabeth Stanton and Susan
Anthony, when a thought occurred to her. She
opened the cupboard where the pile of soft linen sani-
tary cloths were kept and did a rapid calculation. The
pile was short by almost a dozen, which meant that
some were still soaking in the laundry. This meant
that no more than two weeks had passed since Delphia's last infirmity.

She's lying to me.

The thought came not as a surprise, but as an af-
firmation of something Lucy realized she had suspected all along. But when she recalled the red-rimmed
eyes and drawn young face, her anger faded. Though
it was not biology, she knew that something was troubling Delphia. Lucy felt an instant's sympathy, but it
was replaced by irritation as she heard the hall clock
chime the quarter hour. The morning was under way,
and while Delphia lolled in her bed like a Georgia
belle, Lucy had a list of chores so long that she knew
there was no hope of doing everything before the sun
set that night. She and Maureen would work without
stopping, but Delphia. . . .

Her arms laden with linens, Lucy shouldered

open the door and was just turning into the upstairs hall when a wave of too familiar nausea stopped her. The sheets and embroidered pillow slips dropped from her arms and, to keep from falling, she had to grasp the banister. Around the outside of her vision, specks of gold, like dust motes dancing in a ray of summer sunlight, brightened and whirled. The hall ahead of her seemed a dark tunnel, and the three or four pictures on the wall, the silver sconces and the carved woodwork were obscured in granulated shadow.

"Damn!" she muttered, forcing herself down on her knees to pick up the linens. But the effort was too much. She leaned against the wall and sat, covering her face with her hands.

This had all happened before, but it was the kind of experience Lucy knew she would never become accustomed to. She knew without knowing that the spasm signaled something terribly wrong with her. Like the headaches and burning eyes she experienced daily but never mentioned, the black tunnel vision edged in gold could only mean her eyesight was going.

When the spasm had passed, she gathered her things together and continued about her work, trying to push the thought of blindness from her mind. Until it happened, until there was nothing but night before her eyes, she would not think of it. There was too much to do. Besides, she wanted neither Delphia's sympathy nor her mother's and father's. She wanted what she had always wanted, except for the years when she had loved Eben Hopewell. She wanted to be strong and independent, riding the tide of progress with those whom she respected, answerable to no one but herself and the dictates of her own conscience. There was nothing easy about her life as mistress of a boarding house, but it gave her satisfaction to know that she was responsible for her own life and dependent on no one but herself.

Blindness would bring the end to all this. For Lucy Shawn Kilmaine, who had come off the mountain to work in the mills fifteen hours a day and organized her fellow workers for the most successful worker turn-out in the history of Amoset, for Lucy Shawn Kilmaine who had been abandoned by her husband, cheated by her lover and yet survived, dependency seemed equivalent to death.

Once, when his elder daughter was still young enough to toddle after him as he worked the homestead on Cooper's Mountain, James Shawn, then scarcely more than a boy, had told his wife, "She has a will of iron, this one. Like yours and mine together. And then some."

Over the years, Lucy's formidable will had been her greatest asset. She used it now, when concern for her daughter and fear for her own well-being were enough to sap the strength from any man or woman. As if both Delphia and the occurrence in the upstairs hall were incidents of only passing concern, she turned her energies toward the work of running the boarding house and did not look back or pause to let self-pity creep into her thoughts. Instead, she made the beds and cleaned the rooms, lugged the ash buckets down the backstairs, polished the banisters and buffed the heavily waxed parquet floors of the foyer and dining room. She made sure that Maureen, whose job it was to clean the front drawing room where the feminist meeting had been held the night before, went down on her knees to sweep the corners and baseboards with a whisk. She helped her drag the carpets out and pound them free of dust with a heavy wooden beater. Lucy did all this, stopping only for a cup of tea at midmorning. Not once did she stop to think how tired her arms and back were or how her head ached and her eyes still stung. She worked because in this, the simplest of the Yankee virtues, she found distraction for a time and a void of feeling.

At noon, Mrs. Tippits served a light meal. Lucy ate alone, her boarders and guests gone for the afternoon. Just as she was finishing the strawberry tart Mrs. Tippits made so well, for the simple reason that she liked to see her mistress smile, two things occurred almost simultaneously. Patrick Paine came down the stairs from his room on the third floor and a messenger rang the doorbell.

Ignoring Patrick, who had entered the dining room, Maureen came in and placed a letter beside Lucy's plate. "This just came, Mrs. Kilmaine, and from the looks of it, it's been around a bit."

Lucy opened the worn and smudged envelope. As Patrick poured himself a cup of tea from the pot on the sideboard, he heard her cry out, "Uncle William!"

"Ma'am?"

She looked up at him and an expression of irritation crossed her face. As if Delphia and her eyesight were not enough worry for her, here was Patrick Paine looking scrubbed and handsome and every inch the Yankee gentleman. Once again, she drew upon her will and shut the worry out. Her expression became neutral.

"May I be of assistance, ma'am?" Patrick stood at the other end of the table.

"It's my uncle. William Shawn. He's here in Boston."

Patrick, who thought he knew the Shawn family

as well as his own, looked surprised. "I didn't know the senator had a brother, ma'am."

Lucy made a sound that was almost a laugh. "Well, in a way he hasn't. At least not until now. Uncle William's been at sea since I was a child. I think we all assumed he was dead."

"That's good news, ma'am. Can I take a message to the senator? I'm sure he'll be happy to . . ."

"Have you forgotten? He left early this morning to accompany Miss Anthony to New York." Lucy stood up, thrusting the envelope into the pocket of her duster. She went into the foyer to look at the tall clock, then she reread the letter again. "I'm afraid he'll think we've missed him. He might sail out again without seeing us." She glanced at the several addresses scrawled on the envelope. One of them had been crossed off. "He sent the letter to Cooper's Mountain and Mama sent it here." She looked at the clock again. The house had been full of strangers the night before and it would take the rest of the day to set it right again. There were two new boarders coming in that evening; their room had to be prepared. And she still hadn't consulted with Mrs. Tippits about the evening meal. "I can't possibly go. Damn!"

Patrick resisted the impulse to smile. Although he knew that for some reason Lucy didn't care for him, he couldn't help liking her. Like Delphia's, her timid curses were quite charming, he thought. But he knew better than to smile, for Lucy would not be pleased to know she amused him.

"Ma'am, may I help?"

She stared at him.

"Perhaps I could go down to his ship and tell him to come back here. There's space in my bedroom and I wouldn't mind sharing." Patrick had paid a little extra so that he might have a private room, hardly more than a closet, really. He was a studious boy, and the single room gave him the privacy he desired. "Then we can send word to the senator. He'll come back right away, I'll bet!"

Lucy still did not reply. For the moment, she forgot Uncle William and was looking at Patrick. Although he did not resemble James Shawn in any single feature, nonetheless the likeness was bold and unsettling.

"Are you feeling ill, ma'am?"

"Of course not!" She passed her hand across her eyes. Patrick Paine was a Shawn. In Lucy's mind there was no doubt. Her recent realization of this had made it difficult for her to behave normally toward her father. Those who had known Patrick for a long time didn't notice the similarity. But to others, such as Elizabeth Stanton just the night before, the likeness was obvious. A sudden rage welled up in Lucy. For the first time in her almost forty years of life, she thought of her father with a feeling close to hatred. He and Suzannah Hopewell Paine were lovers. They had made this boy who stood before her now, the innocence radiating from him like a new sun on an old world.

Patrick was saying, "I'm going to my cousin's this afternoon and afterwards I could go to . . ."

"You saw your cousin last night with Delphia."

"That was Alexander Duffy. This is my other cousin, ma'am. Uncle Eben's boy. Christian."

The name stung. She thought bitterly that no family in all the world was capable of causing as much pain as the Hopewells. Eben had betrayed her with a black whore, and Suzannah had seduced James from a wife who loved him, children who respected him. Feeling an impulse to punish them all through Patrick, she almost told him the truth before a stronger impulse to be kind controlled her. The boy was innocent. Like Lucy, he was a victim of the Hopewells.

Very quickly and without looking at Patrick again, Lucy handed him the letter. "Very well. Go about your business and then afterward go to the wharf and find the clipper ship *Defiant.*"

"Whom should I ask for, ma'am?"

"His name is Captain William Shawn. According to this note, the ship is his."

Chapter 23

Christian St. Clair had been attending the Quaker
Academy in Cambridge for ten years. As Eben had
predicted, the choice of school was an excellent one
for a whip-smart boy like Christian, who would have
found his mixed racial heritage a problem in larger or
more socially-oriented preparatory schools. The
Quaker Academy, however, had provided a congenial
home, as well as an atmosphere conducive to intellec-
tual growth. A gifted student, he was now, at fifteen,
only a year away from Harvard College and already
gaining a reputation as an orator.

During Patrick's first year at college, he and his
cousin had spent much time together, and both boys
looked forward eagerly to the time when they would
walk together in the Harvard Yard. But when Patrick
mentioned this to Christian now, he was surprised by
his cousin's cool response.

"I don't think I want to go to Harvard," Christian
said quietly. The two were strolling along the path
that bordered the Charles River. To their left, against
a sky of vivid blue, the spires of University Hall were
outlined.

"But you've been planning this for years, Chris.
It seems like forever almost."

Christian stopped, picked up a flat stone lying in the path, and skillfully skipped it across the broad, still river.

"What has changed your mind, Cousin?"

"Last month, I heard Frederick Douglass speak at the Academy."

Patrick's heart sank. He knew what Christian would say next.

"He talked about the Underground Railway. Afterwards, he took me out with him and we walked. Along this path, as a matter of fact."

"Look, Chris," said Patrick quickly, "I know you haven't had much opportunity to speak with members of your own race. Negroes, I mean." Patrick was fully aware of his cousin's mixed parentage, but so accustomed was he to the younger boy, so close had they been for years, that he often forgot his race and made reference to it as an afterthought. "What I want to say is, you shouldn't give up a great opportunity like Harvard on the strength . . ."

Chris laughed and skipped another stone. "You haven't even heard what I have to say, Pat. Or does the college teach mind reading now?"

"All right, all right. Tell me then." As they walked on, Patrick kept his eyes on the path in front of him.

"Douglass is a great man, Patrick. He made me see that no matter how much I feel I belong with you and Aunt Suzannah and my father, I owe something to my people." He grasped Patrick's shoulders. His tawny face with the strong Hopewell brows was as handsome and intense as his father's. "Think of it, Patrick. There are men and women and even children living in bondage, simply because their skin is the color of mine. You saw what the Federal troops did to Anthony Burns."

"I'll never forget it."

"Well, if it affected you that way, how do you suppose it was for me?"

On May twenty-sixth of that year, Patrick and Christian had stood among the silent crowds that had lined the Boston streets from the Federal courthouse to the docks. They had watched as the fugitive slave, Anthony Burns, was dragged by Federal officers to the ship that would return him to his Southern master.

"It's the law, Chris. You can't go against the law." The harsh Fugitive Slave Law had been the price paid for California's admittance to the Union as a free state and part of the government's effort to contain slavery within a confined geographical area. But even as he opened his mouth to explain all this to Chris, who already knew it perfectly well, Patrick knew his arguments were specious. Even he did not believe them.

Christian grabbed him again. This time the pressure of his fingers was painful. "Why should I follow this country's law when it is contrary to God's law? Answer me that, Patrick. How can I support a bad law, an evil law, even if I do so only by ignoring it, by going to Harvard, studying medicine, marrying and living out my life in Hopewell comfort? How can I do that and call myself a man, Patrick?"

The boys were of an age when manhood and its definition were much on their minds. Christian could have presented no argument more persuasive.

"What are you going to do then?"

Christian laughed, suddenly nervous. "If Father gives his permission, I will join Mr. Douglass next year when I finish at the Academy. I will make speeches and help form anti-slavery societies. I'll work on the Railway."

"You could be caught, Chris. Suppose you work

on the Railway and some white man takes you for an escaped slave? No matter how many papers you have declaring your freedom, all some Southern bastard has to do is tear the documents up. You could be . . . sold." Unexpectedly, embarrassingly, tears filled Patrick's eyes. "Sold," he repeated.

"It is a chance I must take."

"And if Uncle Eben forbids it?"

"I'll go with Douglass anyway."

After that, there seemed nothing more to say on the subject. They walked along the riverbank in a heavy silence, stopping from time to time to throw stones or observe the long-necked, skinny-legged birds standing placidly in the shallows of the Charles. As they strolled, a breeze came up and riffled the darkening water.

"We're going to have a storm," Patrick commented. "I suppose I should hurry down to the docks." Earlier, he had told Christian about his errand.

They weren't far from the bridge crossing into Boston. When they reached it, the boys were reluctant to say good-bye. As if Christian were going to leave the next day to begin his journey with Frederick Douglass, the moment had an air of finality that was more than Patrick could stand. He had to try again to dissuade his cousin.

"Come home with me next week. At least speak to Uncle Eben about this before you do any more thinking on the subject. He's your father, Chris. He deserves equal time with Douglass. After all, that man's a stranger to you while we are your family."

"I know, I know."

"You'll come then?"

Christian shook his head.

Exasperated, Patrick demanded to know why not. "Don't you care for us at all?"

"Of course I do. God, Patrick, how can you ask such a question?" Christian looked hurt.

"Then why won't you come home?"

"That's a cold wind," was Christian's reply as he turned up the collar of his light coat.

"Damn it, Chris, answer me!"

"It's . . . the old ones. Our grandparents." He shoved his hands deep into his coat pockets and stared at his feet as he scuffed the dusty path. "Last time I was in Amoset, at Christmas, I had a little talk with Grandmother."

Patrick groaned and reached out to embrace Christian, but his cousin pushed him gently away.

"It's all right, Pat. She's hated me for years. I've always known it. Father prepared me for it on the first day I arrived in Amoset. But until last December, she kept her insults quiet. She did unkind things, but since I knew she was half-crazy, I . . ."

"Unkind things like what?"

"It doesn't matter."

"But it does. The old woman's mad as a coot, same as Grandfather. I want to know what she did."

"When I was little and Father brought me home from the Academy for holidays, I learned to stay out of her way. But sometimes she would sneak into my room at night when I was almost asleep. She'd pinch my skin and pull my hair. She called me names like 'nigger baby' or 'slave brat.' "

"Did you tell Uncle Eben?"

"No. I knew she was crazy. There's no way you can stop a crazy person."

Patrick spat on the ground. When he spoke, his mouth twisted in a grimace of loathing and pain. "I wish she'd die. I wish they both would. I wish that India Man would slip something in their brandy and we'd all be done with them."

"But that won't happen. In fact, judging by what I saw at Christmas, both she and Grandfather are in better health than they have been for years."

Glumly, Patrick nodded.

Remarkably, what Christian had said was true. During the ten years since Sarah Hopewell had come out of the seclusion of her bedroom and chosen to devote her attentions to her husband, both of the senior Hopewells had improved. Though slow, their progress undoubtedly had been steady. Now they had reached a state that, while it did not guarantee either sanity or good health, had brought with it a surprising vigor. And in Martin Hopewell, a will to live had been kindled that surprised everyone. Except perhaps the India Man, Mr. Harahsi, who had nursed the old man for nearly two decades, despite his monstrously evil and thankless temperament. With the passage of time, Sarah had taken over more and more of the simple tasks of his care. She sponged and dressed him daily and saw to it that he ate the special foods she ordered for him. But only Mr. Harahsi had the strength to wheel him in his heavy chair and get him in and out of bed. Martin no longer spent every hour in his study, but took pleasure in being out-of-doors on his own property. On fine days, he would spend the whole afternoon at the observation point overlooking the mill, a structure he had built so many years before when he was an ambitious young man. He spoke little. Sometimes the only sounds he made were untranslatable grunts.

"I saw him on the lookout once," Christian was saying, "and I will never forget his face as he stared down at the mill and the town. It was like a mask, one of those ugly Greek things we saw that time Aunt Suzannah took us to New York. Remember? It was when I was eleven or so." Patrick nodded. The mask of Oedipus the King was vivid to him still: gaping, black, empty eyes and a curled mouth as poisonous as a serpent's.

"You shouldn't worry about the old man," he said without conviction. "Come home, Christian. Please."

"No. It's dangerous there now. I knew it at Christmas. She found me out, the old one, and told me she'd sooner see me dead than sharing the mill with you. I'm afraid of her now. Of both of them."

From the bridge, Patrick hired a carriage to take him to the docks. As always, the trip was a slow one through streets narrow and crowded, but for once Patrick did not mind. He had too much on his mind to care about whether he would be in time to find Captain Shawn. His heart was laden in his chest. He seemed to feel it there, beating painfully against his ribs. And every beat, each pulse, was like the timpani of soldiers, marking time to a funeral dirge.

For Patrick, an only child, his cousins Alexander and Christian were like the brothers his loving heart craved. But where he admired and often looked to Alexander for example, his love for Christian was protective. From the moment they first met, he had known that the slight, dark boy would need him as a friend and ally. He'd been with Christian when he was jeered at, and on several occasions in Amoset he'd gotten himself a bloody nose or black eye from defending him. Patrick didn't care. Though he had no love for fighting, it was something he could do when called upon to defend something in which he believed. But what could he do to protect Christian if he went with Frederick Douglass and rode the dark wagons coming up from the South or ferried boats across the Ohio, guided only by starlight and the beacon of freedom?

For a moment he considered going with him, but he dismissed the thought, realizing that Christian needed to do this on his own. He would not want his protective older cousin along on the journey he proposed to take. The carriage stopped abruptly to let a pedestrian pass in front of it and with that abrupt jarring halt, Patrick experienced a sudden revelation. It was almost as if the motion of the carriage had jolted his brains into some new and startling configuration that enabled insights otherwise impossible in a boy scarcely eighteen years of age. He saw that Christian had to go in order to find himself. Without the risk of that journey, he would remain somehow incomplete. Seeing this, Patrick felt a swift rush of inexplicable envy. Where will I go to find myself? he thought.

Near the docks, the street became impassable. Patrick alighted, paid the driver and continued on foot toward the anchorage where several clipper ships lay. The bracing wind and the salt sea smell, mixed with the aromas of fish and tar and hemp, cleared his mind. The beauty of the ships at anchor lifted his spirits and for a time he forgot Christian. With their mighty sails furled, the ships' masts looked like grids against the map of the sky. Taken by a fancy, Patrick imagined himself with a duffle slung carelessly across his shoulders, striding toward the *Defiant*, his nose itching with the scent of adventure that mingled with the other fragrances of the dockside.

He found the *Defiant* easily. She was a beauty, almost two-hundred feet long with a main mast better than half that size. A clipper like the *Defiant* could make the run to California in less than four months, going far south through Cape Horn. She could go to China and be home in well less than a year. Across her bow the name *Defiant* was painted in bold, dramatic script. All at once, Patrick was excited and eager to know the man who could captain such a vessel.

At the gangplank, he hesitated. A boy on deck leaning over the rail called out to him, "Whatcha want? If you ain't got papers, Cap'n won't see ya." The kid had a cocky, half-toothed grin, and although he was scarcely more than ten or twelve, his arrogant manner was slightly intimidating to Patrick.

He hid it well, however. "I'm looking for Captain Shawn," he called out over the noise of seagulls and sailors and the rising wind riffling the edges of the furled sails.

"You got papers?"

"What papers?"

"Seamen's papers, mate. Where you been?"

"I don't want work. This matter's personal."

"Who says?" The kid grinned.

Patrick was becoming irritable. Doing his best to sound convincing, he bellowed, "Go below and tell your captain I've come on family business. He'll understand."

The kid hesitated as if considering whether Patrick was someone he should obey. Finally, he waved his hand and ducked out of sight. He was gone a long time and Patrick was about ready to go aboard without permission when a man appeared at the head of the gangplank. Burly and bearded, he was wearing a loose, open shirt and a hat pulled down to shade his eyes. He raised his hand and called out something Patrick didn't hear. Then he strode down onto the dock. It was easy to see that this was James Shawn's brother. Though his eyes were disguised by the shade of the hat brim, his smile and the tilt of his head were the same. And there was something else, something undefinable but definitely Shawn. Patrick felt a peculiar stirring in his mind, like a question not quite formed. It distracted him; he wanted to pursue it.

Then William Shawn was there beside him. "You must be Talleyrand!" he bellowed. "I'd know a Shawn anywhere!"

Chapter 24

In his room on the third floor, Patrick could ignore
the reunion party that was taking place downstairs in
Lucy Kilmaine's drawing room. He didn't hear the
clink of wineglasses or the laughter with which Delphia and her mother greeted Captain Shawn's tales of
adventure in the China Sea and the Indian Ocean,
stories of pirates and smugglers and exotic native
peoples that under normal circumstances would have
fascinated a boy of his wit and imagination. Instead,
he lay on his narrow bed beside the one that had
been especially set up for Captain Shawn. His eyes
were shut, but sleep was impossible. Grumbling, he
went to stand before the little mirror on his dresser
and stared at the face that twice in as many days had
been recognized and labeled as "unmistakably Shawn."

Stare as he might, he saw only the face he had
known all his life. Apart from the distinctive browline, which he recognized as the heritage of all
Hopewell males, it was a face that looked like no
other. It was simply his. He tried narrowing his eyes
and turning his head a little to the side, as if hoping
to catch this Shawn likeness unawares. He stepped
away from the mirror and then walked forward
slowly, pretending disinterest in his reflection until

the final moment when he looked at himself quickly, as a stranger might in passing. He tried every trick, but no sign of Shawn appeared to him.

Angrily, he threw himself down on the bed and tried to read. He had arranged with one of his professors to do some private study during the summer, reading classics like Virgil and Homer in their original Latin and Greek. He set his mind to this, but after a little while the voyage of Aeneas only brought to mind the travels of William Shawn. William Shawn who said he would recognize a Shawn anywhere.

After a time, the effort of concentration exhausted Patrick. He put his books away and, after pacing for some moments, stood at his bedroom window looking out on a view that usually pleased him. From the third story of the house on Moon Street, Boston's chimney-potted skyline with its irregular rooftops formed a shadowy landscape against the grey night sky. But tonight nothing could calm or sooth his troubled mind. He had no power to stop his thoughts as they turned to the possibility that James Shawn might be his father.

Patrick was miserable. If ever there had been a man with whom he felt the closeness of a father-son relationship, it was Senator Shawn. But it was Patrick who had initiated the loving friendship by making friends with Helen Shawn. If he had not gone up the mountain that first time long ago and been drawn to the solitary woman in the homestead, it was possible that he would never have known James Shawn. Surely, if they were father and son, the older man would have made the first move. Unless of course he did not know . . . Or did not care.

Patrick's face crimsoned as he thought of his mother. How dare he question her virtue! Self-loathing combined with misery in a way it never had be-

fore. He turned from the window and threw himself
face down on the bed, biting his lip to keep from crying.

A little while later, there was a knock at the door
and Captain Shawn entered. Patrick would not look
at him.

Drink and family had made the captain merry.
He did not seem to notice that Patrick was deeply upset.

"Well, me matey, we've got us berths in the
crow's nest, I reckon, aye what?" He had a gentle
singsong voice like the rocking of a ship at sea. "I'll
say, I'm bushed! The company of pretty ladies wears
me out." He tossed his blue wool coat onto a hook and
sat down heavily on his bed to take off his boots.
When his feet were free, he removed his heavy stock-
ings and wiggled his toes with a sigh. "You know, in
the Sandwich Islands they wear no shoes at all.
Never. Don't have to, for the weather's fine most every day. Rains in the afternoon for a while to damp
the dust a bit. That's all. Ah," he sighed again,
scratching, " 'tis a good life out there. But a lazy one."

Patrick still did not speak.

"I was younger'n you when I went away to sea.
Just up and went, I did. Me old ma didn't like it much,
but she knew when I'd made my mind up, and that's for
damn sure." Captain Shawn laughed and, reaching
out, he nudged Patrick in the ribs. "You don't mind a
bit of cursing, do you, lad? I'll say, it's almost done
me in keeping me mouth clean for the ladies below.
But I did, I did. Sailors' talk ain't suitable for city do-
ings."

"Why did you come back?" In spite of himself,
Patrick was interested in Captain Shawn. It was hard
not to like an old gentleman so full of good will and
ebullient spirits.

"I got to wonderin' what had become of all us Shawns. I wondered about me brother James and where he'd got to."

"Didn't you ever write letters?"

"Aye, we wrote. In the early years, that is. But I was here and there and yonder. Sometimes the letters from James were delayed for years." Shawn became serious. "You see, I never even heard about young Talley's death. I saw you standing on the dock and I just thought . . . Well, never you mind me, laddie. It's no shame to be mistaken for someone else. What counts is you're an uncommonly handsome fellow, Shawn or not!"

Patrick crossed his hands behind his head and watched the captain as he undressed. Naked, he reminded Patrick of an old stallion he had seen once in a field. The years had worn him thin; he was big and sinewy without any fat on him. The way the captain undressed and wandered about the little room stark naked struck Patrick as possible only for a man who had lived most all his life in the company of men only. He didn't seem to mind at all that Patrick stared at him openly. Reaching into his worn canvas duffle, he pulled out a long cotton nightshirt and slipped it over his head. Then he dropped onto the bed and sighed again.

"It's early in and early out for me, lad. But I'll be quiet in the morning, never fear. When I was your age, I remember how I liked to sleep." He raised up on his elbow and, looking at Patrick, winked and grinned. "I was a prodigious sleeper in me youth."

"Shall I turn off the light?" Patrick was still in his clothes, but he thought he might as well go to sleep himself. He had nothing better to do. "I'll only be a moment."

"Take your time, lad. Take your time. The light don't bother me a bit."

But neither the man nor the boy could sleep. Each tossed and turned uncomfortably, their noisy cots creaking from the slightest movement. After a while, rain began to fall. The old man groaned and sat up.

"Rain," he said, speaking to himself. He got up and went to the window.

Watching, Patrick supposed that he was worried about the *Defiant* moored at the dock across town. As if to verify his imaginings, the captain began to speak, his voice as tender as a lover's.

"I've not been away from her even once in all these years. Not since I became her master back in '48. I loved her then and I love her still. Pretty wench. Proud lady." He was quiet and what seemed like a long time passed, interrupted only by thunder and lightning cracks that opened up the sky and lit the room with a sulfurous gold.

Patrick's eyes grew heavy and he began not to care that he had twice been mistaken for a Shawn. The captain had been at sea for more than forty years. What did he know? And Elizabeth Stanton? She was a woman and women were always looking for relationships between folks. Chance had caused the misidentification. Chance and nothing more.

Downstairs, Lucy had just completed her rounds for the night. She always carried a ring of large keys, and every night, not trusting Maureen to do the job, she went from room to room securing the windows and doors. Moon Street was no longer a genteel neighborhood, and at night the street was often full of rowdy Irish immigrants, singing and laughing drunkenly. Though she liked her neighbors the

Flynns and Greens well enough, she mistrusted them and their friends despite her long association with them. Every year, the neighborhood grew less to her liking, and more and more frequently she thought of leaving. But when she confronted the question of where to go, there seemed to be no answer. She would not consider returning to the mountain so long as Delphia was young and unattached. Though Lucy had left Cooper's Mountain more than twenty years before, she remembered the sense of isolation she had felt in the homestead. She wouldn't think of inflicting such a life upon her spirited daughter. So she continued to make her rounds each evening, closing her home like a fortress against the night full of strangers.

Her mood was cheerful as she finally climbed the stairs. Delphia had recovered her good health and joined in the celebration heartily. Uncle William was entertaining and sometimes even wildly amusing. She smiled just remembering his jokes and anecdotes. He loved a story better than anyone she'd ever known. A little wistfully, she thought of the places he had seen, the exotic ports of which he spoke so familiarly and which she would never know. But the yearning mood passed quickly. Lucy had no real wish to travel. She thought it must be some peculiarly male desire, this yearning after foreign places.

Outside Delphia's room she stopped, hearing sobs coming from behind the door.

"Delphie?" she whispered, opening the door and poking her head in the room. "Are you asleep?"

"No."

"You were crying this morning and now again. What is it? Still the pain?"

"Yes, Mama."

"Delphie, are you telling me the truth?"

When her daughter replied something she could

not hear, Lucy stepped closer to the bed. Suddenly, Delphia's sobs became much louder. Sitting up, she hurled herself into Lucy's arms.

"Darling girl!"

"Oh, Mama, I don't want to go away from Boston. Not now. Please let me stay here. You go with Uncle William and Patrick and I'll come later. Please, Mama. Please."

Lucy had no idea what had prompted this outburst, but she saw immediately that Delphia's upset, whatever its cause, was genuine. Her face was puffed and red from crying.

"I promise to go to Madam every day and work harder than I ever have. I swear I'll never miss a day and I'll come home quickly and help Maureen take care of the boarders."

"Maureen doesn't need your help, Delphie. Mrs. Flynn will come in the mornings to do the bedrooms and we'll send the laundry out. And anyway, you know we have fewer guests in the summertime. I always plan it that way so we can visit Nana on the mountain. But why do you want to stay here all of a sudden? Especially after all the convincing it took to get Madam to excuse you for a few weeks' time." Now Lucy's sympathy was diluted with suspicion. She held her daughter away from her and tried to look into her eyes. But the room was dark, lighted only by a candle flame. "What's got into you?"

"Nothing, Mama."

"You say that, but I don't believe you. Why is Boston suddenly so attractive to a girl who just a week ago was talking about how she couldn't wait to be in the mountains? I recall your saying . . ."

"I know what I said, Mama." Delphia sounded petulant. Lucy peered at her and, sure enough, her pretty lower lip was pouting.

"In that case, you can tell me . . ."

"Never mind, Mama. You wouldn't understand."

"I what?" It must be love, Lucy thought. Girls only took such tones and said such things to their mothers when love was the matter at hand. "Is it Patrick Paine?" she demanded.

"No, Mama. Of course not. Patrick and I . . ." At the mention of his name, Delphia's sobs began again, this time with greater volume and intensity. They seemed to prove Lucy's point.

"After we get to Amoset, you must find some way to put him off. I don't care what you say, you must keep away from him. Do you understand me?"

"But, Mama . . ."

"But me no buts, my girl. I know what's best for you."

"You don't understand. You never understand."

"I understand more than I care to. And you must too, or you wouldn't be trying to keep away from him. I'm glad you have that much good sense. There can never be anything between Hopewells and Shawns. As for the trip to Amoset, there is no way I can explain to Nana why you found it necessary to stay in Boston when we've been planning this visit for months. Particularly now that Uncle William's come. You have to go with us, with Patrick and Uncle William and me. But once we get to Amoset, there must be an end to your relationship with Patrick."

Delphia's tears became more violently uncontrolled and Lucy's worst suspicions seemed confirmed. For the first time in years, she thought of passion and of the way it felt to love a man to distraction, to be blinded by desire and willing to risk anything and everything for the touch of a hand, a whisper in the shadows. As if not a moment had passed since her last embrace with Eben Hopewell, the terror of love was in Lucy.

It turned, disguised as rage, and she shook her daughter hard. "You haven't done anything foolish, Delphie?"

"Oh, Mama, don't ask that."

"Answer me!"

"No, Mama. No. You're hurting me."

"I know you love him, I know . . ."

"You know nothing, Mama. Nothing at all." Delphia wrenched herself free of Lucy's grasp and tried to cover her head with her blankets.

"Tell me the truth, Delphia."

"Get out, Mama," she cried. "Damn it, get out!"

Chapter 25

All the way from Boston to Amoset, Delphia kept a sullen silence in her corner of the carriage. Apart from the most inconsequential comments, she made no effort to be sociable. After his avuncular efforts were rejected, William Shawn ceased to try to draw her out. Instead, while Lucy listened, thought and sometimes joined in, he and Patrick made excellent use of the long ride by becoming fast friends. There was a natural camaraderie between them. Strangers a few days before, they were now privy to each other's thoughts and aspirations. Enthusiastically, William shared his adventures at sea and tales of exotic ports with Patrick.

When they arrived in Amoset late in the day, Patrick told the driver to take them along Front Street past the mill and deposit him at the Hopewell mansion before making the long, slow haul up Cooper's Mountain.

"I'll come for a visit in a day or two," he told Delphia. "My mother will want me around for a while, I suppose." When Delphia did not reply except to nod her head and sigh lugubriously, he leaned forward and asked urgently, "Will you tell me what troubles you, Delphie? I've never seen you so . . ."

"Never mind, Patrick," Lucy replied for her daughter. Just the sight of the two young people, their heads bent close together, made her irritable. While on the road, she had been able to ignore Patrick's attachment to Delphia while he and William Shawn talked. Now, she considered her daughter's morose manner proof that she wanted to break off with him. Lucy was determined to do everything necessary to help her effort along. "Delphia is exhausted. She'll need several days to rest."

"But you'll come up and see me, I hope," boomed Shawn, pumping Patrick's hand. "I must say I've enjoyed this ride with you, young man. I don't know when I've talked this much. Why you've helped me recollect things I thought I'd forgotten long ago."

Patrick beamed with pleasure. "I enjoyed myself as well, Captain. And I shall be up to see you." As the carriage approached the gates of Hopewell Mills, he pointed out the huge factory to his new friend. "That's our place. My family's, I mean."

"Well, now, all that's mighty impressive. Myself, I'm not so fond of landlocked things like factories and mills. But I can see as how running a huge concern like this could be as rough as hurricane weather. What did you say you make in there, Pat?"

"Cotton piece goods, Captain. The finest in America. We call it 'Hopewell's family silk.'" Patrick knocked on the carriage roof with the ivory handle of his umbrella and the driver stopped just at the gate of the iron mill yard fence. "Years ago, when I was just a boy, we also had business ventures in Savannah. We could get our cotton cheap then, so we produced something called immigrant cloth that was as hardy as linen but cheap enough for anyone to buy. That's how we made our name. But my mother and uncle changed all that. They've changed a lot of things around here, haven't they, Mrs. Kilmaine?"

Lucy nodded absent-mindedly. She was staring into the mill yard, her thoughts drawn back unwillingly to the days almost twenty years before when she had been an operative at Hopewell Mills. Indeed, a lot had changed since then.

After the liquidation of the Hopewell Southern investments and Eben's permanent return to the family business in New England, he and Suzannah had embarked on a controversial enterprise that had made them unpopular with the other manufacturers in Amoset. In the first place, they had hired Irish immigrant women as well as Yankees and had paid them comparatively well for a ten-hour working day. The Irish women's famed skill in lace-making was utilized to decorate fine quality cotton cloth that was suitable for the most delicate garments. Society brides from every city in the country came to Hopewell Mills to choose the cotton from which the nightgowns and undergarments for their trousseaus would be sewn. It was available not only in white, but in several delicate pastel hues as well. There was even a choice of simple patterns. The cloth, known popularly as family silk, had won every textile prize in America and Europe. And though it had many imitators, none could equal its quality.

Visiting manufacturers and industrialists, often those most critical of innovations like a full hour break for the midday meal, the excellent employee school and female overseers, went away perplexed by the efficiency of the mill. Suzannah and Eben treated their employees with uncommon respect, prompting strong loyalty in return. The women and men who made Hopewell's family silk took as much pride in their product as did the owners. Faulty workmanship and careless habits were tolerated by no one, for they jeopardized the quality of a product all admired. In most mills, the foremen and overseers were ruthless and notorious for such management crimes as keeping "slow time." By contrast, the middle levels of management at Hopewell's were watched carefully and permitted no liberties. They were hired and fired on the basis of their honesty. In the weaving and lace-making rooms, the supervisors were women who had learned the textile trade from their youth. These women were paid at precisely the same rate as their male counterparts, which infuriated the other mill owners.

Patrick explained all this to William Shawn. "And there," he said, pointing to a neat, whitewashed building adjacent to the mill, "is the school where Mrs. Kilmaine's sister has been the teacher for a long time. At Hopewell Mills, children no younger than eleven are hired on as runners and such, but they are required to attend the mill school for half of every day until they're fourteen."

"That's uncommonly advanced," said Shawn. "But with everybody reading and writing and ciphering like scholars, there won't be a man or woman to do the spinning and weaving in a few years' time."

"Sir, my Uncle Eben says that if that ever happens, he'll figure out something. Meantime, he and my mother believe . . ."

"Is Ingrid working today, Patrick?" Lucy didn't want to hear anymore. She had worked in the mill when the labor was a kind of slavery. It had been her efforts, along with those of the other Spindle Sisters, that had enlightened Suzannah Hopewell Paine and her brother and made the innovations at Hopewell Mills possible. Hearing how wondrously wise Suzannah and Eben had become increased her irritability.

She wondered if Patrick had ever heard of Barbara Bolton, who worked at her loom almost until she died. And had he forgotten Talleyrand Shawn, whose neck was broken in the cogs of an unprotected machine? Her eyes filled with tears as she remembered her long dead brother who had loved life so dearly. As much as Eben and Suzannah, Talley deserved credit for the school in the mill yard.

"I'll call up Wiggins and ask him if Mistress Shawn is in the school." Eager to please Lucy, Patrick hopped out of the carriage and rang the brass bell on the gate to summon the keeper. After a couple of moments, the ancient Wiggins appeared at a door in the side of the mill. Bent almost double over a cane, he came slowly toward the gate.

The sight of Wiggins brought back such extraordinarily sharp memories to Lucy that she almost signaled the driver to hurry on. She didn't want to remember the first day she met old Wiggins. Even then, as he let her in the mill gate for the first time, he had the appearance of a man poised on the brink of decrepitude and death. And she didn't want to recall her boarding house "mother," Mrs. Quinn, who had hustled her inside the mill and introduced her to Foster McMahon. Most of all, she did not want to remember him. Time had helped her erect powerful blocks to his memory. She could go for days without thinking of his face, his smell, the way his hands felt on her. "Hurry, Patrick," she ordered.

"It is I, Wiggins. Patrick Hopewell." He had to yell for, in addition to being crippled and half blind, Wiggins was almost deaf. "Patrick Hopewell, Wiggins."

"Sir?"

"Is the schoolteacher here now?"

"Schoolteacher? Who wants to know?"

Patrick was about to begin the dialogue again when, from across the mill yard, the schoolhouse door opened and Ingrid Shawn appeared.

"Sister!" cried Lucy, leaning out of the carriage to wave her handkerchief.

Ingrid ran toward the gate and while Wiggins took some time figuring out what all the fuss was about, Lucy exited the carriage and grasped Ingrid's hands through the open ironwork fence. As soon as Wiggins had gathered his wits and let Ingrid through the gate, the sisters embraced, Captain Shawn was introduced and all but Delphia began to gossip excitedly.

Although Ingrid would not mark her thirtieth birthday for another year, she already had the solid appearance of a middle-aged woman. Her light brown hair was streaked with iron grey and her cheerful face was prematurely lined. It was her sturdy, plump body, however, that most surprised Lucy. She saw her sister no more than once a year and between times always forgot that she was no longer the frail child with weak lungs whom the family feared would never live to her maturity. Lucy wondered briefly why her sister had never married and had a family, she who had a bright and loving heart and cared so deeply for children. It was difficult to accept that no man had ever found Ingrid attractive. True, she had always been plain, but she nevertheless had been a vibrant and bright-eyed girl in her youth. A year or two earlier, Lucy had asked this question of Ingrid, who blushed and ducked her head at the mere mention of love and marriage. "The children are enough for me," she said and hastily changed the subject. Though Lucy supposed she would never know the truth, she suspected there once had been a young man whom her sister had loved. But something must have gone terribly wrong, and Lucy would never press Ingrid to speak of what had brought her pain.

"Mama will be so excited to see you, Uncle William. We still keep that old miniature of you in a blue suit with ruffles. Do you recall it? It used to be on the sideboard in the kitchen, but since Papa became a senator and things improved, you've been given a place of honor on the piano in the parlor."

William Shawn laughed. "There's a parlor in the old homestead? With a piano? I'd say that times have changed."

"More than just a parlor, Captain," said Patrick. "The kitchen's larger and there's a big iron stove and a second floor's been added."

"The loft where Lucy and I used to sleep has two fine rooms with dormer windows," Ingrid went on. "You can see all the way down into the valley now!"

Patrick was describing the new barn, the dairy and the laundry room when, from the interior of the carriage, Delphia spoke up for the first time. "Why are you standing in the middle of the road chattering like magpies? Can't we go?"

Hearing her disgruntled tone, Ingrid pulled a face and raised her eyebrows at her sister. Lucy shrugged, and all at once they giggled as if they were still little sisters with a naughty secret.

"What's the matter with you both?" demanded Delphia. "We came all this way to see Nana, so why are we here at the mill? I'm exhausted!"

"I'll go back to my boarding house for tonight," said Ingrid, urging Lucy back in the carriage. "I have to work tomorrow. But in the afternoon, I'll come up the mountain. We'll have two whole days together!"

After saying good-bye, the four in the carriage resumed their ride along Front Street and up to the knoll. Patrick was deposited at the front door of his home amidst a jumble of baggage. There were more farewells and promises of a reunion in a day or two, but all with an obvious lack of enthusiasm on the part of Lucy and Delphia. For a moment, as the carriage swung away around the ellipse, Lucy felt a twinge of pity for Patrick. Servants crowded about him, gathering up his bags and packing boxes. Standing amidst them, he looked wistful and downhearted. William Shawn noticed it, too.

"I can't say why, but I feel like we've let that boy off on a desert island with only savages for company. Can you explain that, Niece?" He looked at Lucy quizzically, and she responded with unthinking candor.

"Patrick doesn't have the happiest home life. I used to know his mother and his uncle a long time ago. I suppose they're all right as far as rich folks go. Patrick certainly loves them. But from what I hear, his grandparents are both half mad."

"I think he would have preferred to go up Cooper's Mountain with us." He narrowed his eyes at her. "Am I right?"

"I suppose so."

He was quiet for a while. As the carriage began the long pull up Cooper's Mountain, bouncing and groaning over the rutted track, he watched the landscape in silence. Then he said, "Am I right that neither of you cares for that boy?"

Lucy looked embarrassed.

"Now, it's never been my way to ask too many questions. But truth to tell, Lucy, if I don't ask, I'll never have the time to find out. And I'd like to know why Patrick Paine is out of favor with you and Miss Delphie when he seems a fine, intelligent . . ."

"He's not out of favor with me!" declared Delphia, showing more spirit than at any time during the trip. She glared at her mother. "He's been my best friend for years and years. Almost like a brother!"

"Delphia," cautioned Lucy.

"Well, it's true, and you're doing everything you can to spoil it. Patrick and I used to be able to say anything to each other, and now you make me treat him like some horrid leper off one of Uncle William's islands."

"I never said you had to do that, girl. You're exaggerating." Lucy began to fuss with her hair in preparation for meeting her mother. "And even if it were all true, this is certainly not the time for us to speak of it."

William Shawn pulled back at the curt tone of her voice. "Now I know I've said the wrong thing! Begging your pardon, Lucy, my girl. But you must know, I'm a plain-spoken man and unaccustomed to the society of women like yourself. I reckon I've been at sea so long I'm not much good at proper company anymore."

His apology intensified Lucy's embarrassment. As was her way, she tried to conceal her discomfort with anger. "You don't have to apologize because Delphia has become so ill-mannered she speaks out of turn about concerns that are of no interest to anyone but the two of us. Believe me, Uncle William, Delphia's behavior during this whole trip is nothing I am proud of. She knows the right way of behaving, but just lately she insists . . ."

"Stop it, Mother. You don't know what you're talking about. You think you have everything figured out to the last jot and tiddle, like the damned budget you're always working on. But you're all wrong . . ."

"I will not permit you to curse, Delphia. You are a young lady and not some street wench!"

"You curse, Mother! I've heard you."

Chapter 26

Lucy and Delphia were mortified by Captain Shawn's outburst. Although his tone had been light, neither woman could mistake his serious intent. They were bickering in a way he found offensive and he not only wanted them to know it, he wanted them to stop. Immediately.

And so they did. Once they reached the homestead, it was not difficult to forget their anger in the distraction of homecoming. The little farmyard with its well-tended garden plot and neat outbuildings was never prettier than at midsummer. The old bush of climbing roses spread out to cover half the new verandah with red blossoms, and trees that Lucy could remember as seedlings spread their foliage in wide, deep green umbrellas. There had been a time when Helen Shawn had let the farm fall into disrepair, but that time had passed with the period of her great depression. Since then, she had kept herself busy from dawn until nightfall, and in the spring and autumn she hired Irish laborers from the Gully to help with the heaviest chores. Now the farm had a look of prosperity. There were new rooms and gardens to show off and a barn full of modern equipment to tempt a sailor home from the sea.

"What I do is another matter altogether."

"Ho, there!" cried William Shawn. The women stopped arguing and looked at him.

"You want to know something I just figured out?" Shawn chortled a little and shook his head. "I just found out that after everywhere I've gone and all the chances I've taken, about the most dangerous place I've ever been is locked inside this little bitty carriage with two fighting females." Lucy started to say something, but he stopped her. "Hold your peace, girl. Just sit where you are and don't say a thing until we're home and I'm out of earshot." He shook his head again and muttered to himself. "Cursing, indeed! No wonder I stayed away so long."

For all that her attention seemed completely taken up with learning about her brother-in-law and what had transpired during his almost forty-year absence, Helen Shawn was aware of trouble between Lucy and Delphia. She said nothing to interfere, however. It was not that she was incurious. She simply trusted that if she was meant to know what had passed between them, the time would come for telling. Her life on the mountain had taught her that things are best left to happen in their own time.

Helen Shawn was fifty-one. This fact was remarkable to her. For many years there had been no mirrors in the farmhouse on Cooper's Mountain, and having no means or desire to see herself, she had lost all sense of her appearance. But during the most recent renovations of the two-room house she and James had built in the first year of their marriage, her husband had insisted on purchasing a fine gilt-framed mirror for the parlor. For the first time in perhaps as long as ten years, she had occasion to see her image.

She had been alone in the room while James, home on one of his periodic leaves from the General Court, worked out in the stable with the visiting blacksmith. She stared at a stranger's reflection and began to cry. "That's not me."

Before she saw her image, she had been able to ignore the several aches and pains that plagued her regularly. After a full day's work, it had been easy to dismiss fatigue as natural, and when her fertile years had ended, she did not miss that regular reminder of her womanhood and was glad to see it go. James and she had terminated their physical relationship years earlier and lived now as almost brother and sister. Days, weeks, even whole seasons went by without her thinking of her physical appearance. But the mirror in the parlor came to tell her everything she had successfully ignored for years. She was old. Her hair was grey and so thin that when she pulled. it back into a long braid as was her custom, the pink-skinned scalp shone through. There were deep creases in her fore-head and, after squinting into the sun for more than fifty summers, her eyes were red and lined. She'd lost some of her teeth a few years back. She couldn't remember precisely when, but the ache in them had gotten so bad that she had pulled them out herself. Their absence had misshaped her mouth, and it came as a terrible shock to find that she now looked more like her old grandmother than the pretty girl she remembered. Sometime later on the day she saw her-self, James came upon her sobbing in the parlor. He was stunned by such uncommon behavior. But when he tried to comfort her, she pushed him away and covered her face. She felt ashamed to be so leathered and ugly when he was still a handsome, virile man.

Helen liked William Shawn immediately. He, too, showed the wear of time in his lined and sun-darkened face. She felt as comfortable with him as she had when they had played together as children. It was more than a week before James was due to arrive from New York. While they waited for him, Helen and her brother-in-law worked side by side on the farm and spent their leisure rocking on the porch or in front of the kitchen fire, becoming reacquainted.

"Why do you stay up here alone, Helen?" William Shawn wanted to know. "It's a lonely life for a woman."

"Are you lonely at sea?"

"A woman shouldn't be alone."

Helen chuckled softly. "I could never live in Bos-ton."

"Then move to Amoset. At least there you could see folks, get out and socialize a bit."

Helen thought of her last social effort. Ten years ago, she had attended the opening of Reverend Strickland's meeting hall beside the Unitarian Church. The evening had been a disaster. Remembering it, she shuddered. "What do I want with socializing? I keep busy enough up here." And until he had gone off to Harvard, Patrick Paine had been her frequent companion. She told William this and he shook his head in bewilderment.

"You like that boy. I like him. Delphia says he's her best friend. Why does Lucy have such an aversion to him, I wonder?"

Helen reached under her chair for the little pipe she sometimes lit as an evening treat and stuffed it with tobacco. She tore a straw from the hearth broom and stuck it in the embers of the fireplace until it caught. She held the flame to the bowl.

"Seems to me like he's an uncommonly fine boy. But on the ride here, it was all Lucy could do to keep a civil tongue where he was concerned."

Helen puffed hard several times until the tobacco burned, filling the kitchen with its sharp aroma. "It's hard to tell about my Lucy. She's a woman of strong opinions."

Shawn laughed. "Now I wonder how she got that way? As I recall, all you Hildebrands had a reputation for being hard-headed as the devil. Shawns, on the other hand, are more the peaceful, loving type."

Helen shot him a quick, questioning glance he did not notice.

"And that Delphia!" said Shawn. "She's just the same, I reckon."

"Spoiled. Since Thomas Kilmaine left, Lucy's pampered the goodness out of her."

"What happened to Lucy's husband, Helen? Can

you tell me? I allow as how I'll never have the nerve
to ask your Lucy for fear she'll bite me in two."

Helen sighed. "As far as I know, he just went off.
Didn't take to marriage, Lucy told me. Said he
wanted to go west and study up on redskins and
such." Helen stared at the fire as she chewed the stem
of her pipe. "Women in this family have bad luck
with husbands."

William mulled over her words. "What's my
brother like now, Helen? I came home expecting to
find him farming, same as when I left him. Instead I
hear he's a senator and maybe going to be governor
of the whole state. I want to see him, sure enough.
But I confess to being a mite nervous. I'm a sailor,
and the sea and ships is all I know. What do I have
to say to an important man like Senator James
Shawn?"

"I wouldn't worry. He'll be glad to see you, and
that's all that counts with James. But you're right, he's
changed. He's not the man I married."

"I'm sorry, Helen."

"No need, no need." It was not difficult to speak
the truth. "We've made our peace together, James and
I. I belong here on the mountain where I am. He's a
man of the world and happy there. It got so the farm
and the mountain weren't enough for James anymore,
so when the city mood and all got into him, he was
happy to go. And he's good at what he does, William.
He does his work and he does it well. The people
trust him and that's only right. He's a good man.
Whatever he's done, however he's changed, he's a
good man. And he tries to be honest. I never forget
that."

From her room upstairs, Lucy overheard some of
this conversation as she drifted off to sleep. All

through her dreams that night, Helen's words rang in her head: "He's a good man. And he tries to be honest." She awoke before dawn and wondered what her mother would do if she knew the truth about her husband and Suzannah and Patrick Paine. The more she puzzled, the more she believed that for Helen to continue in ignorance was to cheat her of the dignity she prized so highly. Despite this conviction, Lucy was not tempted to reveal the truth to her, however. Lucy had hardened with time and experience, but she could never learn to be unkind to her mother, whether her motive was to punish her father, separate Delphia and Patrick or anger with Suzannah and a sense of righteousness. If her mother was a bit of a fool because she continued in spite of everything to honor her husband, then that was the way Lucy knew it must continue to be.

Throughout the holiday, Delphia's mood was changeable. She was sometimes dreamy-eyed and distracted, at other times weepy and forlorn. At no time did she laugh and enjoy herself like a girl escaping an apprenticeship she abhorred. One day Helen came upon her as she was writing a name in the dust of the yard with a long stick, but she rubbed it out quickly before her grandmother could read the letters. When Helen pried gently, Delphia flew into a rage and stormed off along one of the mountain paths and was gone for more than an hour. Afterward she came to Helen and apologized, but when she wept inconsolably, her grandmother knew the tears were meant for someone else.

On the morning of the day James Shawn was expected to arrive, Helen and Lucy were in the big kitchen preparing all the special food required for the reunion. They had been up since before first light and though it was not yet ten in the morning, the family had been fed and sent out to chores, and the kitchen was already sweet with the fragrance of baking tarts and pies. Mother and daughter worked well together. They moved about the kitchen without getting in one another's way, and there was a feeling of closeness between them that had become quite rare in recent years.

"It's good to have you here, Lucy," said Helen, pausing in her work a moment. "I never have gotten over missing my big girl."

"I like it here, Mama. Even though it's changed, the homestead still has sweet memories for me wherever I turn. When I'm away in Boston, I forget how much I love it, and when I'm home with you, I never want to leave."

"Well, that's a change, I must say!" Helen cracked one of the eggs Delphia had gathered that morning into a blue pottery bowl. "Has city life finally lost its allure for you then?"

"No, it isn't that." Lucy thought of telling Helen about the blindness she could feel stalking her, but it was not necessary to spoil the holiday with bad news. There would be time. Sooner or later Helen and everyone else would have to know, and that day would mark a change in Lucy's life more drastic than any since she had run away from home to work in the mill. Then her life had been opening up with all the promise of the new world before it. Soon it must close like the slow folding of a blossom into and around itself. But not yet. Not yet. Too soon.

"You and Delphia are always welcome here."

"I couldn't bring her to live on the mountain. She's thoroughly a city girl."

"Is that what's troubling her? She doesn't like the mountain?"

"No." Lucy spoke with a curtness that made Helen stop beating eggs and look at her.

"But you do know what the trouble is, don't you?"

"Mama, who can tell about a girl as young as Delphia? A child of sixteen. Her emotions are up one day and abysmal the next."

"When you were her age, you sneaked off to work at Hopewell Mills. When I was even younger than Delphia, I was a wife."

"We were different. Delphia is . . . unreliable."

Helen snorted as if she doubted this and went back to beating eggs. For a time the kitchen was quiet except for the sound of her wooden whisk in the blue bowl. To escape her mother and her questions, Lucy went outside and sat on the sunny back steps, plucking the feathers from the fat chicken Uncle William had killed before breakfast. When she finished, she went back inside and prepared the bird's cornmeal stuffing. She was just grinding some salt when Helen spoke up again.

"What is bothering Delphia, Lucy? I'm the girl's grandmother. I believe I have a right to know. Is she in love?"

"Mother, she's a child!"

"Nonsense, Lucy. What do you think I am, some addled fool like old Edythe Whittington? Do you think I was never young? No matter that now your Papa and I circle around each other like two old neuters . . ."

"Mama, I don't want to hear this." Lucy turned toward the stairs leading to the second floor.

"Stop where you are, Lucy Shawn Kilmaine. Your ears won't burn off, you know, from hearing that your Papa and I once loved each other. I was much younger than your Delphia, hardly more than a little

girl, when I first knew I wanted to marry him. I was
skinny Helen Hildebrand with her hair still in pigtails, pinching her cheeks to make them rosy before
church because I knew that James Shawn would be
sitting with his family and peeking around his papa's
big black hat to catch a look at me. I was once as young
as Delphie. The trouble with you, Lucy, is you've forgotten you ever were."

Lucy's head began to ache and she pressed her
palms against her brow.

"If that child's not in love, then I'm an old fool.
Which I'm not!"

"I don't want to talk about it, Mama. Please, let's
just not mention her again."

"And why not? Let her marry if she wants him so
much, whoever he is." She stopped in her tracks and
looked at Lucy with disbelief. "You mean to say you
don't know who the young man is? You let her traipse
about that city and you don't know who her companions are?" Helen began a lecture on the duties of
motherhood and the risks of neglect. All at once,
Lucy could bear it no longer. She threw down the
stuffing spoon. It hit the edge of the table and clattered noisily onto the stone floor.

"Damn it, Mama, it's Patrick Paine. She's in love
with Patrick!"

Helen hooted and shook her head. "Shows how
little you remember about love, Lucy. You think she'd
be hanging about here mooning if she loved that boy?
You think he'd be staying down at Suzannah's? Those
two between them have twice as much will as any
Hildebrand, and if they wanted to be together they
would be, no matter what!" Helen smiled to herself.
Another cake was ready in the oven, and she began to
clear the messy dishes from the worktable. A kettle of
boiling water simmered on the wood fire. She poured

some of this into a dishpan and sprinkled in some harsh-smelling soap. Without being asked, Lucy took up a dishcloth and dried the steaming mixing bowls and spoons her mother set on a wooden draining rack.

"He's a nice boy, Patrick Paine is. I like him," said Helen.

"You don't know him," muttered Lucy.

"You mean he's got a secret life?"

"It doesn't matter what I mean, Mama. Obviously, you have made up your mind that anything I say is foolishness, so there's no sense in my telling you . . ."

"Telling me what?"

"I said it doesn't matter!" The headache and the stinging soap smell combined with the aroma of baking made Lucy nauseous. She steadied herself by gripping the edge of the table.

"What do you think you know, Lucy?" her mother asked quietly.

"Know?"

"You've got something on your mind. Delphia isn't the only one who's been stewing over secrets this holiday. I know you, my girl. I know you can be sly when you want to be. Now there is something gnawing at your mind and you may as well out with it, because I'm not going to have you spoil this holiday with your papa and Uncle William." She dried her soapy hands on a towel, then gripped Lucy's shoulders and gave her a firm shake. "All right, my girl. The time is now. Out with it."

With a great shudder, Lucy began to weep. Dropping her dishcloth, she swooned in her mother's arms. "Don't you know who Patrick is, Mama? Why must you be so blind? How can you be? He's Papa's boy. His and Suzannah's."

Chapter 27

The kitchen was quiet except for the crackling of the fire in the stove. On the hearth, the sleeping hound clumped her tail as she pursued a rabbit through some canine dream world.

"Sit down, Lucy," sighed Helen, indicating one of the ladder-backed chairs against the wall. Lucy tried to say she was sorry, that she wished she hadn't spoken, that nothing really mattered. Helen shushed her. "You may as well know about your papa and me, though if my own mother ever had had to speak aloud of such things, I know she would have died of shame."

"I never meant to shame you, Mama. Forgive me."

"You haven't shamed me, Lucy. Don't you think I know about your papa and Suzannah? Why, from the first moment I laid eyes on Patrick, I knew he was half Shawn. Sometimes, when he first started coming up here, my mind played tricks on me. I thought he was Talley come back to give me comfort."

Thinking of her own loathing for Christian St. Clair, Eben's son, Lucy asked, "How could you stand the sight of him? I would have been so angry."

"Well, of course, you would have. But I'm not you, Lucy Shawn Kilmaine." As she talked, Helen moved about her kitchen, seeing to the preparations for dinner. Lucy watched her in wonderment. For the first time, she sensed that her mother was more than a mountain woman, bewitched and made a bit peculiar by solitude. She felt Helen's strength and courage and wisdom and began to understand her.

"Let me begin early," said Helen, "back when you were just a wee one. James and I always worked hard. We didn't get married thinking times would be easy for us. When we were building this house, I labored like a man and was happy to do it. We were building something together, and the doing of it gave us both joy. Back in those days, we were as close as any man and wife can be." Helen blushed and Lucy understood her meaning. "But bad year followed bad and no matter what we did, there never was enough. I don't think either of us wished it, but a bitterness began to grow up between us. Once it took root, there was no way we could stop it. Then, the summer when you were just six or so, Dr. Ransome from town paid a call one Sunday and told us how we could make a little extra money."

Helen dragged hard on the pulley ropes that lowered the clothes-drying rack from high up in the rafters over the fireplace. In the summertime, it was used only for kitchen laundry. She began draping the damp dishcloths over the dowels. "Dr. Ransome told us that Martin Hopewell's little girl had a condition that was aggravated every summer by the humidity and heat down in the Amoset River valley. We all knew how much Hopewell hated Yankees, but he was willing to let his girl come to live on the mountain for a few months every year until her sickly condition passed. We told Dr. Ransome we would think about it. You see, Lucy, the money Hopewell was offering to pay was more than enough for the child's keep.

But there was another factor. Although we, like everyone else around here, had good reason to return that man's hatred, we couldn't hold it against the child that her father was a brute. I even got to thinking Suzannah's sickness might not be the weather so much as the atmosphere in that big old house. Even then her mother was a strange woman. It seemed a sad sort of life for a young thing, so we told Dr. Ransome we would be willing to have her here."

When the rack was raised up high again, Helen opened a tall pine cupboard and, removing a broom she had made herself that spring, she began to sweep the kitchen's stone floor. The constant work was necessary, for if she had been forced to stop and look her daughter in the eye, she could not have spoken as honestly as she did.

"I liked Suzannah. It was a pleasure to have her around. I know you think ill of her now, but when you were little girls, you were very close. In fact, the only discipline that ever worked was to threaten you with separation. And Suzannah took to little Ingrid and Talley as if they were her own brother and sister.

"Because her own father was a harsh, unpredictable man, she attached herself to your papa. You and she would spend whole days tagging after him, trying to do men's work in the barn just to share his company. And he enjoyed it. I'd be in the vegetable garden or hanging out wash and I'd hear the three of you laughing or singing some crazy song. I remember feeling a twinge of envy because I wasn't much good at laughing. And even in my church-going days, I was never a singer."

Caught up in a memory of her own, Lucy interrupted. "I remember one year after Suzannah had been in Georgia for the winter. She'd gone to a circus and came up here with the most fantastic story of

clowns and dancing bears and a girl who did pirou-
ettes on the back of a running horse. All that summer,
she and I gave little circuses for Papa while he
worked in the barn." Lucy laughed. "Do you remember the time I fell off the horse? I was trying to stand
up on its back. I was convinced I could do it!"

"You two girls thought you could do anything in
those days. Especially Suzannah. I always knew your
father admired that in her, but by the time she was
eleven or twelve I noticed that the way he looked at
her was . . . different. I can't explain it, but I somehow knew that he was seeing her more like a grown-
up woman than a child. And I saw what that did to
him. How he hated himself for it."

The delicious aroma of roasting chicken began to
fill the kitchen. Helen checked it, ladling fat and
juices over the plump breast with a big wooden
spoon. "James got so he just didn't want Suzannah
around. There was a time or two when I heard him
speak to her in a tone of voice that must have broken
that little girl's heart. She never asked why he changed
toward her, but the question was there in those big
green eyes of hers. I wanted to talk to him about how
he was acting, but the words just wouldn't come. I
guess I was hoping that matters would right themselves naturally. And they did. The summer she was
twelve or thirteen, Martin Hopewell said Suzannah
had to stay in Amoset. After that we only saw her when
she could sneak away."

"Is that why papa didn't want me to work in the
mill?"

"No. I know he changed later, but when you
were sixteen and wanted to go down to the mill, all
he could think about was how much he hated what
Martin Hopewell and his kind stood for. In no time at
all, Amoset had changed from a quiet little trading

village to a small city, a place full of strangers where anything might happen to you. And neither your papa nor I wanted you caught up in a life that would make a wage-slave of you."

"You were right about Amoset. It was a fearful place." Lucy thought of McMahon, of poor Barbara Bolton, of Talley lying broken on the weaving room floor.

Helen wrinkled her brow and tapped her fingers on the tabletop thoughtfully. "I've thought a good deal about all this. As I see it, more than the danger troubled me. It's hard to know exactly why a body feels a given way. But it seemed like I could sense the times . . . moving out on me, so to speak." For the first time in their conversation, she turned to her daughter directly. Her expression was intent as she tried to explain. "Look at me, Lucy. I'm Helen Hildebrand. I married a Shawn, right enough, but I'm still a Hildebrand. And since long before the war, back in the days when these mountains were full of angry savages, Hildebrands have been farmers. We've always been folk who keep to our own places, our own ways. I was just a child when I married your papa. But I knew how to be a farmer's wife because I'd watched my mother and grandmother, same as they watched their mothers and grandmothers." She picked up the broom. "See this? Well, I made it last April, and I did it the same way Hildebrand women have always done it. I think I could have done it with my eyes closed, the work is so familiar to me."

"Comforting," added Lucy without thinking.

"That's right! You do understand. Lucy, you and your papa and Talley and Ingrid all took to the challenge of the city like it was some kind of adventurous game. You might have been afraid sometimes, but that didn't stop you. But I was afraid. I wanted to stay with the old, comfortable ways."

"But, Mama, you've been so alone since papa was elected! I've been as afraid for you as you were for me."

"There's nothing to be afraid of in these mountains, child. Your father knows that. So does Patrick. Do you know, Lucy, that little boy has been exploring the trails on Cooper's Mountain since he was five or six years old? He knows the mountain won't hurt him. He knows it just *is*, same as sky and water."

The mention of Patrick reminded both women of the reason for their discussion. Helen pushed her thin, grey hair back from her forehead, and turning her back on Lucy to stir a pot of fruit stewing on the fire, she said, "I don't know when your papa and Suzannah found each other again. But I do know that after they did, they parted for a long time out of conscience. I couldn't blame your papa for finding another woman. For years I was sick in my womb, and it hurt to be with him in the marriage way. You might say I drove him down the mountain to her."

"If he'd loved you, he wouldn't have done it," said Lucy, thinking bitterly of Eben.

"Lord, child, don't be so sure of things."

"It seems to me that when he betrayed you, Papa betrayed all of us. Even Talley."

"He's a strong man, Lucy, a man with powerful desires. He needs a woman in his bed. I know that, and you must accept it." Helen touched her daughter's cheek tenderly. "You're an unforgiving girl, Lucy."

"I'm not a girl at all, Mama. I'm a middle-aged woman and I know what's right and wrong."

Helen shook her head. "No you don't. You know what you don't like, but there's none of us who truly

knows right from wrong except the Lord Himself. No
matter what the preachers say, there's no single set of
rules to go by. You just have to try not to hurt anyone. That's all any of us can do."

"But they've hurt you."

"Only at first, and not very much even then. You
see, Lucy, I knew when to let go, just like the mountain knows when autumn must end and the winter begin. There was no way I could stop your papa and
Suzannah."

For a moment Helen stood gazing out the window across the clearing toward the road. "And in a
strange sort of way, they made it up to me. If it
hadn't been for Patrick . . . I remember the first day
I saw him. He was creeping along the edge of the
wood like a little fox cub. For just a moment, I was
sure it was your brother, Talley. Then I realized I
was dreaming like an addled old mountain woman,
and it made me so mad I took out after him." Helen
shook her head in disbelief at her own behavior.
"Lord, how I screeched at that child. It's a wonder he
ever came back. But he did. Praise God, he did."

After a moment's silence, Lucy said, "But, Mama,
all of this only proves that Delphia and Patrick . . ."

"They aren't in love, Lucy. Remember what I
said? If they were in love, there would be no keeping
those two apart." Lucy made a half-hearted effort to
argue this point, but Helen dismissed the subject. The
intimacy between them, more intense than any they
had known before, dissipated in the silence that followed. After a time, Lucy resumed her quiet work in
the kitchen. There was much she would have liked to
say, but Helen was no longer in the mood for confi-
dences.

Helen's stoic acceptance of her situation struck
Lucy as remarkable and yet, as she reconsidered it,

quite in keeping with her personality. A disposition Lucy had once seen as slightly off kilter, even a little harmlessly mad, she saw now as so wise and calm that it only seemed strange in contrast to the confusion of her own mind. A longing to share in this peace came over her, intense enough to make her stop what she was doing and stare straight ahead into nothing for some time.

"What's the matter, Lucy?" Helen asked, putting down the pewter jug she was rubbing to a dull sheen. "Is something wrong with you?"

Lucy didn't answer. She didn't even hear her mother's question. She was thinking of herself as an old woman with her sight almost gone, hobbling among strangers in a Boston street, tapping a cane ahead of her.

"Lucy! Wake up! You're dreaming on your feet." Helen's tone was sharp, maternal, the same she had used when Lucy was just thirteen, mooning over her chores. "I expect your papa any minute now. If the kitchen is a mess, there will be no rest for either of us. Move along, girl."

"I want to come back here, Mama." Lucy didn't think of what she was saying. The words took on a life of their own and poured out of her. "To live. I mean I want to leave the city and come home."

The polishing cloth dropped from Helen's hand. "Oh, Lucy."

Chapter 28

James Shawn was pleased to hear of his daughter's decision. For most of his first day home, it was the major subject of discussion when he and his brother William were not reminiscing. After so many years apart, the brothers felt a bit awkward with one another, and talk of Lucy and her sudden plan to return to Cooper's Mountain eased the early tension between them.

Upon hearing at dinner that her mother's return to Boston would be temporary, Delphia tossed down her napkin in dismay. "What am I supposed to do? Live up here like a hermit?"

"No one has mentioned you, Delphia," said Lucy quietly, not looking at her daughter. "You may stay at the house on Moon Street as long as you wish, of course, and continue your apprenticeship."

"Mother! I can't work like a slave for Madame and tend to the boarding house as well. You ask too much of me."

"She asks nothing of you," corrected James. "She never has. Perhaps it would make life more pleasant for us all if you thought of someone other than yourself for a change, Delphia. Your mother has made a decision that makes her happy and gives Nana great joy, as well."

"But I don't understand why!"

Lucy stopped James before he could admonish her further. Delphia's face wore an expression Lucy knew too well. Her feelings were hurt. Her pride had been assaulted. She was the eternal innocent wrongly accused. The next stage would be angry self-protection. For Delphia as much as the family gathered at the dinner table, Lucy wanted to avoid the tears and accusations. "She should know everything, Papa, else she'll fret needlessly."

"Know what?"

"Delphie, my eyes are bad and getting worse."

"Well, you never wear your spectacles. You shouldn't be so vain."

"They would make no difference."

"How do you know?"

"I'm going blind, Delphia. Don't ask me how I know. I know."

The girl opened her mouth to speak, but as quickly shut it. She sat for a time in stunned and sullen silence. Watching her, James struggled to control his temper. He loved his granddaughter, but knew her to be a spoiled and petulant child who had always held her own will and wishes before those of others. James had thought she would outgrow this extreme self-centeredness. But she was sixteen years old, and it was clearly the foundation of her personality. And not an attractive quality. He could not resist thinking what he would have done if she were his own child and not separated from his control by a generation. Delphia's sulky disposition needed a firm hand, not coddling. But Lucy seemed incapable of disciplining her daughter, and James supposed it was because she felt some guilt for the fact that the girl was without a father.

Several days later, James and William walked to the lookout on the western side of Cooper's Mountain, accompanied by Frost, the hound. They talked about Lucy and Delphia, Ingrid, and even Talleyrand. It was important to James that William have some sense of who Talley had been. He described a boy with an impudent tongue whose joy in living had been so extraordinary that even now, after fifteen years, his death did not seem quite real to James. As he talked, his throat constricted and he was overcome by old sorrow. He wanted to deny it all, to cry out that Patrick Paine was his other wonderful son, a boy Talley himself would have admired. Instead, he bit back his grief, and for a time walked beside his brother in silence.

On either side of the deeply worn path, the woods were dense and green with summer growth. Although the lookout was a favorite retreat for the Shawns and the trail often used, that summer it was overgrown and wild in places. William stopped and looked about him.

"Everything else has changed, but the forest is the same." As he continued walking, he said, "When I was a boy, during the first months after I left Cooper's Mountain, I used to dream of this place and all the paths I used to follow. For a while there, it seemed like every night I dreamed I was running up to the lookout or down into the north valley where Grandma's house used to be. There never was a sadder cabin boy than I. Why, I even dreamed of the path to Edythe Whittington's. Whatever became of her, James?"

James told his brother how he had found the old

woman dead in the cave where she had kept Martin Hopewell prisoner for half a year.

"She was mad. The mountain made her that way, I think."

"I've known the sea to have the same effect." William told the story of a young man who had come aboard his ship some years before in San Francisco. "He was running away from something or someone, I suppose. I took him for an Easterner from the way he talked, but, of course, he never told me. Joshua Bolton was his name. I believe he fancied himself a poet. After he went overboard, we found a dozen scraps of paper under his mattress scribbled over with words and rhyming phrases. I should have known something was wrong, the way he used to stand at the bow whenever he wasn't about his duties, staring at the sea with the most forlorn expression." William shook his head. "There's a loneliness at sea that's a little like the mountain. You can't escape it. You can't pretend you're anything but small and insignificant."

Catching a whiff of rabbit, Frost bayed furiously and leaped into the forest. The woods, primevally silent a moment earlier, were suddenly rackety with crying birds, their noisy flapping wings, and Frost's hysterical yapping and crashing through the undergrowth. William laughed loudly, and the sound was a joy to James. Stopping where he was, he whirled and threw his arms about his brother.

"I am so glad to see you, William. My heart is overjoyed. I thought surely you were lost by now. Why did you stop writing?"

William shook his head. "I don't know. I guess I just thought it didn't make much sense anymore. We were like strangers."

"Well, now that you're back, I pray you'll stay, Willy. I've missed you."

"I'll be honest with you, James. About a year ago, in Manila, I had a bout of fever that might have killed me. There's whole weeks gone from my memory, weeks when I sweated out my guts and begged to die. After that, I started thinking I might sell the *Defiant* and come back to the mountain."

"There's always room for you here."

All at once, the forest opened up and they were standing at the rocky edge of the mountain. Before them stretched a heavily forested deep blue valley, and beyond it to the west for as far as they could see, the mountains rose one behind the other like waves in a great sea.

"Helen will be glad to have you," said James.

But William shook his head. "I didn't say I would stay, only that I had been thinking about it. And, James, it's not the life for me. I've been at sea too long. And I miss my lady something fearful."

"You never told me. . . ."

"My ship. The first night I stayed at Lucy's, I knew I could never leave the *Defiant* permanently. I stood at the window half the night worrying about her. Since then, hardly an hour has gone by that she's not in my thoughts."

In spite of his sudden glum spirits, James laughed a little. "You sound like a man in love."

"I wouldn't know about that. In all these years, there's been no woman in my life. Ah, from time to time I've bedded a comely wench from the wharf-side, but apart from that . . . I've left the loving to you, James." William grinned slyly.

"And what is that supposed to mean?"

"Patrick Paine." Before James could disturb the honest moment with denials, William waved his hand dismissively. "I knew he was a Shawn the moment I saw him. It's a wonder to me that everyone doesn't know. You ought to tell him, James. He honors you as no other man."

James sighed and stared out over the horizon.

"I make no judgment, James. But it would be fairer. . . ."

"Would it? I wish I could be sure of that. I love that boy and I love his mother. But he's only just grown out of his childhood. How can I explain that while I love him and Suzannah, I also love Helen?"

"If you'll forgive my saying so, Jamie, you show your love in a strange way. Perhaps another woman is understandable, not even out of the ordinary. But politics! Going away and giving your life to that is like selling your soul to the Devil himself. I will never understand."

James smiled at the hyperbole. William had a point. "There's much about the business I don't care for. I have days, even weeks, when I hate the damn city so much I want to throw away everything and come back to Cooper's Mountain."

"But you don't."

"There's a great deal to be done, Willy. Every day the gulf grows wider between the dream our fathers fought for in the Revolution and the reality of crowded cities and filthy slums. The country's filling up with immigrant folk who've no idea of what America is. But they've heard of the dream, and they want a part of it. I mean to see they have it, and the only way I can do it is by being a senator."

"Or governor."

James shrugged. "It's all talk, Willy. All talk. My name's been coming up in that connection for years, but I doubt anything will come of it. I favor the immigrants and the laboring class, and that makes me unpopular with some of the most powerful men in the state. They'll make sure I'm never governor."

Deep in their own thoughts, the brothers looked out over the valley and distant mountains. It was a content silence, for there were few secrets between them now. The sense of being new to each other, strangers in all but blood, had entirely disappeared. Unspoken was the shared knowledge that when William Shawn sailed his lady out of Boston harbor, he would never come home again. These would be their only days together, and they must live them with intensity. There was no time for deceit or concealment. For William, the memory of his towheaded little brother and of the mountain had been restored like an old painting he had purposely ignored for many years. Now that he knew the land could never satisfy him as the sea did, he could indulge his memories of home and dwell on them without the nagging fear that perhaps, on that long ago day when he slung a duffel across his boyish shoulders, he had made a grave mistake. James was relieved to know his brother was alive and healthy and was thankful for their time together. Paradoxically, the hours he was spending with William were strengthening his commitment to the land and the aspirations of his Yankee family. As he had sometimes in the early years in Boston, James felt himself to be part of a great movement of ideas and people and fortunate to be alive.

For Delphia, such thoughts were constitutionally impossible. And Patrick had no time for any idea that did not relate to his beloved, so consumed was he by his unrequited love for her. He had stayed away from the Shawn homestead for as long as he could bear. Delphia's cold and sullen manner on the trip from Boston had hurt him more than pride would let him show, and he had intended by his absence to make her come to him. But when ten lonely days had passed without her, he forgot his pride and climbed the mountain.

He found Delphia in the low meadow not far from the farmhouse. At the bottom of the slope amidst tall wheat grass and parasols of Queen Anne's Lace, there were half a dozen beehives which she had learned to tend as a little girl. Patrick knew that of all the chores on the farm, this was the only one that gave Delphia any pleasure. She was not afraid of the bees, and though she wore a bee-veil, she worked among the creatures with the arrogance of bare hands, certain they would not sting her. Beside her on the ground was the ancient bee-smoker she used to make them docile. Before announcing himself, Patrick watched her as she worked the bellows, enclouding each white hive. He liked her industriousness. Her quick, decisive motions charmed him and he felt privileged to know a secret part of Delphia Kilmaine, one unknown to her Boston friends, before whom she must always be fashionable and languidly feminine. He found so much to admire in Delphia that he realized he no longer could keep his feelings a secret from her. It would be better to learn that she could never care for him than to continue to harbor the pain of secret love. She was scraping the honey from a comb into a bucket when he called her name.

"Stay back, Patrick. They're restless today." As she returned a comb to its place, he heard her mutter, "Damn." Quickly, she pulled her hand away from the hive. "I've been stung."

A moment later, she showed him the place on her wrist where a small welt was rising.

"I'm not as immune as I used to be," she commented.

Holding her wrist as carefully as if it had been

broken, he wanted to kiss the dainty little puncture and suck the poison out. Instead, he told her, "You need a compress."

"It doesn't matter. Anyway," she blew on the sting, "I don't want to go back to the house. I'm so tired of my family I groan just thinking of them."

Patrick smiled. As far back as he could remember, Delphie was always at odds with her mother or grandfather. "What's the trouble now?"

"Oh, Mama says she's going blind and . . ."

"Delphie, that's terrible!"

"Well, yes, if it's true. Which I doubt. But she hasn't seen a doctor, and she won't use her spectacles. So I don't have much sympathy. But that's not the worst of it. Now she's got the idea in her mind to come back here to live."

Horrified, Patrick thought of Boston without his darling Delphia.

"I'm having no part of it," she said, not noticing the look on his face. "I'll stay on Moon Street with Grandfather."

"What about the boarders?"

"That's one piece of good news. We won't have them anymore. Thank heaven. No more hordes of placard-bearing bloomer girls!" She giggled at her spite. "Don't look so mortally offended, Patrick. I believe in rights as much as anyone, but just now my own concern me most."

They plopped themselves on the ground and lay back in the high meadow grass, squinting into the bright sky. While Patrick thought of how to phrase his declaration of love, he was conscious of the noise of insects rustling the grass about him. Across his field of vision, a large bird glided on an air current, its golden head bright in the sunlight.

"Delphie, an eagle! There!" He remembered from

reading *The Odyssey* that eagles were thought by the Greeks to be omens of good fortune sent by the gods. He hoped this meant Delphia would respond to his proposal the way he dreamed she would. When he was finished at Harvard, they could be married and live in Amoset. He'd build her the biggest, finest house and make sure that she had whatever she wanted.

"Delphie . . ."

"Has your cousin Alexander Duffy come back to Marivale?" Something indefinable in Delphia's voice froze Patrick's declaration in his throat. He swallowed and inexplicably, foolishly, humiliatingly, his eyes filled up with tears. Delphia, her gaze still fixed on the eagle, her thoughts entirely concerned with herself, continued. "Do you suppose I'll ever have a chance to meet him again? I mean, he's going so far away and all. Germany might as well be the end of the world. I suppose he'll be gone for years. Could you arrange another meeting, Patrick?" When he didn't answer, she jabbed him in the ribs, a little harder than playfulness required. "What's the matter, Patrick? You look so funny."

"Nothing," he muttered. Sitting up, he angrily tore up a handful of grass and tossed it away.

"Don't fib to me, Patrick Paine. My family's been out of sorts with me all this holiday, and now you are, too. What in heaven's name is the matter with all of you?"

"You don't love me at all, do you?" His face was crimson with embarrassment, but he had to know.

"Certainly I do. We've known each other all our lives. You're like a brother or a cousin to me."

"I mean the other kind of love."

"Oh, Patrick! Do you want to spoil everything?"

"Are you in love with him?"

"Him?" Now it was she who blushed. Getting to her feet, she dusted the grass from her skirt.

"You know who I mean," he declared, catching her arm as she started to walk away. "Are you in love with Alexander Duffy?"

"I hardly know the man."

"But he's been on your mind since the night I took you to meet him. He's made you sullen and bad-tempered. It's because of him you didn't come down to visit me."

She wrenched away from him, gathered up her bee-keeping equipment and hurried breathlessly toward home, declaring, "I don't have to listen to your insults, Patrick Paine. Why should I come and visit you? Don't I have other things to occupy my time? And don't you have two perfectly adequate feet at the end of those gangling limbs of yours? After all, you're the one who loves this mountain so much you talk about it day and night!"

He kept pace with her. A moment before he had loved her to distraction. Now he hated her and saw all her faults. "You think of no one but yourself, Delphie. You don't know the first thing about kindness or affection. If you're as nasty to your family as you are to me, I don't wonder they've been cross."

"How dare you! Do you think that because you're Patrick Paine I should fall all over myself with gratitude because you love me? Do you think I'd be satisfied with life in horrid little Amoset, seeing the same damned mountains, the same boring provincial people? Do you think . . . ?"

"I think I have been a fool."

She turned and raised her eyebrows. "Aren't you coming? If you expect me to beg . . ." At last she seemed to realize the effect of her harsh words. "Look, Pat, I'm sorry. But I can't force myself to love you.

You wouldn't want that. I don't want to hurt you, and I'm sorry if I did. You know I always speak before I think." She grinned, trying to tease him back into a good humor. "Oh, come on! Don't take it all so seriously. I'm glad you love me, but truly, the feeling will pass. We're friends, you and I."

He shook his head.

"What's that supposed to mean, Patrick?"

"We're not friends anymore."

"Stuff and nonsense, you can't just throw away years and years."

"I don't like you anymore, Delphie. Before, when I heard you criticized, I was always your defender. I thought I knew you better than anyone. Now I see I knew you less."

Delphia's pretty face twisted angrily. But it was her turn to be hurt, and for once she could not pretend otherwise. She bit her lip to keep from crying as her eyes filled with tears. "You aren't being fair," she whispered.

"I'm being fair to myself. That's something you should appreciate. Good-bye, Delphie." Disregarding the grief that just a few moments earlier would have had the power to make him say and do anything, Patrick walked away.

"Damn you, Patrick Paine," she sobbed. "Damn you!"

He could not be sure if he was about to laugh or cry. He only knew that he must keep on walking away from her. He heard her call his name several times more, he heard her curses and her crying, but he did not turn. As the wheeling eagle dipped and glided out along the wide horizon, Patrick found the forest path and ran for home.

Chapter 29

After running a mile or so, Patrick stopped. Although he was accustomed to strenuous exercise, his heaving chest ached as if he had just run a mile in record time. He fell against the hillside and closed his eyes, drawing breath into him in long, painful gulps.

Delphia had done this to him! It was not enough that she had driven a barb through his heart and fallen in love with his best friend, but she had somehow managed to wreck his physical health as well. When his breathing became normal again, he still felt weak and so sick at heart that he had no desire to move. He lay staring at the sky, watching it change from blue to a purplish grey as the twilight deepened.

Had there ever been a man more miserable, more cheated of his heart's desire? The years stretched ahead of him like a line of uninterrupted track across a wasteland. He knew that no matter what, he would never be happy again. He closed his eyes and turned face down against the ground. But it did no good to close his eyes, for he couldn't shut away his memories of Delphia. In his mind, he saw her face, her hair, her hands, her body as clearly as if she were standing before him. All were vivid and brought him more pain.

He loved her. He hated her. He was a fool. Masochistically, he recalled every moment of their visit with Alexander. He read innuendo into each gesture and expression in his friend's conversation, and his spirits fell so low that for a while he thought Alexander had never been a true friend. He had always been laughing at Patrick behind his hands. These thoughts did not continue long, however, before Patrick saw that they were illogical and only the product of his grief. Alex was his friend-and had always been so. It was Delphia who had connived to make him suffer.

He had never really been blind to her selfishness, but he had disregarded it because so much else about the girl enchanted him. She kept him on edge, electrifying their moments together with her sharp wit and the way she had of never giving an inch to anyone unless she really wanted to. Patrick had known plenty of girls his own age. What he disliked in them was the wispy way they smiled and curtsied and sighed a "yes" before and after everything he said. Because he had worked hard for Delphia's approval, it seemed to mean much more than anyone else's.

He grabbed a fistful of grass and yanked it out by the roots. And then another and another. He would have denuded the hillside if it would have helped him vent his anger. Instead, he was left with dirty hands and a feeling of frustration so intense that it almost overcame his hurt. He jumped to his feet and started back up the path toward the Shawns' cabin. He'd tell her a thing or two. She couldn't reject him and expect him to take it. He'd hardly gone more than a hundred feet before he stopped. He wouldn't crawl to her. However much Delphia had hurt him, he wouldn't let her have the satisfaction of denying further pleas. Muttering to himself words he'd heard boys in the Gully use, he turned around and headed home again.

In summer, dusk lingered on Cooper's Mountain as if the light itself were reluctant to leave the forests and meadows. Twilight was the softest time of day, the time when birds and animals appeared from nests and lairs to sing a final, joyful chorus or begin the night's excursions. In spite of everything, Patrick's spirits were eventually soothed by the evening. On a whim, he left the path and set out overland toward the long pasture behind the Hopewell stables. Though the mountain belonged to him as much as it did to the animals and birds, he could not venture into the pathless woods without concentrating hard on the subtle directional signs the wilderness gave him. The lore of Cooper's Mountain was full of stories of grown men and accomplished woodsmen who had been lost in the forest. No matter what his sorrow, he would not add his name to that ignoble list. For a time, he did not think much of Delphia. Sometimes he would be surprised by the heaviness, like an undigested supper, in the bottom of his stomach and then remember her and everything he'd lost that day. But for the most part, he was comforted by the solitude around him.

Once his mother had asked him what it was about Cooper's Mountain that he loved so much. Though he had tried, he hadn't been able to answer her. It was more than the wildness of the place and the varieties of animal life that abounded. Even as a little boy, he had found in it another world, a place so different from his own troubled home that it could make him forget for a while all the hateful things that passed between the adults in his life. Wandering on the mountain as a child, he hadn't thought of how much his Uncle Valentine frightened him, of the ugly smell of his grandmother, or of his great white slug of a grandfather. Once he tried to tell his mother that there was a kind of healing magic in the mountain, but she had laughed at him. It had not been her intention to seem unkind, but Patrick had known better than to explain again. Years later, in his young teens, he had dared to say the same thing to Senator Shawn, though. And he had understood.

The forest thinned. Ahead through the trees, Patrick could see the long pasture and the stable. Beyond, still lighted by the remnants of the westering sun, were the topmost eaves of the great stone house that was his home. He didn't want to go home. His mother would take one look at his gloomy expression and know that something had happened. She would ask a dozen questions until she got an answer that satisfied her. It was even possible, Patrick did not like to think this but he knew it was likely, that she could ease the truth right out of him. If he had to tell her what happened, it would be mortifying. His mother was wonderful and he loved her passionately sometimes; nevertheless, she was his mother and Patrick was a proud young man.

An idea occurred to him. As a boy, his Uncle Eben had built a tree house in one of the big old trees at the edge of the wood. To postpone his inevitable homecoming, Patrick decided to find that tree and climb it. He wasn't sure where it was, for when his uncle had mentioned it when Patrick was seven or eight years old, his mother had shushed him. She said the tree house had fallen down and been carted away. Still, he thought now, there must be something left of it. Even a few boards would do. It would be a kind of retreat, somewhere he could sit alone and think.

He stopped to scan the open woods for a likely tree. There was one not far from him, and beside it stood a man and woman. His mother and James

Shawn! He neither called to them nor walked in their direction. Something made him stand still. Then, without questioning his motives, he slipped behind the trunk of an oak. Taking care that he should not be seen, he peered at the couple.

Their heads were bent close together. Across the silent woods, Patrick heard Suzannah's throaty laughter. It sounded different to him in a way he did not care for. He watched her reach up and stroke James Shawn's cheek, then heard her laugh again in that troublesome way. He was going to look away when she did something he could not believe. Suzannah slipped her hand behind Shawn's head and drew his face down close to hers. James Shawn's arms encircled her waist, their bodies swayed together, and they kissed passionately for a very long moment.

In that same extended moment, Patrick's mind boiled over with thoughts of Shawns and Paines. He was sick to his stomach, too ill to move. He could only stare at the two adults he cared for most, feeling a sick loathing grow in him like a sullen storm. His eyes squeezed shut. He pressed his forehead against the rutted bark of the old oak. As they had before, inescapable visions filled his mind. He sank down to the ground, knuckling his eyes until he saw stars, but the image of their illicit embrace remained encircled by constellations.

He didn't go home until after dark, and then he tried to sneak into his room by using the back staircase. But Suzannah heard him and intercepted him in the hall. She was dressed in a plain wrapper of russet silk that showed the outlines of her body in a way that Patrick had not noticed before. Her hair was long and loose and where once he would have thought it beautiful, it now appeared slutty.

"Where have you been? It's after nine o'clock, and I've been worried to death."

He tried to push past her.

"Well?" She stopped him with her hand.

"I've been on the mountain. I didn't know what time it was."

"You mean to tell me you can't tell the difference between night and day, young man? What do they teach you at Harvard, anyway?" Her face was flushed, and he knew she was very angry. That meant she had been truly worried. Normally he would have been repentant, not wishing to cause her pain, but now he was glad she worried. A woman like Suzannah Hopewell Paine deserved to suffer. "Answer me, Patrick. Where have you been?"

"I told you. . . ."

"You've been at the Shawns?" Suzannah sighed and pushed the heavy hair back from her face. "I suppose you've been with Delphia. Patrick, son, we must talk about that girl. . . ."

"I'm tired," he said over his shoulder as he went into his room. He started to close the door.

"I'm not through with you, young man." She went to his bed and sat down.

Patrick knew there was no use trying to get away from her. Suzannah was not easily intimated by anyone, least of all her son. And when she wanted something, whether goods, services or information, she generally got it. He was terribly weary and so heavy of heart that he thought he might die from the feeling. But he stood before her, prepared to endure her lecture if that was what was required to get rid of her.

"I really don't know Delphia, Patrick. From what I've seen, I like her well enough. But you shouldn't be spending so much time with her. I know you see her often in Boston."

"How do you know that? Who told you?" His questions accused her, and she looked a little confused for a moment.

"Her grandfather mentioned it. The senator."

"When?"

Again Suzannah appeared uncertain, but she regained herself so quickly that only Patrick, fresh with the knowledge of their kisses, would have noticed the slip. "I see him frequently, Patrick. You know that. He represents the people of this valley, and I am on half a dozen citizen committees. . . ."

He laughed.

"Stop that!" she cried. Standing up, she slapped him suddenly across the cheek. "I don't know what your insolence means, but I can tell you this, my friend, I do not like it. I've told you that you see too much of the Kilmaine girl, and I don't want it to continue. Is that clear?"

His face stung and he rubbed it without answering.

"Patrick?" Again, he saw that look of uncertainty and, mixed with it, regret. "If I hurt you, I'm sorry. But I had to get your attention." They looked at one another. "Patrick, you do understand about Delphia, don't you?"

"She thinks she's in love with Alex." He sat down on the bench at the foot of his bed and began to unlace his boots. Suzannah knelt beside him, helping to pull them off.

"It's for the best, Patrick. Believe me."

He looked into her eyes, catching a quick reflection of himself in their depths. All at once, he understood everything that had confused him in the past.

The love of Cooper's Mountain. His kinship with the Shawn family. His resemblance to James Shawn.

"He's my father." He spoke without hesitancy or doubt.

Suzannah said nothing. Slowly, as if it hurt to move, she got to her feet and crossed to the window overlooking the side yard. In the distance, the city of Amoset was lit up like a busy metropolis. While Patrick went into the next room and undressed in silence, she stared out, wondering what to say now that the moment she had dreaded for almost twenty years had arrived. "How did you find out?" she asked finally.

"Everyone says I look like him," he said as he came back in from the dressing room.

"I know. But I thought you accepted that as . . . chance." Patrick was standing in the middle of the room in one of the long nightshirts he had despised all his life. As soon as she was gone, she knew he would strip it off and sleep naked. Thinking that, she feared her heart would break. Her son had become a man, yet to her he would always be the brave little boy who had stood up to Hiram White on her behalf, who had tried to protect her from Valentine. A little fellow, complaining about nightshirts. "Who told you?"

"I saw you in the woods today." He sneered. "You were kissing."

His anger had a quality of quiet intensity that drew her respect, and she feared it could not continue long without doing some permanent damage to their relationship. She had to make him understand before she lost him forever. "I won't deny that James is your father, Patrick. If you had asked me five or ten years ago, I might have. But now you are a man, and I believe you should know the truth. James and I have talked about it many times, but we never knew how to go about telling you. We never wanted you to find out this way."

"I'll bet you didn't."

"Don't take that tone with me, Patrick. I'm your mother, and nothing I've done can change that or the love I feel for you."

"I'm a bastard. Like Christian."

"That's not true. You were born in wedlock."

"You betrayed my father. My father, or should I say Travis Paine, loved you, and you cheated him. No wonder he went away and left you. I wish I could."

"You don't mean that. You're angry and hurt. That's understandable. But nothing can change all we've meant to each other. And as to Travis, you can't know what passed between us. We never loved each other, Patrick. Your grandparents forced us to marry. We were trapped. Try to understand, Patrick, that when a marriage is like a trap it does strange and . . . evil things to men and women. Travis beat me. He hurt me in a terrible way, and afterward he hated himself. He knew we could never live together again and so he went away. Sometimes the only thing two people can do is part. That was the way it was with us."

"You were an adultress."

Suzannah began to cry. The tears slipped down her cheeks. She kept on trying to explain, but with every breath her sense of futility grew. She knew her boy well. Like her, he could be obstinate in his beliefs. He had turned against her and it would take more than words to bring him around. But she had to try. He was her darling. Because of him, her life was more than just a day-to-day existence.

"I have loved James since I was very young. I know it seems wrong to you now, but trust me. When you're older you'll understand that men and women don't always need a marriage ceremony to sanctify their love. We've been together a long time, Patrick, and we love each other as husbands and wives do when their union is good. We care for each other, we respect one another. . . ."

"What about poor Helen? Who cares for her? Do you respect her?"

"I'd never hurt her, darling. Neither would James. We are very careful."

Patrick laughed. "But not quite careful enough. You two, sneaking about in the woods like a couple of children! How could you?"

"Patrick . . ."

"If you weren't so old, I might not feel such disgust." He knew how to hurt her; she cringed and shied away. "I saw you kissing and touching him, and it made me sick. I never saw such an indecent display from two grown people. Two *old* people. If I hadn't been so nauseated, I would have laughed out loud."

"You've been hurt. It's natural to be unkind when you're hurt." She wondered to whom she addressed the words. Was she trying to convince herself? "Tomorrow, you'll feel calmer. We can talk then."

"I don't want to talk to you tomorrow or any other day. I'm not some recalcitrant worker who can be persuaded with words. I know you, Mother. I know how cunning you can be. You think after tonight I'll get used to the idea of you and James Shawn, but I tell you now that I never will."

"Think of James. He's your father. He loves you." She tried to touch him, but he pushed her away so violently that she almost fell against the dresser. Stunned, she could only stare at him.

"Well, do you believe me now?"

She did, she did. Crying out, she fled from the room.

The next morning, he disappeared before dawn. After two weeks time, a letter came. It said that he was gone for good. He had shipped out aboard the *Defiant*, bound for the Caribbean and the South Seas. As far as he was concerned, he had no mother and Suzannah had no son.

Chapter 30

"It's still snowing, Mama, but I think I should go down to the church anyway. Otherwise, I'll never finish the decorations before it gets dark." Louisa Duffy stood in the doorway, her arms laden with aromatic evergreens and sprigs of crimson holly berries.

Margaret glanced at the clock. "It *is* getting late. You'll have to hurry." As Louisa turned to go, she added, "Take a lantern out of the pantry, just in case. And ask May to fill it with oil. But be careful. Let's not burn the church down on Christmas Eve. It makes the Lord so very cross. Not to mention your father."

Suzannah, seated in the corner stringing cranberries, laughed.

"Well, that's a pleasant sound! I don't believe I've heard you laugh all week."

Simon McMahon came into the room, his arms full of firewood. "Do you want me to lay the fire, Mrs. Duffy?"

For an instant, Margaret looked irritable. But as quickly as the expression had marred her pleasant features, it disappeared. "Where have you been, Si-

mon? This room is as cold as Methuselah's toes." She
smiled to take the sharpness from her words.

"Ma sent me to the Gully for that special cider
the vicar favors, ma'am."

"I thought you did that yesterday."

"No, ma'am." He knelt on the hearth and began
to lay a fire in the grate. At twenty-six, Simon McMahon bore a remarkable resemblance to both his
mother and his father. He had May's little reedy body
and the same mass of dark curly hair that stuck out
from his head as if it were electrified. But his face
resembled his father's, the features pinched all together in the middle like an apple doll's. Bigelow
Duffy had told his wife that such faces were the
result of cousins marrying cousins for generation after
generation. Margaret knew nothing of this. She suspected it was one of her husband's many theories,
based on observation and opinion and having no
scientific basis whatsoever. For an Episcopalian
priest, Bigelow Duffy was an uncommonly scientific
fellow. From time to time, it had occurred to Margaret that he encouraged his son in mathematics to
satisfy a secret longing of his own.

Margaret's reverie was broken by the rumble of
logs being thrown into the woodbox.

"Do you need me for anything else, ma'am?" Simon never looked at Margaret directly when he
addressed her. He had a way of staring at his shuf-
fling feet that over the years had worn down her patience to a thin line.

"I'm sure your mother and the cook need help,
Simon."

"Yes, ma'am." He ducked his head and hurried
out. Margaret watched him, frowning again. When
she heard the door to the servant's hall close, she
turned to Suzannah. "That boy . . ."

"He must be close to thirty," Suzannah observed dryly.

"I really used to believe that if we gave him a second chance he might make something of himself. But I confess that now I have most sincere doubts. I truly do. Bigelow says my aspirations were unreasonable to begin with."

"I agree with my brother-in-law. I remember telling you years ago . . ."

Margaret shook her finger at Suzannah. "Spare me the 'I-told-you-so's,' my dear. Despite every effort, I have failed in my quest for perfection. I admit it freely. I've made mistakes and, alas, Simon is one of them."

"Why don't you send him away? The Gully is thriving. It's become a small city, and I'm sure Simon could find work."

Margaret shook her head. Taking a long string of cranberries from Suzannah, she carefully laid it across the branches of the fir tree that occupied one corner of the rosy room. "I couldn't do that to May, Suzannah. Simon may be a wretched specimen by our standards, but he is her only child and she loves him to distraction. That's part of the problem, I suppose. Bigelow says mothers and sons. . . ." She stopped abruptly and covered her mouth with her hand. "Suzannah, darling girl, I am so sorry. I spoke entirely without thinking. It's my worst fault."

Suzannah reminded herself that at forty-one, there was nothing to be gained from crying. On the contrary, tears swelled and disfigured her pretty face and the puffiness remained for half a day or more as a public testament. And of what use were tears? Patrick had been gone for eighteen months, and except for that one letter saying he had shipped out aboard the *Defiant*, there had been no word from him. To change the subject, she asked Margaret, "When do you expect Alexander?"

"He's coming on the late coach. In time for the midnight service, I hope. Bigelow will be cross as tacks if he misses it. I fear the boy has filled up on German philosophy in Berlin. Alexander now thinks he's quite beyond the 'pastoral simplicities' of Christianity," Margaret snapped. Then she sighed, looking deeply unhappy. "Remember how easy it used to be, Suzannah? I wish I hadn't passed my time. I'd like to start again and have the joy of those childhood years. Sons and daughters are such a trial as they mature."

Suzannah held out another cranberry chain. "Louisa is a lovely girl. She'll find a husband in New York City and furnish you with all the grandchildren you can manage!"

Margaret threw up her hands in horror. "You have no idea how I suffer from her! She can be as sweet as butter, but when it comes time to plan her spring wardrobe or discuss allowances, I can barely stand her company. The girl thinks we are made of money! I tell her again and again that her father is a modest country priest, and she repeats just as often and twice as loudly that if she doesn't have the perfect fabrics in the most *au courant* styles, she will fear to set foot out of her Aunt Solicity's house. You would think New York was Paris, for goodness sake!" Margaret clicked her gums noisily, an irritating habit she had recently developed after having several painful molars removed. Standing back from the Christmas tree, she declared, "Another five or six days and we might have enough decorations for this monster!"

Suzannah laughed again. "What's got into you, Margaret? I've never known you to be so out of sorts at Christmas. I thought this was your favorite holiday."

For an answer, her sister-in-law sighed voluminously. Sinking into a chair near the fire, she gazed into the flames.

Suzannah continued with her work, looking up from time to time to watch Margaret's moody expression. Suzannah made a pretty picture, sitting with a basket of cranberries in the lap of her velvet costume the color of bronze. Her dark head was tilted a little to one side, contemplatively, and the late afternoon firelight brightened her skin with gold. In other Christmas seasons, Patrick, Christian, Louisa and Alexander had gathered the fruit themselves, and it was they who had done the stringing up, sprawled on the floor before the nursery fire. Cranberry stringing had been a party then, and not a tedious duty. There had been cups of hot chocolate and potent fruit cake and gales of hilarious laughter. And lovely profound silences, too. But it was the laughter that hurt Suzannah most to remember.

When she thought of Patrick, she always imagined him laughing. He'd been such a bubbling youth, incandescent with life and long-legged Yankee spunk. Without trying, she could recall a dozen special times between them when his smile had brightened her life. Without him, she moved through a colorless world. Even James' love was not enough to make her happy now. They had been together just a few days earlier in Boston, but it had been a melancholy meeting despite their abiding passion. They spent it reminiscing about their lost children.

Suzannah had gone to Boston on the excuse of making a Christmas purchase for Louisa Duffy. Though Amoset was a large, thriving city in 1855 with a population of well over thirty thousand, and close to seventy-five thousand if the Gully was in-

cluded, it was not the place to buy *haute couture* for
a young woman about to meet fashionable society for
the first time. Suzannah went to Jordan Marsh, Boston's foremost department store, and purchased a hat
that her niece had admired in the spring edition of
the *Ladies Quarterly*. It was an elaborate confection
of creamy imported straw, pastel veiling and exquis-
itely wrought straw and silk flowers. Only a very
young woman with Louisa's delicate coloring could
wear such a hat. Back at her hotel, Suzannah tried it
on and was horrified to see how old it made her look.

Forty-one. Was it possible? The truth was in the
mirror. Yet in so many ways, Suzannah knew
herself to be unchanged from the girl she had been.
She could still experience fear at the sight of the
purple nimbus piling up in the sky behind Cooper's
Mountain, and certain cold, starry nights filled her
with the same awe they always had. Even her love
for James had not changed much over the years. She
loved him neither more nor less. He was a given part
of her life, the bedrock of it all.

Her times with James were often planned occasions
with a hint of intrigue about them. Some years back,
they had discovered that it was possible to meet in
her hotel room when she visited Boston, so long as
they took care to be discreet. Had their liaison been
discovered by the management of The Elizabeth Hotel, she would have been ordered out and the resulting gossip might have damaged or even ruined
James' career. But they enjoyed the zest of danger.
The sense of the forbidden added energy to their
conversation as well as their physical intimacy, an excitement that would have been impossible had they
been married and living together every day.

Suzannah was now legally a widow. Early in
1855, she had received a letter from California. The

message, clumsily written, came from a frontier lawyer in a place called Mineral King. The lawyer's
scrawl had been difficult to read, but she had been
able to understand it well enough. A man named Travis Paine had been killed in a landslide in a remote
mountain area. Among his personal effects were the
name and address of his wife. The news stunned
Suzannah. All the hatred she once had felt for her
young husband had long since dissipated. As she read
of his death, unable even to imagine his features
clearly, let alone grieve, she felt guilty. Widowhood
made little difference in her life. She had once
confessed to Margaret that she enjoyed being a scan-
dalous woman in secret. In recent years, she had
come to realize that she didn't really want a husband.
She wanted a lover and a friend. She wanted the mill.
And she wanted Patrick.

"You're unhappy." In the seclusion of their hotel
room, with the curtains drawn in the afternoon and
the bed smelling of the two of them, James leaned
across his pillow and cupped her chin with his hand,
turning her head so she would look at him. "You're
scarcely with me tonight."

"It's not you, James. It's Patrick I'm thinking of. I
never can be easy in my mind so long as he . . ."

"After Talley died, I felt the same."

"Oh, don't say that! Patrick isn't dead. Even if I
never see him again, I must always think of him alive.
To think of his laughter silenced . . . it breaks my
heart, James. I would sooner die than he."

He held her in his arms. "He's safe. I trust
William to see to that."

"Even supposing there is no such thing as a storm
at sea, why would he come back? Patrick hates us
both."

"Perhaps. But I think he may have learned something these many months away. And my brother is a tolerant man. If he and Patrick spend sufficient time together, some of that will rub off on the boy. You must remember, Suzannah, he's young. At his age, a lad is full of ideals. The love of truth and honor is mixed with the sap in his veins. But when he's learned a little of life . . ."

"I think you're wrong. I think his mind is closed. Particularly to me, his scarlet mother. Else why wouldn't he write just to say that he's well? He knows he's hurting me this way. Why is he doing it, James?"

He held her teary face and kissed it. "I don't know."

It had been a bittersweet afternoon at The Elizabeth. Recalling it in the Duffys' front parlor, Suzannah felt the tears rise in her again, followed by an immediate surge of rage with herself. Tears were no longer a helpful vent for emotion. They were a destructive indulgence, one she must overcome if she planned to survive the holiday season and return to her work at the mill's busiest time. At her feet lay coiled a string of cranberries several yards long.

"Here, Margaret. This should take care of that space at the side, and then one or two more . . ." Margaret was still watching the fire. "What is it, Margaret? Is it too much having me here? If it is, you must say so. I will understand."

"Lord, no, Suzannah! You know how much we all love you. And I wouldn't for anything send you home to Sarah and Martin. If this house is gloomy, it's nothing compared to that one!" Margaret started to say something more, then thought better of it. Click, click, click went her tongue in the place where her molars had been.

"Tell me, Margaret. If you're afraid of hurting me. . . ."

The older woman stood up and began to pace before the fire, chafing her hands and punctuating every other sentence with clicks and sighs. "Nothing seems right this year. I should be pleased that it's snowing. In other years, a white Christmas Eve always made me feel festive. Now I sense there's something . . . wrong. I worry so! I worry that Louisa will catch a chill, doing the altar decorations in the cold, empty church. I'm afraid she didn't bundle up enough."

"I saw her wrap that old scarf of Bigelow's at least twice . . ."

"I know. I saw it, too. That thing smells like a cat! But I still worry about everything. There's just too much that seems somehow off kilter. Patrick should be here, and instead he's God-knows-where in some pagan land where they never heard of Christ or his birthday. And poor Christian, all bruised from that beating he took, and Eben having to go out to Ohio to care for him." She clasped her shoulders and shivered. "Why can't we all be together as we were in the old days, Suzannah?" She sniffed noisily and dug in the pocket of her duster for a handkerchief. "I miss our children and all the noise they made. No one ever tracks wet leaves through the house anymore."

Suzannah embraced her sister-in-law and held her close. "We can't go back, Margaret. No matter how hard it is, we must look forward. You've always told me that."

Margaret pulled away. "And on top of everything else, I'm worried sick about Alexander."

"Is he ill?"

"I wish he were!"

"Margaret, you can't mean that. What has he done this time?"

"Maybe I do mean it, and maybe I don't. All I'm sure of is that since he got back from Berlin, he's had hardly a moment for his family. He used to be such a sharing boy, but now he's locked up tight. I don't know what goes on in his mind anymore. Those Germans have advanced ideas, and who knows what atheistic lies he's listened to!"

Suzannah could not, try as she might, keep from smiling. "Now what is it you've always told me Bigelow believes?"

Margaret glared at her with red-rimmed eyes. "Are you going to spout platitudes back in my face?"

"As you have always told me, Margaret, my brother-in-law is an exceedingly wise man. Now what would he say about Alexander and the German influence?"

Margaret made a face. Sounding for all the world like her pedantic husband, she said, " 'God gave us a mind to reason with, and when we go through periods of doubt, it only proves we know how to make good use of the equipment he provided.' "

"There. Isn't that wise? I'm sure Alex will come around. He's a bright young man, and it's natural for him to question and wonder."

Instead of being comforted, Margaret began to cry again. "It's not just the Germans."

"What, Margaret?" Disease? Death? A scandal so horrendous that even the broad-minded Margaret could not bear to speak of it? Suzannah expected the worst. "Tell me."

"He's told Bigelow he wants to get married."

Chapter 31

No matter how cold it was, Louisa liked being alone in St. Thomas' on Christmas Eve. Several years before, she had been put in charge of the holiday decorations in the church. And every year since then, she had implored God to forgive her for the rush of pride she got from hearing people's praise and being called "artistic" for her bows and drapes and clusters on the altar and lecterns, and for all the rows of highly polished walnut pews. This year she was especially ebullient. While her hands busily arranged the greens and berries, her dreams were on the trip she would take to New York the day after New Year's.

Solicity Duffy Dupres was her father's younger sister and the wife of a prominent lawyer in that city. They lived in a fashionable townhouse in Greenwich Village, and from Solicity's gossipy letters, Louisa had gotten the impression that the couple enjoyed an endless round of social engagements. Solicity wrote her brother and sister-in-law of theater parties and exhibits, regattas on the Hudson, strolling parties and concerts, not to mention the balls attended by the governor, the mayor and every man and woman of prestige who visited the city. For many years, Louisa had devoured Solicity's letters with a longing to join

her world. Soon that dream would come true. Solicity
was astringently childless and eager for a young companion to "bring me back to life!"

Ever since the letter of invitation had arrived in
September, Louisa had lived in a fever of anticipation. Faithfully, she counted the days until 1856.
Hardly a day passed when she was not involved in
some aspect of preparation. And she daydreamed constantly. Louisa knew she was a country girl, inade-
quately educated at the young ladies' academy in
Amoset, put together with only bits and scraps of
ideas. But she had inherited a fine and cunning mind
from her father, as well as her mother's instinctive optimism and charm. These qualities had made her eager for adventure and challenge. As she tied elaborate
red bows around handfuls of sweet cedar, she
hummed to herself and her feet tip-tapped uncon-
sciously.

About her, the stained glass windows of St.
Thomas' were alive with colorful scenes from the
Bible. For a while, the late afternoon light filtered
through them, filling the little stone church with rich,
somber tones. When it grew dark, she lit the lantern
May had filled with oil. It was cold, but she dawdled
over her work. Dreaming again. Louisa Duffy just
knew her life was about to open like a deep, dense
novel. She would step into its pages and be swept up
in the lives of beautiful and sophisticated women and
handsome men whose ideas would stimulate and
amuse her. Their stories would never be boring as her
father's so often were, and where the inhabitants of
Amoset and Marivale were utterly predictable in their
pleasures and pastimes, New Yorkers would surprise
her constantly.

The heavy, brass-studded oak door opened, inter-
rupting her reverie. She turned and saw Simon Mc-

Mahon silhouetted in the doorway against a background of white.

"I've come to light the stoves," he said.

"Thank heavens, Si. I checked the woodbox in the back and it's full. Do you mind if I don't help you? I can't seem to satisfy myself with these decorations." She walked to the back of the church and turned, eyeing the distant altar critically. "What do you think? Are there too many berries?"

Simon came to stand beside her, cocking his head a little to one side in imitation of hers. "Looks fine to me, Louisa. Every year it looks prettier."

She beamed at him. "You only say that to make me smile. But Mrs. Darcy of the Guild is not quite so easy to please. She wishes she could be in charge of the Christmas decorations."

"Old bat." Simon McMahon had known Louisa and Alexander for twelve years. They had played together freely as children and, over time, a peculiar relationship had developed among the three of them. They were, on the one hand, perfectly free with one another. But at the same time, particularly as they grew from their teens into their twenties, a sense of class distinction was impossible to ignore. She never thought of him as the son of a murderer, and she had forgotten completely the circumstances of his father's brutal death. Simon was just Si, poor May's son and a permanent feature in the landscape of her life.

Simon walked down the center aisle and ducked through a door on the right side of the church. When he came out a moment later loaded with firewood, Louisa was arranging berries on the lectern on the Epistle side. "Do the stove over here first, will you, Simon? I'm perishing with cold."

He was on his hands and knees in front of the pear-shaped iron stove not far from her when she said, "I think Alex has a surprise for us, Si. I expect he's found someone he plans to marry."

Simon looked up, a spark of interest in his eyes. "Your mother won't like that."

"I know. But Daddy will convince her. Marriage is inevitable. Even you will marry some day, Si. Whom will you choose? I've seen you looking at that Irish girl who works for Mrs. Darcy. What's her name?"

"I don't know, Louisa." He shoved several chunks of coal into the stove.

Louisa giggled. "Well, finding out her name is definitely the first step." She finished her work and went to stand by Simon. As she handed him kindling, she teased, "Don't you want to know the name of Alexander's chosen?" She poked Simon gently with a stick. "Well? Do you want to know?"

"You know I do."

"Well, how was I to know if you never said it? He's gone and fallen in love with Delphia Kilmaine, Senator Shawn's granddaughter."

Simon turned around to look at her.

"You look like . . ." Louisa went white. "Oh, Lord, Si, I am sorry." Her eyes filled with tears of empathy and she knelt down beside him and gave him a quick hug. "I never meant to be so awful. Oh, I could kick myself. You do forgive me? I'm as bad as Mama, the way I go on! It doesn't matter who her family is, Si. If Alex loves her, she must be nice. Don't you think so?" Not for anything in the world would she have hurt her old friend. If she had to talk until sunrise to make him forgive her tactlessness, she would. "Anyway," she declared, digging a deeper hole, "everyone's forgotten what happened. It was years and years ago, and you should have stopped thinking about it, too. Truly. Delphia didn't pick Senator

Shawn for her grandfather any more than you picked your father. And you know we all love you, don't you, Si? I wouldn't say something to hurt you for anything. You couldn't pay me. It's just that I was such a little girl when it all happened, and I put it out of my mind. If I ever really knew at the time, that is, which I doubt that I did because eight is so young and . . ."

"Do you mean that?"

"What?"

"What you said about loving me." Indian-style, he sat on the floor opposite her.

"Well, of course I love you, silly. Do you think I would have said it if I didn't? You're part of my family, Si. We grew up together." Louisa knew this was not true, but she thought the situation called for a bit of gracious exaggeration. She hated herself for having spoken thoughtlessly and for having brought that look of pain into Simon's eyes. She was about to leave for New York and begin the first important chapter of her life. It would be marred if she left misery and hurt behind her.

"If you love me . . ."

"Yes, Si?"

"Will you kiss me?"

She stared at him.

"You said you loved me."

"Well, I do. But kissing is a different matter. A girl must save her kisses for the man who matters most to her." She could think of nothing else to say.

"I wouldn't tell. If you were to kiss me."

"Well, I wouldn't expect you to. But even so," she blushed, "I've never kissed anyone. Except relatives. I always thought I'd wait."

He sneered. "It's because of my father, isn't it?"

"Si, I told you I don't even think about him."

"Then why won't you kiss me? Am I ugly?"

"You know you're not. It's just that I wouldn't feel right. We're friends, not . . ."

"Lovers."

"Well, certainly not that! Look," she got to her feet, "I have to go back before Mama starts to worry. Anyway, you've still got three stoves to light." She tried to smile naturally. "This has been a silly talk and I blame myself, Simon, I truly do. Please say you forgive me."

"Will you help me? I've wasted a lot of time talking to you." He stood up and hooked the latch on the stove's iron door.

Though it was dark and cold and she was no longer in high spirits, Louisa agreed to help with the fires. They did the one behind the choir pews. Halfway down the church on the right side was a third fat-bellied stove, and in the same place on the opposite side was a fourth. They finished the third without incident and were just beginning the fourth when Simon stopped what he was doing and stood before Louisa with his hands dug deep in the pocket of his coat.

"What is it?" she asked.

"Why don't you want to kiss me? Tell me really."

"We've been all through this!"

"But I don't believe you."

"I'm not a liar, Simon, and even if I were, you have no right to expect me to jeopardize my reputation. I told you I was sorry for reminding you of Senator Shawn. I told you and told you and told you. And I've helped you do all these stoves because I wanted to make you happy again. But I will not kiss you."

He grabbed her by the shoulders and pressed his mouth against hers. It was not a kiss, but more of a chew, and it filled her with revulsion. She shoved him away, hard, but he was stronger than she would have guessed. The harder she pushed, the harder he held her to him. His lips opened and his tongue slithered into her mouth and forced her teeth apart. She gagged and tried to scream. She was suddenly in a nightmare of being devoured by a monster. Pounding her fists against his chest, she tried to kick him in the shins and knees and groin, but she teetered off balance and found herself lying on one of the walnut pews with Simon kneeling over her.

His eyes had darkened, and Louisa could feel him staring through her clothing into the very pores of her skin. She felt as if every opening were being invaded. He stuffed a filthy rag into her mouth and began to tug at her overcoat.

Louisa's mind raced. She must make noise. Someone passing by might hear her and save her. But when she tried to kick her heels against the seat of the pew, he sat on her knees. She reached for his throat and grabbed at the space between his neck and the top button. Hooking her fingers in and wrenching hard, she almost pulled him off balance before he undid the frogged closing of her coat and put his hand in to stroke the outline of her breast. She twisted from side to side to escape his touch, but she was losing her strength and each frantic movement took a greater effort. She tried to raise her knees, snatch at his hair, scratch his eyes, but he countered every defense.

And then the door at the back of the church opened.

"Louisa? Are you still in here?"

Margaret's voice was the announcement of a cavalry charge that echoed through the dark church and filled Louisa with energy. She saw the look on Simon's face and squirmed like a pinned dervish. There was no holding her now. With one jerking movement, she made him lose his balance. Simon toppled off her and fell hard against the back of the pew in front. Louisa grabbed the gag out of her mouth and began to scream as she scrambled to her feet. As Margaret ran down the side aisle, Simon leapt up and darted for the door, shoving against her shoulder as he passed. Margaret reeled and fell backward, slamming against one of the stained glass windows. The window was perfect for one last frozen instant before icy shards of vivid blue and green and crimson exploded around her shoulders.

Chapter 32

It was long after midnight when May McMahon was awakened from her nightmares by the clatter of gravel on the window of her little room adjacent to the kitchen. She jumped up and, throwing a shawl over her shoulders, hurried through the kitchen and out onto the back porch. She lifted the iron latch as quietly as possible and opened the door a crack.

"You shouldn't be here!" she hissed at her son, who was cowering on the stoop. "If they knew you was here, they'd call the constable sure." How haggard he looked. His complexion was ashen except for the livid welts on his cheeks where Louisa had raked him with her nails. "Oh, my poor boy!" May cried, opening her arms to him.

But Simon didn't want affection. He pushed past her into the kitchen. "I need money."

She spoke as if she hadn't heard him. "Perhaps you could give yourself up, say you were sorry and never meant to hurt either of those poor women. It's lucky Mrs. Duffy had her coat and hat on, Simon. She weren't hardly cut, so it could've been worse. And Louisa's all right. She's shook up but perfectly healthy. If you said you were sorry, I think the vicar would let you work off the payment for a new window."

"I don't want their pardon or their pity. I've had enough. This house stinks of it."

"They been good to us, Simon."

"You think so? Do you mean to say you like sleeping in a room that's only two by two and eating scraps from their table?"

"After what happened with your father, we're lucky. . . ."

"How much money do you have?" He went to stand by the big cook stove, which was still warm with a dying fire.

May bit her lip, torn by indecision. This was her boy, her only child. No matter what he had done, she couldn't stop caring for him. Frail and pitiful he looked. It almost broke her heart to watch him shiver as if the marrow of his bones had turned to ice. "You need something warm in you. I'll heat up some soup."

"There isn't time," he snarled. But he licked his lips hungrily as he watched her stir the stockpot at the back of the stove. She ladled soup for her son and cut him several thick slices of bread she'd made that morning.

As he stuffed the food into his mouth, he repeated his demand for money.

"But I don't have hardly anything. Not enough for . . ."

"Give it to me."

"What'll you do with it? Where are you going?"

"I don't know, but I got to have something to live on."

May went to her room and dug behind a shelf lined with knickknacks for a small pewter sugar bowl. In it were the few coins she had hoarded since the last time Simon had made her give him money.

"It's less than five dollars," she apologized.

Simon was slicing more bread. With disgust, he looked at the proffered coins and then at his mother.

"What else have you got?"

She looked puzzled.

"Is there anything Da ever gave you? Jewelry?"

"Simon, this is all I have. I told you. . . ."

He grabbed the money and shoved it into his pocket along with several slices of bread wrapped in brown paper. His feral gaze darted about the room. Seeing the scalloped corner cupboard where the silver was stored, he hurried to it and flung open the doors.

"You can't steal from them, Simon!"

Ignoring his mother, he grabbed up some of the larger pieces, a tray and pitcher and serving bowl, and shoved them under his coat. As he dashed for the porch, she tried to stop him, dragging at his arms and shoulders.

"Get away from me."

"Son," she wailed. "They'll catch you. You'll be imprisoned. It isn't right, Son. You know it isn't."

Before she had said her last word, Simon was out the back door and running toward the road at the back of the house. She opened her mouth to call his name again, but thought suddenly of the people asleep upstairs. If they awakened, Simon would have no hope for escape. Part of her was tempted to make sure he got caught, because she believed the good Reverend Duffy and his wife would take pity on Simon and overlook his crazy behavior. "Simon!" she cried out into the night, but it was hardly more than a whisper. She could not betray her son, knowing as she did that he would never forgive her. She had to let him go.

*   *   *

That evening's moderate snowfall was followed by a wind that drove the snow into banks. The road was passable, but slippery. Several times between Marivale and the Gully, Simon slipped and fell into the wet snowbanks. He was aching all over by the time he crested the brow of the low hills surrounding the Gully. Stopping for a moment to catch his breath, he considered his next move.

Though it was after midnight and in a few hours would be Christmas morning, the Gully had its lively spots where drinking and carousing went on regardless of the season. Once, Simon had been head of a gang of toughs that preyed on the folk of Amoset. Over the years of his stay in Marivale, he had not lost contact with his old companions. Unknown to his mother or the Duffys, he had visited the Gully once or twice a month for drinking and gambling with pals like Petey Duff and Kit Mulloon. He could always trust them so long as he made it worth their while.

The Gully had begun to change as some of the immigrant population accumulated a little money. The Lavender and Lily had been rebuilt into a substantial hotel with several upstairs rooms and a dining hall where Peggy Muldoon served country fare reminiscent of Ireland. Across the street was Mickey Quick's dry goods store, which had been built with the aid of Simon's enemy, James Shawn. Simon kept to the shadows and stared at the store. Quick's had a fine glass window in the front with Mickey's name on it in frosted script. Simon's fingers tingled to grab a rock and hurl it through that glass. But he didn't dare. Enough people were after him already.

He scurried from shadow to shadow down the newly cobbled street. There were whitewashed shops and pubs, and Father Snee had a new church with windows almost as fine as St. Thomas' and a deep-throated bell that called the faithful in from every corner of the sprawling town. But away from the main street, the Gully was still a hellhole, stinking of poverty and disease. On either side ran muddy, rutted alleys that had changed little over the years. These were still lined with miserable hovels built of scraps and leavings where the poor managed to survive only because their luck was so bad they could not even die.

Simon stopped and ducked into a doorway smelling of urine and rat droppings. Half a dozen laughing, singing, drunken men came toward him, reeling down the middle of the alley arm in arm. He didn't recognize any of them, but that was not unusual. The population of the Gully was more than fifty thousand now, and every day new immigrants streamed in from Boston and New York and Canadian ports, looking for work in the mills.

Simon spat to show his disgust. He wouldn't get trapped in a filthy bog like the Gully. He went on, turning this way and that, in and along the maze of alleys. Finally, he reached a building that was more substantial than its neighbors, but only barely so. It was a little pub belonging to Liam Doyle and frequented by those who preferred to do their drinking in the shadows.

Simon pushed open the door to The Bull and went inside. It was a smoky, eye-stinging place. Simon peered into the gloom.

"Good evening to you, Simon," said someone to his left. "It's glad I am to see you." Simon recognized the flash of Liam's pride, a single gold tooth in the center of his mouth. "A happy Christmas to you, lad."

Simon grunted something and sat down. As he did, the silver pieces inside his coat made a noisy rattle.

"Are you coming apart or is that your guts rattling?"

Simon wasn't in the mood for games. "I want to do a little business."

"And what did you have in mind?" Liam poured him a drink of strong home brew.

Simon downed it in a gulp, glad for the heat in his belly, and shoved his glass across the table for more. He was soaked through from his falls in the snow, and even the overheated Bull was not enough to warm him. "I need some money."

Liam chuckled. "We all need money, lad. But did you have in mind some trade, or am I to give it to you because of the season?"

Simon removed the silver items from under his coat and laid them on the table. Liam examined each piece carefully. Then he said, " 'Tis fine stuff, lad. No doubt about it. But see here, it's monogrammed and sooner or later the owner . . ."

"Don't give me that malarkey. We both know Petey'll melt it down for you, so who the hell cares about the initials."

Liam's gold tooth glinted as he smiled. "Simon, m' boy, you're overeager. Now how many times have I told you that when doing business, it doesn't pay to hurry the matter along. We need to talk about this."

"I need the money now. And . . ."

"A place to stay awhile, I reckon."

Simon nodded.

"Very well then, I'll see what I can do. There's a mat in the shed behind. You can sleep the night there." Liam leaned across the table and narrowed his eyes at Simon. "What's your rap, lad?"

"A fight. There's Yankees after me."

Liam sighed as if, suddenly, the moral dunghill in which he lived depressed him. His voice was gruff.

"Get on with you, lad. The shed's not heated, but the floor's off the ground, so you shouldn't suffer more than any of the rest of us." He shoved the half full bottle at Simon. "And here, take this. Call me Good Saint Nick."

The storeroom was barely large enough for Simon to stretch out on the floor. He made a backrest of packing crates and covered himself with his coat and some rags he found hanging on nails on the back of the door. The bottle opened with a pop and he took a long drag from it.

He was going to be all right. After two more deep scorching swallows, he was certain of it. Liam was all right. He wouldn't give him up if anyone came looking. And being Christmas Day, Simon thought it unlikely Reverend Duffy would make much fuss. If Simon knew his old benefactor, he'd be more worried about his women and the broken window in St. Thomas' than the loss of fifty dollars' worth of silver. Duffy wouldn't hurry to apprehend him.

But, Simon thought, even if Amoset's entire constabulary came after him, he was smarter than all of them combined. With the help of his pals, he could elude them. He liked the idea of starting up another gang. They'd take what they wanted. He'd make the Shawns and Hopewells regret what they did to his father. He'd make his Da proud of him.

Simon loved Foster McMahon more dead than alive. Alive, he had been a brutish parent, gone from home most of the time and drunk when he was around. There had been a time during which McMahon was employed by Hopewell's when he seemed a different sort of man. Simon had been a student at St. Andrew's then, but it was so long ago that he could hardly remember having expensive clothes and spending weekends in Boston riding in carriages and eating in restaurants with a mother who was pretty and vivacious. For most of his life, May had been timid and dull-eyed, afraid of saying or doing anything that might offend those she called her betters. Simon hated her obsequious nature and admired his father because he was always the toughest man in the room, the one other men feared and stayed away from. Simon still recalled how good it had felt to stand at his father's side in the Lavender and Lily and see Muldoon's eyes go all red and scared. That same feeling of power ran in Simon's blood as he lay on the floor of the shed, downing the last of Liam's burning whiskey. It generated drowsy dreams of power and revenge that warmed him from the inside out. He no longer saw the jumbled shed or felt the draft between the floorboards. He was his father's avenger, flying high, hitting hard. He made them all pay.

Chapter 33

By the time Christian St. Clair was well enough to travel from Ohio to Massachusetts, it was April, and half of Amoset knew the story of his brutal beating by a vigilante gang. In 1856, abolitionist fever ran high in New England, particularly in mill towns like Amoset. Workers formed societies in support of the slaves and contributed generously from their wages to assist the Underground Railway in freeing as many of them as possible. Christian St. Clair became a kind of hero in Amoset. It was not even necessary to exaggerate his injuries to elevate him to this status. Both of Christian's arms had been broken, as well as one of his legs, which would never be straight again. His broken jaw had been wired, and he could take only liquids for nourishment. What hurt Eben the most and made him want to kill his son's attackers was the destruction of the boy's handsome face. His nose had been broken and smashed across his face like a pudding, and his eyes were so badly damaged that it was unlikely he would ever see clearly again.

If it had been in Eben's power to seek out and punish the vigilantes, he would have done so, of course. Money was certainly no obstacle. But Frederick Douglass had assured him that even with unlimited resources, the men would never be found. Like a species of river rat, the men who hated people like Christian and the work they did lived in dives and holes along the Ohio River. They were men without pasts, wearing names they changed on whim, invisible men without friends or families whose sole motive for action was hatred of the black race. Searching for them was impossible.

Throughout the long winter in Ohio, Eben chafed at his helplessness. He stayed by his son's bedside partly to guard him, partly to give him strength. Doctors who treated Christian said the beating obviously had been meant to kill him. But Christian showed immense spirit and seemed determined to survive, and this determination made the difference in his recovery. Daily he grew in strength. Although it would be another six months before he talked and a year before he could walk, the grey film left his eyes and they brightened. By luck alone, his sight began to improve rapidly. As wrecked as his body was, Christian's mind was as clear and sharp as it ever had been.

Eben brought him home in April. As if to welcome the hero who was said to have ferried fifty blacks across the Ohio in less than a year, the season put on its gayest apparel. The day before he arrived, the cherry trees along the driveway leading up to the house sprang into early bloom. And the pink and white dogwoods held their flowers extra long, so that everywhere Christian looked there was color to lift his spirits. As their carriage came to a halt before the porticoed entrance to the Hopewell mansion, however, Christian looked at Eben with what was clearly apprehension.

Eben guessed at the cause. "Don't worry about Grandmama. You'll be upstairs, and Suzannah and I will see that you have everything you need. And Mr. Harahsi will help. If anyone can make you feel better, Christian, it's the India Man."

Christian's room had a new coat of paint, and fresh, sheer curtains had been hung at the windows. To give the invalid a pleasant outlook, the furniture had been rearranged so that his bed was very near a window. From it, he could look out across the gardens toward the river valley and town.

Although Eben had written Suzannah a full description of Christian's injuries, she was not prepared for the battered wreckage of a man she saw before her. Just a year before, his face had been the face of a boy. Now it was a mash of features, an ugly reminder of what had happened. She thought of her son in a world full of strangers on the other side of the globe and feared for him in a way that was more painful than ever.

Suzannah bustled about the bedroom. It was easier not to think when she was engaged in this kind of domestic fidgeting. "Here's the servants' bellpull. Mercy will bring you all your meals, and the India Man will look in on you throughout the day to see if he can be of assistance. I know he's rather strange, Christian. But he's been with us so long now he's almost one of us. This wretched family couldn't have gotten along without Mr. Harahsi. And he's a natural healer. There must be some magic in him, I think."

Certainly Mr. Harahsi had accomplished miracles with Martin Hopewell. Though her father still did not walk, over the last year there had been a marked and disquieting improvement in his appearance. He was terribly old, almost seventy, Suzannah thought, though she was not sure of his birth date. But his constitution now seemed impervious to time and suffering. She saw her father every day for a discussion of the business, and every day he looked more like his old, vigorous self. When Sarah said he would soon work in the mill again, Suzannah half feared this might be true.

"Christian, I've arranged for Ingrid Shawn, the schoolteacher from down at the mill, to come here in the afternoons and read to you. Your confinement must be very boring for you. But you'll enjoy Ingrid's company. She's a bright, intelligent woman, and I've given her free access to the library downstairs."

Life in the huge stone house was little changed by Christian's arrival. The mansion was so large that half a dozen guests could have resided in the upstairs rooms without causing inconvenience. The kitchen staff adored Christian. They made a cause of him and tried to fatten him up with wonderful liquid concoctions of cream and sugar and whipped eggs. And he had no shortage of company. A committee from Reverend Strickland's Unitarian Church presented him with a laudatory plaque and took turns visiting him. And Margaret Duffy brought him charcoal and an easel that fit across his bed. During her own recuperation after the terrible incident with Simon McMahon, she had taken up sketching and now proclaimed its therapeutic value to everyone. Missing her own children, longing for something to take their place in her daily routine, Margaret spent many hours every week with Christian.

At first, Christian thrived under all this care. His surprised doctor thought perhaps he would be able to get out of bed before the fall. But sometime in May, he began to lose ground. The deterioration in his condition was scarcely perceptible at the outset, but by early June Mr. Harahsi had begun to worry. One day he went to see Eben in his office down at the mill.

Harahsi had chosen a day when Eben was particularly overworked and harried. Hopewell's family silk was in such demand that the mill could not meet all its orders without running extra shifts. This involved training new workers and reorganizing work crews. Orders for patterned and laced cotton were especially high that spring, and operatives with the necessary specialization were difficult to find. There were circles around Eben's eyes, and long fatigue lines in his cheeks drew his expression down, making him appear more somber than usual.

"I don't have much time, Harahsi. What can I do?" He tapped his stylus on his desk impatiently.

"Christian is no longer improving, Mr. Hopewell. Gradually, he is weakening."

"That's impossible. The doctor says he's doing fine. You're imagining things. The boy is making a remarkable recovery." As he spoke, Eben scanned a column of figures before him and did some mental calculations. He was listening to Mr. Harahsi, but not with his full attention.

The turbaned Indian shook his head. "I cannot say what is happening to the young man. But I know he is suffering in some new way. If you would permit, Mr. Hopewell," Harahsi bowed slightly as he used his employer's name, "I would like to take Christian to Cartland House for the remainder of his care. At the shore the air is vigorous. It makes the blood run more quickly through the veins." He bowed again.

"No," said Eben. "I don't want him out of my sight. We can't be separated again until he's entirely mended. I won't risk it. You say he's failing, but after all he's been through, I have no doubt these ups and downs are to be expected."

"It is more, sir. Something . . ."

"I know you think so, Harahsi. After years in this

family, I can't say I blame you for expecting the worst. But I'm not convinced."

After their conversation, however, Eben observed Christian more carefully and questioned others who spent time with him. The boy was listless and not much interested in either drawing or eating, and often fell asleep when Ingrid or Margaret read aloud to him. Eben decided such dull spirits must be natural for a boy forced into a long convalescence.

While everyone else in the house tried to brighten Christian's life and hasten his recovery, Sarah and Martin kept to themselves and appeared to ignore his existence as they did most other things. But every day, behind her husband's locked study door, it was clear that Christian was much on Sarah Hopewell's mind.

Sarah was in her middle sixties now. Although she was younger than her husband, who seemed to grow stronger almost every day, the years had shrunk her into a thin, brittle insect-woman who moved in jerky fits and starts. Her eyes, faded to a whitewashed grey, darted constantly from side to side, as if she expected predators. Once Sarah Hopewell had been a lovely, soft-featured woman with cloudy fair hair and a vague, airy manner that some had found endearingly vulnerable. But as her body aged, the softness evaporated from it and what remained was hard.

"They'll give your mill to that nigger baby upstairs!" she declared, pushing her face close to Martin's. "You wait and see if I'm right. As long as you stay planted in that chair, those two children of yours think they can do what they want." She hissed at her husband, who was staring in front of him at nothing, his lizard eyes only half open. "Listen to me, Martin. She'll do it. She hates us both. And Eben!" Sarah laughed bitterly. "He's even worse."

She paced the rug before the wheeled chair in which Martin spent all his days. She knew he was listening, for he had no choice, and she took his improving health as proof that nagging did him good. In the old days, Martin would not have permitted her to meddle in business affairs. That was when she was weak, and he so powerful that he held the whole city in terror of his will. Now that the balance of power between them had shifted in Sarah's favor, it pleased her to spend her days pacing and nagging, pacing and nagging. Her former addiction to tonic and brandy had been replaced by the new and more satisfying compulsion to rouse her husband and see her arrogant children ruined. Valentine had abandoned her, but he was still the only one she loved. If her favorite son could not have the mill, then she would see to it that Suzannah and Eben didn't have it either. She would rather see the whole establishment burned to the ground than given into the hands of Christian St. Clair or Patrick Paine. A worm of hate had gnawed at her insides for decades now, and she had grown dependent on the feeling. It gave her life meaning where once there had been a void.

"They're plotting some way to get rid of you, Martin. I know it because I've heard them talk about how you're stronger now than you've ever been. They know if they don't stop you, you'll soon have what it takes to overcome them. They know you're almost ready to stand up and demand your control again, and they're afraid, Martin. You have the power inside you to ruin them, but you'd better do it fast before they find some way to get rid of you once and for all."

Martin raised his lids and looked at her. Was there perhaps a little fear in his eyes as he imagined himself helpless before his children? Sarah liked to think there was, for as much as she despised her children and grandchildren, she hated Martin, too. In a secret part of herself, she was glad to see her husband stuck in that chair year after year. It pleased her to raise her voice a little and put a shrill edge to it, knowing as she did the way it irritated him. There was nothing he could do without her. She was his window on the world. In spite of everything he might have wished, he was as dependent on her as he was on Harahsi.

She heard the sound of bells out on the driveway. Without saying anything to Martin, she turned and hurried out of the room. A servant was just going to the door, but she waved her away. "I'll do it! I'll do it," cried Sarah. She did not even wait for the boy delivering the mail to reach the porch, but darted down the steps and met him in the middle of the drive. His beribboned and belled mule leaned down to munch a bit of the grass.

"Don't let him do that!" Sarah screeched, slapping the animal's head sharply. "This is not a pasture."

Quickly, the mail boy tugged the mule away from the lawn. He was well-acquainted with Mrs. Hopewell, and if there were some way of avoiding her, he would have. But every day when she heard the mule's bell, she rushed out to grab the mail and heap insults upon him and his beast. When he handed her the envelopes and packets she wanted, Sarah didn't bother to thank him. He heard her muttering to herself as he turned away from the house. Like everyone else in town who came in contact with Sarah Hopewell, he was relieved to be away from her as quickly as possible.

Standing in the drive, Sarah riffled through the envelopes quickly. Seeing the familiar chunky handwriting, she squealed with glee. For the third time that week, she had intercepted a letter from Patrick Paine. Tearing it open, she read the message and began to laugh aloud.

The poor boy wondered why his mother never wrote. Didn't she believe that Patrick knew he'd made a mistake? Didn't she accept his apologies? Didn't she want him to come home?

The tone of the letter was so sad and homesick that Sarah relished the words over and over. She had never been able to figure out what had driven the boy away in the first place, but the details seemed unimportant. It was sufficient that both mother and son were miserable over their separation. Sarah would do everything possible to see they stayed that way.

I miss home. I miss the mountain. I miss you. But if you cannot forgive what I said and the stupid childish way I behaved, then I will stay away. Just tell me, Mother. Just write and tell me.

Upstairs in her dresser, Sarah had a dozen such poignant letters. Sooner or later, she knew Patrick would stop writing them and give up hope of mending his relationship with Suzannah. Eventually, Suzannah would stop expecting word from him and assume he was dead. Shoving the envelope into her pocket, Sarah skittered up the front stairs and into the house, a smile on her face and a little tune on her lips. She saved the letters for times when she was most angry with Suzannah. Then she liked to savor them one by one and laugh to think how she was fooling everyone. The whole house believed she was a harmless old crazy, but Sarah knew differently. Sarah knew she was dangerous.

If Valentine couldn't have the mill, then no one would.

Chapter 34

In late July of 1856, the engagement of Delphia Kilmaine to Alexander Duffy was announced in the Amoset paper. The young people, it reported, came from two of Massachusetts' foremost families, and the September wedding would be attended by friends, family and dignitaries from as far away as New York and Philadelphia. The Reverend Bigelow Duffy was to perform the ceremony, which would take place at St. Thomas' Episcopal Church in Marivale, and the bride would be given in marriage by her grandfather, Senator James Shawn. A large reception would follow at the home of the bridegroom's aunt, Suzannah Hopewell Paine.

It should have been a happy time, but from the moment the announcement was made and the plans under way, Delphia showed signs of acute distress. She was tearful in the mornings just on waking, short-tempered when attention was not focused on her, distracted during conversations at the dinner table and melancholy on long, rainy afternoons. Observing her daughter, Lucy sighed, laughed to herself and wondered if any of the family would survive to enjoy the wedding day.

It was the reception that worried Lucy. Understandably, she hadn't liked the idea of having it at Suzannah's. On the other hand, there simply weren't adequate facilities at the remote homestead and, besides, the trip up the mountain would have been difficult for the visiting dignitaries. And then there was Delphia. The very idea of refusing the offer of the mansion threw her into a frenzy. Lucy sighed again. Soon she would have to face Suzannah and be pleasant. Soon she would see Eben.

Eben figured more prominently than Delphia in Lucy's thoughts during the days preceding the wedding. This was partly because Ingrid, who had been given a few days of special leave from the factory school to help in the frenzied trousseau preparations, spoke often and at length about the Hopewell family.

"They've suffered terribly, don't you think, Sister?" Ingrid and Lucy were sitting on the sunny verandah of the homestead, sewing. Lucy's eyesight had deteriorated to the extent that she could sew for only a few hours in the morning before her vision became blurred. She liked working on the verandah because it relaxed her eyes to sometimes lift them from her handwork and stare into the distance.

"Life isn't meant to be easy, Ingrid," she said, biting off the silk thread with her teeth. "I don't suppose life has been harder on the Hopewells than on any of the rest of us."

But Ingrid shook her head, unconvinced. "I watch Eben Hopewell sometimes. He seems . . . haunted. It's as if he has some great sorrow wrapped about him like a cloak."

"You are too romantic, little sister."

Ingrid, who was no longer the child Lucy always remembered her as being, was not easily put off. She said in a schoolmarmish way, "I know the family well after spending so many afternoons with poor Christian. And I know Eben has suffered."

Lucy said nothing more, but her mind stayed with the subject. She would never let Ingrid guess, but her curiosity about Eben was piqued. Thomas had been gone for so many years that she knew it would be possible to have him declared legally dead. For a few irresistible moments, her thoughts floated into and around the idea of marriage to Eben, but she quickly stopped herself. After so long was it possible that she still cared for him? Foolish woman! A year earlier, when she was caught up in her Boston life and a houseful of interesting guests, she would have denied such an idea without hesitation. Now that her Moon Street life was over and the house had been sold, she was not so sure how she felt about Eben Hopewell.

"And Mrs. Paine is wonderful!" Ingrid was saying. "She is totally committed to educating the children at the factory. I do believe our little schoolhouse is as well furnished as some of the private academies in Amoset." Ingrid looked up and saw her sister staring across the clearing toward the woods. "Are your eyes bothering you, Lucy?"

Lucy looked embarrassed. "I can work a little longer. I only got distracted."

"What was I saying? Oh, yes. About Suzannah Paine . . . as you might suspect, the other owners don't like her. Her advanced ways make them look bad. But she doesn't seem to mind what anyone thinks of her. I admire that in a person, don't you, Lucy?"

Lucy did and said so. While Ingrid went on to list all of Suzannah's admirable qualities, her older sister listened only half attentively. It was impossible for her to hear Suzannah's name without thinking of

Patrick and her father. During the last year, her attitude toward the three of them had begun a gradual transformation. She had observed her father and mother together and seen that though the passion between them had disappeared, their relationship was nonetheless warm and strong. She tried but could find no fault with her father when it came to his responsibility toward the family. James Shawn spent weeks at a time in Boston, but he came home whenever he could and wrote frequent letters. Helen was not a part of his political career, but she was not separate from it either. He confided his concerns and ambitions freely and often asked for her advice. It was a marriage unlike any Lucy had known of, and it was with reluctance that she acknowledged its strengths. And had she any right to criticize her father's infidelity when every day spent on Cooper's Mountain reminded her of the man she had loved instead of her husband?

"Do you think Dada will be governor?" Ingrid asked.

"It seems likely they will nominate him. Apart from that, who can guess?"

"Would Mama go to live in the governor's mansion?" Ingrid giggled. "I can't see it, can you?"

Lucy could not. Nevertheless, there was no doubt that many powerful figures in Massachusetts state politics had decided James Shawn was the man to be governor. All across the state, he had a reputation for fairness and honesty. He was admired partly because these were rare qualities, and partly because he was a Yankee pragmatist who knew how to get things done while still retaining his honor. The working population had made him a hero. In every mill town on the Amoset, the Merrimack and all the other great rivers rushing out of Massachusetts, he was known as the working people's friend, a man who had fought hard for the ten-hour day. The immigrant population swore their loyalty to him as if he were a clan chief. And if women had voting rights, he would almost surely be elected governor, for his work to elevate women to equal citizenship was widely known. It was, however, just these admirable qualities and constituents that had made many enemies for James Shawn. If he were nominated to run for governor, the fight would be hard and dirty.

Lucy rubbed her eyes. They had begun to sting and water. With a sigh, she put down her work. "I can't do any more, Ingrid. I'm sorry to leave you with so much." She didn't want Ingrid's pity, but it was there. She couldn't miss it. The sorrow emanated from her in waves. "Don't say anything. Please." Lucy got up and walked to the edge of the verandah. "I think I'll just wander up to the lookout before it's time to help with the meal."

As she walked, Lucy was particularly sensitive to the forest around her. In another year, she might not be able to see so clearly the details of the leaves, the play of shadow and light along the forest floor. She was consciously hoarding up memories to light the dark ahead. She could not keep her mind on the present, however. It kept drifting back over the years to her childhood and the time when she and Suzannah had played in the woods like happy little savages. She was surprised to find herself aching with yearning for her old friend. All at once she realized it didn't matter about her affair with James or that they came from vastly different worlds. The years had blurred the edges of those worlds until they were almost the same. Lucy was no longer single-mindedly intent on finding her place in the world of working women. That place had been discovered, relinquished, and recovered in a half a dozen different ways. And Suzannah was a woman of formidable strength, and not the flighty girl of twenty years earlier. It was possible that Lucy had misjudged her friend even then. Lucy saw that the future no longer stretched like a broad and busy highway toward the horizon. Instead, like the path to the lookout, it had become shadowed, uncertain, twisted and not the place to be alone.

At the lookout, she discovered Delphia.

"You should be down at the house helping Aunt Ingrid," Lucy scolded. "Marriage is not an excuse to have your family wait upon you hand and foot, Delphie."

The girl was hunkered against the stones, her head turned slightly away toward the west.

"And are you sure you want to sit in the sun? You'll brown your skin."

"I don't care. I like the sun."

Lucy laughed. "You are a difficult person, Delphie. A week ago you would have made a fuss if I suggested that the sun would put roses in your cheeks."

"I don't want to talk, Mama." Her voice broke. Resting her head on her knees, Delphia began to cry.

"My darling, what is it? Tell me."

"I've been sitting here thinking what a horrid person I am."

Again Lucy laughed.

"It's not funny. I've been thinking of Patrick and missing him. Alex talks about him all the time and how he wishes . . ." She turned into her mother's arms and wept. "I drove him away, Mama. If I had been anything but selfish and short-tempered, if I had tried to understand him just a little, he would still be here."

Lucy held her girl close and tried to comfort her with caresses. Whatever had transpired between Delphie and Patrick, she didn't want to know. She was only thankful that the problem of a love affair between them had not arisen. Alex Duffy was an excellent match for Delphia. Someday Patrick might return and be a friend to them both. For now, Lucy was glad he was gone.

"Aunty Ingrid says Mrs. Paine cries every day because Pat's gone away. And it's my fault. I'm such a horrid, selfish girl! How can Alex possibly love me. When he finds out . . ."

"You're only young, Delphie. Don't be so hard on yourself."

"Oh, Mama," she looked up at Lucy, tears streaking her pretty heart-shaped face. "You don't know how bad I am. When you first told me you were going . . . blind, I didn't believe you. I thought you were only being stubborn about wearing spectacles and seeing the doctor. I purposely didn't help you with close work because I thought I could force you to use your eyeglasses and then you'd get better. I've been sitting up here thinking of how hard you've worked to give me a good life and how I've never said thank you for anything. Oh, Mama, I wish I could crawl into a rabbit hole and never come out. I'm so ashamed. How can Alexander love me when he's so good and kind and wise and I'm so . . ."

"Ah, Delphie, you may as well know now as later that neither of you is perfect. Not even Alexander. I know he's a fine young man and good in so many ways, but he's not perfect. If you're wise, you will learn to love him because of his imperfections. Don't demand perfection of life, or nothing and no one will ever satisfy you. And there's no good trying to change yourself, trying to make yourself perfect. Just let Alexander love you the way you are. That's real love, Delphia." She held her daughter's damp face, rosy from the autumn sunlight, between her hands. "It's taken me all my life to understand that we must love each other as we are and not expect changes to suit our wishes."

Lucy paused, thinking of Eben. Now she could admit to herself that she loved him, had always loved him. The bitterness she had felt about Marianna and Christian dissolved as she realized that she had used it as a shield to protect herself from the pain of losing Eben. "Delphie, in the past I lost some people I cared for deeply because I didn't accept them and love them as they were. I beg you, Delphie, don't make my mistakes. Just love Alexander as he is, for what he is, even after you know he's not perfect."

Chapter 35

In years to come, most would remember the wedding party for Delphia and Alexander Duffy as a gala splendid enough for royalty. For a few, it would be recalled as a day of drama and passion that marked both an ending and a beginning.

For two days in advance of the day of the wedding, it rained. But on the afternoon before, the sky cleared and a baking sun came out to draw the moisture from the soil. All around the ellipse, the fall rosebushes blossomed in a sudden profusion of yellow and red. The rain left everything with a sparkle. Even the cold grey stone of the Hopewell mansion had a crystal gleam in the bright light. And down in the Amoset valley, there was enough breeze to blow away the smoke from the factories. Looking out over the town, the wedding guests were incredulous. There hadn't been such a clear day since before the mills had come and captured the great power of the Amoset Falls on their wheels. Margaret Duffy, reigning resplendent as the proud mother of the groom in peacock green taffeta and a massive gauze and straw hat, confided to Suzannah privately that such weather was an omen. "Bigelow says I'm still a pagan Celt, but I don't care. I do believe in omens. A day like this means my Alexander's made a wise choice. He and his Delphie will have a good life together."

Though at first Margaret had felt a shock of betrayal and jealousy, she had adjusted to her son's engagement quickly. On the weekend when the banns of marriage were announced at St. Thomas', the Duffys entertained the whole Shawn clan for two days. Margaret felt comfortable with the Shawns and began to anticipate the benefits of Alexander's match with Delphie. Chief among them was the prospect of grandchildren. Margaret had made a thorough assessment of her new daughter and had concluded, accurately, that Delphie would not find much satisfaction in mothering. The little ones would spend a lot of time with their grandmama, who already was happily imagining a parade of wet leaves tracking across her favorite carpet.

More than two hundred guests had come to the Hopewell mansion after the ceremony to drink to the health of the young bride and groom. It flattered Margaret's vanity that the affair was attended by everyone from Harvard boys and millinery apprentices to feminists and abolitionists and politicians. Still, in the early part of the long and festive afternoon, she was a bit awed by the assembly and felt uncharacteristically shy. She kept thinking how remarkable it was that she, Margaret Paine Duffy, whose beginnings had been humble in the extreme, had so risen in the world that lawyers and doctors and senators had come all the way from New York to attend her son's wedding. Until she regained her courage, she stood alone on the steps of the porticoed porch and watched the party. Her glance fell on Louisa and the young man she had brought up from New York. He was involved in some sort of banking enterprise and would be going to Paris in a year or so. Margaret suspected he would want to marry Louisa and take her with him, but Louisa was still too independent for marriage. With the resilience of youth, she had recovered from the shock of Simon's attack on her and now was entirely happy with the New York life she'd found. Her eagerness for life permitted no backward glances for fear an opportunity in the present might be missed.

For Margaret, recovery had not been so swift. Her physical injuries had mended in less than six weeks, but inside, she still hurt. She suspected it might always be so. With Simon's betrayal, her dearest belief had been destroyed. She had discovered that not every soul could be redeemed. Knowing this had cast her faith into an abyss. It drifted there still, unable to latch onto anything. Margaret didn't care about the stolen silver. And though the destroyed window and her own injuries had been most upsetting, even they had not damaged her as much as the realization that it was Simon, the boy she had befriended, who had brought this grief upon her family. At this time, it seemed that reality and faith could not co-reside in Margaret. But she was by nature too optimistic to accept the chance that trust in God would forever be eclipsed by reality. Margaret prayed every day for her own redemption and believed that it would come.

On the flagged terrace to the right of the ellipse, a long table had been laid with bright white linens and all the finest Hopewell silver and cut crystal. There were platters of meat and fish in aspic, fruits, vegetables, oysters in their shells, caviar and cheese and an assortment of sweet concoctions, including flans and tortes. The highlight of it all, of course, was a ten-tiered wedding cake, frosted in butter cream and decorated with glacé fruit. Servants moved among the crowd, refilling champagne glasses and offering savory canapes. Under the blue autumn sky, the party mood was teased into gaiety by all this food and drink. Casual acquaintances felt like dear friends with much in common, and everyone's conversation seemed stimulating and delightful. The ellipse was a swirl of laughter and color.

On the far side of the front lawn, James Shawn kept a protective arm about both Lucy and Helen as he engaged in a spirited conversation with several Amoset officials. As soon as James appeared at any occasion, business or social, he was surrounded by local power brokers pressing their favorite opinions and causes. Lucy listened with interest to the talk of mills and laborers' rights and occasionally made comments in support of her father's egalitarian principles. Her mind was on the conversation or Delphia, of whom she caught an occasional glimpse through the crowd. She did not notice Eben as he came and stood beside her. When she did her first reaction was a schoolgirl's. She blushed and looked down at her feet shod in gold slippers that matched her gown and the highlights in her hair.

"Will you walk with me, Lucy?"

Before she could say no, James interrupted his conversation. Giving her a gentle nudge, he said, "Go along with you, Daughter. Enjoy yourself."

She wanted to say that she would not enjoy herself with Eben, that she would feel awkward and shy and foolish and tongue-tied after the many years and all the misunderstanding between them. But she was a grown woman and the mother of the bride. She was no longer a girl, despite her embarrassing blushes. They strolled along the drive and slightly away from the crowd to where the lawn sloped down, making idle comments about the weather and the bride and groom. Then they wandered onto the path that led to the observation point. Once she had begun to walk with Eben, Lucy did not consider asking where they were going or even reminding him that as the mother of the bride, she should not leave the reception. It was enough just then to stay by his side and go where he led her.

"It's changed so much," she murmured, looking at the mill and the town sprawling out around it. Once, and not so very long ago, Amoset had been only a trading post on the wild river. Martin Hopewell was the first man to harness the power of the fast-falling water to generate energy for manufacturing, but others had been quick to follow him. Now all along the river there were huge, multi-storied mills and factories. In addition to family silk, Amoset produced cotton and woolen and worsted piece goods, saddles, shoes, boots, machinery and household items. The city on the Amoset River was thriving, and its crowded streets were lined with hotels and boarding houses, churches, shops, theaters, halls and gaming parlors. From the observation point on the Hopewell estate, the city hummed with the motion of a hundred thousand wheels turning for industry.

"Is it possible that I actually worked down there from before dawn until after dark? It seems so long ago." Lucy spoke as much to herself as to Eben. There was a soft fuzziness about her vision now, so that only those things she saw up close were distinct. Soon she would have only her memory of Amoset, the city that had both thrilled and terrified her.

It was a Saturday, and as they stood looking down on the mill, a din of half-day bells rang out from all the mills in Amoset. The noise startled her and she stepped back, bumping against Eben. The sound carried memories bitter and sweet, clearer than any vision. As if no time had passed, she remembered how much she hated the bells that had controlled her life as an operative. It was a warm autumn day, but she shivered, recalling those pre-dawn winter mornings in Mrs. Quinn's boarding house. Her bare feet, just out of bed, had stuck to the icy floor of the top story room she shared with girls like Barbara Bolton. She wondered what had happened to the others who had survived the mill life. Had girls like Kitty and Beth and Faith and Marie found the happiness they had fantasized about when work had not exhausted them to the point where their faculty for hoping and dreaming failed altogether.

As she was thinking these things, hundreds of women and girls streamed out of Hopewell Mills and through the gates on to Front Street. The voices the breeze carried up the hill seemed different from those of twenty years before. They were lighter, more energetic and optimistic.

Lucy spoke on impulse. "Thank you for what you've done down in the mill. Ingrid has told me so much about the changes, and it seems to me . . ."

"I did it for you, Lucy."

"You did not," she scolded with a smile. "You run a fair business because you are a fair and just man."

"Does that mean you have forgiven me?"

"Forgiven? Oh, yes, Eben." Lucy paused, remembering the day on the lookout with Delphie, when she had gone beyond the facade of bitterness toward Eben and found the love that had always been in her heart. "It took a long time, but I finally realized that I regretted my words even before you were out the door and onto Moon Street. A part of me wanted to call you back and say that . . . well, it doesn't matter. It was a long time ago." She looked away from him, back toward the city. She didn't want to see his expression that her words were true, that it didn't matter.

He spoke so close to her that she felt his breath stir the ringlets at the back of her neck. "For me, nothing has changed, Lucy. I still love you."

In the twelve years since they had parted, Eben had led a monkish life, devoting himself entirely to running the family businesses. He had been highly successful, tripling the Hopewell fortune with ease. During this time he had shown no interest in women, and there were those among his business associates who disliked and mistrusted him for this peculiarity. Periodically, efforts were made to match him with this or that eligible daughter or niece, but no arrangement had sparked so much as a flicker of response in Eben. "Lucy," he said gently, "is it true what Ingrid told Christian? Are you going blind?"

When she nodded, he groaned, turning her toward him and pulling her close. "Tell me what I can do."

"There is nothing anyone can do. Not even a Hopewell. I finally saw a doctor in Boston, and he told me it is simply a progressively degenerative condition."

"It wasn't the mill? All the lint in the air. I thought . . ."

"This would have happened even if I had spent my life in a nunnery."

"How much do you see?"

She looked around. "I'm tired now, so it's a little worse than usual. At the center of my vision, I have a clear image of you, Eben. Around you, there is a mist, and then at the edges a fog through which nothing, no light or image, passes." She saw his look of pain and touched him gently. "It's all right, Eben. You mustn't grieve for me. My life has been full and interesting and . . ."

"What, Lucy. Tell me."

"You know, when I was a little girl, everyone always said what a brave child I was. Ingrid was sickly, Talley was cheerful, and I was brave. I didn't feel brave, but after a while I guess I came to believe what people said about me. I didn't dare be anything but courageous for fear of letting down my family and friends. I began expecting myself to act bravely. Whenever I didn't, I felt I'd shamed myself. I wouldn't ever turn my back when a challenge was offered. You know, I married Thomas because the family needed money. As the brave one, it seemed right that I should act on everyone's behalf. I told myself that I would make the best of it. It was a mistake; I know it now. But at the time . . . I've done so many things I regret and . . . except for losing you . . . it was always because I couldn't risk not being brave. But it's a peculiar thing, Eben, that now, when I have a real need of courage, I have found it. This time, for the first time, I truly am not afraid."

"But blind or not, you need me, Lucy. And God in heaven knows I need you. You don't know how many times this last year I have wanted to climb that goddamned mountain and tell you, but I thought you'd never even hear me out. Then I heard about your eyes. Now that I know, I can't let you go. Not ever. I want to care for you. Let me be the last one you see, Lucy."

"Eben, I can never be anything other than I am. An aggravating and opinionated woman. I will entertain feminists and abolitionists in the front parlor. I will tell you how to run your mill, and I will agitate for labor." She laughed. "I will complain about those damned bells until I am dead and in my grave."

"But do you love me?"

"Oh, Eben. I never have loved anyone else."

He grabbed her up in his arms and whirled her about. Not knowing whether to laugh or cry, they clung to each other as if they feared that some new threat might appear.

Lucy stopped and pulled away. "What about Christian? Ingrid says . . ."

The joy drained from Eben's face. "He's in the house. Upstairs. He wanted to come down for the reception, but he's too weak."

"Is it very bad, my love?"

Eben nodded. "He was all right until I brought him into this house, but it's as if the atmosphere has poisoned him. He's weaker every day. Nothing we do helps him for more than a few hours." Eben covered his face with his hands and rubbed his eyes hard. "Jesus, I wish I knew . . ."

"Take me to him, Eben." She drew his hands away from his face and brought them to her lips. She kissed the fingertips. "I love you, Eben, and I have been a fool. Not just about you, but about Suzannah and . . . that poor boy up there. Now, before it's too late, take me up and let me know your son."

Mr. Harahsi had cared for so many Hopewells since coming to the house when Eben was a young man that he felt there was nothing he did not know about the peculiar and tormented family. As the wedding party continued on the lawn, he looked in on Martin Hopewell. The old man was sleeping in his chair, the remains of his afternoon meal on the tray beside him. He closed the door softly and went into the kitchen to prepare a tray for Christian, knowing all the while that the food would probably go to waste. The boy's illness troubled Harahsi in some indefinable way that was different from his feeling about Martin Hopewell. The old man's disability had been created by a severe ordeal, by months of isolation and inhumane treatment. It was understandable that he might never recover enough to walk or speak more than an occasional monosyllable. Harahsi was perplexed by Sarah's demand that her husband walk and talk and even, this was most ludicrous, assume some control of the family business. Christian, however, was a young man. His progress had been startling for a while. Then suddenly, mysteriously, he had begun to lose more ground every day. Now, he could not digest even the soothing chicken and vegetable broths Harahsi ordered the cook to prepare for him. It appeared to hurt him to swallow, and so he went without food and daily grew more thin.

Harahsi was a man who did not seek to understand his employers. Rather, he was an observer of life and, for the most part, uncritical. Nevertheless, he found old Sarah and Martin pitiful and rather disgusting. He had seen a look in Sarah's eyes that made him think she probably felt the same about him. As a further irony, Martin's eyes told him that though he knew he could not have survived without his care, he hated Harahsi for giving it. Martin's unblinking reptilian stare emanated frustration and rage, and Sarah seemed obsessed with manipulation and revenge and punishment. Harahsi saw their sickness as more than the mental and physical deterioration of old age. It sprang from their hearts, which were so bitter that they were beyond his comprehension.

For Suzannah and Eben, he felt some pity and affection. He had watched them change from foolish, greedy children to clever and ambitious adults. However, at the same time, he was acutely conscious of their unhappiness. For all their power and intelligence, they seemed doomed to lose those people for whom they cared most. Upstairs, Eben's son was wasting away from a disease no doctor could identify, and Suzannah's son was lost amidst the oceans and seas of the world. Though he gave no indication of being emotionally involved with the family, Harahsi had known them all too long to be as aloof as he appeared. He cared, and if there had been some way for him to root out the evil that poisoned the Hopewell family, he would have done it.

On his way upstairs with the tray, Harahsi stopped in the front hall to pluck a rosebud from a huge vase near the door. He laid it across Christian's linen napkin in its flat, rectangular silver holder and hoped the boy would be strong enough to notice. As he climbed the wide staircase, the house around him was as silent as a mausoleum. It seemed to have no connection with the laughing merriment of the party going on out-of-doors. A string quartet had begun to play on the terrace, but the sound seemed to come from a great distance, almost from another world.

At the bedroom door, he stopped, sensing that someone was in the room with Christian. He placed the tray gently on the carpeted hall floor and pushed against the door. It opened without a sound.

Beside Christian's bed stood Sarah Hopewell. She was turned at such an angle that Harahsi could see her hands. She held a glass of what appeared to be juice in one hand, and in the other was a small vial containing a white powder which she was sprinkling liberally into the juice. Harahsi did not speak, and Sarah was so intent that she did not hear or see him. He saw her lips move and thought he heard her mutter something about Valentine. She turned her back to the door and leaned over Christian's bed. Harahsi saw the boy's legs move as he struggled feebly.

"Stop what you are doing!" cried Harahsi.

Sarah whirled. The juice glass dropped from her hand.

She stared at Harahsi, a vial labeled "Arsenic" clutched in her hand.

Chapter 36

Sarah screamed as Harahsi grabbed for her arms. Curses gushed from her mouth as from a ruptured sewer. She used words he had never heard from a woman, language so foul he was disgusted, and to touch her was revolting.

From down the hall, there was the sound of running feet and anxious voices. Eben rushed into the room. "Mother! My God, what's happening?" In a flash, his gaze took in everything. Arsenic. He stopped in the doorway. "Sweet Jesus, what have you done, woman?"

Thrashing against Harahsi's grip, Sarah yet had strength to rail at her son. She did not appear to notice Lucy standing just behind him, her eyes wide with horror. "I won't let him have it! No filthy half-caste brat will take what belongs to my Vally. He'll come back and when he does, you'll see, you'll see!" Moving with the swiftness of a much younger person, Sarah whirled in Harashi's grip and spat directly in his face. The astonished man let go of her hands for just an instant, enough time for her to plunge past the others and tear out of the room.

Eben was stunned. "Christian. How is he?"

"Go after her," cried Harahsi. "Stop her before she hurts someone else."

"My son . . ."

"I'll take care of your son. Go!"

Eben darted from the room without further talk. With Lucy close behind, he raced to the head of the stairs. Sarah was at the bottom. Standing in the foyer, the light from the stained glass window high above the door casting lurid lights across her face, she laughed hideously. Instantly, Eben saw that his mother had fled into a madness from which there would be no return. She flung herself against the door of Martin's study, which burst open.

Inside it was cool and dark, smelling of old papers and forgotten treasure. Martin was in his chair, facing the door. As Eben and his mother lurched into the study, he opened his heavy-lidded eyes and glared at the intruders.

Suzannah, who had just entered the house, heard the commotion and ran to the study door. "Eben, what's happened? Lucy . . ." Suzannah stared at the scene before her, bewildered. "I had begun to wonder whether Christian was all right. I didn't know . . . Eben, what's happened here?"

Her brother was too distraught to hear her. He grabbed Sarah and shoved her ahead of him until she was standing directly in front of Martin.

"See her? She's been poisoning my son with arsenic. She tried to murder my boy!"

"Whoremaster!" cried Sarah. "That half-breed has no right to live. He should have been drowned at birth." This cruel thought struck Sarah as terribly amusing and she laughed wildly. The look on Eben's face delighted her. "I wish I'd drowned you the day they told me I had a son. A son!" She sneered at

Eben. "You poisoned my life with every breath you took."

"Mother . . ."

"Stay away, Suzannah," said Eben. "You don't know what you're dealing with here."

Now Sarah turned her spiteful tongue against her daughter. "And yours won't get anything from this family either. That boy you prize even more than the gold you grovel for like a man, that boy is gone! Gone!"

"Shut up!" cried Eben. "Close your filthy mouth and listen to me. Do you know I could have you arrested for what you've done to my son? I could call the magistrate and have you put in jail for the rest of your life. I could do it, Mother. He's right outside, drinking champagne and dancing."

"But you'll do nothing. You're a Hopewell and it would be too horrible if all the world knew the truth about us." Sarah began laughing again. "The wonderful, the successful," she looked at Suzannah, "the beautiful Hopewells! But it's your insides that tell the tale. Full of corruption you are, stinking with it!"

"It is you who are vile, Mother. Don't try to interrupt. I'll speak my piece, and for once, you will listen to me." Eben looked at Lucy and Suzannah. "I want you to hear this, too."

Lucy touched his arm. "My love, you are punishing yourself."

"No, Lucy, let him say it. It's been a long time coming." Suzannah stood beside her childhood friend and without self-consciousness, they put their arms around each other for comfort and protection. Neither woman had ever seen Eben so intent and fierce. Taut and strained, his handsome face was distorted almost beyond recognition. Even his voice, normally as resonant as an echo through a deep well, was unfamiliar, changed to an animal's snarl.

"If ever there was a marriage made in hell, it was yours and father's. It surely must have been planned by Satan himself, for you are both the spawn of demons." Martin Hopewell's heavy lids lifted just perceptibly, but his expression remained frozen. "I've never told a soul what you did, Father. But now I think it's time to get it out into the open. Maybe that's what I should have done in the first place. Perhaps if I had, all the degradation and pain and suffering could have been avoided. But I didn't go to the authorities that night in Savannah. Instead, I let you get away with murder." Martin blinked slowly several times. "Now, however, I want everyone to know that you pushed your own father against the stone fireplace and beat his head until it was bloody. You killed my grandfather, just as this woman would have killed my son. I couldn't understand it then. I thought a monster had taken you over and that you couldn't possibly be as evil and rancid a human being as you seemed. But I was wrong. You hated your father because he stood for fairness and order in the world. Greed didn't dominate him and drive out all sense of right and wrong the way it did in you. You hated him, and you were able to kill him. Well, I hate you, too, Father. But I am not going to kill you any more than I am going to kill this woman, my mother. I am going to see that both of you are exposed for what you are. Maybe then this family can go on and find some happiness. Maybe then, after the truth is known, after the name of Hopewell has been dragged through the mud . . ."

Martin Hopewell grunted something.

"What's that, old man? You deny your guilt?" Eben laughed scornfully. "I don't care. You can try to say what you like, but I'll make your wretchedness the talk of every town between here and Boston. You and my mother will be the scandal of the century!"

Again Martin grunted, and he shifted in his chair.

"That's it!" cried Sarah, clapping her hands together like a little girl enjoying a performance. "That's it! Get up! Show him who's the man here. Show him he can't lie and threaten . . ."

"Murdering old fool, do you think you can frighten me? I know you now. I am your son, and you have no power over me any longer."

Martin put his hands on either arm of the chair. His eyes were fully open now and fixed unblinkingly on Eben. Grunting again, he raised himself on stiffened arms until his legs were straight and his feet flat on the floor.

"My God," whispered Suzannah, stepping back, "he's going to do it! He's going to walk."

He stood without support for an instant, then his hand reached out and he steadied himself on the desk beside his chair. Still his inhuman eyes were fixed on Eben.

"You . . . are . . ." His hand groped about on the desk and fastened on a large brass paperweight."

"Yes," hissed Sarah. "Yes. Yes. Yes."

"You . . . are . . . a . . ." Martin swayed precariously, then took one step and then another toward Eben.

"You . . . are . . ." His face was purple. "A . . . dead . . ." As he raised the paperweight, it appeared that some invisible force, perhaps the devils with whom he'd made an ancient bargain, gripped him by the throat. His eyes bulged in their sockets. His mouth opened for a scream, but all that came out was a strangled gurgle as the little of humanity that was left in Martin Hopewell fled into eternity. The paper-weight dropped as he fell to the floor, dead.

Harahsi saw to everything. He took Sarah up-stairs and gave her a draft of something that quickly put her to sleep. He sent a messenger for the doctor who had been treating Christian, then he prepared Martin Hopewell's body for the undertakers. While all this was going on, Eben and Lucy stayed at Chris-tian's bedside. Suzannah sat alone, numbed of every feeling, in the front drawing room. Outside, the string quartet was playing dance music, but she was only dimly conscious of the sound. For the longest time, her mind was totally without thoughts. Then, slowly, her awareness returned.

On a sideboard was a cut-glass decanter of brandy and some glasses. She poured herself a gener-ous portion and drank it quickly. She filled her glass again, and sipped the burning liquid as she wandered about the room, touching familiar ornaments. Each one brought fresh memories of the years she had spent in the house of her father.

It did not surprise her to discover that he was a murderer. She remembered the day he and Eben came back from Savannah, and the way Martin had announced Theron Hopewell's death in a voice that was peculiarly calm. Looking back, it seemed that even then she had sensed something false in his story. Even more clearly, she remembered Eben's crazed, angry sorrow and the eagerness with which Martin had sent him off to Cartland House to stay until it passed.

Sarah's culpability, however, she could not accept so easily. All along, through every vicissitude, she had clung to the belief that her mother was a basically good woman whose only real fault was a weakness for alcohol and nerve tonic. At her worst, Sarah had seemed irritating yet essentially harmless to Suzannah. The idea that for months she slowly had been poisoning Christian St. Clair was impossible for her to believe at first. But when she remembered her mother's eyes and heard her voice hissing "yes, yes, yes," she realized with a shock that the charge was true. Sarah was utterly insane and capable of the most despicable act.

She watched her guests from the window. If she and Eben and Lucy had been missed, the well-entertained guests did not seem perturbed. In a while, she supposed, Margaret would come into the house to find out what had happened to them all, but for now Suzannah didn't want her to know. She watched Delphie and Alexander standing together, their fingers interlocked. She saw the misty, romantic gazes they exchanged. She didn't want anything to spoil their wonderful day. There would be times ahead, she knew, when the memory of a purely blissful day, a day before disappointment and disagreement, would be cherished and clung to for love's survival.

She thought how little the couple really knew of life. They were young, and optimism was their guiding star. It lighted every move they made, together or apart. Suzannah could almost read their minds. Now, on this shining day, she knew their only concern was the question of how quickly they could arrange to be alone together.

For today, let them be invincible, she thought.

Her gaze sought and found James on another part of the ellipse. He was facing the house, and sometimes he glanced away from the people he was talking to and shifted restlessly. Suzannah knew he was looking for her, but the rules by which they had chosen to live demanded that he not leave Helen. His wife stood by his side with a small, proud smile on her face. Suzannah felt no need or desire to interrupt their moment. It was as if Suzannah were spying on the wedding from a distant world. She and James were two planets spinning in their own separate orbits, and she knew there could be no shift in proper placement. If there were, James would be lost to Suzannah forever, and both their worlds would be destroyed beyond mending.

Strange, she thought, I am content to have it this way. James was her lover and friend. She had the mill. . . . If only Patrick had not left her.

A gentle knock at the drawing room door disturbed her thoughts. It was Harahsi.

"I have seen to everything, Mrs. Paine," he said in his high-pitched, precise voice. "I have washed your father and done what is necessary to prepare him for the morning."

"Thank you, Mr. Harahsi," she said. He was about to say something more to her, but she interrupted him. "You have known us for more than two decades, Mr. Harahsi, and I wonder . . . what is it in the Hopewells? Are we all mad? Or are we doomed somehow?"

"I do not know what it means to be doomed, Mrs. Paine." His expression was maddeningly passive, despite the horrors of the day.

"Surely, you believe in some kind of . . . fate. Or destiny?"

He shook his head.

She pressed him for an answer. "Is it that we are evil then?" Still he didn't answer. Damn the man! He never had been able to give her a direct reply to any question, but this time she would not let him escape behind inscrutability. "I think you know us as well as anyone. How did it all go wrong?"

"You must know that for me, Mrs. Paine, there is no right or wrong in families. Even your poor mother and father cannot help being themselves."

Suzannah stared at him, waiting for more. But Harahsi had given her all the answer his code permitted. He would not invent easy truths or facile explanations to ease Suzannah's mind.

She spoke without thinking and was surprised by her words. "A long time ago, my aunt told me that if ever I was to find contentment, I would have to accept who and what I am." She smiled ruefully. "I cannot escape Sarah and Martin Hopewell, can I, Mr. Harahsi? I am their child."

As the memory of Bronwyn faded, another, almost forty years old, quickly took its place. She was dressed for a party, and she was running from her mother on the stairs to her father, who was standing in the open front door. He was a big, handsome man who lifted her off her tiny feet and threw her in the air while she giggled in terror. She could still hear her mother laughing and scolding Martin to stop. How many years had it been since she thought of her parents with a fully loving heart? No matter. For the space of a moment, as dance music drifted in from the terrace and Harahsi stood by watchfully, she felt the wrenching, passionate attachment once again and knew that the bond between parent and child was the strongest of all. She was the child of Martin and Sarah. Nothing would ever alter that.

"You have a home with us for as long as you like, Mr. Harahsi," she said. "You've done so much for us all. Even now, here, you've helped me. I can never thank you enough."

He dipped his head, the perfect servant. Or was he a servant? That was something else Suzannah had never gotten straight in her mind. She realized now that she probably never would.

He put his hand inside the placket of his plain white coat. "As I was helping Mrs. Hopewell, I found these in her bureau." He held out Patrick's letters.

Suzannah took them. Her hands were trembling.

"I think your mother intercepted them in the hope that she could keep Master Patrick away. It was her obsession . . ."

". . . that no one would have the mill unless it was Valentine."

"Exactly." He watched her face as she scanned the letters. He watched just long enough to see her smile.

FIRST IN THE HOPEWELL SAGA

Broken Promises

by
Drusilla Campbell

Suzannah Hopewell is a young woman of eighteen in *Broken Promises*, the first in the HOPEWELL SAGA. In this powerful and moving story of her life in Amoset, her first love for Travis Paine and her friendship for Lucy Shawn, all the elements of nineteenth-century New England life are woven into a dream of a young woman's pride and passion. But it is far from the Hopewell Mills—in a villa on the shores of Sicily—where Suzannah learns the true character of her family history and faces her own troubled destiny. And when her brother Eben witnesses a cruel and tragic struggle for family power, Suzannah too must bear the scars of her brother's suffering. . . .